Reykjavik

ICELAND

FAEROE IS.

Shetland IS.

NORWAY

SWEDEN

SCOTLAND

NORTH SEA

DENMARK

IRELAND

Limerick

ENGLAND

Padstow

BRITTANY

FRANCE

Burgundy

Provence

WALES

ENGLAND

Severn

London

Bristol

Thames

Bath

Canterbury

BRISTOL CHANNEL

Shaftesbury

Winchester

Glastonbury

Romsey Abbey

Southampton

Tre-Uther

Launceton

Corfe Castle

ISLE of WIGHT

Padstow

Lydford

CORNWALL

Tavistock

ISLE of PURBECK

ENGLISH CHANNEL

The Lizard

Bay of the Seine

avalon

avalon

ANYA SETON

HOUGHTON MIFFLIN COMPANY BOSTON

THE RIVERSIDE PRESS CAMBRIDGE

avalon

chapter one

THE FOGS were still dripping in from the Atlantic when Merewyn met the stranger by the Camel River.

The last plodding hours through rainy mist and mud had scarcely discomforted the girl, for she was very young and eager, nor had ever left home before. Besides she was certain that this overnight pilgrimage to the Holy Well at Roche would help her mother. St. Gundred's Well was famous for its cures. The gentle St. Gundred (who had once lived beside the well and given it her name) had a particular closeness to the angels, and also tenderness for the maladies that bedevil the aching flesh or disordered mind.

To be sure it would have been far better if the sufferer could have made the pilgrimage herself, and bathed in the cool dark water beneath the granite cross; but Breaca, Merewyn's mother, was far too weak for the journey. So Merewyn made it for her. She prayed by the well, dropped into it a precious silver half-penny, and a tiny piece of her mother's sleeve, so that there would be no doubt for whom the cure was intended. She also brought back some of the holy water in a lead vial.

Merewyn had company on her march along the wild lonely

tracks, over moors where the furze was golden now in April, around rocks and ruts and through deeply mired fords. One of her companions was her dog — Trig. Trig came of no particular breed. He was simply a large hound, with a long nose, fierce wary eyes, and complete devotion to Merewyn. He would have attacked either wolf or robber in her defense, though such valor had not been needed.

Merewyn's human companion was her serf, an enormous youth of eighteen, whose body was as thick and solid as a yew trunk, whose shaggy black-thatched head rose a foot above the heads of most men, and who had never learned proper speech.

His name was Caw. Breaca said Caw's wits had been addled on the Day of Death fifteen years ago in the year of our Lord 958, when he had witnessed the horrors inflicted by the devil raiders from the sea.

Yet despite his handicaps they were lucky to have Caw; he could fish and tend the pigs, and his great strength helped the two lone women in many ways. Nobody had been left alive in the household after the dragon ship full of helmeted and bearded murderers sailed away. Only the baby Caw in his hiding place and Breaca herself. She had been sorely injured; a sword wound in her thigh and an arm wrenched from its socket which even today hung limply at her side.

It felt like early afternoon to Merewyn when she and Caw trudged into Pendavey; there was a tinge of pearly yellow overhead above the swirling mist. At Pendavey the river Camel widened, and here she and Caw had hidden the coracle on the way to St. Gundred's. It was a rounded little boat made of bent withes and covered with greased cowhide. Now they might float home to Padstow on the current and the tide. The rest of the journey should be quick. The coracle was waiting where they'd left it, amongst reeds under a bank, and Merewyn was about to step into it when Trig stiffened, his hackles rose and he began to snarl.

Caw never looked up; he went on stolidly holding the coracle against the current, but Merewyn peered through the mist. Piskies? she thought anxiously. Yet the little folk were seldom abroad in daylight. Who else then in this lonely place?

She heard a man's muffled voice. "Help me, maiden," it called. "I am lost."

Trig started to bound forward, the girl put a restraining hand on his thong collar. She waited, heart fast beating, until a man on horseback appeared in front of her. He had seen her before she did him, because of a rift in the mist and because she wore — as did most Cornish women — a red woolen cloak.

"I've been lost all day," the man said. He glanced at the straining, snapping dog. "Don't be afraid of me. I'm a stranger from far off."

"Ah —?" said Merewyn, thinking this over. A stranger. She had never met one. Not a real stranger with odd clothes and an accent.

She examined him. While she did so the mist broke and the sun poured down. The sunlight made of the young man a figure as vivid as the painting of St. Michael she had seen in the chapel at Roche. The stranger was dark, like her mother, like Caw, like all the folk she had ever seen. Yet he did not resemble these folk in any other way. His black hair, glossy as a raven's wing, was cut short above the ears, he had no beard on his lean jutting chin, and instead of coarse homespun he wore a soft blue mantle furred with squirrel and embroidered at the hem. The mantle was held at the shoulder by a glittering enameled brooch. He had long leather shoes with a design on them, and his legs were covered by blue trousers, then cross-gartered to the knee with linen strips.

The expression of his thoughtful brown eyes was pleasant. She knew she need not fear him. The dog also knew this. He ceased snarling and sat down.

"You're lost?" said Merewyn. "Where do you want to go?"

"I'm bound for England, to King Edgar's Court," said the young man, smiling.

Merewyn looked blank. Not only was his accented speech hard for her to follow, but in all her fourteen years she had never heard of anyone going to England, and barely knew that there was a king somewhere up there.

"England?" she repeated, and when he nodded, she said, "That's so *far*. I've just come from St. Gundred's," she added proudly. "I spent the night — but I don't know the way into *England* where the wicked Sawsnachs live."

"Where are you bound for now, maiden?" he asked, eying her with amusement. She looked like many of the Cornish girls he had been seeing on isolated farms as he passed; the bare, dirty feet; the drab homespun kirtle; the red muddy mantle; the long flowing hair, somewhat tangled; and yet her coloring was different. The hair was ruddy — like a horse chestnut — not black. Her eyes were not dark either, they were like rippled seawater, blue, flecked by green lights. He did not consider her pretty; on her rosy cheeks and short snub nose there were freckles, and she held herself awkwardly, being embarrassed by his scrutiny. Yet her earnestness was appealing. And she looked intelligent.

"For home —" she said, pointing at the coracle. "Down the river a league or so."

"Is yonder giant yours?" he asked, indicating Caw, who was still holding the coracle, and waiting incuriously for orders. "Does *he* know the way into England?"

She shook her head. "Caw knows only what we tell him." She hesitated a while, added reluctantly, "At Padstow where I live there are some monks. Perhaps they could tell you."

"Come with me then," he said, patting his horse's rump. "Up here to guide me. That lout can take the boat down himself, can't he?"

After a moment, she assented. She told Caw what to do, then clambered up on the horse behind the stranger, putting her arms around his waist as he directed. The feel of a man's body so close was peculiar. She did not understand the rush of warmth it gave her, or the giddiness. Perhaps it was the scent of his mantle, she thought — like the sweet smoke from burning turf, like gorse. Strange that a man should smell fragrant. Caw smelled of sweat and dung. "What is your name?" she whispered.

"Romieux de Provence," he said, over his shoulder. "That's hard for the Celtic tongue to say. Call me Rumon, as they did in Brittany. I'm used to it."

"Brittany!" She had heard of that land across the sea to the south. One of the Padstow fishermen had been to Brittany. "That is your country?"

"Oh, no. I spent four months there — that's why I can speak your language. Breton is like Cornish."

"Where *do* you come from?" she persisted. Riding there behind him, savoring the scent of his mantle, her nose almost touching his hair which was clean and shining, her arms clasping the lean waist where she could feel the rib cage rising and falling, she was seized by a poignant curiosity. Her arms tightened around him involuntarily.

He felt this and stiffened. "A shipwreck," he said briskly. "On the southmost point of your country called Maneage, or the Lizard — a dreadful place — they're heathens down there. For the rest, it would mean naught to you." His tone was courteous enough, yet it silenced her.

As they rode Rumon went on thinking. "Where do you come from? Where are you going?" The latter, at least, had always been the question since five years ago, when he was fifteen, and had had the vision.

The horse jogged along the track, which was plain now that the mists lifted. The dog trotted beside them. Here and there a guiding stone cross was set along the way. The sea smells grew stronger, and gulls wheeled shrieking overhead. Soon he would see the Western Sea, if he had understood the girl aright. I'm a wanderer, he thought. A searcher. And I bring shame to my blood that I do not wish to be a warrior. That was what his grandmother, Queen Edgive of Arles, had shouted when she finally lost her long patience with him. "You will not fight to regain our shattered kingdom, you will not even fight the Saracens, which is every Christian's duty, you moon about with books, you dream of angels and fairylands where no human has ever gone. You shame your royal blood, your doubly royal blood! You sicken me!"

He had felt the shame she wished, and also confusion and sorrow. He could barely remember his parents. His father died in battle, his mother a month later of plague. And he loved his grandmother who had raised him. She was English, a granddaughter of the great King Alfred who had rid England of the Vikings. Her husband had been Louis L'Aveugle, King of Arles. Blinded by his enemy, Bérenger, Louis had yet managed to rule over Burgundy, which included Provence and parts of Savoie and Italy. He had died long before Rumon was born. His empire dissolved gradually, for lack of a strong hand, while the Saracens encroached on the south, and the Frankish kings encroached on the west. At times the Hungarians, wild hordes from the center of Europe, also harried Burgundy. Rumon's childhood had been hideous with the clashing of steel, and battle cries; the stench of blood; and the screams of torture. He shrank woefully from these. He dwindled and pined and had dreadful nightmares. Edgive finally put him for safekeeping in the great hill fortress of Les Baux, not far from his birthplace at Avignon.

Les Baux castle was a stone stronghold built high on a weird rocky spur which overlooked surrounding valleys. It was inhabited by a fierce Baron and his knights, and was shudderingly called "The Nest of Eagles" by the rest of Provence. The Baron had remained friendly towards Edgive, the old dowager Queen. He revered her royal blood and her spirit, though her power had vanished with the death of her husband. The Lord of Les

Baux consented to raise her delicate grandson in his impregnable fortress.

At Les Baux, Rumon was given servants and a couple of rooms to himself. He gained strength and lost his fears. He learned avidly from the castle priest who was something of a scholar and delighted to have a worthy pupil at last.

Rumon soon knew how to read and write Latin. He spoke excellent English too. Edgive saw to that. She brought him an English slave and drilled him in her mother tongue on each of her frequent visits.

He had but one real friend during those years — a blind harper. This was an odd, gentle man called Vincent, who had traveled widely before he was blinded. He knew a hundred songs, describing a thousand marvels. These he sang so movingly while accompanying himself on his little harp that even the old Baron would sometimes listen and applaud. Vincent taught Rumon to play the harp, and to make up songs in the Provençale language. But Rumon, who was devoted to the harper, preferred the times when the blind man would lift his thin face towards the sun, and tell of the old legends he had learned on his travels to the West.

In this way Rumon first heard of a heroic bygone king called Arthur. He heard too of a blessed island called Avalon where all folk might be happy and at peace. He heard the story of St. Joseph of Arimathea who had fled from Calvary bearing Our Lord's precious blood in a chalice called the San Graal and that the very sight of this holy cup might bestow eternal Joy. Where was Avalon? Where was the San Graal? Rumon would ask. The harper always sadly shook his head. He did not know. And heeding the disapproval of the Baron, who thought Rumon far too much given to sedentary pursuits, Vincent would dismiss the boy, and send him to the knights.

The knights at Les Baux taught Rumon how to ride. They tried also to teach him manly arts — the use of sword and spear and shield; the joys of drinking, and the seduction of women.

Rumon listened to them because he had to, he learned swordplay and hawking, but as he grew older he felt himself increasingly apart from the brawling warriors.

Vincent died one day of an issue of blood from the lungs, and after that Rumon was lonely. Yearning ever for he knew not what. Except perhaps the return of a dream he had had at fifteen, some weeks after Vincent's death. The dream or vision was of great beauty, though when he mistakenly tried to recount it to Edgive, Rumon could hear that it sounded like nonsense . . . a blessed island suffused with golden light floating somewhere in the West. A transparent ruby-red cup shimmering beneath the wings of a white dove. The light beams from the cup which shot down and touched Rumon's face as gently as flower petals. There was music in the air and a Voice whose words he could not remember, except that it had urged him on a Holy Quest. The Voice had spoken of the brotherhood of all men, and of peace. It had spoken of love. It had induced in Rumon such awe, such joy, and such a sense of dedication that he awoke in tears.

Edgive was exceedingly sharp in her ridicule of this vision. She had lost her sons in honorable war. She had no intention of losing her cherished grandson in a morass of dreamy inertia which appeared to her very like cowardice; or — almost as bad — she had no intention of allowing him to drift into the cloister. Such a life was not for a prince who descended from the two most victorious kings known to mankind — not only her own line from King Alfred, but Louis L'Aveugle's line from Charlemagne.

So Edgive treated the vision with contempt, saying that youths of his age were always having peculiar dreams, and she trusted that his would soon take the usual form of voluptuous maidens and lustful dalliance. In the meantime she would search

out a suitable heiress for him to marry, since he seemed to be so
laggard in finding women for himself.

Edgive found several heiresses. Rumon was agreeable, he sang
songs to them, he paid them compliments, he kissed their hands.
Yet he did not fall in love, and he continued to make the extraordinary assertion that he did not wish to lie with a woman unless
he loved her. He also continued to make the other more extraordinary assertion that he did not wish to kill anyone — even an
enemy. He had the audacity to quote the sixth Commandment
to his grandmother, and to the knights at Les Baux who were
urging him to join them in arms against the Saracens. And
Rumon followed up the commandment by quoting the Lord
Jesus Christ's injunction to love one's enemies.

The knights were disgusted. They said that all that fiddle-
faddle was well enough for saints, or might have been a thousand
years ago, but the Lord Jesus would certainly be the first to
command Christians to kill pagans. Rumon announced that he
did not think so. The knights sneered at him, avoided him.

Queen Edgive was baffled and upset. Yet she loved Rumon
deeply, perhaps all the more because of his calm almost sorrowful
defiance of her wishes.

One day she summoned him to her chamber. They eyed each
other in silence for a while. The dowager Queen was old. Her
white face was deeply lined, beneath the golden crown her hair
was gray and scanty, as it hung in two bound plaits across her
bowed shoulders. Yet her eyes were still of a piercing blue —
eyes accustomed to obedience. She stared at her grandson seeking
to fathom him.

He was dark, fairly tall, rather slight of build as his father had
been. His face was thin, though the lips were mobile and full.
He was very pleasing when he smiled. Women liked him, they
had all shown that — from the high-born damsels she had provided, to the luscious peasant girls she had asked the Les Baux
knights to tempt him with. He always dressed magnificently in

velvets, gilded embroideries, and furs — as a prince should. He
was extremely clean, even his fingernails. He insisted upon the
servants hauling water for a daily bath. Another eccentricity
which set him apart from others.

"Grandson," said Edgive at last, and in English which she
used for grave moments. "I don't understand you." She closed
her wrinkled lids, said with difficulty, "Surely it cannot be that
you are the kind of man, who — who takes pleasure only in
men — like the Comte de Toulouse."

Rumon shook his head, he gave her a tender smile. "No, my
royal grandmother, I am not like the Comte de Toulouse, or any
of those. Do not fear that. I cannot tell you what I am. Except
that I have a great yearning to wander and to search, that this
causes a fever in my breast, and dulls my interest in what most
folk consider pleasures."

Edgive sighed. "I don't understand you," she repeated. "But
if this is the way you are, then I have decided what you must
do. No, you will not object again," she said as she saw him
start. "For I give you leave to wander, at least I send you from
here, sad as this makes me. You shall go to England, to my
nephew, King Edgar. You demand peace — and his country is
peaceful. An envoy, who came to me at Arles last month, says
that England is the most peaceable land in the world at present.
You will go to Edgar and give him my greetings. Tell him that
I miss my native country, that if I were not too old I might have
come myself. Tell him that I pray him to find some occupation
for you commensurate with your own royal birth. You have
talents, I suppose, though they are not to me specially admirable.
You can write, and draw, you have book learning, you have a
quick ear for music and languages. Perhaps the *peaceable* Edgar
can make use of you. And it may be that in England you will
find what you seek."

Rumon was so astonished and relieved that for a moment he
did not speak. Then he ran to her and kissed one of the blue-
veined hands.

"Ah, my lady, my dearest grandmother. This plan of yours makes me happy. I have always longed to see England." England lay in the Western Sea. It was an island. He knew that in some mysterious way this island was tied into his vision, or at least was not antipathetic to it, as everything here had been. And he was heartily sick of Provence where he had no friends.

Rumon set out in September with two servants; they were all well mounted on fleet horses from the Camargue. There was a donkey too, which carried the luggage and sundry presents for King Edgar.

Edgive had not required him to hurry. She suggested that he see something of the countries he would pass through, and also — from her own vivid memories — implored him not to brave the wintry seas, to wait until spring before crossing them.

Edgive wept when they parted, and he was moved out of his youthful self-absorption into realizing how bitterly she would miss him, disappointing to her as he had been. They both knew that there was little chance of their ever meeting again.

In the chapel he knelt beside her in prayer, but could scarcely keep his mind on the prayers for looking at a little wooden image of a ship which hung near the altar. It contained the carved figures of the Three Maries and Martha, and their companions who had all fled from Judea after the Lord Jesus had been translated into Heaven, and the persecutions began. The boatload had miraculously landed on the shores of Provence. Rumon had himself carved the little figures of the Three Maries — Mary of Bethany, Martha's sister; Mary, the mother of St. John and St. James; and Mary Magdalene. A monk had carved Lazarus, Maximus, and Sara, the black servant. Rumon used to imagine himself in the boat with them on that sacred voyage. The legend of it always stirred him. He liked to think of such things.

When they finished praying, Edgive hid her sorrow under her usual sharpness. "So — farewell, Romieux de Provence! I shall

pray daily that you are not so great a worry to your cousin, King Edgar, as you have been to me!"

He kissed her and mounted his horse.

For the first time in his life Rumon was at ease as he wandered north through the Frankish kingdom, stopping at monasteries when the fancy took him. His safe conduct assured him a welcome. It had been illuminated on vellum by one of the monks at Arles and signed by his grandmother as "Edgiva Regina." At the monasteries they read the Latin script and were impressed by the arrival of a scion who descended from both Alfred of England and Charlemagne. Rumon stayed a week at Fleury-on-the-Loire, the great new Benedictine monastery. He was repelled by the strict Benedictine rule, yet fascinated by the tranquil radiance which emanated from many of the black-habited brethren. He had some pleasant talk with them, but no desire to join their order. The necessary vows of chastity, poverty, and obedience he found distasteful. Chaste he was, though had no intention of remaining so when he finally met a woman he could love, and he wanted children too — someday. Obedience he had attempted all his life with mediocre results. As for poverty, it held no charms whatsoever. Poverty went with dirt and shabby garments, both of which he abhorred.

Besides he had escaped from one sort of prison at Les Baux, and despite Edgive's fears, he had no wish to be imprisoned in a cloister. He relished his freedom, and like everyone with a keen observant mind he delighted in travel.

In December Rumon reached Brittany, and was at once stimulated by this land so different from any he had known. The dark forests, the stone temples from the forgotten days before the Romans came, the costumes, the Celtic speech which at first he could not understand — all these were of interest.

On Christmas Eve, which was his twentieth birthday, he arrived at the monastery of St. Brieuc on the coast. It was snowing. The first snow Rumon had ever seen. Past the abbey church

the sea pounded against icy shores, black waves roared in and thundered down in cataracts of white.

Rumon thought of the heat, the sun-baked barren hills of his old home, a languorous heat, ripped through once in a while by a screaming wind — the Mistral, but otherwise of a glaring wearisome monotony.

Rumon stood for some time gazing exultantly at the sea, breathing in the snow-filled air. As though to share in his exultance, the Abbey bells began to peal. They rang to announce the last Mass before the midnight one which would celebrate the birth of Christ. The bells and the sea, thought Rumon, made a wondrous personal salutation to his own birthday. Edgive had ever deplored the date of Rumon's birth. It was bad luck to precede the Lord Jesus by a few hours. Discourteous. Such a birthday was known to invite the attention of demons, of witches and warlocks — all the dark ones who would presently be routed at midnight when the Holy Babe Himself was born. To this unfortunate birthday, Edgive attributed many of her grandson's peculiarities.

Rumon, of late years, had been inclined to think that his grandmother's superstitions were silly. Yet some uneasiness remained, and he was always relieved when midnight came.

It would seem that ill luck was indeed his portion on this December 24th, for the monks of St. Brieuc would not receive him in their monastery.

Rumon and his attendants, the horses and the donkey were all tired, hungry, cold. Snow fell on them as they stood by the postern gate. A monk appeared, shrugged when he heard Rumon's mixture of Latin and the few Celtic words he knew, then vanished with the safe-conduct parchment to show it to his Abbot. The monk returned in a few minutes, gave back the parchment, shrugged again, clanged shut his heavy oaken door in Rumon's face, and shot an iron bolt inside.

"By the Three Maries!" cried Rumon, stunned and furious. "What ails these stupid Bretons!" He did not get the answer

that night. None of the village would unbar doors to his knock. In the end Rumon's party went supperless, drank some snow water, and spent the night shivering in a deserted barn.

Next morning Rumon rode to church, and assailed the Abbot after Mass. The Abbot was identifiable because he wore a pectoral cross, and because he held a kind of bishop's crozier, otherwise these bearded Celtic monks in shabby white robes were like none Rumon had seen.

"Reverend Father," said Rumon peremptorily in Latin. "Is it the custom in this land to turn hungry wayfarers from your door?"

The Abbot raised his grizzled eyebrows. "Your tone is rude," he said in halting rusty Latin. "And we do not like foreigners."

"Did you read my parchment?" said Rumon, tilting his chin. "Did you see who I *am?*"

"I read last night that you descend from an English king and a Frankish king. Both those nations have cruelly persecuted my race. And I see *now* that even on this day of rejoicing for the birth of Our Lord you have no humility."

Rumon swallowed. He knew in a vague way that the Celts had been crowded west and farther west throughout the centuries. Pushed to this peninsula in France, pushed to Wales and Cornwall in England. But so accustomed was he to instant respect for his rank that the Abbot's resentment amazed him.

"Mea culpa, Reverend Father," he said slowly. "I had not thought." And he smiled.

The Abbot's scowl gradually relaxed. "What are you doing in St. Brieuc?"

"I was told I might here find a ship to take us across the Channel to England."

"In this weather!" The Abbot gave a dry cackle. It had stopped snowing, but the northeast wind whistled by, and the breakers pounded below them.

"I have money," said Rumon, touching the heavy coin-filled

pouch under his tunic. "I can pay for our board until a ship does sail."

"In that case," said the Abbot, suddenly twinkling, "come, join me at Christmas dinner."

As it turned out, no ship sailed until the first of April. The weather grew fierce. The north winds continued to pile icy waves into the harbor. The cargoes were not ready, either.

Rumon passed the time by learning Celtic and listening to legends of the saints which the monks would occasionally tell him. One evening he particularly wished to hear the story of his namesake — or what the Abbot soon decided was his namesake. "Romieux" was obviously only a barbaric form of Rumon or Ronan or even Ruan. So said the Abbot, who could not pronounce "Romieux." The first Rumon was a much revered saint in Brittany. He had come from Ireland centuries ago with St. Patrick. How many centuries? Nobody knew exactly. Five, six, maybe. About the time that King Arthur had crossed the Channel to save Brittany, as he had saved the Britons in England from the marauding Saxon heathens. Blessed King Arthur!

"Blessed King Arthur," repeated all the monks obediently in chorus.

Rumon bowed his head politely, though he was not interested in King Arthur. "Pray tell me about St. Rumon," he said, "since you consider me his namesake."

It was the recreation hour before Compline. The monks were gathered around the central fire in the refectory digesting a meal of rye bread and salt fish washed down with hard cider. Sleet hissed on the wooden shutters; now and then from nearby forests a hungry wolf howled.

The Abbot dozed in his chair, the monks crouched idly on stools; only the chamberer was busy mending a torn habit, squinting near the firelight. Rumon had already observed how much this order differed from the Benedictine abbey he had seen at Fleury. Here, beyond the Offices, and essential tasks of wood-chopping and cooking, there seemed to be few disciplines. There was also boredom, especially in winter.

The old almoner was by general consent the best taleteller. Presently he cleared his throat and began the story of St. Rumon.

"It was in the days of Grallon, King of all Brittany," said the almoner and went on in a kind of chant, "that the holy Rumon came to us from the Western Isles of Scotia."

Rumon thought the long story of St. Rumon both naïve and repellent. It had to do with werewolves and the Devil (here all the listeners crossed themselves), it had to do with a seductive, heathen woman called Keban who was justly smitten with leprosy after she had tried to murder St. Rumon. "And when he died," said the almoner, "his most holy body was put in a shrine at Quimper, where the blessed relics have cured many of their ills. May he intercede for us all!"

The almoner folded his hands to show that he had finished.

The Abbot nodded slowly. "A most edifying account." He turned to Rumon. "You will see from this history of St. Rumon how dangerous women can be, my son. Profit by the lesson."

"Yes, Reverend Father," answered the guest. Yet he had not found the tale edifying. He found it puzzling. If the woman had been possessed by the Devil, if indeed she were mad, as it sounded, and if the saint could work miracles, why could he not have routed the Devil, have converted her, and spared her the loathsome affliction of leprosy? Was then the Lord's injunction to love one's enemies, to turn the other cheek, as stupidly impractical as Edgive believed? Yet, to be sure, murder must be punished. Keban had tried to do murder. Did the Lord Jesus anywhere say that murder must *not* be punished? Aye, He had said it on the Cross. "Father, forgive them —" Yet was that the same, was it not blasphemy to think so?

Rumon's mind buzzed with questions. The crowded refectory was stifling; he escaped and went riding in the chill twilight.

That night he dreamed about a beautiful naked woman. He knew she was naked though her yellow hair fell around her shoulders like a mantle. Ivory and gold she was except for rosy nipples on the round uptilted breasts. He could not quite see her eyes, yet knew that they were looking at him with desire and defiance. A strange expression. Rumon felt a thrill of excitement in his dream.

There was cruelty in the woman's face, in the set of the short, square jaw, the outthrust lower lip which disclosed ever so slightly the white teeth behind. Cruelty, power, and an immense allure. She continued to look at him unsmiling, arching her neck, thrusting forward her breasts. He moved toward her fascinated, and saw that she held low down against her side a small jeweled dagger. From its point, blood dripped steadily. When he saw the dagger Rumon was afraid, yet he could not stop going towards her, his hands outstretched as though to cup her breasts.

From somewhere there came a peal of laughter, a harsh, malicious sound which awakened Rumon, who found that he was sweating, and much disturbed. It was the first time that he had felt lust in life or dreams, and it was the first time since his childhood that he had felt such fear.

Too much strong cider, he thought as the impression faded. And perhaps that gruesome story of Keban. Yet he knew that the dream had nothing to do with Keban. Though it undoubtedly came from the Devil. Rumon shivered, and touched the golden crucifix which hung at his neck. "Libera nos, Domine, ab omnibus malis —" he murmured, and rising hastily from the fine-sheeted feather bed the monks had provided for his comfort, he strode into the chapel.

Rumon's jaded old horse stumbled as it plodded along the path towards Padstow. Merewyn clutched hard on Rumon's waist as he jerked the bridle up. "Ai-ee-e," she cried. "It will fall?" She had never ridden a horse before. She did not like it much. She was not exactly afraid of this great beast, not if the Stranger were there, and in all this adventure there was a kind of excitement, yet she knew that the man who was called Romieux de

Provence — a meaningless jumble of syllables — was not in the least aware of her.

"I won't let it fall," said Rumon kindly as to a child, which he thought she was — a very young gawky peasant girl. "How much farther have we to go?"

She considered the landmarks, the broadening of the Camel on their right, the squat thatches in a palisade, which she had gone to visit alone some years ago, and her mother had been angry. Breaca never wanted Merewyn to explore anywhere except on the empty headland of Pentire.

"More on," said Merewyn. "Not very far, to my home at Tre-Uther."

Rumon sighed. He did not care about her home, wherever it was. The monastery she had mentioned was the only hope for a night's sleep — and a meal. Though what hospitality there was in Cornwall, he had so far found very peculiar.

"Move this way a little," said Rumon, indicating the middle of the horse's rump, "I don't suppose you weigh much, but still a double load for this old nag . . ."

It took her a moment to understand his meaning in the oddly accented Celtic. "I can walk," she said, "I always do." She slid off the horse.

"If you like," said Rumon, with the courteous smile he had long been drilled to by Edgive. That it was an abstracted, as well as courteous smile, Merewyn knew very well, despite her inexperience with any being such as this. Or indeed with any men.

"If you get tired," Rumon said, "you must mount again." He looked at her bare, dirty feet, which actually went along faster than the horse. It occurred to him that she had a grace of carriage, and that her "Thank you" was nicely said. Then he forgot her again as the horse ambled along and had to be guided out of potholes and between rocks.

Rumon's nether thoughts slipped back to the shipwreck which had brought him to Cornwall.

On the first of April, though the weather was still unsettled, Rumon had most thankfully sailed from Brittany. He bought room for himself, his beasts, and servants on a large Frisian coasting vessel which touched at St. Brieuc and was bound for Plymouth with a miscellaneous cargo of wine, silk, and spices that had come overland through Venice from the Byzantine Empire.

A favorable shore breeze blew into the one square sail, the sailors scarcely had to row, and there was hope that the passage of a hundred or so miles would be made by tomorrow.

The hope soon vanished. As they passed the Isle of Guernsey, and left its lee to starboard, an east wind came tearing down the Channel. The waves mounted and began to break. The sailors hauled down the sail and rowed desperately while the captain struggled to hold his course with the steering oar. The frightened horses and the donkey neighed and plunged, straining against their tethers. Rumon, though drenched like the others with rain and spray, was exhilarated by this new experience, and he had felt an immediate love for the sea. He did not know when they were swept far out past Plymouth nor could he understand the captain's despairing cry in Frisian that they must try to head for the open ocean, lest they end up like many before them on the rocks along the South Cornish coast.

They raised the sail again to try to scud before the wind. The sail cracked, tore asunder, and disappeared in the murk ahead.

Rumon knew then that they were in danger. He spoke to his Provençal servants, but in the fury of the storm they could not hear him, and he saw that they were praying. How many hours passed he did not know. It grew dark. He became very quiet inside, as he clung to the gunwhales which were constantly awash. He did not know what was to happen to them, yet he felt that he would not die. The memory of his vision long ago came close to him, and with it the sense of dedication and purpose. It is Thy Will that I should not die now, he thought with certainty.

The ship struck, lifted high by the force of a tremendous wave. She cracked down on the Craggan — off the east tip of the Lizard.

Rumon hit his head against the gunwhale. For some minutes he was dazed. He heard the screams of his companions, he felt the ship breaking up beneath him. Water gushed over him. He struggled, suffocating. He could not swim, but even if he could have, his wet clothes and the money pouch on his chest would have weighed him down. Gasping, he got his head above water, standing for an instant on the Craggan rock itself, as the wave ebbed. Something oblong and dark pushed against him. It was one of the oarsmen's benches. Instinctively he grabbed it. Another wave came and washed him away, yet the bench held his head up. He clung to it frantically. The tide and waves were with him. Presently he felt ground under his feet. He staggered up onto a little pebbly beach, surrounded by cliffs.

He got beyond the line of foam that gleamed in the darkness, before his legs began to shake. He lay down abruptly, his arms outstretched on the welcoming sands. The terror he had not felt earlier rushed through him, to be followed by a passion of gratitude.

He pressed his lips to the sand, turned his head and fell into exhausted sleep.

When Rumon awoke, the sun shone full on him. The sea lapped gently a few yards away — translucent shimmering green, so innocent in the sunlight.

A noise behind him made him start. Two people were staring at him, a beady-eyed crone and a stunted black-haired man, both naked to the waist, around which were tied rabbit-fur aprons. While they gave him sidelong, wary glances, they also crouched over a driftwood fire, on which some large spitted animal was roasting. Still a trifle confused, Rumon discovered that he had lost his sword and helmet somehow in the shipwreck. His clothes and fur-trimmed blue mantle were nearly dry. He must have been lying in the sun for hours. He got up and approached the pair who drew back, muttering and holding out their hands to fend him off. The man had a long skinning knife which he fingered.

"Where am I?' said Rumon in his native Provençal.

They shook their heads, still backing away. Rumon tried English. They looked at him blankly, — a wary beastlike stare. The man made a tentative gesture with his knife.

Rumon's wits began to clear. Where *could* he be? He summoned his scanty knowledge of geography, and the memory of a map he had once seen. "Is this Cornwall, my good folk?" he asked in the Breton he had recently learned.

There was a slight flicker in the man's dull eyes. "Ya, Kernuow," he answered slowly.

"Thank you," said Rumon. He approached the fire, the roasting animal gave forth a rank odor, but Rumon was very hungry. He started to ask for a piece of meat when he saw what it was. Parts of the donkey he had brought from Provence. Its bloody head had been flung aside and was recognizable by a black star between the eyes.

Poor beast, he thought. It must have come ashore as he had. But where were the others? Not only the horses, but the men. The ship's captain, the sailors, his own two devoted servants.

"Where are the men?" he cried. "Many men with me in the ship!"

The old woman hunched her shoulders, and turned the donkey's leg on the spit. The man answered after a moment. He waved his hairy hand towards the sea. "Out there." He frowned, glowering at Rumon. "Only *you* the sea would not keep. You are a Bucca." The old woman sucked in her breath, and shivered.

It took Rumon a second to understand that they thought him an evil spirit or ghost, and it was obvious that they were afraid of him. Otherwise, he thought, I suppose I would have had my throat cut like that donkey's. He walked away from the fire, the sizzling meat now disgusted him, and realization of the catastrophe began.

There had been thirteen men in that ship. Could they all be drowned? He crossed himself and whispered, "Omnibus in Christo —" If so and some bodies were washed ashore, he should arrange for a Christian burial. Or if by the same miracle which had saved him someone living appeared from the sea, he should be here to help. There would certainly be no help from this uncouth pair.

"Where is the nearest priest?" he said. "The 'Papa.'"

They stared at him with the same blankness they had shown before he spoke Breton to them. The man shook his head, and slicing a hunk from the half-cooked donkey, gobbled a huge mouthful. The old woman did the same.

"The Papa," repeated Rumon sternly. To clarify his meaning he pulled the golden crucifix from under his tunic and held it up.

They gazed at the crucifix without interest, returned to their meat.

Can they be heathens? thought Rumon. Strange, because at St. Brieuc they had often talked of the conversion of Cornwall hundreds of years ago. Many saints, including St. Rumon, had christianized the country, before continuing on their missions to Brittany.

Rumon secretly fished in his pouch, aware that they might plan to rob him. He brought out a small silver piece, and tendered it towards the man. "Here is money. I need food. You must have bread at least somewhere."

They glanced at the silver and showed as little interest as they had in the gold cross. It was apparent that they had never seen either metal, and did not know its meaning.

Rumon sighed. He thought that his conscience would not let him leave this coast for some days, and the first requisite was food.

"Listen!" he cried in the tone of command his rank had long

since taught him. "This donkey you are eating was *mine!* Oh, I permit you to eat it!" They had both ceased munching, their faces showed fresh alarm. "But in return you must find me something else to eat. Now!"

The old woman wavered, her hands shook; she put down her hunk of meat. She nodded sullenly, and beckoned. Rumon followed her up a steep hill from the cove, clambering over strangely marked serpentine rocks. A track led inland across a heath of bracken and gorse, an occasional patch of buttercup-spotted grass. There were no trees and there seemed to be no habitation, until suddenly they came on a round turf hut like a beehive. It was set against a thicket of brambles. In front of the hut stood a nine-foot upright stone, roughly oblong. A menhir from the old days, thought Rumon who had seen some in Brittany, though he had never seen one like this — covered with blood both fresh and dried, and speckled with bits of bird feathers.

Jesu! he thought as he stared at the great stone. They must worship the thing, make sacrifices to it. He averted his eyes from a soggy red mess of what looked like liver which was placed at the menhir's base. He stooped low through the open door and followed the old woman into the hut. The stench nearly drove him out again, though he paused as something on the ground gave a long wail of fear.

It was a young woman, and in her arms she held a naked new-born infant. She struggled to rise from a soiled bed of grass and bracken, fell back again panting, trying to shield the infant with her arms.

"I won't hurt you," said Rumon. "Don't be afraid."

The dense black eyes were glittering bright, even in the gloom he could see the unhealthy flush of her dark square face, the sweat glistening below matted black hair.

"She's ill!" he said to the old woman, who shrugged and announced, "I've done what I can, I gave the afterbirth to the menhir god, shall I give it the baby too?"

At this the young mother screamed, clutching the squirming infant tighter to her bare breasts.

"No," said Rumon, grabbing the old woman by the shoulders and shaking her. "You must not touch the baby!"

She cringed away from him. "There's bread," she whispered, pointing to a pile of dark flat objects in a corner of the hut. "Take, and leave us alone."

Rumon picked up a "loaf" and bit into it. It was tasteless, burned and dry, a flat cake made of barley meal, yet he ate two of them while gnawing hunger pains decreased. "Water," he said. The woman pointed towards the door, where he saw a spring bubbling some yards away. He cupped his hands and satisfied his thirst at the spring. He washed his face and hands, tried to comb his hair with his fingers.

As he did so, he was seized with a passion to be gone. The heath and the sea below, and this spring were sweet enough. The human beings were nothing but the vilest of animals. Finally he arose and went back to the hut.

He stood just inside the doorway, while the roof grazed his head. The young mother looked up at him awed, at the blue velvet mantle, at the glittering belt and brooch, at the white linen tunic which had been bleached in the sea.

"I'll not leave just yet," said Rumon. "If you were Christians you'd understand this. *Our* god is merciful. He is the only God. As it is, you will take orders."

He gave orders and the old woman sulkily obeyed. Rumon made her cleanse the mother who was lying in a mess of childbirth blood and excrement. He himself brought her water, a great deal of it, which she gulped down frantically. He saw to it that her man fetched her a slice of donkey meat. These things he did in exactly the way he would have commanded the servants to tend a sick horse or dog at Les Baux. Fecklessness and disorder must be rebuked. Then Rumon tried to make them bury the afterbirth and cleanse the menhir. But this they would not do. The man snarled and brandished his skinning knife as near to

Rumon's throat as he dared. The old woman flung a rock which grazed his cheek, and fell in terror to her knees expecting retribution.

Rumon made a disgusted sound, and let them be.

The weather was fine, he slept in a thicket on the far side of the spring. And next morning he patrolled the crumbling cliffs along the sea. Once far out he saw a pallid corpse drift by. He could not possibly have reached it, and it disappeared towards the Lizard Point as he watched. He murmured a prayer and gave up, though he had meant to wait longer.

That afternoon he left.

The young mother had improved. She was nursing the baby whom they called simply Map, which is to say "Boy." None of them had special names, they addressed each other as Man, Old Woman, Young Woman. He learned nothing else about them, nor tried to.

He was frantic to be off, and braving the renewed filth in the hut, he extorted some vague directions from the girl who was slightly less brutish than the others. He was to follow a track through the downs until he came upon another hut like theirs. In it she thought lived a man who had been as far as a place where there were several stone huts together. This was all she knew.

Rumon nodded decisively. The old woman's eyes showed relief. But on the girl's face was a peculiar look of pleading. She touched her baby's head, as though to ask something about it. Rumon ignored both the expression and the gesture. It never occurred to him that the young woman might feel gratitude for his help the day before, or that she might have listened if he had tried to tell her of a faith which forbade blood sacrifices to phallic stones. The baby repelled him, its purplish head was covered with scurf, and the young woman was nearly as filthy as she had been yesterday; while the other two, he regarded as on a par with an ape the Lord of Les Baux kept shackled in a cave beneath his castle.

Rumon escaped from the hut, and set out along the track in the direction indicated. From then on his lot was easier. He found the next hut, which also had a bloodstained menhir beside it, yet here the occupants understood money. The silver penny Rumon gave them procured him a dinner of stewed rabbit, and a guide.

The next day he passed several tin mines, mostly abandoned, one still operating, and that night he reached civilization, or what seemed like it, since the village of Redruth boasted several stone houses, and a tiny church. It even had something approaching a hostel for travelers, where Rumon, to his great relief, was able to buy a horse.

He inquired for a priest, thinking to get some intelligible directions, and found that the "Papa" was on a journey to another parish. So Rumon refreshed himself for a day, eating ravenously, drinking sour barley ale, washing himself, shaving, and ridding himself of stray lice.

This very dawn he had set out on the northeastern track towards a place they called Bodmin which the hostel keeper thought might be on the way to the "Pow Saws" or English country.

In no time the dripping fog closed down, and he had been wandering ever since, until he met this girl who had sat behind him on the horse clasping his waist with thin, tentative arms.

"Look," Merewyn said suddenly, looking up at him and pointing ahead to a dazzle of yellow sands and a glimpse of foaming emerald breakers between two dark headlands. "Padstow, my home." Her voice quivered, and Rumon was startled out of his thoughts.

"You aren't happy to be home?" he asked.

"I'm afraid for my mother." Merewyn caught her breath. "Afraid the saints haven't listened to my prayers. They didn't listen when the horror happened fifteen years ago. Nor did the monks help. That's why my mother hates the monks."

"Oh," said Rumon uncomfortably. "I'm sorry, but I'm sure

your prayers have been heard." He did not wish to hear of whatever horror had happened fifteen years ago, he wanted to find the monastery and rest himself and his horse.

"Tre-Uther," said Merewyn. "Stop!" Rumon jerked the reins. He noticed then they were at an opening in a circle of stones, and that there was a house inside the circle, quite a large house for Cornwall, built of granite slabs and roofed with thatch.

"Tre-Uther," repeated Rumon. "The homeplace of Uther? Is this where you live?"

She nodded, looking up at him; her glinting blue-green eyes were steady, she squared her shoulders and raised her chin. "Uther was my father. He was in direct line from King Arthur. So *I* am."

"Oh?" said Rumon, astonished and somewhat amused. Her pride was so evident. He wondered if she knew how very long ago King Arthur had lived — or what indeed was true about him. Vincent's songs about Arthur had been full of marvels, some of which Vincent himself admitted that he had made up.

"I salute you, Princess," said Rumon smiling, and refrained from mentioning his own royal lineage.

Merewyn did not hear him, she had turned and gave a gasp. "There's no smoke!" she whispered, staring at the peaked center of the thatching where the smoke hole was. She ran stumbling through the stone enclosure and into the house. The dog leaped after her.

Rumon sighed and dismounted. He could not in decency go searching for the monastery until he found out if the girl's mother were still alive.

He waited some time, first watching the fishermen paddle their coracles into the harbor along the estuary below him, then gazing out between the headlands towards the great western sea which had no limits.

Merewyn came back slowly, her feet dragging, her little face blanched of its rosy cheeks. "My mother is very weak," she said.

"I've rubbed her chest with the holy well water. She wants to see you."

An instinct of denial, of foreboding leaped up in Rumon. He did not wish to see another sick woman. He wanted no more delays and entanglements on his journey. He wanted no further reminders of death.

"I pray you, sir," said Merewyn softly. Tears started from her eyes, and rolled down her face.

Rumon tightened his lips, and nodded. He followed the girl into the house.

Chapter Two

At first when Rumon entered the hall at Tre-Uther, he was
relieved. Merewyn's mother, Breaca, was standing near a window, her hand resting on the stone sill. She was quite young —
not yet forty — and her face, though haggard, was still handsome. She had fine dark eyes which examined him steadily, and
there was no appeal to pity or impression of weakness in her
stately greeting.

"Welcome, Rumon," she said. "Merewyn tells me that is
your name, and that you are bound for the court of the English
king. Welcome to this royal house of Arthur, though we are no
longer able to entertain you as once we might have before this
child was born." She indicated Merewyn.

"No need to entertain me, madame," said Rumon smiling.
"Surely the monks will receive me tonight."

He gaped at the change in her face. It stiffened while her
eyes widened slowly with a frightening glare.

"The monks," she cried. "Those fat mewling cowards. What
can *they* do for you!"

"Mama —" whispered Merewyn, running to her mother.
"Mama, don't."

Breaca pushed her aside and took three halting steps towards Rumon. "Look!" cried Breaca, pointing to her left arm which Rumon now saw was crooked, dangling from her shoulder like a rag. "And look!" she cried, raising her skirt so that he might see a jagged purple scar on her thin thigh. "That day the red devils landed from the North — that day they did this to me and more —" She paused, glancing at Merewyn. The wild light left her eyes, the momentary strength visibly drained from her. She put her hand across her mouth, as though to hush herself. She dragged to a wooden bedstead in the corner of the hall, crouched down on it, still holding her hand over her mouth.

Merewyn went to her mother with little soothing sounds, trying to make her lie down, which she would not.

Rumon too moved towards the bed, noting that a large roughly hewn wooden crucifix hung above it. He was shocked, and sorry for the girl, suspecting now that whatever else might be wrong with Breaca, she was also touched with madness.

The woman's hand dropped from her mouth, and she spoke again in a dull vague voice, looking at neither of the young people.

"They killed my serfs except some of the women whom they took with them. We had many serfs then. They seized our sheep and cattle and threw them in their ship. They ransacked our house and set fire to it. Then when Uther came home — he had been across the river to — to — where was it he was? I don't remember. He saw the serpent ship drawn up on the beach. He hurried to help us, but he had no chance. They murdered him with their battle-axes the instant he touched shore. I saw his head cloven in two, his brains spilling out."

"Mama —" breathed Merewyn. "Mother, I pray you —" She seized the vial of holy-well water, and sprinkled the rest of its contents over the huddled woman.

Breaca looked at her daughter, and touched the girl's forehead. "Ah, you are a good child, it is because you come from the wondrous line of Arthur. Never forget it."

"No, Mama." She put her arms around Breaca, who had not done speaking though her face had gone gray with pain. "Come here, young stranger —" she said, beckoning to Rumon.

Breaca breathed heavily for a moment. "Do you know what the monks did while this was happening to us? They ran and hid in their church. They heard our screams for help, they had weapons — scythes and axes, pruning bills. There were a score of them in those days, and they had time to prepare as we did not. But they did nothing. They barred themselves in the church and cowered there, until long after the murderers had sailed away. Do you wonder that I hate the monks?"

"No, madame," said Rumon. "Yet monks are not trained to fight," he added uneasily.

"Ah —" said the woman. "They are trained for nothing but chantings and mealymouthed prayers which do no good. And they are trained to lie. Remember that. They *lie!* They would tell you lies." Her weakening voice held a special emphasis. She glanced suddenly at Merewyn, then fell back against her pillow.

The girl made a gesture and preceded Rumon outside into the sunlight. "She's not better — yet," said Merewyn, wiping her eyes on a corner of her skirt. "Though she's not often as — as you saw her. It was meeting a stranger, I suppose."

"Haven't you friends, neighbors to help?" he asked. "You shouldn't be alone like this."

"There's nobody. Only the fisher wives, and they're afraid to come here. They think — that my mother is a witch. But I have Caw," added Merewyn, staunchly pointing towards the pigsty, where the huge serf was feeding the swine. He had returned earlier in the coracle and was doing his accustomed chores.

Rumon thought that the dim-witted giant was hardly the prop most needed by this distressed household, and he looked at Merewyn with the first unalloyed sympathy he had ever felt.

"You're brave, my dear," he said, and put his hand over hers.

"I'm going to the monastery now," said Rumon, relinquishing her hand. "You need not tell this to your mother, don't distress her."

Her eyelids dropped. "So this is farewell, Rumon? I'll not see you again."

"Yes, you will. I'll stop by tomorrow, on my way north."

Merewyn nodded. She watched him mount his horse, and pointed down the river in the direction of the monastery. "Is it true all monks tell lies?" she said. "Mother has always forbidden me to speak to the Padstow monks."

Rumon frowned. He did not understand Breaca's hysterical accusations, even granted that fifteen years ago the monks had failed her so badly. "I do not believe they all tell lies," he said. "I believe there must be some men of God amongst them, and despite your mother's feelings, I believe that they may help you."

She shook her head, and started to protest, but Rumon did not wait. He turned the horse and cantered off along the riverbank. A night's lodging for himself had now become secondary to finding help for the girl and her mother. The woman had the look of death about her. She must be shriven. Despite the crucifix above the bed, despite Merewyn's pathetic journey to the Holy Well, it was obvious that the forlorn family was bereft of any spiritual comfort.

A half mile from Tre-Uther, Rumon came upon the church. It was small, but staunchly built of granite and roofed in slate. A carved wheel-headed cross stood by the entrance; a crude plaque above the door gave in Latin a dedication to St. Petroc, whose sacred bones were entombed therein.

Beyond the church and up the hill Rumon saw what must be the monastery though it did not look like any ecclesiastical foundation he had ever seen, being nothing but a collection of various-sized huts inside a wooden fence. Outside the fence were fields green with flourishing crops of barley, leeks, and beans. Sheep were pastured nearby, the newborn lambs frolicking around their ewes. A score of beehives attested that the monks were not short of honey, nor of the strong mead which was made from it.

As Rumon dismounted, he was amazed to hear feminine laughter, and a snatch of song which sounded extremely secular.

Nobody answered his call, so he tethered the horse and walked up to the largest hut, from whence the noise emerged.

The door was open to the mild spring dusk, and Rumon stuck his head into a smoky room, well lit by six tallow candles.

Several monks were lolling around a table, holding leather tankards and munching gustily on chicken legs and chops between drinks. There was also a woman, a buxom wench who leaned over the table giggling while she tickled the fat roll at the back of a stout monk's neck.

If they *were* monks. They certainly wore grayish-white robes, but their tonsures were extraordinary. Their hair was shaved back from the forehead to a line across the scalp above the ears, giving them a naked half-headed look. The fattest monk wore a round gold disk or breastplate on his chest. This marked him as the prior, and he started when Rumon cleared his throat. All the others and the woman turned to stare.

"Who're *you?*" said the fat one, putting down his tankard and frowning.

Rumon held out his safe-conduct parchment. The monks all gazed at the illuminated vellum, the fat prior waved it away.

"How're we supposed to know what it says? We don't read." He shrugged and pursed his mouth above the double chins, then cried, "Oh, I know what *you* are, ye're a spy!"

"I'm not!" cried Rumon, taken aback. "What nonsense!"

"Oh yes, ye are. You've come from Wulfsige, that Saxon bishop they've foisted on us in Cornwall, or worse yet, you've been sent by that sour old meddlesome Dunstan. Fellow they made Archbishop of Canterbury — wherever that may be. Oh, we've heard all about it and been expecting some prying busybody to disturb us."

"Maybe so," said Rumon, smothering a laugh. "Someone may

indeed disturb you, for you seem to me a singular monastery. But I'm not the man. I come from the southern part of France, and am bound *for* England to see King Edgar."

The young woman had been staring openmouthed at Rumon. She now leaned forward and said to the fat monk, "I think he's honest, Papa Poldu. And maybe he's hungry."

Father Poldu gave her a pinch on the cheek and a playful slap on the buttock. "If *you* say so, m'dear," He turned to Rumon. "Sit down and eat. Me wife vouches for ye."

"Your wife . . ." repeated Rumon faintly.

"To be sure. Some of us are wed. We belong to the good old church, no matter how they try to Romanize us."

"Well . . ." said Rumon. He sat down and took a chicken breast from the heaped platter. Ecclesiastical squabbles and points of view were no concern of his. He ate and drank plentifully, while all the monks except Poldu, the prior, drifted from the table and out to their cells to sleep. They were a plump and incurious lot. Once having accepted Rumon as a chance wayfarer and no menace, they lost interest in him.

Presently Poldu's wife yawned and said, "I'm for bed. The stranger can share a pallet in Conan's hut. Tomorrow's the Feast of St. Petroc," she added to Rumon. " 'Twas the day he landed here in a silver bowl, or maybe the day he flew up to be man i' the moon. Anyway we have Masses 'n' dances wi' a hobbyhorse so fierce 'tis a treat to see, bonfires later on Pentire Head." She reverted to the prior. "Don't drink too much, Papa. Ye'll have a full day."

"I'll drink as I please, m'dear," said Poldu amiably, folding his hands on his belly. "Go along with ye."

Rumon was daunted by this domestic interchange, and uncertain how to begin on the tragic subject which had filled his mind upon his arrival.

"Reverend sir —" he said urgently, seeing that the monk's popeyes were watery and vague, while a flush had spread up through the shaven scalp. "Reverend sir — were you here about fifteen years ago, when the *Vikings* landed at Padstow?"

Poldu slowly focused his wandering gaze on the visitor. "What d'ye know of that time?" he said. " 'Twas only a random raid from the north. They've not been back since."

"I know that at Tre-Uther most of the household was massacred."

"So 'twas," said Poldu, belching comfortably. "Too bad."

"You knew what was going on, but you hid in the church with the other monks?"

"We hid all right. What else could we do? No sense getting ourselves slaughtered. As it happened, the raiders never did come near the monastry, they crammed their ship with what they got from Tre-Uther, and after they killed Uther himself — they sailed away." Poldu waved a pudgy hand to show how the Vikings had departed. A massive silver ring twinkled on his forefinger. It caught the prior's attention. He began to shine the ring carefully on his sleeve.

Rumon, who loathed violence, and had glibly exhorted the Les Baux warriors to forgive their enemies, could not in justice rebuke Poldu's eminently reasonable attitude. He abandoned the subject of the long-past raid. "The woman, Breaca, is dying," he said. "She must be shriven. And the girl, Merewyn, needs Christian help."

"Have they asked f'r it?" The prior, having done rubbing his ring, began buffing his round gold breastplate.

"No," admitted Rumon. "Yet if you sent one of your monks there in charity, the girl at least would be grateful and might persuade her mother."

"Bah!" said the prior. "The woman's a witch, known to practice black magic. M'monks wouldn't go near her, nor would I. Nor, young man, should *you!*" Poldu added, banging his tankard.

"But they are descendants of King Arthur!" cried Rumon,

remembering how the monks at St. Brieuc had reverenced the British king's name.

"Who is?" said Poldu impatiently. "Oh, I believe Uther made some such claim and our old prior, m'father, ye know — and I've got a son to be prior after me. A bouncy li'l lad he is too. Talks already. Why t'other day he —"

"To be sure," interrupted Rumon sharply, quelling paternal anecdote and accepting the oddness of hereditary priorship. "But what did your father think of Uther's claim? I've heard no mention of Arthur's descendants."

"Oh, he had 'em all right. Foreigners wouldn't know. M'father always respected Uther. However, that doesn't apply to the women."

"Of course it does!" Rumon cried. "At least the girl has royal blood."

"Not a bit of it." The prior yawned and hiccuped. "The girl's a Viking brat. One of 'em raped the mother. The big red-bearded chief, I saw him doing it on the beach, while his men scurried round killing the serfs and hauling off the cattle."

"This is monstrous!" cried Rumon, after a stunned moment. "Now I know why Breaca said you would lie. You couldn't possibly know this."

"Mind your manners, young man. I do know this because I hadn't time to get to the church, I was up in a tree down there and watched the whole thing."

"No matter what you saw, or imagined, no matter what happened to that poor woman, you cannot possibly know that Merewyn is not Uther's child."

"Ye weary me," said the prior. "Yet I'm sorry for ye, since that witch must certainly have cast some spell. So I'll answer once more. The girl's not Uther's because he'd been on a four-month voyage, and got back just in time to be killed as he landed. That was in July, and Breaca's brat was born the next April. If she was Uther's she was thirteen months i' the womb, an' that's against nature, m'lad."

"How do you know when Merewyn was born?" said Rumon, his voice wavering.

"Because m'father, the old prior, heard o' the birth from a fisher wife. He went to Tre-Uther and christened the little bastard, though the mother was wild — shouted blasphemies, insults, and woulda done him harm had she been strong enough." Poldu chuckled. "Ah, I see ye've no more questions. Cheer up an' have a drink! Can ye sing any merry songs? I'm very fond o' music. Very, very, very fond!" caroled the prior, thumping out a rhythm with his tankard. "Fond o' riddles too. Here's a sly one . . .

> What's sweet as flowers when it wishes
> Other times can stink like fishes?"

The prior leered across the table. "Come! A lusty young man 'ld be able to guess that!"

"I'd like to retire, Reverend Sir," said Rumon rising. "Kindly direct me to the hut where I may sleep."

Rumon left the monastery next morning, greatly regretting his promise to revisit Tre-Uther. He had not only failed in his mission to get help for the women, but he had discovered the miserable secret that was probably responsible for Breaca's intermittent madness. Nor did he doubt its truth. Rumon had acute intuitions. The prior was fat, lazy, dissolute and heartless, but he was neither cunning nor devious. Besides there was Merewyn's appearance. The hair with its auburn tint, the blue-green eyes, the freckles and fair skin differed greatly from the dark Cornish.

He thought of her pride of descent from Arthur. He thought of the troubles she had endured, sustained partly by that pride. With all his heart he wished to be rid of the two women and their woeful predicament. They're nothing to me! he thought angrily. I can do nothing for them. What reason to see the girl again, especially now that she did not even possess the royal blood which Edgive's training had taught him always constituted kin with other royalties, no matter how remote. I'll not stop by, he thought. The weather was still fine. He had received clear directions as to how to find Bodmin, the next town on the way to the English border. He was sick of delays, sick too of discomforts. He longed to reach the English Court where there would be intelligent people to talk with, and good music; there would also be servants and fresh clothes.

Cornwall had provided nothing except squalor and distressing problems. No, I'll not stop by, he thought.

But Merewyn was waiting on the road outside Tre-Uther. She ran up with a wave and a shy smile. "I was wondering when you'd get here!" She wore a clean brown frock. Her glossy hair was neatly braided. Her little face glowed with the pleasure of seeing him.

Rumon pulled up his horse and said, "Good morning," in a restrained tone which the girl did not notice.

"My mother's better," she said breathlessly. "The terrible pains went away in the night. She's most eager to see you again — I pray you come in," she added in surprise, as he hesitated. "I've made girdlecakes for you."

Rumon sighed and slowly dismounted. He followed Merewyn once more into Tre-Uther.

In the hall, Breaca was propped up in bed. Her face was much whiter than the homespun pillowcase, her dark eyes were enormous. They gazed at Rumon with sad resignation and understanding.

"You've breakfasted?" she asked calmly. "At the monastery?"

He reddened, and nodded. "Then Merewyn's girdlecakes can wait." She addressed her daughter, "Go outside, child. Hunt for eggs. I heard the hens cackling. Don't come back until we call you."

The girl, looking puzzled, at once obeyed.

"Sit here," said Breaca, to Rumon, indicating a stool by the bed. "I've little time, you know. A few hours at most."

"But you're better, madame. Merewyn said the pains stopped."

She shook her head. "My death is near. I believe I've waited for you to come. Nay, don't draw back. I understand you well. You meant to get help for us, and you found none. Isn't it so? And then they told you," she paused, went on quietly, "about Merewyn's birth. Don't fear me now. The hatred burned out of me last night. And the madness which has been my bitter lot at times — it too has gone. Rumon!" cried Breaca, sitting up in bed. "The child must never know about her birth. Never know she was not Uther's!"

"No, madame," he said gently. "I hope she never knows."

"Swear that you won't tell her. Swear on the crucifix!"

"I?" he cried. "Why should *I* tell her! I'll never see her again."

"Swear!" cried Breaca. "I command you to swear you'll never let anyone know she is not Uther's."

"Very well," said Rumon, thinking how little this mattered. "I swear it by the crucifix. Pray calm yourself."

"*Kiss* the cross," she cried. He did so, reluctantly.

She sagged on the pillow. "I see I push you too fast, but I've so little time. You're going into England to see the English king. Why is that?"

"He is my cousin, madame. My grandmother, who is dowager Queen of Arles, has sent me to King Edgar."

She sighed as though satisfied, and was silent while she fought against the mounting weakness. At last she spoke in a thin whisper. "Uther's sister went to England — many years ago, before the — day — the Vikings came. She was a dear woman. She wanted to become a nun. She went to a nunnery called Shaft — Shaftesbury. Aye, that was it. Her name was Merewyn. I loved her. When the baby came I called her —"

Breaca's face contorted, under the sheet her heart began to pound visibly. Rumon jumped up and seeing a jug on the table, poured out a cup of ale. She moistened her lips and pressed her hand hard against her chest.

"You will take my Merewyn into England with you," she said in a stronger voice. "Take her to her aunt, for there is nothing else to do."

It was a command, not a request, and Rumon's dismay was such that he could not speak.

"You are young and free," said Breaca, watching him. "You do not wish to be encumbered by anything. And yet you have a good heart, which fights always that selfish, restless side of you. Your heart must win this time. Take Merewyn away from here, bring her to her aunt, who I feel is still alive. It is not much to ask."

Yet he was silent, and she twisted herself around to look up at the crucifix. "For the love of God, and Our Lord, Jesus Christ — have mercy now, Rumon," she said. "I have hitherto known no mercy."

Rumon lowered his head and crossed himself, and yet he could not give assent. Why should he take responsibility for a girl he had met but yesterday, a girl scarcely more than a child? How was he to find an aunt — somewhere in England called Shaftesbury — or believe that such an aunt still lived, despite Breaca's fey assurance. How true it was that he did not wish to be encumbered with any other human being. And what was really in Breaca's mind? Did she wish to trap him, by desire — by propinquity — into an association with her daughter which would ensure Merewyn's future? He thought of Edgive's efforts to lure him with heiresses. But *they* had been girls of noble birth, while this poor little misbegotten thing, the fruit of sickening violence and a half-mad Cornish woman — what had he to do with *her*?

"I wonder, madame," he said slowly, "that you would subject your innocent daughter to a situation in which her virtue might be lost. That you trust me — or do you? Is that aspect unimportant?"

Breaca strained, as though trying to understand his words. She pressed her hand harder against her chest. "I trust you," she whispered, then gave a low moan. "Call Merewyn! I can stand no more."

The girl came hurrying in, smiling with pleasure. "Look!" she cried. A white dove was perched on her shoulder. "Look, Mama! It flew into the courtyard and came straight to me. It's so pretty. Where could it have come from?"

Breaca scarcely stirred. Her breaths were harsh and shallow.

Rumon looked at the dove, which fluttered off Merewyn's shoulder and flew up to perch on the crucifix. A shiver went down his spine, for as he stared the dove began to shimmer and give forth a pale golden light. The light streamed on towards Rumon, and he heard the lovely faraway sound of voices singing. The chiming voices, though so soft, drowned out Merewyn's cry of fear and the rattle Breaca made in her throat.

"Mother!" Merewyn screamed. "Mother, what is it?" She threw herself on the bed, shaking and kissing the woman, who did not respond.

Rumon could not move. The singing faded. The golden light grew dim. The dove folded its white wings and hopped along the crossbar of the crucifix; it preened its feathers and flew clumsily out of the open door into the courtyard. Rumon sat on half dazed; held by a great and joyous awe. The vision had come again. Not quite as it had been the first time — no voice had spoken directly to him now, but the ever latent yearning was rekindled. The Quest was real.

He emerged with reluctance to hear Merewyn sobbing wildly. To see Caw, looming in the doorway, his huge face puckered by fear, while the dog cringed in a corner, whining.

Rumon stood up and looked at the bed. He put his hands on Merewyn's shoulders, and lifted her away. "Hush —" he said to her. "It's finished. Your mother's sufferings are over. Her soul has gone to God."

"That bird!" Merewyn cried. "I shouldn't have brought it in. Birds in the house mean evil tidings. Oh, dear Lord, why did I bring it in!" She covered her head with her arms.

"Merewyn," said Rumon sternly, "Perhaps the white dove came from God. Raise your head and look now at your mother!"

She shuddered but she heard, and slowly obeyed him.

From Breaca's upturned face all marks of pain had gone. It looked as young as Merewyn's, and on the pale lips there was a faint delighted smile.

They left Tre-Uther the next morning . . . Rumon and Merewyn on the horse, Caw shambling behind with a great sack thrown over his shoulder. It contained the girl's few portable possessions. The dog trotted beside them.

They had buried Breaca below the house on the river shore as she had once told Merewyn she wished to be. She could not, of course, be put in consecrated ground. She had died unshriven. That she had nonetheless died in a state of grace, Rumon was sure, but he knew the impossibility of explaining this to Poldu. He did not attempt it; though he did see the fat prior again, long enough to arrange the sale of Tre-Uther's pigs and chickens to the monastery. Nobody wanted the house or the land, which was now Merewyn's.

"Haunted — that place is," said Poldu. "Was before an'll be worse *now* wi' that doomed witchwoman's ghost wailing round it. So ye're taking the lass wi' ye! Bit o' risk considering her blood, but lads must have their fun no doubt, an' she's not an ill-looking wench. I saw her once last autumn."

"Spying from a treetop, I suppose," Rumon said acidly.

The prior chuckled. "I'm too stout now for such games. I saw her as I was passing Tre-Uther on the way to Bodmin. By the bye remember we've a frolic in our village tonight, honor o' St. Petroc. Like to go?"

"No," said Rumon, gathering up the silver which Poldu had reluctantly disbursed for Merewyn's livestock. "And I bid you farewell."

"God be wi' you," said the prior mechanically. "Ye've

diddled a good price from me for that brat's chattels, now mind in return, don't ye go stirring up aught against my comfort when ye leave here."

Rumon shrugged. "I assure you, Reverend Sir, that I hope never to think of you or Cornwall again!"

It was a pity, Rumon thought, while he and his charges jogged along the track up the Camel River, that Merewyn could not feel the relief that he did at leaving. She had wept bitterly this morning. She was crying now. He could feel the quiverings behind him on the horse and hear stifled noises.

Poor thing, he thought impatiently, I hope she'll get over it soon. He had no wish to cart a sobbing damsel into England; they were an odd enough party as it was. He glanced back at the gigantic Caw and his great bumpy pack. Then it began to drizzle, and Rumon frowned, trying to decide just when they *would* reach England, and from those conjectures he thankfully turned to the memory of the vision he had seen above Breaca's bed. It warmed and contented him like a fire. Yet he knew that this had been only a glimpse of the mystery, which had revealed itself more fully years ago. Or was it a fringe of the same mystery, or had he perhaps been deluded, as Edgive would certainly have said. He could hear her voice of scorn.

"Foolish boy. You were wrought up by the dying woman's pitiable state, though you didn't want to do as she begged. And after all it was a *real* dove, wasn't it? You've seen a hundred like it at Les Baux. You'll be trying next to tell me that you've seen the Holy Ghost. Ah, Romieux, will nothing knock the fancies out of you!"

Merewyn had no visions to sustain her. Again and again she turned, straining to see the stones and thatching of Tre-Uther, to see the spot on the riverbank where her mother had been laid. When she could no longer see those she gazed back at the great headland of Pentire where she had so often wandered on the seaside cliffs collecting odd-shaped stones and wild flowers to bring home. She remembered Breaca's pleasure and the pretty designs they made together. She remembered her mother's rare tender smiles and the wonderful stories she could tell by the fireside on winter nights — stories of piskies and mermaids, and of King Arthur, his courage, his gallantry, of the way he slew giants and routed foreign demons who threatened their beloved country. And always when these tales ended, Merewyn would hold her head high, feeling a little sorry for her mother who might not also claim the hero's glorious blood as her own.

Ah, I must be worthy of him — she thought. And worthy of my father, Uther.

Yet she could not stop weeping. Every thud of the horse's hoofs carried her further away from all she had known. "Alone, forlorn, alone." The words rang in her head like the dirge of the passing bell from the church as it often tolled from the Padstow hillside at someone's burial.

"Merewyn," said Rumon over his shoulder. "I know you have great sorrow, but I also think you have courage. Have done with this sobbing. I believe I see Bodmin ahead."

"Ah, you're ashamed of me," she cried, choking. "I know you don't want me here. And I don't want to go!"

"Needs must, my dear," he said with a shrug, startled by her vehemence. "It won't be too long before I deliver you to your aunt."

"And glad of that you'll be!" she cried so wildly that the dog stopped trotting and looked up at her.

Why shouldn't I be glad? thought Rumon, a bit annoyed by this feminine inconsistency of which he had no experience. He said nothing, and he was relieved to hear that she too grew silent. He returned to his thoughts while they entered a huddle of wooden houses on the outskirts of Bodmin.

They spent the night in wretched lodgings, and the next day they started into Bodmin moor. At noontime they were swathed in a sudden drifting white mist, and Rumon stopped to ask the way from a shepherd who was sitting on a stone which formed part of the many prehistoric villages dotting the moor.

"Straight on yonder," said the shepherd. "Leave Dozmary pool to your right. Mind ye don't get pisky-led into the pool. 'Tis haunted."

"Dozmary pool?" said Merewyn suddenly. "Isn't that where King Arthur's sword was thrown before he died?"

"I've heard some such tale," said the shepherd, staring at the simply dressed Cornish girl, then at the disdainful, elegantly clothed young man.

"I am a descendant of King Arthur's," announced Merewyn. "My mother told me about Dozmary pool."

"Be ye so, now!" said the shepherd, staring harder. "I've heard tell there was a family of Arthur's blood living over Padstow way."

"That's ours!" she cried. "That's Tre-Uther. My father was Uther!"

"Merewyn!" Rumon interrupted. "We must hurry on." He kicked his horse's flank, and the beast broke into a trot leaving the shepherd behind.

"Soon," said Rumon, "we'll be across the Tamar and into England. I'm sure they've scant interest in King Arthur there. I wouldn't mention him again." He spoke more sharply than he meant to because her childish pride in what he knew to be a miserable falsehood made him uncomfortable. "And by the bye, that reminds me, you'll have to learn some English. We'd best start at once."

The girl sighed. How had she displeased him now? All morning they had ridden in harmony. She had controlled her sorrow, and tried not to think of the past. They had chatted of the sights along the way — the bleak mysterious moors, the sharp cone of Brown Willy rising in the distance. They had shared a youthful, excited interest. Now he had gone stern and aloof. She glanced at the back of his head, at his shining black hair from which came the delicious clean scent.

"Cornish 'den', " said Rumon, "is 'man' in English. 'Benen' is 'woman.' Repeat it."

She did so, in a small subdued voice. The lesson continued. Rumon was a good teacher, and Merewyn was quick to learn. By the time they approached their night's stop at Launceton she could translate several words and was delighted by his praise. "Good," he cried, smiling. "From now on I'll speak only English to you. You'll learn quicker thus, and you must be as tired as I am of my very foreign brand of Cornish."

"Oh, no!" she objected. "Please don't stop speaking Cornish to me, it'll be lonely, and English is ugly."

"I don't think it is," he answered after a moment in Cornish — exasperated by the reminder of how dependent she was on him. "I believe most unfamiliar things seem ugly at first, unless, of course, one has a zest for travel and change, as I have. Perhaps women don't," he added. "The girls I've met were always wanting to settle down."

Merewyn was silent, conscious of her ignorance about what most women wanted — or men either. She knew however with sad certainty what *she* wanted. She wanted Rumon to take her in his arms and hold her close while she laid her cheek against the blue velvet mantle on his shoulder. Her thoughts went no further than that, and she was perfectly aware of their impracticability. He had not touched her since the morning he arrived at Tre-Uther and took her hand in sympathy. Yet surely he treated her less as though she were a troublesome child than he had when they started the journey. And surely now and then she pleased him, because he would smile at her with friendliness.

She had walled off the memory of her mother and all the years at Tre-Uther; she was too young and too reasonable to indulge in useless grief even if she had not seen that it vexed Rumon. Yet though sorrow for the past could be quenched, dread of the future could not. If only this journey might last indefinitely. She had no wish to find the baleful-sounding

"Shaftesbury" or the unknown aunt, no wish to meet the English king, who would — according to Rumon — at once settle the disposition of her person, and dispatch her to her aunt.

They reached Launceton by sunset, and Rumon found them lodgings in an inn below the Castle hill. This inn was the most elaborate place Merewyn had ever seen, since it had several sleeping chambers, and a lofty public hall through which servants scurried with steaming dishes and foaming tankards for a motley collection of patrons.

Caw, who had so far eaten with them, was now sent off to the kitchen, while Merewyn shrank down on a wall bench indicated by Rumon and listened nervously to some incisive English voices which mingled with the slower lilting Cornish.

Rumon consumed his blood sausages and ale, then left her to join a party of English merchants who were singing lustily and playing catchpenny. He came back in ten minutes crying, "We're in luck! The Court is at Lydford across the river, not two hours' ride from here. We'll be there at noon tomorrow."

Her eyes widened, and she shook her head. "I don't understand."

"To be sure," said Rumon. "I forgot I was speaking English." He translated his news, and added more.

"I couldn't have come at a better time. It seems King Edgar is to be crowned at last on Whitsunday at Bath, but is at present visiting his Queen's old home at Lydford. Most of the Court is with him."

"Oh," said Merewyn, in a small voice. She had never seen him so enthusiastic, or so handsome. His eyes sparkled, his voice rang out and attracted the attention of a Launceton man who was supping alone further down the table. He was a silversmith, a meager, pointed-nosed little man, with a taste for gossip, which his calling gave him an opportunity to enjoy for he sold his silver thread and silver-gilt brooches not only here in the Cornish castle town but across the Tamar in England. He cocked his brows and said sardonically to Rumon, "You'd best stick rowan in your shoe and tell your beads before you meet the Queen, young sir."

"Why?" Rumon stared at the little man, who shrugged and gave a wary glance around.

"From what I hear, ye'll be in trouble if she don't like ye, and in worse trouble if she do."

"Bah!" said Rumon laughing. "I believe I can take care of myself. What's her name? Eneda?" He dimly remembered his grandmother mentioning Edgar's Queen.

"No," said the silversmith. "That was the first one. Eneda the White Duck they called her for she was plump and fair. Eneda was the first one the King *married*, but he was a rare one for the wenches, slaves, maids, ladies or nuns he'd yank 'em all to his bed."

Merewyn drew in her breath and stared at her lap. Why would he want all those women in his bed? She didn't know, yet she was shocked. Neither man noticed her.

"Well," said Rumon, "kings always have special opportunities, but you speak as though this wenching was past. Why's that?" He was anxious to learn all he could of the Court he was bound for. He signaled to a servant and ordered an ale for the silversmith, who was gratified and answered promptly.

"Ah, they say he's right under the Queen's thumb — besotted by her. Also there's the Archbishop Dunstan. Strict in his views Dunstan is. That's why he wouldn't crown the King all these fourteen years he's been reigning, sort of penance for that early lust."

"Oh," said Rumon, thoughtfully. "But what's the Queen's name?"

"Aelfryth, or some such Saxon bungle they won't pronounce themselves, for I understand everyone calls her Alfrida."

"Latinized," said Rumon nodding. "Have you ever seen her?"

"Once," answered the silversmith, warmed by Rumon's ale, and quite ready to oblige since the young man had the dress and manners of the well-born. Besides he spoke Cornish, and there was no danger of a touchy Englishman overhearing. "There's a royal mint at Lydford," said the silversmith," and I go there now and again to buy silver from the moneyer. That's where I saw Alfrida. Lydford was her home. She was born there, daughter of Ordgar, Earl of the Western Shires. Now her brother Lord Ordulf lives there. A great hulking mountain of a man, *he* is — most as big as that servant o' yours I saw going to the kitchen."

"And is Queen Alfrida a great mountain of a woman?"

The silversmith shook his head. "She's tall, maybe as high as you, sir, but she's slim like a hazel wand and has yellow hair to her knees. She's reckoned the most beautiful woman in England," he lowered his voice, " — *and* the most wicked."

"Indeed. What an interesting tribute. Just how has she earned the latter distinction?"

"Murders," whispered the silversmith with relish. "She's stopped at nothing to be queen. She was wed early to the East Anglian Earl Athelwold, but when King Edgar saw her — and they say she gave him a love potion — he had to have her. So he lured her husband to Wherwell Forest, and stuck a spear in the Earl. Then there was Eneda, poor duck, the King repudiated her and married Alfrida, but Dunstan he said the marriage was irregular as long as Eneda lived, another reason he wouldn't crown the King properly. And this winter Eneda died. So you see . . ."

"You suggest that Eneda was poisoned?" asked Rumon coldly. The judicial side of his nature made him view the silversmith's assertions with skepticism and by counterbalance he felt some sympathy for the slandered Alfrida, who was royalty, and therefore kin of his own. "Folk often die quite naturally, and it appears that Alfrida had no hand in her *husband's* death."

The silversmith looked offended. "She's a witch," he said, "and makes others do her bidding. I'm only repeating what I've heard. You asked me, and I can see you're not a Sawsnach —

so I answered. Well, I must be off to m'smithy. The Lady
Buryan at our castle has ordered brooches and buckles to wear
at the coronation, for I'm the only able silversmith in Cornwall."
The little man rose abruptly, and bowing, quit the inn. Rumon
suddenly remembered Merewyn, who was plucking at a fold of
her red cloak and frowning.

"Don't ever be worried by rumors and gossip," said Rumon
kindly to her. "I'm sure we'll find that the Queen's wickedness
is as exaggerated by report as is, no doubt, her beauty. And
besides you'll have nothing to do with the royal family, I'm
sure."

The next day, having forded the Tamar and entered England,
they came into Lydford at noon.

Lydford, the seat of the Devonshire earls, was a straggling
wooden village, surrounded by moorland streams, earthworks,
and a palisade. It was dominated by its castle, built of stone and
timber, perched high on a hill. From the topmost wooden
turret there billowed a large green flag with a white horse
embroidered on it, denoting that the King was in residence. The
lanes and alleys at the foot of the castle were crammed with
soldiers in chain mail and bright helmets. Rough shelters had
been erected both inside and out of the earthworks for the
accommodation of the court's overflow. There were even
hastily built huts on the south bank of the Lyd. The air was
filled with a constant din, such as Merewyn had never imagined;
not only the raucous shouts of English soldiers, the lowing of
oxen, the pealing of the church bell, the hawking of peddlers,
but a clanging tooting racket near the church where some musicians were practicing on cymbals and trumpets. Rumon held
his head high, and approached the castle bridge at a trot. Merewyn had slipped off the horse, suspecting that he would not
want to be embarrassed at this important moment by the presence of a Cornish peasant girl, clinging to him around the waist.
She waited nervously behind across the castle ditch with Caw
and Trig, and was for a time sufficiently busy preventing dog-

fights while Trig exchanged insults with the Lydford curs which
rushed at him in all directions.

At the bridge the sentry indifferently challenged Rumon
and as indifferently waved him into the castle when Rumon
gave his name. Lord Ordulf perforce kept open house during
the King's visit. In the paved courtyard there was a welter of
merchants, housecarls, black-habited monks, and two richly
dressed mounted thanes from other parts of Devon, who
watched the mob superciliously. All were apparently waiting
their turn to ascend the circular stone steps to the upper stories.
Rumon paused uncertainly, looking for someone in authority,
when there was a sudden hush. The milling crowd drew apart
to form an aisle, and Rumon saw a smallish black figure slowly
emerging from the bottom of the stairs.

All those not mounted fell to their knees.

Now who can this be, Rumon thought, startled by the tokens
of respect around him — homage worthy of a king. Yet it was
certainly not the King. This was a man in his sixties, clothed
in the black Benedictine habit, yet with additions; a gold-
embroidered cope fastened at the neck by a jeweled cross; a
pearl-studded skullcap with two flaps half concealing a grizzled
tonsure. He carried an elaborately carved ivory and silver T-
headed staff on which he leaned heavily, limping a trifle.

Rumon heard someone murmur "Dunstan" and was enlight-
ened. So here was the redoubtable Archbishop of Canterbury,
who did not look redoubtable at all. He had ruddy cheeks, a
snub nose slightly askew, and a vague benign gaze beneath bushy
gray eyebrows.

The benign gaze, however, altered as the Archbishop paused
in his progress and instantly perceived Rumon. The wrinkled
lids parted and disclosed burning eyes sharply focused.

Ever watchful of his King's and country's interest, it was
Dunstan's business to recognize and investigate any stranger. He
advanced at once towards Rumon, held up two fingers in benediction, and said, "Christ's blessing on you, sir. I've not seen

you before." The voice was mellow yet most authoritative. So
was the gesture that Dunstan made.

Rumon dismounted and knelt. The Archbishop extended a
delicately molded hand, and Rumon duly kissed a huge amethyst
ring on the forefinger.

"You may rise," said Dunstan, noting with surprise the grace
of the stranger's gesture. The Archbishop had been laboring
for years to instill proper ceremonial observance amongst the
unruly earls and thanes of Edgar's court, and the results were
still often disappointing.

"You are gently born?" said Dunstan, "And from overseas,
I think?"

"Yes, my lord." Rumon pulled his Latin parchment from
under his tunic and presented it.

Dunstan scanned it rapidly and was astonished. An *atheling?*
he thought. A prince descended from the right line of Cerdic
and of King Alfred? He didn't look it, he carried no sword, his
mount was a plow horse, poorly harnessed, while the man himself was too dark complexioned to have Saxon blood, he thought,
and though we've peace in the Daneland and Northumbria, yet
who's to be sure of what those Norse heathens are up to overseas.
Also passports may be forged or stolen.

Dunstan examined the young man, while Rumon reddened.
It had never occurred to him that his word might be doubted.

Dunstan at last said sternly, "You have a retinue outside, sir?
You have come for the coronation?"

"Neither, my lord," answered Rumon. "No retinue, and I
knew nothing about the coronation. I was shipwrecked at the
tip of Cornwall." He gave the Archbishop his slightly rueful
smile. "I swear by the Blessed Blood of Our Lord that my safe-
conduct speaks the truth."

"Well —" said Dunstan. "That is a mighty oath but I've
heard others like it which were false. There are some questions
I wish to ask." He glanced at the kneeling figures who were

muttering and shifting, curious to hear what went on. "In here —" said the Archbishop, gesturing towards a doorway and preceding Rumon.

The door lead into a small guardroom, empty now since Ordulf's men were at dinner in the lower hall. The Archbishop shut the door and sat down on a bench. "Now —" he said twining his fingers around his crozier. "I'm an old man, and I've much experience in judging people. You have a frank face but so has many a villain. You must see that it is my duty to guard the King from impostors, or from any threat of danger. In eleven days Edgar will, at last, become the Lord's Anointed. He will receive Divine Sanction for the ruling of his realm. It will be the happiest moment of his life — and of mine. No untoward incident of any sort must mar it."

"I see that, my lord," said Rumon, "and I assure you that my only wish is to serve King Edgar, who is my cousin."

The Archbishop shrugged. "Tell me your tale from the beginning."

Rumon obeyed, starting slowly, stammering a little, then finding confidence. He told of his early years at Arles, then of those at Les Baux. Dunstan listened so carefully, never shifting his eyes, that Rumon said more than he meant to about his fears, about his hatred of battles and his distaste for wenching. He spoke of Vincent, the blind harpist, and even to his own astonishment mentioned the vision he had had at fifteen. Here Dunstan raised his eyebrows, and a different light momentarily softened the steady gaze, but he said nothing. Rumon went on to tell of Edgive and her disappointment in him. Of her decision to send him to the English Court. Then Rumon told of his travels through the Frankish kingdom, of the winter in Brittany, of the shipwreck on the Lizard, and the uncouth heathen family there. Here Dunstan interrupted.

"Did you not try to convert them?"

Rumon shook his head. "They were animals, my lord."

"They have immortal souls," said Dunstan coldly. "But go on."

Rumon told of his wanderings, of his meeting with Merewyn, of his night at Poldu's monastery, though not of what Poldu had told him about Merewyn. His oath to the dying Breaca precluded that.

Rumon paused to moisten his lips, and the Archbishop said thoughtfully, "There have been none of those Viking pirate raids since Edgar started to reign. The Lord has protected us under his merciful wings. Glory be to God! And what you tell me of that so-called Cornish monastery is indeed disgraceful, yet reform takes time. The whole of England was as lax but recently." He recollected himself and concentrated on the young man he was investigating. "Continue."

Rumon went on to tell of Breaca's death, when suddenly his voice trembled, and he paused again.

"This poor Cornish woman's death moved you so much?" asked Dunstan dryly.

"When it happened, I had a vision." Rumon spoke with reluctance, nor did he describe the advent of the white pigeon.

Dunstan himself had had many visions, mostly prophetic, but he asked no questions. He waited.

Rumon then hastily described his unwilling guardianship of Merewyn, and the journey out of Cornwall. "That is all, my lord, we arrived here some two hours ago."

"Where is the girl now?"

"In the village with her slave and dog."

"And you indicate that she is as much a virgin as when she left her home in Padstow? You have not bedded her?"

"Holy Mother of God — NO!" cried Rumon. "It never occurred to me."

A smile twitched the corners of the Archbishop's lips. "You seem to be quite an odd young man, and you tell a remarkable story. I still desire proofs. You claim an extraordinary education. Can you read this?" Dunstan fished in the pocket of his habit and brought out a small exquisitely illuminated vellum book in Latin. "Can you read this prayer — which you certainly don't know since I wrote it myself."

Rumon read the indicated prayer in Latin.

"Now translate it into English."

Rumon did so.

"Now into French, and then Celtic."

Rumon obeyed, with a touch of complacence.

Dunstan nodded. On his journey to Rome to obtain the Archbishop's pallium from the Pope, he had perforce heard much French, while the Irish monks at Glastonbury had taught him some Celtic. "I believe your translations are correct," he said, "I congratulate you."

We indeed might use a man like this, he thought. Use him in the Church for which he obviously has a leaning. But the Archbishop was thorough, and none of this linguistic prowess was proof of the high birth the young man claimed.

Dunstan leaned forward. "When I was a child at Glastonbury, I saw the Queen Edgiva who you say is your grandmother. It was just before she sailed for France on her way to marry the blind King Louis of Arles. She had gone to take communion in our most sacred church in England — the little old wattle one built by Christ's angels for St. Joseph of Arimathea, and dedicated to Our Lady. Do you know anything about what happened in the church that day?"

Rumon thought a moment. "I don't know what you mean, my lord. Except something my lady grandmother once told me as a — a bad example. While the Abbot was celebrating High Mass for her, and just as she was about to sip from the sacred chalice, a frog hopped through the door. It hopped up the chancel steps and hid itself beneath the Abbot's robes. My grandmother, who was very young, burst into laughter, even spilling the consecrated wine. The Abbot was shocked. He stopped the Mass and upbraided her from the altar steps. She was much ashamed and never forgot the disgrace of that moment."

"Aha!" said Dunstan, slowly. He had been an acolyte and well remembered the episode. He was now nearly convinced, yet he did not show it. He still questioned. "And later did the Abbot — whose name was Aelfric — did he give her anything?"

"Yes, my lord. A reliquary which she must always wear secretly in her bosom, as indeed she has."

"But you have seen it?"

"She opened it once to show me before I left her, saying that she would pray to it for my safety."

"What was the relic that she showed you?"

"A thread from the Virgin's robe, my lord."

"And what color was the thread?"

"Blue, my lord."

Dunstan's hands fell from his staff, he gave a long quivering sigh. "Forgive me, my son," he whispered. "Forgive me. No one else *could* have known these things." His eyes blurred and filled with tears. "You *are* the prince you claim to be," he said almost on a sob. "You *are* cousin to King Edgar and therefore distant kin to me." Copious tears dripped down his cheeks.

Rumon viewed these with gratified astonishment. He did not know that the Archbishop often wept — from humility, or pity, from the contemplation of a virtuous deed or a beautiful manuscript — or when singing praises to Our Lord.

"What can be sharp as a dagger, yet soft as spring rain?" was a popular riddle, which one of his monks had made up about Dunstan.

"Now," said the Archbishop, drying his eyes on his black sleeve, "I will take you to the King, but stay — what about that girl — Merewyn you call her, she must be hungry, poor child. And it's not fitting that a woman of high blood should be left outside with the rabble. You said that her father is descended from King Arthur?"

Rumon compressed his lips. "I had not thought that the Cornish king of so long ago would be well thought of in England."

"On the contrary. King Arthur and his Queen Guinevere are buried at Glastonbury. Our Celtic monks — of which we have many there — reverence the graves. It is my desire — and King Edgar's — that all the different nationalities of our island shall respect each other and live in harmony together — as you will see, we even have several Danes at Court. But the girl. I know her Aunt Merwinna well, a most holy woman. She is no longer at Shaftesbury, she has become Abbess of Romsey."

"Then Merewyn can be sent to her at once?" asked Rumon eagerly.

Again a flicker of amusement crossed Dunstan's face. Such zeal to escape from a woman's company might mean that she was ugly, but more likely it came from a true monkish vocation, as yet unacknowledged, and the Archbishop was delighted. Here in this young man was perfect ecclesiastical material waiting to be molded by skillful hands. A bishop, someday, he thought. He looked tenderly at Rumon, whom he now liked immensely, and all the more so from sorrow at having suspected him.

He smiled and said, "It would not be wise to send the girl to Romsey at present, since the Abbess will be traveling to Bath for the Coronation, as are all the dignitaries, secular and clerical in the kingdom. As *we* shall be. No, I'll summon the girl and see that she is properly received here first."

The Archbishop rose with decision, and Merewyn's future was changed from that moment.

chapter three

RUMON and Merewyn were ushered together into the Great Hall of Lydford Castle. Dunstan waved the girl back as he led Rumon towards the dais at the far end, where the King was sitting in a carved red armchair.

Merewyn shrank into a corner near the entrance. She was dazed by the rapid events of the last half hour; ever since a servant of the Archbishop's had retrieved her from her long wait across the castle ditch, and made it plain by gestures that she was to follow him into the castle. She had been startled by the Archbishop's extremely courteous greeting, puzzled by Rumon's constraint, and the curtness with which he explained in Cornish that they were both to be presented to the King.

While they had waited in an antechamber for Dunstan's reappearance, they drank ale and ate bread brought them by another servant. Merewyn caught glimpses of several court ladies trailing up and down the stairs. The ladies were visions in multicolored robes trimmed with fur and embroideries, flashing with gold chains and brooches. Merewyn became miserably aware of her brown homespun kirtle, her worn sheepskin sandals, her old travel-stained cloak. She decided that Rumon was increasingly ashamed of her, and did not blame him, though she was hurt by his silence. Now she sat down on the edge of a bench and waited.

The huge raftered Hall was lit by high windows open to the May afternoon sunshine which glowed on the gaily painted wall hangings depicting war scenes, ships, and odd beasts, including a blood-red dragon. Above these wall cloths a continuous row of decorated wooden shields made a glittering frieze when the sun caught the central gilt bosses. The shields belonged to Lord Ordulf's men — his thanes and housecarls — and were ready for instant use if there should be a battle call. Though there had been no such alarm in anyone's memory. Not since the days of Alfred. As for the Cornish (against whose raids from across the Tamar this castle at Lydford had been originally built), *they* had caused no trouble for a hundred years.

Yet men still enjoyed hearing of great battles — those of Charlemagne and Alfred, of Arthur, of Julius Caesar, and particularly the exploits of Beowulf.

The Hall benches were empty; the dinner hour had passed and the company all gone. Only the High Table was occupied.

King Edgar sat in the state chair, sipping occasionally from a flagon and listening critically to Ordulf's bard who stood a little behind the King, plucking at a harp and chanting the lay which the King had requested — "The Battle of Brunanburgh."

Edgar was fond of this song since it celebrated his uncle, King Athelstan, and his father, King Edmund, and the glorious victory they had won in Northumbria against the Norsemen, thirty-five years ago. Edgar knew the lay by heart, and once corrected the bard who forgot a line; but he smiled as the chanting voice deepened emphatically for the triumphant ending. "Then the two brothers, both together — the King and the Atheling sought their kin in the land of Wessex, exulting in the conflict . . . never was an army put to greater slaughter by the sword since the time when hither from the East the Angles and the Saxons came, seeking Britain over the broad ocean, and the haughty warsmiths overcame the Britons and won for themselves this land!" The bard rippled up his harp strings and bowed.

"Good," said Edgar, his blue eyes shining. He tossed the bard a silver penny.

Next to Edgar, Queen Alfrida's chair was vacant, but two most powerful noblemen were seated further down the table, playing chess.

One was Ordulf, royal thane and brother-in-law to the King. He was, as the silversmith had said, "a mountain of a man." Few horses could carry him, and his pink fingers looked like sausages as they rested on the ivory chess pieces. He was indolent, amiable, a trifle slow-witted and very devout. He even acted as a kind of lay abbot at nearby Tavistock Abbey which his father, Earl Ordgar, had founded. Ordulf inclined his flaxen head towards the King in gratitude that his bard had given satisfaction. The other chess player — Earl Alfhere, the Lord of all Mercia, instantly seized upon this moment of inattention, and soon put Ordulf's king in check. Then he gave a peal of derisive laughter, before pursing his shiny red lips, and eying his opponent maliciously. Alfhere was a handsome hawk-nosed man of forty, who usually succeeded in any game of wits, though he had not so far succeeded in ousting the Monastic party, especially as represented by Dunstan whose influence over the young King Alfhere resented. The Earl owned a quarter of England, or had done so, before Dunstan had made the King filch land from him for the new Benedictine monasteries and nunneries the intrusive Primate kept founding. Not only that — Dunstan; Oswald, Archbishop of York; and Ethelwold, Bishop of Winchester were all briskly ejecting secular clergy, thus crushing many of Alfhere's relations who now looked to him for support.

It was therefore with marked annoyance that Alfhere's hooded gray eyes watched the arrival of Dunstan and Rumon, and the latter's presentation to the King.

The Archbishop addressed Edgar for some moments, though

he had already prepared him for the appearance of a cousin. Then Dunstan waved his hand and Rumon kneeled before the red chair, saying humbly, "My Lord King, I bear the loving greetings of your aunt, Queen Edgive of Arles, and I bear also the hope that I may be of service to you."

The King jumped up. He leaned down and kissed Rumon on both cheeks, crying, "Welcome, welcome, Cousin!" in such glad ringing tones that Merewyn could hear the greeting at the other end of the Hall. She watched Rumon rise, and saw with surprise that though he was not uncommon tall he towered over the King who was a small chunky man, scarcely bigger than a lad, though his straw-colored mustache and beard precluded immaturity, and he was in fact twenty-nine. His hair was tawny as a fox's pelt and curled over his ears. He wore a simple circlet of gold, and a squirrel-trimmed, gold-threaded cape over shoulders which were very broad for one of his height.

He drew Rumon down beside him into the Queen's seat and showed warm delight. His laugh which was deep and pleasant rang out.

There ensued a round of drinking from gem-studded beakers in which the lords and the Archbishop joined. The King kept his arm twined affectionately around Rumon's neck, while they drank from the same cup, and altogether the evidences of welcome and good-fellowship pleased Merewyn for Rumon's sake, though she did finally begin to wonder if everyone had forgotten her again. And if so, what was she to do? She longed to run away but there was no place to go.

Dunstan, however, who never forgot anything, had kept a distant eye on the girl while he waited for the excitement of Rumon's arrival to abate. He interrupted the King quietly and said, "My lord, your newfound cousin has brought with him a most piteous child, whose story will, I know, move your tender heart. She is an orphan. A maiden of royal blood — the ancient British blood — yet destitute."

"Indeed?" said Edgar, his eyes sparkling. "Tell me about her, my lord of Canterbury!"

Dunstan inclined his head. "I will, unless the Atheling wishes to?" He gestured towards Rumon who drew back, and showed his discomfort so blatantly that the King began to laugh.

"On the contrary, I believe," said Dunstan smiling. "Lord Rumon has but done his Christian duty in conducting her here. Her tale is this . . ."

Whereupon Rumon perforce listened to an account of Merewyn's life which was remarkably accurate except for the central premise which alone ensured her ceremonious reception. The King was interested. He best loved tales of battle and adventure, yet he enjoyed novelty, and in Dunstan's skillful telling the pathos of Merewyn's situation became vivid. And Edgar had a particular fondness for the legends of King Arthur whom he sometimes fancied he resembled. At his palace in Winchester he kept several bards, and the Welsh one knew many songs about Arthur, who had fought so bravely for his country against the Saxon invaders, five hundred years ago. That those Saxon invaders were also Edgar's own ancestors no longer seemed important.

The Saxons had adopted Arthur as one of their heroes; after so long a time the conquerors felt no animosity towards the old Celtic stock; nor had need to.

"Where is the maiden?" Edgar cried as his Archbishop finished. "She shall be cared for at once by the Lady Alfrida. Summon the Queen!" he said to a servant.

Merewyn, blushing hot, walked timidly down the Hall, and imitating Rumon, fell to her knees before the King. He seized her gently by the chin, and raising her face, examined it with a connoisseur's eye. Pretty lass, he thought. Unusual appearance. A rosy skin unfortunately marred by some freckles across a blunt little nose. What he could see of the downcast eyes was good. They were large and light, and of a color between green and blue. The lashes and brows were dark, but the hair — very abundant to judge by the thickness of her plaits — was of a hue the King had never seen before. Almost dark red, rather like the color of the great garnet which decorated his mantle brooch. Figure seemed undeveloped — one couldn't be sure what lay under the hideous homespun shift and cloak. Once I would have tried to find out, Edgar thought, then he glanced guiltily at Dunstan, who stood watching.

"Rise, Lady Merewyn," said the King. "I have heard your unhappy story, and bid you heartily welcome to my Court. We will befriend you, and treat you with the honor due to the last of King Arthur's line."

Merewyn blushed harder, she understood the gist of what the King had said, stammered "Thank you, sir" in English, and could not forbear darting at Rumon a look of puzzled triumph. He had told her that nobody in England would care about King Arthur, had forbidden her to mention her lineage, and yet he must have done so himself. How strange.

Rumon's face showed a mixture of annoyance and resignation. Yet there was a slight smile on his lips. He gave a shrug, raising his hands and letting them fall again — a foreign gesture, of which he had several.

There came a rustling at the door behind the dais; everyone turned and then stood up, except the King, who said tenderly, "Ah, here you are, my love!"

Alfrida walked towards them with a graceful glide, her tall slender body seeming to undulate. Merewyn gasped; Rumon also drew in his breath and held it, while he stared.

Nobody upon first beholding Alfrida ever questioned her flawless beauty, possibly because she never questioned it herself, and worshiped it for the power it gave her. She was twenty-eight and enchanting. Her wavy hair — the exact shade of buttercups — fell loose to her knees. Her eyes were violet, so was her silk gown, its bodice cut low enough to expose her round provocative breasts down to the pink nipples. A gauzy white veil framed her face, softening a determined clefted chin. In repose her full moist mouth, reddened by cochineal paste, had a slightly protruding lower lip, which disclosed the lower row of small perfect teeth. A seductive, and at times sulky mouth, one that many a man had ached to kiss, while some had succeeded. High cheekbones and a short straight nose completed a face whose proportions were exquisite.

Her skin, constantly tended with rosewater and unguents, was like creamy velvet. On her head, anchoring the gauzy veil, she wore a little golden circlet like the king's. She exuded waves of a flowery oriental perfume, which the King had had exported for her from the Levant.

Merewyn and Rumon were at one in their awed admiration. The King stared up at Alfrida with doting pleasure. The noblemen, one her brother, Ordulf — and the other, Alfhere, who had long desired her, paid her the momentary tribute of silence, before returning to their chess game. Alfrida seated herself beside the King, gave Rumon and Merewyn each a brilliant smile, then placing her hand over Edgar's, said in a soft voice that she was eager to hear about the newcomers. Edgar kissed her hand and started eagerly on the narration. Rumon and Merewyn sat speechless, gazing at the Queen.

Dunstan, alone, was unmoved. He stood apart leaning on his crozier, waiting for the King to finish. He had long ago observed that those violet eyes were deepset, not large, that they could narrow with a hard purpose; that the underlip could jut out further if the Queen were vexed, and that sudden temper could contort the lovely face. He alone always noticed her hands. White and rosy-palmed, they were nevertheless square, powerful, with blunt spatulate fingers which sometimes flexed in a grasping motion.

Dunstan distrusted the Queen, though he liked most women, and Alfrida had always accorded him punctilious courtesy. He had perforce accepted the hold she had on the King, he had even persuaded himself that Edgar's passion for her was beneficial since it prevented the lustful crimes Edgar had once committed.

For the other crime which had made her Edgar's consort — the murder of her husband in Wherwell forest — Dunstan had exacted a long severe penance. Though there had been extenuations.

Nine years ago the King, being in search of a wife, had heard men praise the beauty of a Devonshire girl, the daughter of Earl Ordgar. Edgar was then engaged on one of his numerous journeys throughout his realm, enforcing the laws in person, visiting the new abbeys he had founded, cementing many a loyalty by his personal interest. He therefore sent his close friend and confidant Earl Athelwold of East Anglia, on a mission here to Lydford, so that the Earl might report on Alfrida's looks and behavior.

Athelwold's report was damning. He described the girl as skinny, gangling, pockmarked, loud-voiced, ill-mannered, and altogether unfit to be enthroned. Edgar accepted his friend's verdict, and married the plump pretty daughter of another Earl — little Eneda, the "White Duck." It was not long, however, before Edgar heard that Athelwold had most astonishingly married Alfrida himself — moreover, the Earl disappeared from Court on some lame excuse. Edgar scented betrayal and set off to visit Athelwold, who was terrified by the news of his King's arrival, and implored Alfrida to make herself ugly, to wear a tiring-woman's shapeless gown, to cover her face, giving as reason that it was disfigured by a rash. Alfrida, of course, did nothing of the sort. She used every art and bedazzled the King like a sunburst. In addition she sealed her husband's doom by pathetic complaints of him, of his meannesses and cruelties. When he left her Edgar was violently in love, and as violently determined to revenge himself upon the man he had trusted.

Even so, Edgar had not committed base murder. On that hunting expedition in Wherwell forest, though Edgar gave no previous warning of his plan, he had not thrown the javelin at the Earl's back. He had given Athelwold a moment to understand what was coming before hurling his spear into the left breast, and the King himself had said prayers for the dying, and made the sign of the cross over his erstwhile friend. Then he had made full confession to Dunstan.

The Archbishop sighed as he thought of the next tragedy caused by the King's passion to possess this woman who was even now smiling gently and casting unfathomable looks at Rumon while she listened to Edgar's explanation of his arrival with Merewyn.

Though Athelwold was dead, there was another impediment — Eneda. So Edgar decided to repudiate his wife, who had begun to bore him even before he saw Alfrida. Legally it was a simple matter to get rid of Eneda; the King had only to assert the sudden discovery of consanguinity within the prohibited relations, shut her up in a nunnery and announce that the marriage was dissolved. This procedure even Dunstan could not stop; it had been the manner of kings since the beginning of time. Nor could he delay but for a while the King's marriage to Alfrida. The uncanonical rite was finally performed by the lax Bishop of Ramsbury after Alfrida had used the age-old stratagem and got herself pregnant by the King. That child of shame, little Edmund, was never healthy and presently died, leaving his brother, Ethelred, to occupy Alfrida's whole attention.

Dunstan had not been able to prevent the marriage, but he refused to recognize it or give it blessing.

Thirteen years ago Edgar had been properly elected king by the Witenagemot — the Council of Wise Men who helped rule England. He was therefore King in the eyes of men, but not — Dunstan held — in the eyes of God, nor could be until the religious rites had been fulfilled. The sacred church rites of anointing and investiture, the laying on of hands, the consecration like a priest, the mystical union which alone could guarantee his royal recognition in heaven too.

Dunstan would not perform this ceremony until the King's crimes had been expiated by years of penance, and by the founding of many Benedictine abbeys to the glory of God. Nor would he perform the ceremony while Edgar was living in mortal sin with a woman who was not his true wife. The King, goaded by Alfrida, had protested often during these years, he had grown angry, but he was deeply devout, and afraid of hellfire. Moreover, Dunstan's stand was backed by the other two prelates who labored for England's much-needed religious reforms; Oswald, the kindly Danish Archbishop of York, and Ethelwold — the harsh, dogmatic Bishop of Winchester.

Well, the situation was resolved now. Eneda was dead. She had died last winter in the royal nunnery at Wilton. Piteous, silly, fluttering creature; her wits gradually grew addled as time passed. She wept incessantly, she alternated between bursts of outrageous gluttony and dangerous fasts. Her death resulted from the former phase. She had somehow escaped the abbey cellaress and broaching a vat of fermenting mead, had consumed a quarter of it. They said her belly burst. Anyway she died.

Alfrida did not conceal her pleasure at this news, and though slander whispered that she had somehow encompassed the death of the despised hindrance herself, Dunstan thought that to be untrue. Unless by black magic — ill-wishing and incantations. Those things were possible. Love potions were possible too; it was hard to explain Edgar's unabating passion, and yet — thought the Archbishop with a shudder — there was the mighty thralldom of the bed — of lechery. And this was a woman who obviously excelled in lewd arts. Though to do her justice, nobody had even whispered that she practiced her arts with anyone but Edgar. Nor was she irreligious, thought Dunstan, chiding himself for lack of charity. She attended Mass regularly. She kept the fasts. She founded nunneries.

And now the Lord had seen fit to reward her great ambition. Her marriage recognized, she would be crowned at Bath on Whitsunday with Edgar. She would be a legitimate Queen. She could surely find no higher goal for her designs — unless —

Dunstan thought with sudden foreboding — she now exerted herself to forward Ethelred, her miserable eight-year-old son, at the expense of poor Eneda's Edward, the first true-born atheling.

Dunstan never thought of little Ethelred without repugnance. At Ethelred's christening, when Dunstan lowered him into the font, the baby's backside exploded into farts and feces, thus loathsomely defiling the Holy Water. A bad beginning. And there were other nastinesses. It had been reported to Dunstan that the child was still often incontinent, and had been caught at the sin of Onan. Moreover, he was a coward, afraid of snakes, storms and hunting; forever lying himself out of punishment for his frequent faults.

Edward, on the other hand, was a manly little lad; short like his parents, yet good at sports, honorable, brave — and already something of a scholar, so his tutor, the Bishop of Creditor, reported. Edward could be fashioned into an excellent king — as his father had been fashioned — with God's help.

The Archbishop glanced fondly and proudly at Edgar, who had finished his narration and was now talking to Rumon.

Alfrida arose. She turned gracefully to Merewyn, holding out her hand. "Come with me, my dear. One of my ladies is attacked by rheumatism and completely useless. I should think you could replace her."

Merewyn smiled nervously, she did not quite understand. She glanced towards Rumon for help, but his dark eyes were fixed on the Queen. "I — I — if you please?" said Merewyn, groping.

Alfrida gave her sweet tinkling laugh. "You'll soon learn," she said, and settled Merewyn's uncertainly by grabbing the girl's wrist in a firm grasp. They went out together to the Ladies' Bower.

After a week at Lydford the Court was preparing for its march towards Bath. And Merewyn had learned a great deal. She learned that though the Queen had six ladies around her, and innumerable serving maids, there was always a great deal to do for the pleasuring of Alfrida. Each lady had a special talent. Wulfsiga of Kent could sing and strum on the harp, and the Queen often demanded her services. Hilde came from York and was the dark-haired Danish wife of Thored, a great fighter and preeminent northern thane. Hilde was a quiet, middle-aged woman who commanded respect even from the Queen. She was expert at embroidery, and Alfrida kept her busy mending and decorating the royal gowns.

The Lady Albina was Ordulf's wife, and therefore the Queen's sister-in-law, and exempt from much duty since she was heavy with pregnancy; but the Queen often desired her to play chess or backgammon with her. Britta, Earl Alfhere's daughter, was a thin ugly girl who had the dual tasks of tending Alfrida's elaborate wardrobe and of caring for her white Persian cat — Frez. Alfrida was fond of her cat, and constantly sent Britta to the kitchens for dainties to tempt its capricious appetite. Elfled, a wispy little thing, was the youngest and exactly of Merewyn's age — fourteen. Perhaps it was this which made Merewyn feel an immediate sympathy for her, added to the quick recognition that Elfled was very unhappy. The Queen gave her tasks which should have been done by the servants. Elfled would be peremptorily commanded to empty chamber pots, to wash soiled linen, to clean up the vomit made by Britta, who had a squeamish stomach. Elfled was the Queen's step-daughter, child of the murdered Athelwold whom she greatly resembled. Her selection as Queen's lady had been Dunstan's doing — which Alfrida resented. She hadn't liked the girl's father and she certainly did not like this constant reminder of him.

Elfled was Merewyn's bedmate, and the latter heard the frequent sound of stifled weeping beside her. The Queen's ladies slept on bench beds in the Bower, two in each. The Queen, of course, returned to her husband's bed at night, and so did Lady Albina to Ordulf's. Merewyn inherited the space left by her rheumatic predecessor. She did not inherit the duties.

"I'm sure I don't know *what* I'll do with you!" said Alfrida airily on the first day, after presenting Merewyn to her other ladies. "Descendant of some old British King," explained Alfrida. "Niece to the Abbess Merwinna of Romsey. Destitute, poor thing. Britta, find her some gown of mine, and a mantle. I'll pick a brooch for her myself. She can't go about looking like this!"

Merewyn understood little of the questions the Queen asked her. Could she sew? Embroider? Sing? — Well, what *could* she do? Merewyn's English was not yet up to replying that she could tend pigs, chickens, cook a little, and weave. She could only shake her head and look frightened.

Alfrida laughed, thinking that she wouldn't be saddled long with this little dolt — only until Bath where the girl could be delivered to her aunt. Saddled with her she must be since Edgar had suggested it, and pleasing Edgar was of prime importance. Also there was Rumon who had brought the maiden here. Rumon had interested her immediately. A strange, dark young man, unlike anyone she had seen. That he had felt the impact of her beauty, she knew very well, and she was amused to find that Merewyn also felt it.

"Would you like to comb my hair?" she asked on the second night as she saw Merewyn staring with awe at the golden shining flood rippling down the Queen's back.

Merewyn silently obeyed. She already felt great gratitude to Alfrida for letting Britta bestow on her a yellow silk gown and a green velvet mantle from one of the chests in the Bower. Alfrida herself had inspected these gifts, tilting her head and considering what best became her new lady's peculiar coloring. The Queen entered into these decisions with gusto. She understood the enhancing of a woman, and she had no jealousies of this kind. She had capped her generosity with the gift of a small gilt and enamel brooch to hold the mantle on the shoulder. Merewyn choked with pride and excitement.

She combed Alfrida's gorgeous hair so gently, so skillfully that by the next night the Queen decided that nobody else should do it. Moreover, after one trial she gave Merewyn a new duty. The massaging of the lovely white body with a lamb-fat and rosewater unguent.

"You do that well —" said Alfrida, when she at last gestured for Merewyn to cease rubbing. "Better than any lady I've had." She pulled the girl down and gave her a quick, careless kiss on the cheek.

Merewyn's heart swelled. Nobody but her mother had ever kissed her and then only in the long ago. Her famished affections settled themselves on the Queen, who was pleased. She knew very well that her other ladies did not accord her the same degree of uncritical worship, and she treated Merewyn with indulgence, even permitting hours off to visit Caw and Trig who had been relegated to quarters across the Lyd River. Merewyn did not enjoy these visits. Trig had picked up some ailment and would not eat. He greeted her only by feeble whimpers and a quiver of his tail. Caw was healthy enough — they had put him in a smithy, blowing the bellows and stoking the forge — but his little black eyes were dull with bewildered homesickness. When he saw Merewyn he would grasp her hand and mumble in his thick gobbling way, "Tre-Uther? Tre-Uther?"

She shook her head. "We can't go home, Caw. 'Tis better here."

He turned dumbly back to the forge while his fellow slaves chuckled and jeered at him behind their hands. Merewyn was sorry for him and Trig, yet little seemed important anymore except the castle life.

She saw nothing of Rumon, save at the dinner hour when she might look at him sitting near Alfrida at the High Table, while Merewyn was naturally placed at a side table amongst the lesser ladies. Rumon also had new clothes; a scarlet mantle edged with miniver, a white silk tunic, a gilt-pommeled sword presented by

Edgar, and a gold circlet on his head like all of the very high-born. He had acquired servants too, and lodged with them in a guesthouse next to the palisade; he had a new horse, a black stallion, and spent his days riding the moors and hawking with the noblemen. In the evenings he read Latin to Dunstan or — at Alfrida's request — took the harp from Ordulf's bard and sang plaintive songs in his native Provençal. When he had first seen Merewyn dressed in Alfrida's gifts he had given her a smile of astonished greeting. She knew from his look how much he thought her appearance had improved, and she hoped that he might come and tell her so. Almost at once, however, he turned back to Alfrida, magnet-drawn. Merewyn did not blame him.

In the radiance of the Queen all other women dimmed like daylight stars. Yet Merewyn could not repress her longing.

On the morning of the Court's departure for Bath there were several incidents. The Ladies' Bower was in a frenzy of packing coffers, searching for a lost pot of unguent, getting their mistress dressed while she changed her mind repeatedly as to which gown she wished to wear. In the middle of all this while Alfrida was still in her shift, the hapless Elfled managed to upset a pan of dirty water over the Queen's new red velvet shoes.

Alfrida's underlip jutted out, she began to tremble, and seizing her long-handled polished steel mirror she belabored the girl furiously on her head and shoulders. Elfled screamed, "Blessed Jesu, save me!" while she fell to her knees, and blood ran down her face from the sharp-edged mirror. Merewyn stood by stunned. Britta and Wulfsiga, who had seen these rages before, nervously went on with their tasks. Hilde, however, the Danish Thane's wife, wrenched the mirror from Alfrida and put it on the dressing table. "You must not kill the girl, Lady," she said dryly. "It would be most unfortunate just before the Corona-tion." Her quiet Danish voice with its foreign lilt always calmed Alfrida.

She bit her underlip; her eyes, which had been glittering as jet, slowly widened. Her hands stopped trembling. "Get up!" she said to Elfled. "Stop sniveling there!"

But Elfled was dazed, and lay in a huddle, whimpering, "Jesu, Lord Jesu, save me!"

At this moment the door curtain was pushed aside and the King came in with his two sons. "What's this, darling?" he cried to Alfrida. "You're upset!" He looked down at Elfled. "What ails *her?*"

"Naught, my lord," said the Queen, and instantly turned her most caressing smile on her husband. "Except that I've given her a beating she richly deserved. The clumsy fool."

Edgar nodded slowly. "You must, of course, regulate your women as you see fit, particularly this one to whom you stand in place of a mother. And I'm sorry she proves exasperating."

"*You* put her here, my lord," she said softly, adding on a lower note, "Or Dunstan did."

Edgar frowned, watching Lady Hilde and Merewyn who carried Elfled to her bed, where the girl gave a moan and slumped down. Edgar always tried to ignore the antagonism between Dunstan and his beloved. "Well!" he said with a curt laugh, "This seems to be the day for unruly children. Here are two more."

He gestured towards his sons who had hung back near the doorway. Both were flaxen-haired and blue-eyed. Aside from that, each resembled his own mother. Edward, at eleven, was plump and sturdy, his hair was straight and hung in a shock over his ears. His square face was often anxious, he revered his father and was continually afraid of offending him, yet he *could* stand up for himself if he had to, though the effort brought on a stammer. He gripped his hands tight, and waited, breathing hard.

Ethelred was eight, he had long slender bones like Alfrida, and was nearly as tall as his elder brother. His hair was a mass of curls, his eyes beneath the flaxen brows were wide and innocent, his pink mouth pouted adorably. He ran now to his mother and buried his face on her thigh. "I never did," he wailed. "I never did! Edward's lying!"

Alfrida patted his head, and said, "The athelings have been quarreling again? Have we time for such nonsense, my lord, when we should be starting our journey?"

"Ethelred needs correction," said the King. "Since you will not permit anyone to punish him, you must do it yourself, my dear. You don't spare the rod in other cases." He gestured towards Elfled. "This child has done two dishonorable, sly tricks, designed to injure his brother."

"I want to ride *first* in the procession," whined Ethelred, looking tearfully up at Alfrida. "You SAID, Mama, that the son of the real King and Queen should go first!"

"N-No," interjected Edward, his hands gripping harder. "I am the oldest atheling. All the thanes s-say I should ride ahead."

"With this view I concur," said the King. "I had no idea that Ethelred dared to think otherwise, or could invent means of degrading his brother."

"He p-painted my new horse green all over!" said Edward, his voice shaking. "Made it s-sick, so I'll have to ride a m-mule like a woman!"

"I never *did!*" cried Ethelred. "A serf must've." He saw a secret smile in his mother's eyes, and clung to her harder.

"You were *seen* painting the horse, Ethelred," said the King, and there was no smile in his eyes. "And worse than that, you stole Edward's sword, the Sword of Athelstan. It was found hidden under your bed."

"Childish pranks, my lord," said Alfrida softly. "He doesn't understand."

"Then he must be made to. An atheling may engage in brave fights, he may show anger, he may even play pranks, but he may not steal and lie, and cringe when he's caught. I am much distressed."

"I wonder," said Alfrida in a silky voice, "that you did

not go to Dunstan about this, my lord — as you usually do."

The King drew himself up. His mouth hardened. "The Archbishop has already left for Bath. And *I* wonder at your tone, my lady."

Alfrida quivered. The King never combated her wishes. Stern as he could be to others, he had never addressed her like that. She pushed Ethelred aside, and threw herself down on her knees before Edgar, seizing his hand and covering it with kisses. "Forgive me, my dear lord." The upturned violet eyes sparkled with tears.

At once Edgar softened. She was considerably taller than he, and he was sometimes vaguely distressed by this, nor did he realize how Alfrida with instinctive coquetry usually managed to minimize the discrepancy. He seldom saw her standing up beside him, and in bed, of course, it made no difference. Now he looked down into the beautiful tearstained face, saw the superb breasts and delicate flanks outlined by the clinging shift. The kisses on his hand kindled the beginning of desire which her touch always awakened. Was there time before they started for Bath? No, there was not. The procession was already beginning to form. He leaned down and kissed her on the mouth. "Hasten and dress, sweetheart. I'll leave you to deal with Ethelred as you think fit. Come, Edward!"

His eldest son followed him miserably from the Bower. Nothing had been gained by this interview. Ethelred would certainly not be punished. And I shall have to ride the mule, he thought. Every horse in Lydford was bespoken. There was no time to cleanse his own horse of the thick coat of green paint. Besides the poor beast had colic. She always won. Edward clenched his fists and quelled the unmanly sob he felt in his throat. He reckoned, however, without his father's sense of justice and of rank.

The King commandeered a horse from a Mercian thane who was exceedingly angered but dared not show it. And Edward,

wearing the famous sword which King Alfred had given to little
Athelstan, rode ahead of Ethelred in the procession.

On the Feast of Pentecost, Whitsunday, May 11th, the
nobility and high clergy of England were packed into St. Peter's
new Abbey at Bath, waiting for the Coronation to begin.

The Abbey was lit by a thousand tapers, it smelled of incense
and of sweat; the May day was warm, and there were several
hundred excited people crammed on tiered benches in the
transepts, or standing in the nave.

Outside in the sunshine the royal procession was slow in starting because Dunstan must supervise every detail. The Coronation was his triumph. He had worked for years on its "Ordo"
or directions for performing the sacred rituals which would make
of Edgar the first divinely appointed king in England. Dunstan
had fashioned his "Ordo" from examples of coronations abroad,
those of French kings and of Popes, yet he had added many ideas
of his own. For these he had searched the Bible, and prayed for
heavenly guidance, which he knew had been sent to him. He was
exalted, as he stood near the Abbey cloister beside Oswald, the
Archbishop of York, while they endured the inevitable delays.
Elfstan, Bishop of London, was late but sent a breathless messenger to say he would arrive shortly. Lady Britta, who, with
Lady Hilde, was to hold up Alfrida's pearl-studded white
mantle, suddenly had an attack of nervous vomiting, and was
given laudanum by the Abbey monk-physician. Then Ethelred
decided to play with his mother's Coronation ring, and managed
to lose it, which set a dozen people anxiously searching for it
until it turned up in the grass.

Dunstan waited patiently enough, listening to the pealing of
the church bells, and the chanting of the monks inside the
Abbey. "This is a most joyous day," he said to the other Archbishop, who smiled. "You haf vorked hard to make it so, goot
Dunstan," Oswald said with a slight Danish accent. "Ah, my

heart svells ven I see this fine new Abbey, and think of all the abbeys we haf founded, or purged of vickedness and brought under the Benedictine rule. God must be happy, and very pleased vit you, Dunstan, for your success in molding this fine young King."

Dunstan grasped his friend's hand and his eyes moistened. "I love Edgar like a son — a very dear son. And today he becomes a Holy Emperor on earth, as surely as Our Lord Christ is Emperor of Heaven."

Oswald nodded. It was truly an empire over which Edgar reigned, now that all Northumbria was subject to him, and the Danelaw, and that the Welsh kinglets avowed his supremacy. Even Kenneth, King of the Scots, had arrived for the Coronation to do homage.

"I see a cloud of dust on the London road," said Dunstan peering at the hilltop to the east. "Let us pray that 'tis Bishop Elfstan arriving. And then we can begin." He moved off to alert the King who sat inside the cloisters looking pale, and sipping water — the only substance which had passed his lips since midnight.

Within the Abbey, the great congregation waited. Merewyn was seated in the ladies' section of the north transept, beside her long-sought Aunt Merwinna. There were several black-habited abbesses, scattered amongst the vividly gowned earls' and thanes' wives in this privileged place. All the Queen's ladies were there except Britta and Hilde who, by reason of their rank, were to assist in the actual ceremony.

The south transept contained abbots, thanes and the King's own housecarls; in the choir were the Abbey monks; the nave seethed with lesser priests, and whatever members of the general populace who had been able to squeeze themselves in.

Merewyn sat demurely beside her aunt, trying to imitate that lady's perfect composure. The black wool habit and black veil were motionless, so were the precisely folded hands. The golden crucifix on the Abbess's shapeless breast was unstirred by her quiet breathing. Merwinna, Abbess of Romsey, was as famous for her decorum as she was for her piety and kindness. She was short, slight and dark-skinned; thirty-five and looked older, because of the hollows around the large black eyes; and a bony beaked nose, and compressed mouth which nonetheless could curve into smiles or even laughter. Her nuns revered and obeyed her; most of them also loved her.

The monks in the choir finished one chant and began another. The great western doors still did not open to admit the procession.

Merewyn sighed and thought about the meeting with her aunt three days ago.

Upon her arrival in Alfrida's train three days ago Merewyn at last spoke again with Rumon. He had arrived in Bath earlier, but was waiting for them near the Avon bridge. Waiting for the Queen, no doubt, Merewyn thought, though her heart jumped at the sight of him.

He looked magnificent to her, sitting his new stallion so proudly, his dark hair shining, his shoulders thrown back with an easy grace. He bowed low to the Queen as she rode past, then to Merewyn's flustered delight, he came up to her as she crossed the bridge.

She was riding pillion behind young Gunnar, Lady Hilde's eighteen-year-old son who was body thane to Prince Edward.

"Good evening Gunnar —" said Rumon, smiling, "*and* Merewyn. I've found your aunt. She's waiting for you. Will you come with me? I'll take you there."

She slipped joyfully off Gunnar's horse, while Rumon dismounted. "Tarasque is too weary to carry extra weight," he said, throwing the reins to a servant. "We'll walk."

Merewyn asked nothing better. The sunset air was fresh; the grass brilliant green and spangled with pink daisies; a cuckoo called three times from an alder copse — three times for the Trinity meant good luck.

"How have you been?" asked Rumon, as they strolled along. "Do you enjoy your duties to the Queen?" As he said "the Queen," his voice faltered, took on a deeper note.

"Yes," said Merewyn slowly. "She's so beautiful, and she is kind to me."

"Ah —" he said, sighing. "She's an angel." *Alfrida la toute belle,* he added to himself.

"She's not always an angel," Merewyn objected, thinking of Elfled. "She can get very angry."

"Why not? In a righteous cause. Even our Lord Jesus could be angered at times. Remember that, Merewyn, and do not presume to judge so lovely and exceptional a woman."

"No, sir," said Merewyn, wondering if the drenching of velvet shoes were a righteous cause, yet herself so much under Alfrida's spell that she accepted Rumon's rebuke.

"Your new clothes vastly become you," said Rumon kindly. "They were *her* gift, I suppose?"

She nodded, hoping that during the entire walk they would not be constantly discussing Alfrida, but Rumon continued.

"Generous, virtuous and devout is our lady. How fortunate the King is!" He stopped abruptly. The emotions he felt for Alfrida were as disquieting as they were thrilling. He did not understand them. He tore his thoughts back to Merewyn for whom he still felt responsibility; now at last to be discharged when he delivered her to her aunt, as he had promised the dying Breaca.

"Did you enjoy your ride with young Gunnar?" he asked, chuckling a little. "He's a pleasant youth, and I thought he looked at you tenderly as you said farewell."

Merewyn had been too much engrossed by Rumon's appearance to notice what kind of look Gunnar had given her. She lifted her chin and said, "I hate the Danes. They're Northmen.

It disturbs me to find so many at Court. I fear them. Why should I not, after what they did at Tre-Uther?"

"I know," said Rumon slowly. "But, child, you must see that these Danes are different from those heathen Viking pirates. These are Christians, they are becoming Englishmen, they are loyal subjects of the King, who has handled them superbly. Besides, remember that way back hundreds of years ago, the Anglo-Saxons were of the same stock as the Danes."

"I'm not," said Merewyn proudly. "I'm Cornish — British."

Rumon frowned. "It is Edgar's and Dunstan's hope that all races in this island shall live together in harmony," he said after a moment, and changed the subject. "How are Caw and Trig?"

Merewyn drew in her breath, staring at the ground. "Trig died. Caw was left behind at Lydford, working in the smithy. He's very homesick."

He heard the tears in her voice, and took her hand out of sympathy. "*You're* not homesick anymore, are you Merewyn?"

She clung to his hand, while her bones seemed to melt, and a honey-sweet fire run through them. "No," she said, and added so low that he was not quite sure of hearing, "Never, if I can be near you."

He dropped her hand and spoke briskly, "Ah, there's the Abbey guesthouse. Now we shall find your aunt."

Guesthouses had been put up all over Bath to accommodate the Coronation visitors. The one for the Abbesses was near a bubbling sulphurous hot well, which had been used by the Romans, and was still used for the cure of skin afflictions.

The Abbess Merwinna was waiting for them in a small parlor off the refectory. As the two were ushered in by one of the nuns, she rose, bowed to Rumon, and reaching up, kissed Merewyn on the forehead. "So, here I have a little niece," she said gently in Cornish. "Lord Rumon has explained to me your trials — and I did not even know that you were born! I heard

nothing from Uther or Breaca since the day I left for England.
Now I know why."

Above the beaky nose, the Abbess's large dark eyes examined
Merewyn, and into them came a puzzled look.

"You are nothing like your parents," she said with a shade
of astonishment. "Not like Breaca, and certainly not Uther,
whom *I* perhaps unfortunately resemble." And she smiled, a
transforming smile which gave sweetness to her sharp thin face.
Still she examined the girl, her height, her auburn braids, her
freckles, and the green-blue eyes.

Rumon drew back against the wall. He found that he did not
now wish the secret of Merewyn's birth discovered. He did not
wish her to be thus devastated, and he had an instinct of protection. "No doubt, Reverend Mother," he said casually, "there
might be some ancestor in Breaca's line whom Merewyn re-
sembles."

"Very possibly," said the Abbess in her composed way.
"Breaca came from the wild southern parts of Cornwall, and I
knew little about her family. My dear —" she turned to Merewyn, reverting to Cornish, "you may be sure, that with God's
grace, I'll look after you for the sake of my poor brother, Uther
— God rest his soul." She crossed herself slowly, while the
other two followed suit. "You will stay here at the guesthouse
with me, and when the Coronation is over, return to my convent
at Romsey."

But then I'll *never* see Rumon, thought Merewyn overwhelmed — nor the Queen. She dared not speak, but the
Abbess, who had much experience with girls, looked at her
shrewdly.

"It was to be under my care that you have made this long
journey," she stated. "And I believe it is high time, considering
your youth, that you be removed from the perils and temptations
of the world."

Nobody ever gainsaid Merwinna when she spoke in this tone,
and Merewyn was aware that she should be grateful, that this

result was precisely what her mother and Rumon had intended.

Still her mouth grew dry, and into her chest there came a lump. The lump grew heavier as Rumon took his leave, smiling at her, patting her on the shoulder like a child. And in the refectory later sitting next to her aunt amongst the other silent abbesses, Merewyn could eat nothing. After the bustle, chatter, music — yes and even the strife of the Queen's Bower — this hush was formidable. The black-robed abbesses of Shaftesbury, of Wilton, of Barking, of Winchester — and Merwinna of Romsey all sat with downcast eyes, their lips moving only to receive the morsels of food which they plucked delicately off the plates their attendant nuns put before them.

I can't stand it, Merewyn thought. I can't, and she gave a gulp, at which her aunt shook her head slightly, and put a restraining hand on the girl's arm. Please, Blessed Holy Virgin! Please, dear Lord Jesus! Please, St. Petroc! Merewyn prayed desperately, clasping her hands tight on her lap.

Her prayers were answered promptly. Answered through the very earthy medium of Lady Albina, Ordulf's large indolent wife, who was waiting in the parlor as the abbesses and nuns filed out of the refectory.

Lady Albina had been sent by the Queen. "Merewyn is to return with me, Reverend Mother," said Albina, drawling a little and yawning, for the journey had wearied her. "The Queen will not retire for the night until she has Merewyn's combings and rubbings."

The girl's head flew up, her face was transfigured, while a crease appeared between the Abbess's dark brows. "I would prefer to keep the girl with me, as everyone has planned."

Albina shook her head. "It is a royal command," she said indifferently. "The Queen wishes Merewyn to return and perform her usual duties."

After a moment the Abbess inclined her head. "I cannot ignore a royal command. Just what are your duties, Merewyn?"

"Oh —" said the girl eagerly. "Combing her hair, polishing

it with silk, or washing it in honey oil. Then I rub and stroke perfumed creams all over her body. She loves it."

The Abbess's nostrils wrinkled with distaste. "Singular duties," she said. "And when the Queen has no need for you, I shall expect you to be here with me."

"Yes, Reverend Mother," said Merewyn faintly. And so it had been these past days — a shuttle between the scented noisy Bower in the palace and the austere offices and silences of the black-robed women. She admired her aunt and tried to please her — she did not yet love her. She loved Alfrida who be-glamoured her with compliments, an occasional caress, and the loveliness of the slender white body which stretched in languid pleasure. Alfrida almost purred like her white Persian cat under the touch of Merewyn's hands.

At last there was a bustle near the Abbey's west door, which swung slowly open and let in a burst of trumpets while the new organ swelled in triumph throughout the taper-lit Abbey. The choir struck up the antiphon, as the two Archbishops entered first, walking down the nave with stately steps. They were followed by the premier earls of England — Alfhere, Britnoth, Athelwine, Oslac. These bore the King's regalia — the sword, the ring, the sceptre and the rod. The earls were dressed in purple mantles lavishly furred with ermine, yet Merewyn scarcely glanced at them, because Rumon followed alone behind, his hands clasped in prayer, a strange dreamy light on his face as he gazed up towards the altar.

Next came the athelings — Edward and Ethelred, both boys dressed in green gold-embroidered satin, both looking frightened.

There was a pause, and then appeared the King escorted by the Bishops of Winchester and London. Edgar wore nothing but a white lawn baptismal shift, the thin gold circlet on his crisp straw-colored hair. At Dunstan's request he had shaved off his beard, since in all details this was to parallel a priest's ordination. He looked very young.

The Queen came last, followed by her two ladies — Hilde and Britta. Alfrida too was in white; but no simple shift like the King's. She wore a gown and mantle of silver-threaded tissue embroidered with tiny freshwater pearls. The serving women had been sewing them on for days. Her chaplet was made of lilies. Her tremendous plaits of shining hair were intertwined with threaded pearls. She was breathtaking as she undulated down the Abbey, a faint smile on her full reddened lips when she heard the murmurs around her. For some moments nobody looked at the King, who had prostrated himself on the altar steps while Dunstan led the choir in chanting a *Te Deum.*

The bishops raised the King, while Dunstan put a gold crucifix in his hand. Edgar stood silent for a second on the altar steps, his eyes were shut; he began to take the Coronation oath in a shaking voice which quickly gathered strength.

"These three things to the Christian peoples subject unto me I do promise in the Name of Christ:

"First, that the Church of God and all Christians under my dominion in all time shall keep true peace;

"Second, that acts of greed, violence and all iniquities in all ranks and classes I will forbid;

"Third, that in all my judgments I will declare justice and mercy; so to me and to you, may God, gracious and merciful, yield His mercy — Who liveth and reigneth forever and ever."

"Amen!" Dunstan cried, and all the congregation kneeling, whispered back, "Amen."

That was beautiful, Merewyn thought. Justice, Mercy, Peace were English words she by now understood. Comfortable words. Only one other could be more consoling — Love. And that word she caught in the prayers for Edgar which followed. It came in Dustan's prayer or Oswald's for the two archbishops alternated. "Govern them with Thy love — give to this Thy servant Edgar the spirit of wisdom . . ."

Shall I ever have a spirit of wisdom? thought Merewyn. All her sorrows, passions and rebellions dropped away, she felt herself as pure and dedicated as the King they were now consecrating up there. Half dreaming, lulled by the chanting and the organ, she watched the distant figures. This was the feast of Pentecost, and perhaps the great white dove had already descended. Perhaps it was hovering over the Abbey, enfolding them all in its wings, sending peace into their hearts.

Up in the choir, Rumon, who had erstwhile been the one for such visions, now had none, because he had been placed near Alfrida and the athelings. She was seated on a small chair near the choir entrance, waiting for her part in the ceremony. Rumon tried not to look at her. He knew it to be blasphemous that not the solemn ritual, nor the King, not even the altar and its crucifix, affected him like the sight of Alfrida in her shimmering white robes, her unfathomable violet eyes resting on the scene, her red lips parted slightly.

He was, however, forced to look at her, because when the choir commenced the antiphon of the Anointing "Zadok the Priest . . ." and Dunstan led the King behind a screen held up by four bishops, Ethelred suddenly began to whimper and clutch at his middle. Young Edward had never moved since the ceremony began except to kneel. He stood sturdily, his feet far apart, gazing rapt at his father. He did not move now, while Ethelred's whimpers grew louder.

"Be quiet!" hissed Alfrida, shaking her son's shoulder.

"I can't!" he cried, thrashing his arms to escape from her. "It's hot in here. Besides I've a bellyache!"

His voice shrilled through the reverent silence.

Ethelwold, Bishop of Winchester, frowned over the corner of the anointing screen. Rumon had turned at the commotion and met Alfrida's imploring eyes, while Ethelred began to wail and thrash more violently.

There were of course no housecarls or even thanes near them in the sanctuary, nobody to deal with this disruption.

Rumon did not hesitate. He scooped up the struggling, malodorous child and ran out with him through the choir entrance
into the cloisters.

A lay brother was spading the cloister garth. Rumon went
towards the man and dumped Ethelred on the ground. "Here,
take charge of this little wretch. Beat him if you like. And
cleanse him, for he has obviously soiled himself!"

The monk looked puzzled, then his face cleared. He seized
Ethelred by the arm.

"You daren't touch me!" the boy quavered, twisting in the
monk's stolid grasp, and staring at Rumon with fearing disbelief.
"I'm the Atheling!"

"You're not THE Atheling," said Rumon. "And you act like
the most vulgar of serfs. I cannot conceive how you sprang
from such a mother — or father either," he added after a second.

"The lad is still very young, sir," said the lay monk, unex-
pectedly. "I've a brother like him at home. Soils himself when
he's nervous. I'll tend to him."

Into Ethelred's round blue eyes came confusion. He was used
to inspiring fear, anger, annoyance, indulgence, occasionally
praise. He had never encountered the voice of simple kindness
before. "I want to be in the Coronation — I'm *supposed* to be,"
he said tentatively, looking from Rumon to the monk.

"And so you may," said Rumon, who had also noticed the
gardener's kind tone. "After you're cleaned, and *if* you can
behave yourself." He turned to the lay brother. "Bring him to
the Abbey, later."

Rumon hurried back into the sanctuary, and took up his stand
near Alfrida, who gave him a long look of gratitude — gratitude,
and something else which sent a shiver down Rumon's spine.

The King had reappeared from behind the screen, and was
now dressed in cloth of gold, accepting from Dunstan the in-
signia of investiture handed up by the premier earls — the gold
ring with *Christus Rex* enameled on it; the jeweled sword which
had been his father's, King Edmund's; the scepter topped by a

cross; the rod of Equity topped by a dove. Then, at Dunstan's gesture, the King sat down on his throne. Dunstan walked to the altar and fetched the crown which was lying before the tabernacle.

The Archbishop — an expert goldsmith — had made the crown himself. It was square (for the four-square city of God), each angle was surmounted by an elaborately chased trefoil (for the Trinity), and along the high band of gold were studded all the gems mentioned in Revelations as pertaining to the heavenly Jerusalem. Emerald, chrysolite, sapphire, topaz, amethyst, and the others, blazed in the taper light. It had taken many years to collect these jewels.

The congregation held its breath as Dunstan lowered the sparkling crown onto Edgar's head; then when Dunstan cried out in a great voice — "Will ye have King Edgar to be your liege lord forever?" the Abbey resounded with shouts of "Aye, we will! Long live the King!" while the monks chanted, "Vivat! Vivat! Rex!"

The choir burst out in another triumphant *Te Deum*, during which Edgar turned and beckoned to Dunstan. "Alfrida?" he whispered. The Archbishop nodded, concealing his reluctance. He walked over to her and led her by the hand to a small throne lower and to the right of the King's.

Alfrida's ceremony was brief. Dunstan anointed her with the holy oil on forehead, cheeks, and breast. He invested her with the Queen's ring, on which was enameled an image of the Blessed Virgin. And when Lady Hilde had removed the chaplet of lilies, the Archbishop placed on the bowed head a small crown studded with little pearls and crystals, while praying aloud that she would "be a faithful, diligent consort to her lord, tender mother to his children, and a queenly example of mercy, graciousness, charity and virtue to all Christian subjects."

Alfrida kept her head modestly inclined while cheers burst forth again, and cries of "Long live Alfrida." Nor did she raise her lovely head throughout the ensuing ceremony of homage.

The Archbishop of Canterbury did homage first, kneeling before the King, placing his hands between Edgar's, kissing him on the brow, and intoning, "Your liege man of life and limb, and of earthly worship . . ." The Archbishop of York followed him, and all the bishops. Then Kenneth, King of the Scots, seeming dazed by the magnificence around him. After him the athelings, for Ethelred had returned in time to see his mother crowned. He was subdued, and did not even try to elbow Edward out of the way as that prince went first to pay homage to their father. Rumon came next. He had noted the procedure in regard to Alfrida. Dunstan had decreed that it was not *homage* which should be paid a woman, only a bended knee in token of respect.

Rumon was glad that he need not touch her; as it was, while he bowed, her nearness and her flowery perfume made his head swim. He retreated quickly, and stood in his former place watching the earls from all over England, and the Danelaw, and Northumbria each pledge to Edgar their allegiance and the allegiance of those who lived in their particular domains.

The Coronation ended with High Mass in which Edgar himself offered bread and wine, and made his personal oblation — a heavy ingot of gold.

The procession re-formed, and filed slowly out of the Abbey.

Dunstan was exultant as he stepped into the sunlight. In the entire history of England there had never been such a Coronation, not one in which heaven had also participated, and endowed the King with the divine right to rule. Edgar was now a Holy Christian Emperor, and great triumphs were still ahead. They would proceed to Chester next week where the seven western kinglets of Cumbria, the Isle of Man, and the various parts of Wales would all be gathered to swear allegiance to Edgar.

Ah, Dunstan thought, my vision has come true through God's grace. He thought of the angelic voice he had heard on the night of Edgar's birth. It had said, "Peace to England as long as this child shall reign, and our Dunstan survives." He murmured a prayer of thanksgiving.

Alfrida too was exultant, though the tenor of her thoughts were unlike Dunstan's. At last she had achieved the highest glory open to a woman. At last her power was secure, and she need no longer be quite so careful. A consecrated and anointed queen could not be put away on a pretext as Eneda had been. Not that she feared any loss of her hold on Edgar — it was rather that she need not respond so slavishly to his ardors, and that she might now pursue certain plans of her own. She smiled as she thought of this, and the populace who were kneeling and avidly watching the royal procession to the banquet hall murmured admiration. One ragged old beggar woman broke from the crowd crying, "God Bless our beautiful Queen!" and clutched at the hem of Alfrida's white robe. The housecarls rushed up to beat off the old woman, but Alfrida stopped them.

"I thank you for your blessing," she said smiling again, and tearing one pearl off her mantle, put it in the woman's withered hand.

She breathed deep at the cheers which rose on all sides. Though the pearl was not worth a penny, the old beggar slobbered her gratitude.

All the mob had cause for gratitude today. Twenty oxen were a-roasting at open fires, tuns of ale were being broached. Even the lowliest slave would be fed from the King's bounty.

Alfrida glided into the Banquet Hall where her table was set across the Hall from the King's. Dunstan had arranged this too. At a Coronation banquet the King must entertain the lords, both spiritual and temporal. To the Queen fell the lesser folk — the ladies including abbesses, and a stray abbot or two for whom there wasn't room at the High Table.

Alfrida took care to wave charmingly across the room to her liege lord, and to murmur a pleasant word to Wulfrid, the Abbess of Wilton, who was seated at her right. That Wulfrid had once long ago been Edgar's mistress, and borne him a daughter, Edith, did not in the least disturb Alfrida. Whatever attractions had awakened Edgar's lust were gone now. Wulfrid was fat, pompous, and thoroughly satisfied by her position as Abbess of England's most fashionable nunnery — an honor she owed to Edgar's conscience. She grunted some polite reply to the Queen's remark, and thereafter applied herself to the spiced venison slices which had been laid on her trencher of thick white bread.

Nor had Alfrida need to concern herself long with the lady on her left. This was Alfhere's wife, Godleva, and a most unfitting mate for the robust, resplendent Earl of Mercia. Godleva was sickly, a trait inherited by her daughter, Britta. Godleva had headaches and a perpetual cough. She was terrified of strangers and spent her life sipping broths in a darkened apartment in Shrewsbury Castle. Only her husband's threats had brought her here for the Coronation. She sat silent, lost in a fog of headache and timidity, while picking nervously at a roast woodcock.

Alfrida, seeing that further courtesies on either side of her were unnecessary, gave herself up to various pleasing thoughts.

The realization of power was far more intoxicating than the wine from Burgundy which filled her gold cup. Power to get certain material things she had long wanted. Lands of her own — Edgar could no longer put her off "until after the Coronation." Those rich grants in Dorset and Hampshire she had asked for. And then she wanted an ermine cloak — fine as the one they said was worn by the Holy Roman Empress. Too there was the rebuilding and furnishing of the rickety royal palace at Winchester. And she must have a suitable crown, not this trumpery little thing of base gold and the quartz called "Scotch diamond." It had been ordered by Dunstan, of course.

Dunstan. Alfrida looked across the Hall at him, sitting next to Edgar — of course. The Archbishop was smiling in a smug way, Alfrida thought, like a well-fed hound. What a pleasure it would be to eliminate that smile forever, to eliminate this meddlesome autocratic old man, and his ever-present influence on Edgar. That was one of the uses of power — to pay off old scores. Her violet eyes moved slowly down the High Table until their gaze rested on another — the Earl Oslac of North-umbria. Here was a man she also hated. An ugly, grizzle-haired Dane, hand in glove with the Monastic party — with Dunstan, Oswald, Ethelwold, and the rest of the sour churchmen who were rapidly turning England into a land of penances, mortifica-tions, and celibacy. Though it was not so much for his eccle-siastical policy that Alfrida hated the Earl. There were more personal reasons, which had been reported to her, jestingly by her brother. Oslac had tried to dissuade Edgar from marrying her, from putting aside Eneda. Worse than that — Oslac did not think her beautiful.

Alfrida's easygoing brother, Lord Ordulf, had thought this a great joke and had chuckled while he repeated a remark of Oslac's which he had happened to overhear. "Alfrida's a schem-ing wench, and *I* don't see why such a pother is made about her looks. Why, you can find a hundred yellow-haired lasses just like her in London or York any day of the week."

The remark was made nine years ago, when Alfrida was newly widowed. She had never for a moment forgotten it, though she had never mentioned Oslac's name to Edgar. Oslac seldom visited the South, and when he did Alfrida kept out of his way. Someone else shall be appointed Earl of the North, she thought. Aye, indeed — someone else. And why not Thored?

She turned her gaze on Thored — a dark middle-aged Dane who already ranked second in those murky northern lands, and whose wife was Lady Hilde. Fortunately, Alfrida had not been forced to accept one of Oslac's womenfolk as attendant, since he had none.

Alfrida nodded to herself, and took a sip of wine. And the Bower Ladies. There would certainly be changes there, and at once. Elfled must go. That stupid Wulfsiga of Kent must go. Britta would certainly have gone, except that she was the daugh-ter of Alfhere. And HE was an ally. More than an ally — a would-be lover. . . . Aye, probably a good lover, she thought, examining the Earl of Mercia as he lifted his beaker to receive more wine from his weedy young son Cild Aelfric who was acting as his table thane. The Earl was a big, lusty man with a knowing eye and a note in his voice which always made one feel naked and desired. A strong crafty man who might well provide adventures in bed which the unimaginative Edgar would never dream of.

She shook her head and took another sip. That kind of thought was still too dangerous. And there was another matter of the Bower Ladies to decide. The matter of Merewyn. The Abbess Merwinna should not have her. Of that there was no question. Let the Abbess take that sniveling Elfled to Romsey instead of Merewyn, Alfrida thought, and was so amused at this neat switch that she gave a sudden laugh.

Wulfrid went on eating her way through a saffron pasty, but Godleva jumped, her frightened eyes stared at the Queen. "You spoke, Lady?"

"No," answered Alfrida. "Ah, look! The gleemen are coming. That's why I laughed."

A troop of jugglers and a bearward cavorted into the Hall.

Alfrida watched the bouncing balls, the balanced knives, the performing bear for a moment, she tapped her fingers to the rhythm of the tabor, but she went on thinking.

She looked across at the athelings, noting that Edward was seated nearer to the King than Ethelred. This must be altered from now on. Edward would retire from Court, send him on a pilgrimage to Rome perhaps, and Ethelred would be proclaimed Edgar's rightful heir. Then there must be a betrothal — a more ambitious match than Edgar or these stupid clerics would think of. A Frankish princess? A German one? He's not too young for betrothal, she thought, and he is such a pretty lad. He has my looks.

Ethelred had been half asleep, but he awakened at the arrival of the gleemen. He squealed with excitement as he watched the unmuzzled bear, lunging to the end of its rope and snapping its jaws at the tumblers who dexterously kept out of reach. The bear, prodded with a stick from behind, was in a frenzy, its little red eyes murderous. The King and his nobles, most of them half drunk, laughed at the antics of the bear and the tumblers, who hopped and leaped and did somersaults around the bear. They laughed harder when the bear's trainer, puffed by success, seized a burning fagot from the fire and thrust it into the bear's hindquarters. Ethelred jumped up and down in delight as the stench of burning flesh and fur filled the Hall. There were three, however, who did not laugh. Dunstan sat quietly, his hands folded, frowning occasionally as the tumblers made lewd gestures. Edward did not laugh. He turned his eyes away, like the little prig and milksop that he was, Alfrida thought angrily. And Rumon did not laugh. He contemplated the spectacle without expression, that remote considering look in his dark eyes which Alfrida found intriguing. He was a strange young man indeed. Never boisterous or drunken like the others, and as much given to book learning as a monk. It seemed that he had felt her gaze, for he now looked across the Hall and his eyes met hers during a long somber moment, which had in it the essence of all that was most flattering. Alfrida sighed voluptuously. He was in love with her, she knew, and perhaps one day — when all was safe — he would be rewarded. No, he should be rewarded at once in a practical way. She was grateful for his prompt help with Ethelred in the Abbey, and the conferring of favors on friends was almost as sweet a fruit of power as the destruction of enemies. Rumon should be given land, rich properties commensurate with his rank. A King's grant, near mine, she thought. Or better yet, one of the new monastery grants in Mercia which would both infuriate Dunstan and delight Alfhere.

Ah, there were no limits to the intricacies of power — a game far more fascinating than the chess at which she was adept.

Edgar is King, but *I* shall rule this realm, she thought, for I can rule Edgar, and soon need no longer bow to Dunstan.

The bearbaiters and the tumblers finished their act. The bear was hauled off, half dead — his burned hindquarters dragging. The King and the nobles threw pennies to the tumblers and awaited the next diversion, which turned out to be a troup of musicians from France: four men who played harp, lute, viol, and flute, accompanied by a scarlet-gowned woman who sang in a low, true voice.

Nobody except Rumon had any idea what she was singing about, and most of the sodden noblemen were bored, while the abbesses were shocked. They had never heard of a female entertainer and suspected besides that this new-sounding music was not only secular, but indecent, since the woman danced provocatively as she sang.

Alfrida was interested. She enjoyed music, and had a sufficiently good ear to appreciate the unaccustomed harmonies. The gay tune was followed by a mournful one, a piece so sad and plaintive that Alfrida's assurance was suddenly pierced. The woman was singing of lost love, you could tell from her expression, her gestures, from the music itself.

I *couldn't* lose Edgar's love, Alfrida thought. The lure of her body had never failed — yet as one aged . . . ? She felt a pang of terror. It was followed at once by relief. The witchwoman would help her. Old Gytha, who lived in a hovel outside of Winchester. Alfrida crossed herself secretly.

Danger there. Traffic with such a one was very dangerous. Not only in this world, where the punishment might be death, but in the world to come where it was the fiery agonies of hell. Yet, thought Alfrida, I know *nothing* of Gytha's potions, I know nothing of what goes on in her hovel. I've but dropped a hint or two through the years, given her money as I do to all the poor, and bought from her certain odd-tasting drugs. No harm in that. No harm in the liquid I put in Edgar's ale ten years ago. I've never done it since. No harm in taking that powder she gave me, so that my courses might come regularly. It is natural that I should not wish to disgust Edgar again with a body swollen and deformed by childbearing. There was no harm in simply *saying* to Gytha that Eneda's death would be a mercy.

Gytha is naught but a mad old woman, and I don't believe she can weave spells. All these things simply happened by Providence. I need no power except that of my own wits and beauty. Alfrida's strong hand closed tight around her goblet, and she drank deep of the wine. "Wassail, Alfrida the Queen!" she whispered to herself and smiled.

The Coronation Banquet ended when the King came across the Hall and held out his hand to Alfrida. "Come, my dearling," he said, bending over and giving her a hearty kiss on the mouth. " 'Tis time to retire." He had drunk as heavily as his lords, some of whom were already sprawled and snoring on the benches, yet he showed little sign of tipsiness.

The Queen came around the end of the table and joined him, bending her knees inside her flowing skirts so that she might not look too tall beside him. He drew her arm through his, and they proceeded slowly down the Banquet Hall. "I have been thanking Our Blessed Lord all evening for the great happiness of this day," said Edgar solemnly. "And I'm sure *you* have." She gave him a soft look and did not answer.

"I'll not make love to you tonight, sweeting," he went on. "The holiness of my consecration is yet too near to me for that, and Dunstan would not think it seemly."

She stiffened slightly, and inclined her head. As they passed the end of her table, she saw Merewyn, looking very sleepy, drooping next to her aunt, the Abbess. Alfrida decided to win one small victory at least — this very moment. "My lord," she said, stopping his walk by pressure on his arm, "will you grant me a favor?"

"Of course," he said smiling. "You've only to ask."

"Merewyn. I want her appointed as one of my permanent Bower Ladies."

"Why, I thought she was going to Romsey with the Abbess?"

"I don't wish her to, if you please, my lord. I wish the Abbess to take Elfled instead; surely one high-born boarder will do as well as another."

"If you like," said Edgar, finding this a trivial matter.

"Tell the Abbess NOW, my lord," said Alfrida urgently.

Edgar shrugged and walked back to Merewyn and her aunt, who both sank to the floor in bewildered curtsies.

chapter four

On Tuesday morning, July 6th, in the year of our Lord 975, when the urgent summons came from Winchester, Rumon was sitting with Dunstan in a sunny corner of Glastonbury Abbey's garden.

For the past two years since the Coronation, Rumon had made his home at Glastonbury. Rooms in the Abbey guesthouse had been assigned to him, and he had furnished them luxuriously; their plaster walls were covered by vivid frescoes; the bed, table, and chairs had been carved by the most skillful of the Glastonbury monks. There were always clean rushes on the floor and sweet-smelling herbs mingled with the rushes — thyme, verbena, rosemary. An elaborate crucifix hung above the bed, but in the other room a marble bust of some Roman goddess was enshrined on a pedestal. Rumon had bought the head at Bath and found it beautiful. He thought it looked a bit like Alfrida.

The Archbishop came each summer to visit his beloved Abbey. He had been born nearby at Balstonborough, he had been educated here and eventually became Glastonbury's Abbot. He had himself been responsible for enriching and restoring the old building, for making Glastonbury known as "Roma Secunda" to

the whole Christian world. On this visit, after conferring with
Abbot Sigegar, and praying in the little old wattle church which
was the holiest spot in England, Dunstan went in search of
Rumon. The old man's eyebrows twitched as he noted the
increased luxury of Rumon's chambers; he stared at the pagan
goddess and suggested that they sit in the garden. "God has sent
us glorious sunshine today, we must enjoy His bounty," said
Dunstan, "nor should you be forever stuck with your nose in a
book, my son. 'Twas thus I found you last year."

"I do other things, my lord," said Rumon, "I hunt and hawk.
I ride out to inspect my land, and I've labored much at the
copying and illumination you asked of me."

"Ah, yes." Dunstan eased his aching joints on the bench,
savoring the warmth of the sun. "Pliny's *Natural History*. I'm
eager to see your progress, though still regretful that you did not
choose to work on one of the *sacred* histories."

He looked keenly at the young man, noting lines of discontent
around the full sensitive mouth. "You've not yet found the peace
of God here at Glastonbury, Rumon? Have you had any more
visions to assure you that this is indeed the Avalon you once
dreamed of?"

Rumon shook his head. He looked at the great square Abbey
church, a veritable basilica which Dunstan had built next to the
old wattle church to enclose the many precious relics. He looked
in the direction of the Tor, the high mysterious hill topped by a
guardian chapel to St. Michael. He thought of the lakes and
water meads surrounding the town, the Abbey and the Tor, so
that in spring this place was truly an island.

"It is a holy spot, my lord," he said. "Yet it is not the Avalon
I dreamed of. I have tried to think so. I have prayed much to be
rid of this feeling, but always something urges me on, away, and
over there . . ." He gestured slowly towards the west.

Dunstan sighed. He had hoped that by now Rumon would
have felt some certainty as to the vocation he had seemed
obviously fitted for. That he would have moved from the

guesthouse to the novices' cloister, and exchanged the gold circlet on his head for a tonsure. That there would not be this talk of hunting and hawking, though Rumon *did* eschew the other usual activities of a nobleman . . . brawls, gaming, and intrigue. Not to speak of casual wenching.

"You're not happy, my son?" said the Archbishop. "Surely you're not still bedeviled by — by the — the iniquitous passion for which I sent you here?"

Rumon's dark skin reddened. He tore a rose from the wall beside him and crushed the flower in his hands. "No, my lord — I never think of her!"

Neither of them knew that this was a lie.

They sat in silence a moment, both remembering the painful night of Rumon's madness.

It had happened at Winchester a fortnight after the Coronation. Edgar was still with his fleet, somewhere off Wales, after receiving tribute from the western kinglets at Chester. Rumon had been invited to accompany the fleet, whose annual circumnavigation of the whole island had entirely quelled foreign invasions. This show of naval strength was Edgar's own idea, and indeed he was a superb admiral.

Rumon's love of adventure and the sea had not been as compelling as the new obsession which tortured him like St. Anthony's fire. He had refused to sail with the King, had gone instead to the royal palace at Winchester with many of the royal household — and Alfrida. Dunstan, wearied by the Coronation and anxious to return to Canterbury, also stopped at Winchester.

Rumon did not wish to remember the events which led to the climax; Dunstan did not precisely know them, yet he felt that the sure hand of God had been leading him on that Saturday night. He had been praying in the new Minster, praying for some hours after Compline, and further delayed by a conference with the prior. It was therefore dusk of the June night when he limped out of the Minster and walked across the cemetery towards Bishop Ethelwold's mansion, where he lodged.

As he groped for the gate, motion caught his eye. Figures moving at the far end of the cemetery, amongst some yew trees.

He stiffened and crossed himself; the figures were very like ghosts. Then he heard voices, a man's hoarse tone, and a woman's excited laugh. Servants? Churls? Dunstan thought, annoyed. Whatever they were they had no right to defile consecrated ground by their low amours. He turned and walked towards them over the thick grass. As he approached, and could see clearer, the man fell to his knees, and from him came a torrent of pleadings, almost sobs.

The woman laughed again, very low, seductively. She leaned down, holding her arms out. In an instant the two were locked in a violent embrace.

Dunstan inhaled sharply. He now recognized the woman's laugh. He stood appalled, then he cried, "In the Name of Our Blessed Lord, what is this!"

The pair sprang apart. Alfrida gave a whimper of fear. And Dunstan, sick at heart, saw that the man was Rumon.

The three confronted each other, while a raven cawed and the night wind rustled through the yew trees.

"This is how you repay your King!" said Dunstan, his voice cracking. "My amazement is not great in regard to you, Lady, but Rumon — ah, Rumon —" he faltered. "To betray your cousin who has shown you nothing but kindness, to shame your own blood — no matter how she tempted you!"

Rumon stood staring at the grass, panting.

" 'Tis not her fault, my lord," he said finally. "I lured her here. She's not to blame. I've been possessed. We've not betrayed Edgar, there's been nothing between us — except what you saw."

"Nor shall there be!" cried Dunstan, in deep relief. He knew that he could trust Rumon's word. "Go to your chamber, Lady, and whatever confession you make to your chapel priest is between you and God. I shall never mention this. Rumon, come with me!"

All the rest of that night, Dunstan wrestled the demon for Rumon's soul. He prayed, he exhorted, he wept, and he won a complete victory. Rumon could not withstand the Archbishops' strength, nor could he withstand his own guilty shame.

He accepted all Dunstan's arrangements. He would leave Winchester at once, nor see Alfrida again. He would live at Glastonbury, partly as penance, partly to make himself useful to the Abbey by employing his talents as scribe. And so that he might not have to depend on the Court for favors, Dunstan would see that he got a substantial land grant from the King. A grant which might enrich Glastonbury Abbey someday when Rumon finally renounced the world, thought Dunstan, who was a practical man.

The grant was duly made after Edgar's return. It was of a thousand acres near Cheddar, and had been part of the royal domain. There were forests and rich meadowland, there was a small section of the Mendip Hills, which included a cave and a lead mine. An affectionate letter from Edgar accompanied the generous grant. The King regretted the loss of Rumon's company, but quite understood the attraction of a semi-religious life, especially at Glastonbury. It concluded by asking Rumon to pray for his soul, and for the continuing prosperity of England.

The Archbishop returned from his memories to see that Rumon had plucked another rose from the vine and was absently tearing it to pieces, while he stared into the sky.

"Perhaps you should marry someone, my son," said Dunstan sadly. "Though it would impede what you know I hope for you, and — except for that one incident — I would have thought you a man made for holy celibacy."

"I don't want to marry, my lord."

"We could find a desirable girl," pursued the Archbishop, wishing as always to explore a situation fairly. "You can build yourself a fine house on your land, have children to carry on your exceptional line. After all, you're twenty-two, aren't you? I am distressed to see you drifting — neither in the world nor

out of it. By the way, have you heard aught of that little Merewyn, she whom you brought to Lydford and who became
Queen's lady?"

Rumon shook his head. "She's still serving the Queen, I suppose. As you know, I've had no contact with the Court."

"Yes," said Dunstan. "I know that you have faithfully kept
your promises to me and God. I saw Merewyn last month when
I was at Winchester. She is pretty, and has several suitors, I
understand, though favors none of them." Here he cocked an
inquiring eyebrow towards Rumon. "Romsey Abbey is flourishing. The girl, whom I find charming, will doubtless bring some
sort of dowry." As Rumon said nothing, and seemed to be
scarcely listening, Dunstan went on more plainly. "I believe
she's very fond of *you*. She asked me several questions. If one
does marry it is well to take a wife who loves one."

"Wife!" cried Rumon, startled into awareness of the old
man's drift. "Merewyn! My lord, you're jesting!"

"Not at all. The girl is estimable, her royal Celtic line is quite
fit to mate with your own. And I would like to see her removed
from the Court influence. From the Queen," he added. "Here
I quite agree with her Aunt Merwinna. But marriage seems the
only way in which the child's bond to Alfrida may be broken."

"Let her marry, then," said Rumon tartly. "One of those
suitors you mentioned." He opened his hand and let all the
crushed rose petals fall to the ground. Even his liking and
reverence for the Archbishop could not allay vexation. The
thought of Merewyn was painful either because he alone knew
the pathetic secret of her birth, or because the girl naturally
called up memories of Alfrida — memories he had some minutes
ago denied ever having. In that instant he thought the old man
both tactless and tiresome. He changed the subject. "The glassblowing progresses well, my lord. Have you inspected their new
beakers?"

Dunstan raised his brows and contemplated the scowling
young face before answering with a certain quiet amusement,

"Not yet, my son. But you may be sure that I shall give my closest attention to all the matters which interest me, and for which I am responsible at Glastonbury . . . the glassblowing, the goldsmithy, the scriptorium, the spiritual and physical welfare of the brethren. Nor shall I neglect to examine the bed of oriental poppies I ordered sown by the infirmary wall, nor even the clogged drain from the lavatory which Brother Cuma — on my last visit— held to be the cause of illness amongst the novices. All these and many other matters I shall deal with presently. At this moment I am concerned with *you*."

Rumon flushed, accepting the Archbishop's rebuke. " 'Tis kind of you, my lord. But there's no need."

"Have you friends, Rumon?" asked the Archbishop. "Who are your companions?"

The young man shifted uneasily. Had he ever had real friends? Men for whom he felt affection, whose company he cherished, except Vincent, the blind harpist, long ago — and then, yes — Edgar. For a little while there had been Edgar. "Why," he said, "I go hawking, or hunting with several of the neighboring thanes — Oswerd, Elmer — you know them, my lord. And I see a good deal of Brother Finian, here at the Abbey."

"Finian the Irish monk, recently elected subprior?"

"Yes, my lord."

"You find Brother Finian congenial?"

Rumon assented, and Dunstan felt surprise as he considered what he knew about Finian, who was a spare little man of forty — his tonsure already graying. He had darting green eyes and quick nervous motions rather like a sparrow. He had been born to humble parents — fisherfolk — somewhere in the western parts of Ireland — Connemara, was it? Anyway he had no high birth to recommend him, nor even adequate book learning. There had been some question about his appointment to the post of subprior. But Finian was a good administrator, particularly apt at handling his own countrymen of whom there were many at this famous Abbey which boasted the remains of both St. Patrick and St. Bridget. Finian was also useful in matters pertaining to the lay community, "Little Ireland" down by the river.

None of this, however, explained why Rumon — out of the hundreds of brethren at the Abbey — should select Finian for mention.

Rumon might have explained that Finian not only had a mordant sense of humor — mother wit which tickled Rumon — but that he also had a deeply hidden mystical bent. That he could sometimes be persuaded to talk of the eerie lands to the west, from whence nobody ever returned, and about the Culdees, Irish monks who had during the centuries fled westward — ever westward in search of peace.

There was no time for explanations because a young man came dashing through the garden gate, came panting up to the Archbishop, and kneeling to kiss the ring, explained at the same time, "My lord, my lord — I bear dismal news! The King lies ill unto death at Vinchester. He has sent for you — and for you too, Lord Rumon." added the messenger in a distracted way. "He vants to see you both before the end."

"Blessed Lord Christ!" exclaimed the old man. "How can this be! I saw Edgar last month. He was hale as ever!"

"Not now, my lord."

Rumon, almost as shocked as the Archbishop, now noted that the messenger was Gunnar, Thored's son and body thane to young Edward.

Even while the Archbishop questioned anxiously, Rumon had a sharply irrelevant thought. Was Gunner one of Merewyn's suitors mentioned by Dunstan? He was short and dark — a dark Dane — yet he had matured since Rumon last saw him into manliness and he looked to be a dependable sort — trustworthy. He and his father were highly placed at Court, and a girl might do worse for herself — far worse. She could hardly expect to do better, thought Rumon with a spurt of anger he did not examine, and which vanished as the tremble in Dunstan's voice recalled him to the news.

"The King *cannot* be very ill," said the Archbishop. "He is but thirty-one and leads a temperate life nowadays. Moreover he has no enemies."

Gunnar shook his head. "There's no question of enemies, my lord, nobody vishes him ill. Our King has had a cruel griping and blood in his guts for two weeks. He burns vith fever and is sometimes lightheaded. He cannot eat, even the best wine he vomits. Bishop Ethelwold's Spanish monk — the physician who has effected marvelous cures on others — even he has lost hope. The King expects to die. That is vy I am sent to summon you."

Dunstan made the sign of the cross and raised his old eyes towards the serene white clouds lazily drifting across the summer blue. "We will leave at once," he said.

Two days later, on Thursday afternoon, July 8th, the Archbishop, Rumon, Gunnar and a group of attendant monks arrived at Winchester.

They went immediately to the Palace and were met inside the gate by the young Prince Edward, who had been crouching on the well curb and eagerly arose to greet them. "My father still lives," he cried, trying to smile though there were tears on his round cheeks above new golden fuzz. "My lord D-Dunstan," Edward continued, "The King has been p-praying steadily that you would reach him soon."

"He's better then?" asked Dunstan, while Edward knelt to kiss the amethyst ring.

"I don't rightly know, my lord," said the boy with a gulp. "They won't let me in. One of the thanes brings me n-news . . ."

"Won't let you in to see him?" asked Dunstan frowning.

"No, my lord. The Queen is there with Ethelred. She's given orders."

"Come with me now," said Dunstan. "You too, Rumon."

The King lay tossing and moaning on a feather bed while

Alfrida bent over him, stroking his temples with vinegar water. The chamber was darkened, because the sunlight hurt Edgar's eyes, but a huge clock candle in the corner made it possible to see.

Brother Pedro, the Spanish physician, stood by the bed; his long austere face set in gloom. A monk whispered prayers from behind a wooden screen. Ethelred, who was now ten, stood at the foot of the bed where Alfrida had placed him. The child kept licking his lips and staring in horrified fascination at his father. At the emaciated body, which, constantly tossing, threw off the coverlet to disclose a grossly swollen belly sprinkled with pink dots; at the sunken face between sweat-darkened hair; at the trickle of blood which ran from the right nostril; and at his mother, dabbing the hollow temples, and murmuring "Jesu, Jesu, Jesu . . ." beneath her breath.

Alfrida looked up as Dunstan, Rumon, and Edward entered the chamber. Her eyes narrowed, and her underlip thrust out, but Edgar suddenly gave a loud cry, and clenched his hand on his belly. She whirled back to him. "Oh, what is it, my love?"

"It is the end, Lady," said the Spanish monk. "Or will be shortly. The gut has ruptured. I've seen many of these cases. He will now have a few moments of respite, and he may know you all."

"Holy Mother of God," murmured Dunstan. "He's been shriven? Last rites?"

"Aye, my lord. This morning by Bishop Ethelwold. And afterwards we thought he rallied. We were hopeful."

Edgar lay suddenly quiet, propped up on pillows. The pain furrows smoothed from his forehead. Full consciousness cleared his eyes. "Bring near the candle," he said. "Ah, Dunstan, my teacher and my friend. I'm glad you're with me, and know how able will be your prayers for me . . . Rumon? Is it Rumon — my cousin? I've missed you, yet know you've found the peace you sought in Glastonbury."

Rumon bowed his head and murmured something.

The King's gaze roamed over the faces near him. "Edward!"

he said. "To you I give my Kingdom. It is for *you* to carry on
— with God and Dunstan's help — the peace and unity of
England."

Alfrida gave a gasp. "My lord!" she cried. "My lord, you
promised me that *Ethelred* should be your heir!"

The King slowly turned his head and looked up at her with a
sad smile. "I've loved you very much, Alfrida, but I never
promised you that. It would be a crime against reason and
justice. I've tried to please you, I banished Earl Oslac at your
request, and many other things I've done for you. But I command that the Witan elect Edward to be England's King when
I'm gone."

Alfrida collapsed on Edgar's chest in a torrent of inarticulate
sobbing, highly appropriate to the tragedy of the moment. Only
Dunstan thought that this heartrending grief sprang as much
from the frustration of her desires as it did from the imminent
loss of her husband.

Edgar raised his fleshless hand and stroked her golden head.
"There, my dear, there —" he whispered tenderly. "Think of
this only as a temporary parting between us — and we've had
many. If our Dear Lord is merciful, we shall meet in Heaven."

Alfrida sobbed harder. Dunstan leaned over and pulled her
off Edgar's chest. "Hush —" he said. "The King is still trying
to speak."

The face on the pillow had gone livid, the lips gray. Edgar's
life blood gushed out beneath the coverlet. "Edward," he
murmured. "Kiss me — and promise you will remember what
I have tried to teach you."

The boy leaned over and kissed his father on the forehead.
"I p-promise, m-my lord."

There was a moment's silence while the King struggled for
breath, then he spoke again. "Ethelred — my son — come here,
I can't see you."

The child was so frightened that his knees shook. He seemed
unable to move, and Dunstan pushed him towards his father,

who said, "Poor little lad — you are afraid. Death is not fear-some, and you must learn *not* to fear anything. You must be a brave atheling — obey your brother and your mother — I give you — my blessing . . ." The last word was scarcely audible as a convulsion shook the King's body. He closed his eyes, and his mouth sagged open.

"In manus tuas Domine —" whispered Dunstan to the silent room. He made the sign of the cross and continued prayers for a passing soul while tears coursed down his cheeks. The others knelt; Ethelred still trembling, pressed close to his rigid mother.

Rumon's own eyes were wet as he bowed his head on his clasped hands and listened to the two monks join Dunstan's intoning of the Latin prayers. A great King is dead, Rumon thought. Dead in his prime, and for what? Why did God permit him to die like this of an inglorious rotting in the belly! Edgar's early sins were atoned for long ago. He was beloved by all his people, he brought prosperity to England, and he loved life. Was God then — not the all-merciful Father de-scribed by Lord Jesus, but the Old Testament God of senseless, jealous vengeance? A bleak misery came into Rumon. He thought of his Quest, so long in abeyance; of his early visions which now seemed but childish vaporings.

Of what use were these mouthing clerics and their cringing beseeching prayers for the dead? Where was this heaven they talked about so glibly? The dead were dead, that body would dissolve in dust. And as for that soul they kept speaking of — had anyone ever seen a soul? Nobody, thought Rumon angrily. It was life that mattered, life and the body — which contains life.

He shivered, and in a sudden great revulsion felt the clamoring of his own life through his veins, his sinews, his manhood. Why was he letting it drift away — this great force, unused, un-explored.

That thing on the bed had been Edgar — the warm, brave, virile Edgar — and look at it now!

He did look for an instant, then turned his gaze slowly towards Alfrida.

She knelt where Dunstan had thrust her, motionless, while Ethelred whimpered unnoticed into her green skirts. If two years had altered her at all, no trace of alteration showed in the wavering candlelight. The golden hair, the grace of her body, the lure of her averted face, and especially the indefinable magnetism which seemed to exude from her like her perfume — all these were unchanged. So Rumon felt. And he allowed himself to feel, while the prayers continued, and from outside there began the sounds of lamentation — wailings, and the ponderous tolling of the Minster bell.

Dunstan ceased his prayers as the chamber filled with people, tiptoeing, hushed — Bishop Ethelwold, other monks, the ranking thanes.

The Archbishop wiped his tears and spoke to the newcomers. "Aye," he said. "It is finished. Do what is needful, for he must lie in state before the Minster's High Altar, that his subjects may take leave of him." The Archbishop bent down and put his hand on Edward's head. "Rise, my lord —" he said gently. The boy slowly obeyed, and Dunstan addressed the gathering. "This is your new King. This is England's future. May God and His Son and all the saints in heaven guide him aright."

Rumon was watching Alfrida, whose lovely face was suffused, while her hands clenched each other so violently that the knuckles whitened. She trembled, her lips moved, but Rumon could not read the explosive soundless words they were forming.

She was the very image of anguish, and Rumon's desire mellowed into sympathy. He moved near her, and said to Dunstan, "The Queen is suffering from shock and grief. She must be tended." He put his arm around Alfrida, and after a dazed look at him, she swayed against his shoulder.

The Archbishop's mouth tightened, yet he could not deny that Alfrida looked very odd — like a sleepwalker. "Take her to her bower, Rumon," he said. "Her women will care for her."

Rumon and Alfrida walked from the death chamber. She leaned against him and his steadying arm. They moved in silence through anterooms and the Great Hall, while little Ethelred trailed behind them. They climbed stone steps to the Queen's Bower, where her group of ladies were weeping. When they saw Alfrida, they surged forward clamoring their pity.

"Merewyn . . ." said Alfrida faintly. "I want Merewyn."

The girl rushed with outstretched arms towards the Queen, then stopped as she saw who Alfrida's escort was.

"Merewyn," said Rumon acknowledging her vaguely. "Take care of her, help her. She has need."

For an instant, Merewyn stood rooted. The King's death, the Queen's need were eclipsed by the sight of Rumon whom she had never managed to forget. She noted the tenderness in his eyes — in his voice — as he spoke of the Queen. Merewyn had hitherto not seen tenderness in that dark lean face which she knew she still loved.

"He's gone —" whispered the Queen, shuddering again. "Gone. Gone. Gone. And all my hopes with him. I can't bear it. Can't bear it!"

"Lie down, my poor lady!" cried the girl. "We'll bring you wine, and I'll stroke your back for you. Please, dear lady."

Alfrida allowed herself to be led to her couch, and Rumon, sighing deeply, bowed himself from the room.

Merewyn bent over her mistress with soothing sounds while she removed the gem-studded girdle, loosened the green robes, began the stroking and massaging which had never failed to calm the Queen. This time they failed. Alfrida shook her off. "I can't bear it," she repeated, stiffening, the violet eyes narrowed, staring past Merewyn towards an embroidered wall hanging of Salome's dance before Herod. "I WILL NOT bear it," said Alfrida, loudly and distinctly. "They shall see who wins!"

Merewyn was transfixed by the venom in Alfrida's voice, but the Lady Britta, who was hovering anxiously, whispered, "She

raves, poor thing. Grief has unsettled her wits." An explanation
the girl tried to accept. One of the housecarls came running in
with a beaker of strong mead but Alfrida would not touch it.
She continued to stare at the wall hanging, her penciled brows
drawn together intently.

King Edgar was buried at Glastonbury, as he had always desired. Dunstan and Abbot Sigegar officiated, and during the
High Requiem Mass Dunstan felt a mystical union with all the
exalted Beings who pervaded this most sacred place. Though
there were skeptics, he knew.

Alfhere, the cynical power-mad Lord of the Mercians, had
dared to question Glastonbury's possession of St. Patrick's and
St. Bridget's holy remains. He had contemptuously doubted that
the old wattle church was built by angels at Our Lord's direct
command, or that the Arimathean Joseph had arrived here bearing the cup which contained Christ's precious blood. And he
had blasphemously jeered at the event which to Dunstan was the
most moving of all — that the Lord Jesus Himself had visited
Glastonbury as a lad when he accompanied his great-uncle —
Joseph of Arimathea — on a trading voyage to the Mendip
lead mines.

The report of Alfhere's blasphemies had greatly angered
Dunstan. He bitterly resented slurs on the unique holiness of
the Abbey, and he threatened Alfhere with excommunication.
But the Earl blandly denied everything, saying that he must have
been misunderstood by some of his drunken thanes. Dunstan
thereupon wished to put Alfhere to the Ordeal — the plunging
of an arm in boiling oil — which would have remained unscathed
if the denials were true. But Edgar intervened. Edgar, the
mediator and the merciful, had calmed the Archbishop's just
wrath. Edgar — whose Requiem Mass they were now celebrating, and whose spirit was mingling with those of the other
sacred dead.

A shiver ran up Dunstan's spine as he elevated the Host and

the altar shone with a gentle radiance. A heavenly sign, he thought. Edgar is happy amongst the blessed saints.

The old man's ready tears flowed while the droning voices of the monks became an angelic choir, and the sip of wine from the chalice permeated his tired body with the warmth of fulfill-ment and certainty.

He had great need of that transfiguring moment, for no sooner was the funeral over than the strife began.

The emergency Council of Wise Men — or "Witenagemot" — was demoralized, split into factions which astounded even Dunstan. He was accustomed to man's senseless rages and greed, but had not expected that anyone would dare to oppose Edgar's dying command.

Yet they did, led by the enemy — Alfhere. Alfhere's group included Lord Ordulf, Alfrida's brother, and most of the other noblemen present.

This first Council meeting took place in the Abbot's Hall at Glastonbury, and the battle lines were at once drawn up. Alf-here, ignoring proper procedure, remained standing, his burly legs widespread, nor even bowed to Dunstan who presided.

"Edward is quite unfit to rule," Alfhere announced in his loud, confident voice. "He is bad-tempered and weak, look at the way he stammers. Besides, his mother was no Queen, and the marriage was dissolved. The idea of crowning Edward is ridiculous."

The other earls and thanes nodded agreement. Across the Hall from the temporal lords, the bishops were gathered. They looked at each other, and they looked at Dunstan who sat hunched in his Archbishop's throne. Hostility crackled through the chamber which was stifling in the July heat.

"You are surely not proposing to elect *Ethelred*, in the face of King Edgar's express command," said Dunstan, while his right hand trembled on the crozier. "The boy is scarcely ten, and has shown no desirable character traits since his birth."

"Oh, he can be molded," said Alfhere airily, flicking a louse off his red velvet sleeve.

"By whom?" asked Dunstan, straightening up. "You and his mother?"

Alfhere shrugged and cocked his head. "Not by bishops, abbots, and monks anyway. You'll find, my lord, that England is heartily sick of your grasping monasteries, and that foreign Benedictine Rule you foisted on us. It's unnatural. I, for one, am chucking out the monks and putting back the old-time canons on my lands. WITH their wives and wenches too. Let a priest enjoy himself like a man."

"You can*not!*" Dunstan cried, rising, and clutching the chair arm. "You haven't the power!"

Alfhere's contemptuous laugh was echoed along the benches amongst the lords, Ordulf joining in with a belated guffaw. Only old Britnoth, Earl of the East Saxons, looked grave, and sent a worried glance across the Hall towards the bishops.

"Am I to assume," said Dunstan in a voice of terrible control, "that you have no concern for your soul — Alfhere of the Mercians? That you do not fear God's punishment? Do I understand that you would lead England back to paganism? That we have an Antichrist amongst us?"

The Archbishop's eyes glistened as he glared at his adversary. His bent little body stiffened; he seemed to tower through the Hall.

Alfhere drew back very slightly. He tugged at his brown mustache. "Need we make such a pother, my lord?" he said after a moment. "Between a child of ten and a child of fourteen — what difference? Neither is old enough to rule."

"Aha," said Dunstan, sitting down. "I perceive that you are not quite so impervious to the threat of eternal damnation as you would like to think. And so you quibble."

The Earl flushed. Blood ran up his heavy shaven cheeks into the greasy brown hair. His hand clenched on the pommel of his sword. "I do not quibble," he said in a thick voice. "Ethelred shall be England's King, and this choking spiderweb of greedy monasticism shall be torn into a thousand shreds!"

"Aye, aye! Hear! Hear!" chorused all the other lords except Britnoth.

Dunstan expelled his breath sharply. A great weariness clouded his wits while nausea churned his stomach. He longed for the comforting Oswald, the Archbishop of York, but he was not there. Nor were other faces across the Hall who would have been his friends. Athelwine, Earl of East Anglia and his brother. Oslac of the North.

It had seemed unnecessary to summon a full Council of the Witan for so simple a thing as ratifying Edward's kingship. Nor had Dunstan foreseen this other and far graver issue. Antichrist, he thought, Satan is amoungst us. Once he had fought the devil in a dream — if it *was* a dream — long ago. He had felt no fear and routed the fiend with a pair of red-hot pincers, tweaking the black snout until the enemy roared for mercy, and vanished howling. Whence came that sure strength of mine? he thought, where is it now? His head drooped.

"Why, you've bested the old man!" cried Lord Ordulf in admiration to Alfhere. "He's gone to sleep."

Ethelwold, the grim Bishop of Winchester, had been staring at Dunstan in consternation. "My lord! My lord!" he said, tugging at the hunched black shoulder.

Dunstan moistened his lips, and whispered, "You help me — Ethelwold."

The Bishop did not hesitate. He was a born authoritarian, and renowned for his stern measures. He stalked down the Hall and faced Alfhere, while his voice rang out.

"The Archbishop is unwell, and this meeting of the Council is hereby dissolved!"

"Not until we've voted for Ethelred," roared Alfhere, "and there's more of *us* than *you!*"

"The Witan is hereby dissolved," said the Bishop as though

the Earl had not spoken. "And will reconvene in a month at Winchester, when ALL the Councilors have had time to appear. I decree this in the Archbishop's name. I'm quite sure nobody will care to invoke the penalty by demurring."

"What *is* the penalty?" asked Ordulf, his oxlike face gaping at the Bishop.

"Anathema!" answered Ethelwold in a spine-chilling voice.

Ordulf looked frightened though he had no idea what "Anathema" was. Alfhere began to bluster, but was cut short by Britnoth, the grave old Earl. "It is proper that this Witan be dissolved," he said, "and I am leaving now. A brawl here is unseemly and as insulting to the memory of King Edgar whose funeral we are attending as it must be painful to Our Lord Jesus Christ and His gentle Mother." Britnoth turned on his heel and walked out of the Hall. Slowly, sheepishly, one by one the other noblemen followed him. Alfhere said no more. He sat down on a bench, and glanced up once towards a high window which gave on a little gallery outside the Hall. As he had expected, a beautiful face half hidden by a white veil peered quickly down through the window.

Alfhere shook his head, and waved his hands in an angry gesture. "Not this time, my pretty one," he said aloud as though Alfrida could hear him. "We'll have to wait a bit. God damn those whoreson monks!" His hairy dirty hand clenched hard on the pommel of his sword. At that moment a clap of thunder exploded through the sultry air above the Abbot's lodging. There was a flash of lightning, and more thunder. Alfhere's hand dropped from his sword. He stared anxiously around the empty Hall. "Naught but a thunderstorm," he said. "Nothing supernatural about it." Yet his heart beat fast, and he made the sign of the cross several times until the thunderclaps diminished and he bolted from his seat towards the far door yelling for his son. "Cild! Cild Aelfric! Where are you, you fool! I want some wine!"

A month later, at the full meeting of the Witenagemot in

Winchester, Edward was elected King of England. The opposition had not subsided, Alfhere and his friends were prepared to fight — with swords if need be. But Dunstan, who recovered soon from his weakness, had dispatched messengers as far as York. He had summoned the godly thanes from the Danelaw and East Anglia. His co-Archbishop Oswald had arrived, and exerted his benign authority over his fellow Danes. Rumon too had been appointed to the Witan, by Dunstan's wish. "We need you, my son," said Dunstan. "Need every God-fearing soul who is eligible." He did not note the young man's hesitation, nor know how often Rumon had seen Alfrida recently.

The Witan was held in the chapter house of Ethelwold's new Minster, beneath a huge silver crucifix, which contained a fragment of the True Cross and was reputed to work miracles. It worked one on that date, just before the voting started. For it spoke. A deep hollow voice emerged from around the crucifix, saying, "Edward will be crowned, and Dunstan's rule is to continue as before."

The restless, arguing Assembly was struck dumb. They gaped at the crucifix which repeated in a louder thrilling voice, "It is My Will that Edward be crowned and that Dunstan, My vicar, be obeyed."

Astonishment held them frozen; then Ordulf fell to his knees even before the bishops did. "Forgive us, Blessed Lord," he said to the crucifix while he clasped his huge hands in supplication. "Forgive! Forgive! Misericordia!" came murmurs throughout the chapter house. Dunstan spread out his arms in blessing, his weary face was transfigured as he cried joyously, "A miracle! Our Merciful Lord has vouchsafed a miracle!"

Even Alfhere blenched. Sweat glistened on his forehead. He was silent when the voting commenced.

Rumon too was silent. For an instant he shared breath-cutting awe with the others, hypnotized as they were by the shining crucifix from which came this actual Voice of God. Then he chanced to look at Ethelwold, across whose gaunt face there flitted a very strange expression. Of sardonic triumph? Not of amusement, the Bishop's face was not formed for that, yet of something akin to it.

When the Witan had voted for Edward in a chorus of subdued "Ayes," the Voice spoke again from the crucifix, saying, "It is well. I am content with you."

Rumon thought of Alfrida, of the maternal hopes for Ethelred she had confided in him. Hopes now so conclusively ended. He thought of her soft wooing ways, of her pleading violet eyes, and the fragrance of her body and shimmering hair. They had not touched each other during this month of mourning for Edgar, not so much as a handclasp, yet each time they met their intimacy grew, and Rumon knew that he loved. The thought of the cruel disappointment she was soon to know, roused in him a passion of protectiveness and anger.

The Witan, after prayers of thanksgiving led by Dunstan, filed out of the Chapter House, solemnly, whispering to each other about the miracle. Rumon hung back, making pretense of fixing the cross-gartering on his legs. Soon he was alone except for Bishop Ethelwold, who stood watching him.

Rumon saw that he was not to be allowed solitude, and moved fast. He ran to the silver crucifix, and swung it aside, swiveling it on the supporting peg. Behind in the painted wooden wall, there was a slit, as wide as the Christ's head. The slit was funneled to the outer wall and showed a glimmer of daylight. Rumon knew that the light came through from some hidden angle of the cloister.

Ethelwold did not move. He continued to observe Rumon steadily.

"How simple," said Rumon. "How extremely simple it is to impersonate the Divine Voice! Which one of your obedient monks had the honor?"

"There are many ways of expressing God's manifest will," said the Bishop. "It is not for you to judge them." He walked over to the crucifix and replaced it to cover the slit.

"Trickery!" Rumon cried. "Deceit! And not for Edward's sake, I vow. Done solely so that you monks can keep your stranglehold on England!"

The Bishop refolded his arms into his sleeves. "That is a strange remark from one whom Dunstan trusts, and whom he considers almost one of us."

"Dunstan!" Rumon repeated uncertainly, remembering the excited joy on the Archbishop's face when the crucifix spoke. "*He* cannot be party to this shameful fraud! The poor old man is gullible as the rest of these dupes you had here."

The Bishop compressed his pale lips. "He has certainly been gullible in respect to *you*, Lord Rumon. Your words are obnoxious. You will leave my Chapter House at once!"

Rumon tossed his head. "Ah yes, I'll leave. And I shall tell Alfhere, and — and the Queen exactly how the 'miracle' was worked to insure the ends you wanted. I shall tell *everyone!* They shall see the proof!"

Ethelwold shrugged. "Rash, foolish youth! Who will believe your so-called proof? I admit nobody to the Chapter House I do not wish to, and in any case you have had a hallucination, brought on no doubt by the excesses of wine in which noblemen indulge. What did you think you saw behind the crucifix?"

The Bishop reached out his hand and pushed the heavy silver cross aside a little. The wall behind was whole. The even lines of painted boards showed — at least in the dim light — no signs of having been tampered with.

The Bishop drew back and lifted his eyebrows. "Another miracle, you see, Lord Rumon. Now relieve me of your unwelcome presence."

Burning with helpless rage, Rumon went. He went to the Palace, and directly to the Queen's Bower which he had not approached since the day of Edgar's death. Merewyn opened the heavy plank door to his thunderous knock. Her sea-green eyes widened as she saw his face. "Oh, Rumon!" she whispered, touching his arm in quick sympathy. "What's happened?"

He stared past her into the Bower where two of the ladies were embroidering, another folding linen, and Ethelred was curled up on a cushion cradling a shapeless straw doll and nervously watching his mother's white cat devour a mouse.

"Where is *she?*" asked Rumon hoarsely.

"Gone to the chapel to pray for victory in the Witan," said Merewyn after a moment.

"She may save her prayers," Rumon said. He turned and as he hurried off, Merewyn distinctly heard him add, "My poor tender, trusting love." She slammed the door hard and walked towards the little window which looked down on the privy garden. As she passed Ethelred the boy looked up. "Play with me, Lady Merewyn," he pleaded. Often she did so, and also made up stories for him. But now she gazed out the window. The roses and gillyflowers blurred as she stared down at them.

Alfrida was alone in the candlelit chapel; she rose quickly from her knees when Rumon burst in. She stood there, swaying a little, one hand on the prie-dieu, her favorite white gauze veil covering her beautiful head. "We've lost again?" she whispered. Her pink underlip thrust out and quivered. She put her hand over her heart.

"Wicked. Wicked," Rumon cried, hardly knowing what he said. "My darling, I can't bear to have you hurt."

"I've not been *sure* you were on our side," she said dully. "You're a friend of the monks, of Dunstan."

"No more. Never more! The depraved hypocrites! I want to help you, Alfrida. I love you! *I love you!*"

His vibrant young voice echoed through the chapel. She glanced around quickly. "Sh-h . . ." she whispered. "A priest might come in."

"No matter!" he cried. "Edgar, God rest him, no longer stands between us. I want to marry you, my love. To live with you and protect you, always!"

Alfrida swallowed, she glanced aside as she considered rapidly. She had, of course, known Rumon's passion for her, but barring the ill-judged episode in the graveyard, there had been no more awkward incidents. This last month while she had been influencing him to her course, his decorum had rather amused her. She had put it down to his monkish traits, or to youthfulness and lack of the sort of forthright vigor she admired in Alfhere.

Yet Rumon showed no lack of vigor now, and the proposal of marriage was interesting. Not impossible, in view of his rank, yet one couldn't be certain how useful it would be. These things must be thought out.

"Rumon —" she said softly. Teardrops sparkled on her lashes, and her smile seemed to him like that of the Blessed Queen of Heaven.

He fell to his knees on the chapel tiles, and kissed the hem of her dark blue robe.

chapteR five

EDWARD was to be crowned immediately at Winchester, before the effect of the miraculous crucifix could dim, and the opposition again rally its forces. There would naturally be no elaborate ceremonies, nor the priestly consecration Dunstan had instituted for the boy's father. The two archbishops were to follow the older simpler ritual. Yet Edward, on the Coronation Eve, acted very much as his father had — pale, exalted, and tense, praying constantly in the chapel, refusing to eat or drink.

On this same Coronation Eve, Edward's body thane, Gunnar, arrived at Alfrida's Bower, bearing a polite and searing message, which he delivered with embarrassment.

Gunnar said that Alfrida's presence was not required at the Coronation, since women were not expected to render homage. A widow — who had no blood kinship to Edward — was no longer officially dubbed "Queen." She would be called "Old Lady," the immemorial and respectful title for the widows of kings. So would the noble "Old Lady" now begin to consider her retirement from the Court? To whichever of her properties she selected for a Dower House. Edward knew that she was well provided for. She need not hurry herself unduly, but Edward wished to dispense with all women in his palace. Until, of course, he married — which event was not now in question.

Alfrida perceived that her prestige had vanished as quickly as she had always foreboded, yet she showed remarkable control. "These are Edward's wishes?"

"Yes, lady" — which was true, though Edward's wishes had been much influenced by Dunstan.

The delicate rose deepened on her cheeks, and she was aware of possible advantage to be gained by winning over this young thane so close to Edward. She smoothed one of her golden braids, fingering the intertwined pearls absently, then gave Gunnar her softest glance through her lashes. She bowed her exquisite head in sad resignation, murmuring that to be sure the new King's wishes must be obeyed, though they burdened her heart and she had so *hoped* that he would consider her as his mother. Gunnar, who had never suspected her of any such hope, was puzzled, and wondered if Edward's antipathy to her were quite justified.

He looked uncomfortably towards Merewyn, who had withdrawn to the weaving corner with the other women.

"My dearest Merewyn will share my banishment, I'm sure," said Alfrida gently, having long ago noted his interest in the girl. "You must come and visit us at Corfe."

"*Corfe!*" cried Gunnar. "Corfe Castle in Dorset! That ees far, lady."

"It is the best of my properties," she answered sighing. "Poor widows cannot be particular. And my little Ethelred will be strengthened by sea air. We will leave tomorrow morning, since we are not wanted here."

"Tomorrow!" Gunnar flushed with concern. "That ees the Coronation, lady! Ethelred must do homage to hees brother!"

"Quite impossible, I fear," she said sweetly regretful. "The child is too nervous for the strain of such a ceremony, besides he's feverish. You see —" she gestured towards a silver cup on the table, "I was preparing a draught to give him when you came."

"But lady —" began Gunnar, not daring to ask how Ethelred could be well enough to travel if he were not fit for the Cornonation.

"Say no more, Gunnar —" she interrupted with a pathetic smile. "Tell Edward that he will not be troubled by the unwanted members of his family, and that I forgive him."

Gunnar bowed and hurried down the winding stairs from the Bower. Perplexity and dismay were stamped so obviously on his broad honest face that when he bumped into Alfhere outside the Great Hall, that Earl caught him by the shoulders. "What's wrong with you, Gunnar? Can't you look where you're going?"

"Sorry, my lord. I've been with the Lady Alfrida. She ees taking Ethelred to Corfe *before* the Coronation. I don't know how to tell Edvard this, it vill upset him much."

"Oh," said Alfhere, chuckling. "Alfrida's in a temper, is she?"

"No. No, my lord. She vas so sad. So regretful."

The Earl chuckled again. "No doubt. I'll have a word with her myself." He turned and mounted the stairs.

He burst into the Bower without knocking, and found Alfrida standing in the middle of the floor panting, hands clenched, eyes blazing, underlip thrust out. "I thought as much," said the Earl. "Though you certainly diddled Gunnar."

He looked towards the ladies who were huddled fearingly behind the loom, each one — even Merewyn — knowing that at any sound from them the mirror might be hurled their way, or the brass candlestick, or a stool.

"Clear out! All of you!" said Alfhere to the women, who sidled thankfully out the door. "*Now*," he went on, grabbing Alfrida roughly by the arms and shaking her. "Sit down!" He pushed her to the ermine-covered bed, and sat beside her — a bulky man in wine-stained crimson velvet. His bold prominent eyes contemplated Alfrida before he said, "What's all this I hear about Ethelred not being at the Coronation?"

"He'll not go," she said through her teeth, still panting. "They've insulted me."

"He *must* appear," said Alfhere. "This isn't the moment to call attention to our future plans. Also the crucifix spoke. I heard it."

"Oh, you coward!" she shouted. "Surely you will not render homage to that stuttering bastard — that usurper!" She had begun to tremble violently.

"I shall," he said shrugging. " 'Tis only a mummery, and don't you see —"

She saw nothing but a flash of red around Alfhere, and she struck him in the face with all her force.

He reeled, clapping his hand to his jaw. "You bitch!" he cried. "You stupid bitch! Only one way to deal with a wench like you!" He ripped up his velvet robe, and before she could move he hurled himself on top of her, pinioning her arms, biting her breasts until she screamed, and finally slackened. Then he raped her brutally.

There was a silence of some minutes, broken only by the cawing of rooks, and the distant ringing of church bells. The Earl rearranged his clothes. Alfrida looked down at her breasts, where teeth marks were bleeding. "It hurts," she said in a small voice.

"Ah, but you liked it." He smoothed his brown mustache, got up and drank from a flagon of mead on the table. "Now, perhaps your wits are clear enough for reason." He glanced rapidly around the Bower, and lowered his voice, "Have you been to the witch?"

"To Gytha?" she whispered, shrinking. "No."

"Then you must go, at once. Her — shall we say arts — have much helped you in the past. I think of Eneda's death, for one. The puppet and the pins, I suppose, much safer than something unwholesome given in a drink."

"You mean Edward . . . ?" she breathed.

The Earl assented by a nod. "We may still have to wait a

while. You must learn *patience*. But you see how important is the Coronation." He looked at her face which had regained its luminous beauty. "You and I, eh, my dear?" he said, putting his sweaty hand on her neck. "Godleva can't last long. My physician says her lungs are rotted. Then we'll wed, and rule England through Ethelred."

"Ah — h," she said on a long sigh, and added half smiling, "*Rumon* wants to wed me."

Alfhere laughed in perfect confidence. "That dreamy, bookish foreigner? A bit young for you, my girl — ten years, is it? And he'd bore you to death. Amuse yourself if you like. *I* don't mind, but I wager you'll find he's a timid virgin, and he'd never understand your nature as I do. However, if you've detached him from the monks, that's one in the eye for that wretch of a Dunstan, and it won't hurt to have Rumon on our side."

"True, my lord," she said softly. "We understand each other well, and I shall go to Gytha this very night."

Edward was duly crowned — then Ethelred, Rumon, and all the noblemen knelt to do him homage and swear fealty. Thereafter Dunstan was delighted by the anxious sense of responsibility the boy king showed in his new position. And he kept his head throughout the continuing conflicts with Alfhere's party. The Earl retired to his own Mercia, where he systematically ousted the monks from all the religious foundations and replaced them by loose-living canons who in return filled Alfhere's coffers with gold. The wicked sedition spread too; other earls followed Alfhere's example, monasteries were destroyed, even nunneries. The disgruntled abbots, priors, monks escaped south to Wessex, or to East Anglia which remained staunch, thanks to Athelwine and Britnoth. Something very like civil war threatened England, but the monks could not bear arms, and Edward's royal guard was tiny and untrained. Edgar had not needed one.

Dunstan agonized over the breaking down of the Holy Benedictine system he, Ethelwold, and Oswald had labored so long to implant. He resorted to fasts and frenzied prayers. Particularly, and with Edward kneeling beside him, Dunstan prayed to St. Swithin, Winchester's especial saint, whose precious bones had been moved into the new Minster by Ethelwold and performed more miracles than all the other relics put together.

Undoubtedly the next event of that autumn was one of St. Swithin's miracles. A blazing comet appeared, streaking through the night, and was seen all over England. Certainly a portent of some kind, and so stated by Dunstan, who interpreted it in many a sermon as a sign of God's wrath at the evildoers.

Alfhere tried to scoff, but it was noted that he abated his persecution of the monks, and retired to winter in seclusion at his castle in Shrewsbury.

By spring a worse disaster hit England. Famine. Bitter cold, even snow, continued into June, and the crops failed. The herring shoals did not arrive as they always had. And then murrain — the cattle plague — swept the country. Starving beasts were consumed by starving men, who became themselves diseased. There was scarce a cottage in the land without a corpse, in many places whole villages perished.

The remaining Benedictine monasteries did what they could, though suffering themselves. The almoners handed out doles of bread and ale in ever diminishing quantities, as day by day the famished throngs increased outside their gates. The royal Palace at Winchester was equally generous — after Edward, upon returning from a stag hunt in Wherwell Forest, saw a moaning young mother die of hunger right on the Palace doorstep. Her skeleton body, her bloated belly, and the wizened dead baby in her arms shocked him into awareness of his people's misery. He ordered the stag to be roasted for them. He announced that during the famine the death punishment for poaching in the royal preserves would not be enforced. He had his housecarls issue the dole, and when even the royal stores began to dwindle, he himself subsisted on fish from the Palace pond, or birds brought down by his falcons.

Now when the serious sturdy lad rode out through the streets of Winchester, his people swarmed around to bless him and kiss his hand.

Little by little the ghastly monsters of famine and murrain loosed their hold. The church bells no longer tolled hourly for the dead. Amongst the strong or lucky who had survived, there was new energy to replace the apathy of doom. Young Edward was happy. He knew himself beloved by the people, and in the autumn of 977, he himself fell in love.

Edward's love was Gunnar's sister, daughter to Thored — Earl of Yorkshire — and of the Lady Hilde. The girl had come from York on a visit to Winchester with her father, and stayed at Bishop Ethelwold's guesthouse, since the Palace no longer received women. Her name was Elgifu, and she was not quite fourteen — a gentle, pretty thing; modest, quiet, with chestnut curls, and a soft adoring gaze rather like that of Edward's favorite hound. He longed to fondle Elgifu, and though they were both shy he never stammered when he spoke to *her*. Dunstan was in Canterbury, and not available for advice, but Bishop Ethelwold whom Edward tentatively consulted was not averse to the thought of union between the two, except on the grounds of youth. The Earl of Yorkshire's daughter was suitable enough for the English King. The alliance would further cement to the throne, all of the Anglo-Danes.

Ethelwold added that he and Dunstan HAD considered marrying Edward to Britta — Alfhere's daughter — which move certainly might quell that insubordinate earl's renewed persecution of the monks. "But," said Ethelwold, eying the young King's start of alarmed disgust, "My lord Dunstan has already decided against that. Britta is too old and ugly, she is sickly like her mother. We doubt she would be a breeder. Were it not for that, I'd expect you to sacrifice inclination to duty. Dunstan is more softhearted, and concerned for your happiness, even in this life. So we will find some other way of defeating Alfhere and speak no more of Britta, nor even search amongst the Welsh or Scottish kings to find a bride for you. Since you haven chosen well enough for yourself."

Edward heaved a tremulous sigh. His round blue eyes lit up, he gave a boyish joyful laugh. "Thank you, my lord. With Elgifu b-beside me, I shall be a g-good ruler. I know it! My prayers are answered."

The happiness in Winchester did *not* extend sixty miles southwest into the Isle of Purbeck, where a great many other emotions centered around Alfrida at Corfe Castle. But not happiness.

For Rumon there was the dark, violent slavery of passion, often thwarted, since Alfrida was most sparing of her favors and insisted upon the maximum discretion. Consequently their trysts took place outdoors — in the forest, or the prehistoric rings deemed haunted by the Corfe villagers, or on the riverbank. He rebelled against these arrangements. Each time when her favorite and stupid housecarl, Wulfgar, appeared at Rumon's lodging with a scrawled summons from Alfrida, Rumon clenched his jaw and vowed he would not go. Yet each time he went. And was rewarded by the fragrant softness and the knowing wiles of her body. When the rapture had subsided, he would rebel again.

"WHY must we meet like this, my love? Like loutish serfs afraid of their master! Why won't you wed me, so that I may share your bed in open decency? You say you love me. You give yourself to me as though you love me. Or is it I am such a fool I do not know?"

Always she soothed him, pressing her mouth on his, her naked breasts against his chest, murmuring in her sweetest voice, "Be patient, darling — yet a little while. Of course I love you, but be patient."

"Patient! *Why* must we wait and lurk in hedgerows?"

And she would answer sadly, her golden hair covering him like a cloak, her scented breath close to his ear, "You know why, Rumon. I cannot reconcile it with God and my conscience to wed so soon after Edgar's death. It would be heartless."

At first this silenced him, and he respected her scruples, while blaming himself bitterly for having led her into sin.

As time went by and her summons to the trysts grew fewer, he chafed mightily and yearned for her with an obsessive hunger he could not control. He and three servants lived in a house at the end of the village near Corfe common. Alfrida had maintained that her poor little castle on top of the hill lacked room to lodge him properly, and that the temptation to expose their love would be far greater if they were under the same roof. Also there might be moral detriment to little Ethelred. Rumon could not but agree, and admire her character even as he lusted for her body. So white and lovely and pure was she that despite that which was between them, he often thought of her with worship as he had in the Royal Chapel at Winchester.

By the Yuletide of 977, Rumon was frantic. He had not lain with her for a month, and then but for a hurried hour in a deserted shepherd's cot on the heath.

That tryst had not gone well. Alfrida was distracted, captious. Though he had covered a pile of straw with a bearskin, and lit a fire for her, she complained of cold. She drank several draughts from the wine flask he had brought, then said she was sleepy. When he put his hands gently on her breasts and started to kiss her, she pushed him away.

"Oh, Rumon — can you think of nothing else? Or at least a different —" Her voice trailed off and she smothered a yawn.

He stiffened, his hands dropped from her breasts. "I weary you, my love?" he said, and heard his own voice trembling, abject. "What can I do to please you?"

She threw him a quick speculative glance, and laughed. "Jesu! Don't look so woebegone! Here, go on — have done with it." She unfastened her girdle, and pulled off her gown.

He flinched, and the sign of desire left him. Nor, though now she smiled at him and murmured endearments, could he for some time regain it. The consummation when it came left him miserable and uncertain instead of triumphant.

After that and as usual Rumon saw her often at her castle but always amongst others of her entourage — her remaining ladies, Merewyn and Britta, her chapel priest, her housecarls. He went to the castle because the excuse for his dwelling at Corfe had been the tutoring and guardianship of Ethelred. Each day he conscientiously spent time with the boy. He took him riding in the forest or to the sea. He taught him hawking. He tried to teach him Latin, reading, writing. Ethelred enjoyed the outings, but he was no scholar. Lessons bored him. He fidgeted and spilled the ink. His long-lashed violet eyes stared mutinously and without the slightest comprehension at the alphabets Rumon drew for him.

Once in exasperation, Rumon switched him, and the boy ran howling to his mother who expressed her displeasure during their next tryst.

"You must not lay hands on my kingly son, Rumon. Such an act gives me doubts as to our marriage. I had not thought you cruel."

So much in thrall to her was Rumon that he humbly apologized. And though he was not fond of Ethelred, the boy's extraordinary likeness to Alfrida often tore at his heart. The same eyes, and purity of feature, the same curly golden hair, the same grace of movement. Moreover, he knew with some sympathy that Ethelred was often lonely. He was twelve now, and in little Corfe there were no companions of his rank and age. Indeed Corfe was a backwater, and Rumon had often dreamed plans for his beloved after they married. He would take her to his property in Somerset, build for her there a beautiful castle. Or they might travel together — see new lands. Ireland, he thought, instinctively choosing a land to the west, though the old pull towards these, and the visions of a Quest had long been

forgotten. Other interests of his early life had also lapsed . . .
reading, study, translations, had lost their savor. Even his harp
hung untouched on the wall unless Alfrida commanded him to
play at the castle.

During all the period of his enslavement he had but twice left
the Isle of Purbeck and those were journeys to buy presents for
his mistress. Once to Southampton where a Levantine ship had
put in bearing damask, attar of roses, and the fine gold-threaded
gauze she loved.

And later, he went to London. She needed a new comb which
must be made of the smoothest walrus ivory, the handle carved
with her name and a motif of crowns. She also wanted a new
girdle clasp from France — gold, of course, enameled and
studded with gems. London seemed the best place for Rumon to
find goldsmiths and craftsmen able to fill these needs. He jour-
neyed there eagerly, anxious to please her, proud of his ability
to do so, saddened only by separation from her.

He was impressed by London — its Roman walls encircling
stately brick or marble Roman villas, crammed into the bustling
city amongst new wooden Saxon houses. He might have enjoyed
himself in the taverns where there was music and superb French
wines, had he not been in such a fever to return to his en-
chantress.

Alfrida was delighted with his gifts, and for some time rewarded him by frequent trysts.

On this Christmas Eve in his lodging Rumon sat sadly by his
empty table, his head in his hands remembering how fervently
she had returned his lovemaking then, how their eyes had met
secretly when she wore his girdle clasp in public, or combed her
magnificent hair with his ivory comb. Yet this morning, when
he went to fetch Ethelred for a ride in the forest, she had worn
the clasp, but there was no message in her glance. She bade him
a casual "Good day," then turned away.

If I got her another gift, he thought, a New Year's offering?
A magnificent ring, perhaps? He pondered gloomily how this

might be arranged. There were no foreign ships in the harbors. The nearest skilled goldsmith was at Winchester. Moreover, Rumon had spent most of his cash on the earlier gifts. His Somerset property would have supported him well enough if he had lived there to supervise his reeve, his tenants and serfs. But from Corfe, he could not control laxness and dishonesty on his estate. Then there had been the famine last year and greatly decreased revenue. What could I sell? he thought, looking around his sparse little Hall. It must be land then. Nothing else would provide a ring worthy of Alfrida. As he thought of her, he was seized by a spasm of yearning so sharp that he groaned.

At that moment the church bells rang out through the chilly twilight drizzle, and Rumon was suddenly reminded that this was his twenty-fourth birthday. I should go to Midnight Mass, he thought dully. I always did. Yet of what use to go to Mass, since he dared not go to confession to the village priest in Corfe, and therefore could not take Communion. Last Christmas he had ridden four miles to Wareham and confessed a vague tale of fornication to a hurried priest who did not know him and gave him a light penance. This year the trip seemed not worth the effort.

He got up and began to pace the rush-strewn floor. Alfrida took the Sacraments in her tiny private chapel. She had told him so, recounting with a wistful smile all the scoldings and penances she endured from her chapel priest for Rumon's sake.

He had felt horribly guilty and loved her the more, yet he could not forbear saying that these sins need not be. She had but to marry him.

To this she replied only by another sad smile.

He stopped pacing and listened in surprise to a distant commotion from the Castle end of the village — heavy thumps of galloping hoofs, and the long drawn-out blare of horns. Visitors? he thought. Or some Yuletide celebration? Would not this unusual hubbub provide an excuse for going to the Castle, even though Alfrida had said that Ethelred should have no lessons through the twelve days of Christmas, and had issued no invitation for Rumon to join the festivities.

Rumon sank down in his chair again, marshaling the nearly vanished remnants of his pride. I am an atheling, he thought, a prince of England. And I am her lover. Why then should I fear to intrude on her, why do I fear that she would scorn me as a beggar, a supplicant?

His legs tensed as if to carry him to the Castle of their own will, and yet he did not move. Some time went by, and so profound was his interior conflict that his mind dulled to apathy, and he stared unseeing at the leaping flames on his hearth.

He did not hear a knock on his front door, but he emerged to awareness at the rattling of the wooden latch. *Wulfgar with a summons from her!* he thought in a great burst of relief.

He rushed to open the door and saw Merewyn standing on the step. "Yes, it's me," said the girl quietly. "You are disappointed, I see." She walked to the fire, and warmed her wet hands. The hood of her amber cloak slipped back disclosing her garnet-colored hair which was darkened by rain around her small square face. Her eyes, smoky-blue in the firelight, regarded him with a kind of rueful sadness.

"You expected a message from *her*, no doubt," she said in a flat voice. "Take heart, for in a way I bear one, though it is really from the King."

"The *King?*" repeated Rumon, staring. "Young Edward? What are you talking about, Merewyn?"

"The King has just arrived in Corfe for a surprise visit to Lady Alfrida. Many noblemen are with him including —" she paused, "Alfhere of the Mercians. As you can imagine, the Castle is in turmoil. The housecarls are all frantic, running hither and yon trying to prepare a feast. That is why *I* was sent to you."

"I still don't understand," he said.

She sighed, and shook her head. "Rumon, Rumon — there is so much that you don't understand, alas. Nor did I, once. I was be-glamoured like you. Oh, poor Rumon," she cried.

"You've grown so pale and thin! You have a look of suffering."

He heard the sorrow in her voice, he saw the softness in her eyes and was vaguely touched, but clearly — as though etched in the air beside her — he saw another face.

"What did *she* say? What were you sent to tell me?" he asked vehemently.

"The King bids you to the Christmas feast tomorrow. And Lady Alfrida wonders how many of the thanes you can accommodate here tonight, and for the duration of their stay."

He swallowed. This was not the message he had hoped for; still it was not reasonable to expect Merewyn to bear anything more personal, and at least he would see Alfrida on the morrow. Amongst the bustle of all that throng, there would certainly be some way to see her alone, to tell her about the ring, to rekindle the love he felt sure was only dormant.

"I suppose I could take a half-dozen thanes," he said. "On the benches here," he gestured around the hall, "and one or two clean ones," he smiled faintly, "might share my bed."

She nodded. "The Castle is cramped, as you know. The King will share *Ethelred's* bed."

That startled him. "This all seems very odd," he said frowning. "Heretofore, Edward has shown no desire to see those whom he in effect exiled to Corfe. He behaved with the most unjust enmity to — to the Lady and Ethelred. Nor do I understand why he appears here with Alfhere who has done his best to split the kingdom and ruin the monks."

"I believe Alfhere has repented," she said. "At least they say that he came humbly to Winchester and made his peace with Edward, who himself has altered. He is brimming with happiness, and wishes well to all the world. It seems that at this Christmastide he wanted to make friends with his half brother."

"How extraordinary! Do you know what caused this remarkable change?"

She was quiet a moment, looking at his strong, lean face, the shining black hair which he kept short, the dark somber eyes under heavily marked eyebrows. "The King is in love," she said very low, and blushed. "*Happily* in love," she added, "which I observe — now that I'm full grown — is not the common lot."

For the first time he looked at her attentively. Aye, she was full grown, must be eighteen or so. Despite the freckles on her blunt little nose, the width of her pink mouth and all that strange dark red hair, no doubt most men found her attractive. She had full breasts, outlined as were her full hips by her green wool robe though the embroidered girdle between proclaimed a small waist. He noted that her shoes were muddy, and that there was a smooch of mud on her round cheek, and though the mud was natural considering the dirty walk she had had from the Castle, he nevertheless at once contrasted her with the slender, elegant, and fragrant Alfrida.

"You've so far found no happiness in love?" he asked kindly, and remembered with some effort what Dunstan had said long ago. He never thought of Dunstan willingly. "Gunnar, perhaps? I suppose he came with the King?"

"He did." She tossed her head. "But I shall never marry Gunnar, that *Dane!* Rumon — as soon as Yuletide is over, I am leaving Corfe. I'm going to my Aunt Merwinna at Romsey Abbey."

"What!" he cried. "But you can't. Alfrida needs you, she'd never let you go, nor should you! What possible reason have you?"

Merewyn was silent, longing with all her honest soul to tell him the truth. She answered him only in her mind. Because I can no longer bear to watch your senseless infatuation for that woman, nor watch your anguish when you finally understand what she is. As you certainly will — for there is danger coming. And don't you think I know — that all the Castle knows — for what purpose she has so often slipped out of an afternoon when she is supposed to be resting? Don't you know how you give yourself away when you look at her? This I can no longer bear to watch. Why do you think you've seen me so seldom when you are at the Castle? But you don't think of me — you never have. Yet I love you too much to torment you. Or I could tell you of the letters I know she has received from Earl Alfhere. I could point out that while there was never room at the Castle for *you*, Alfhere this very night is to sleep in the small chamber adjoining hers. I could tell you that there is evil seeping through the Castle, I don't know what it is, but I'm afraid. Sometimes I've slept near Alfrida, and she has talked in her sleep. She talked of murder, of a bleeding clay puppet bristling with pins. She suspects that I heard, and as I am repelled by her, and am no longer deft at stroking and tending that white body you keep desiring — I'm sure she will let me go.

"Merewyn!" he said sharply. "Why don't you speak? You haven't answered me!"

Merewyn sighed. She clasped and unclasped her hands in the old childish way he remembered. "My Aunt Merwinna is unwell. Her heart isn't strong. She wishes me to come."

"Bah! As though she didn't have a hundred nuns and novices to care for her!"

"She wants someone of her own blood."

But you aren't! It nearly burst from him, in his anger that she should be so callously deserting Alfrida. Indeed his death-bed vow to Breaca now seemed as vapid as did all the other prayers and trappings of religion. He might have broken his word this minute, had not Merewyn lifted her chin and said fervently, "The thought of my descent from King Arthur has helped me through many a desolate hour."

Rumon softened despite his annoyance, and he reflected that if her lack of rank were known she would not be considered a fitting lady to serve Alfrida. And he wanted Merewyn to stay at the Castle. For it occurred to him that though she was earthy, a bastard, and of lowly stock, yet there was a charm and comfortableness about her. He would persuade her not to leave Alfrida.

"I must go now," Merewyn said, rising. "The Christmas feast

is at eleven tomorrow. Rumon, isn't this your birthday? Will
you attend midnight Mass?"

"No," he said.

She pulled her cloak about her and spoke in a dry, cool voice,
most unlike her. "I can guess why. Well, I shall pray for you
tonight — no matter how presumptuous you may think it."

"Pray for *me?*" He smiled and said in the amused tone he had
so often used to her, "What would you pray for me, child?"

"For your redemption." She bowed slightly and was out of
the door before he recovered from astonishment.

At the Castle the housecarls and serfs worked all night —
slaughtering pigs and sheep for the feast, turning spits to roast
the meat, building a bonfire on the level slope below the Castle
gate where villagers and other humble folk would join in welcoming their King (as well as the Christ Child), by devouring
an ox. The baker sweated at his ovens, serving wenches scurried
from the cellars bearing flagons of wine, while the men trundled
casks of mead and ale to the courtyard before Alfrida's great
Hall.

Upstairs in the Castle, Edward and Ethelred slept side by side
in bed, oblivious to all the commotion below them. Gunnar
dozed on a pallet near them — ever aware of his duty as the
young King's body thane.

Ethelred had been flattered by his half brother's warm kiss of
greeting and delighted with the presents Edward brought, especially a well-trained falcon from the far North. Ethelred's spite-
ful jealousy of Edward had waned since the latter actually
became King, especially as Alfrida never mentioned Edward
anymore.

Before going to bed the boys played a lively game of tipcat
together, followed by a wrestling match which Edward allowed
Ethelred to win, thereby puffing up the younger lad with pride
and a satisfaction which he seldom found in life. Before they
slept they talked in mutual excitement about the boar hunt which

would follow the feast tomorrow. They made plans for a bear-baiting too. Ethelred had previously shrunk from the dangers inherent in either boar- or bear-hunting, yet now Edward's good humor inspired him to confidence and a touch of hero worship for this brother who was four years older, and also a king. They linked arms before they slept.

In the Bower, Merewyn did not sleep. She listened to the turmoil outside and to Britta's hiccuping snores, while she had many dreary thoughts.

There was no sleep in Alfrida's chamber, where Alfhere was sitting on her bed guzzling mead. Shortly before, they had both been naked in the bed together violently satisfying their mutual lust. Now he was robed, and she had wrapped the ermine coverlet around her. The December night was chill, the fire scarcely warmed the room.

"Well, my dear —" said the Earl, wiping his mustache. "You've not lost your skill at bed sport. Been having practice?"

She shrugged. "Not really. Now and then. Hardly matters."

"Rumon?" asked the Earl chuckling, "Or some brawny housecarl?"

"Certainly not a housecarl," she snapped. "What do you take me for!"

"It's hard to say." He chuckled again and pinched her thigh, then frowned into his mead tankard. "And there are more important things for us to talk of. The least — that Godleva worsens, but she doesn't die. Who would think there'd be such strength in that withered, coughing, bleeding body! At times I feel pity. May God relieve her soon."

Alfrida sighed. "I have been patient," she murmured, her golden head drooping, "patient as you told me to be, but you can't conceive the boredom and humiliations I've suffered — mewed up here in this benighted little dower house!"

He shrugged and getting up, made a tour of the chamber. He opened the door, inspected the empty passage outside, pulled down the latch again and wedged it.

"Gytha's sorcery seems entirely ineffectual," he said, hastily crossing himself. "On the contrary Edward flourishes stronger every day. You *did* go to Gytha?" he added angrily.

"Of course. I gave her three pieces of gold with promise of more when — it happened. And since then I've sent Wulfgar to Winchester with urgent messages and silver."

"Wulfgar — that clumsy dog-faced housecarl? You *trust* him?"

She nodded. "Because he *is* like a dog, and devoted to me. He'll do anything I say but you needn't think he understands his errands. He's not got the wit."

Alfhere clenched his hairy fists while he scowled at her lovely anxious face. "We can't wait much longer for Gytha's efforts to succeed. Edward is to be married at Easter, and nine months later for sure there'll be an heir to the throne nearer than your precious Ethelred — Or me," he added beneath his breath.

"*You?*" she repeated, staring at him.

"Aye. Haven't you thought of that, my sweet? I'm of the line of Cerdic, I was kin to Edgar. You might be full Queen again . . . Ah, that thought pleases you!"

She had opened her eyes wide and they shone like amethysts.

"Unfortunately, we must face certainties. With Dunstan, Oswald, Ethelwold, and all the rest of the gaggle of monks against me, I'd not stand a chance of election by the Witan. Nor am I strong enough to take the throne by force. At present. We must still count on Ethelred and after that, we'll have power enough."

She shivered voluptuously, pulling the ermine coverlet tighter around her naked shoulders. "What is in your mind, Alfhere?" she whispered. "What plan have you? Not here and now, surely?" her pupils darkened in sudden fear.

He shook his head and tugged at his mustache. "Not now when Edward has brought along fifty of his loyal thanes, and has Gunnar always beside him. No, we must show the greatest friendliness, we must lull any suspicion. That is why I went humbly to Winchester to make my "peace." You will charm Edward, as you know so well how to. This Christmas feast shall be one of perfect amity. Edward shall enjoy it so that he will soon return. And then . . ."

"And then . . ." she repeated. Her heart was fast beating, but she looked exultantly into his eyes. He gave a grunt and drank some mead. "Enough of that for now," he said. "Shall we return to more amusing matters?" He ran his hand up her bare thigh beneath her robe. "Oh, but this reminds me — keep Rumon besotted over you, so that he suspects nothing. His good will might be invaluable later."

She nodded slowly. "As you wish, my lord. Though one wearies of bread and milk when one has a taste for other diets."

Alfhere threw back his head, laughing, then grabbed her around the waist.

chapter six

THAT Yuletide passed merrily at Corfe. Every day there was hunting, or bear-baiting, or a troup of dancing tumblers to watch. Every night at dusk there was a feast, while the King's gleemen chanted new songs and twanged their harps. Edward enjoyed himself mightily, and was amazed to find how sympathetic was the stepmother he had once detested. Alfrida listened, smiling, to his stammered confidences about little Elgifu, how he missed her and wished that her parents had not requested that she go to York for the holidays, how he wished that the wedding might take place earlier, but knew that there was not time for proper preparation before Lent, and that during Lent, of course, nobody might be married. So wasn't it fortunate that Easter was early this year — the last day of March!

Alfrida assented to these raptures, assented too when Edward said that she and Ethelred must attend the wedding as honored guests, that Winchester Palace would open all its chambers for the occasion. Her conduct was perfect, as Alfhere assured her in private. He was delighted with her. And so for different reasons was Rumon.

Alfrida found occasion to see Rumon alone on Christmas Day

and all her recent coldness had vanished. She gave him tender looks, pressed against him and stroked his hand while whispering that she longed for another tryst, but they must discreetly wait until the King and his company left and then she added, touching his cheek with her lips, they might really make plans for their marriage — at Eastertide perhaps like Edward. Rumon had gone off to his lodging that night in a joyful daze.

Why then should he have suffered so appalling a nightmare? It was a repetition of the dream five years ago in Brittany and never thought of since. Here again was the beautiful naked woman, ivory and gold except for rosy nipples on uptilted breasts, here again a face not quite seen, yet emanating cruelty, power, and great allure. But this time in his dream Rumon knew who the woman was, and when he reached towards her as he had before, horror seized him. He saw blood behind her, cataracts of blood, streaming, falling, splashing, he saw that her white feet were dabbled with blood, her clenched hands were stained crimson, and as before from somewhere there came a peal of harsh malicious laughter. The laughter of a demon.

He awoke with a shout of fear to find that the young visiting thane who shared his bed was shaking him. "Jesu!" said the young thane crossly. "What ails you, Lord Rumon? You've been groaning and shouting fit to wake the dead. For sure *I* can't sleep!"

Rumon sat up, pressing his palms to his eyes; he was trembling and waited a moment to control himself. "I'm sorry," he said. "The Devil sent one of his monsters to beset me. Only a dream," he added quickly. He touched the golden crucifix which he still wore around his neck. "And one should give no credence to dreams. They are a mockery."

"No doubt," said the young thane yawning and rolling onto his side. "I never have 'em myself." In a moment he was snoring.

Rumon got out of bed and poured himself a mug of wine. By the time he had finished it the horror had faded; he began to feel wry amusement and shame for having groaned and cried out like a child. And how ridiculous to have thought the nightmare woman was Alfrida since he had not really seen her face.

By consequence of feeling that his dream had somehow so grossly wronged her, his love had increased when he saw her at the Castle Gate early next morning. The drawbridge was down, as it always was, and she was standing near the inner end, between two small square brick towers which had been built to house the archers and guards who had in Alfred's time been necessary for defense against Viking marauders. King Alfred, himself, had seen to the fortification of the little Castle, which was of strategic importance by reason of its position high on the hill at "Corfe Gate" — the passage through the Purbeck range.

Alfrida was dressed in the ivory-white she so often wore, a fine new wool gown embroidered with gold thread; and Rumon who had seen her in it yesterday assumed that the young King had presented the expensive gown as an early New Year's gift.

The day was unusually warm for the season; she wore no mantle though her head was covered by a white veil and golden circlet, for she had just been to Mass in her chapel. She looked as fresh and sparkling as the sunlit morning, and Rumon's heartbeat thickened.

She made a slow gesture, rather as though she were pointing out something, and as Rumon came nearer, he was unpleasantly startled to see that she was deep in converse with Alfhere. Rumon thought her as repelled by the Mercian Earl's coarse manners, braying laugh, and bold cynical stare as he was himself. Why then was she chatting alone with the Earl at so unlikely a place as the Castle Gate? And why, as Rumon crossed the drawbridge, did she start and frown, saying angrily, "Ah, you're very early today!"

"Forgive me," Rumon said flushing. "I didn't mean to be intrusive."

Alfrida recovered at once. "You're most welcome, always." She gave him her warmest smile, holding out her hand for him to kiss. "I was asking the Earl's advice. As you see the steps here are somewhat rotted. I was wondering if they could be replaced by stone ones. The Earl has much building experience."

They all looked at the narrow steps which led from behind the mounting block by the gate up to the Castle's inner ward, and Alfrida's private apartments.

"I believe," drawled the Earl cocking his massive head and surveying Alfrida with amusement, "that she might at least have the bottom steps replaced with marble from that old quarry the Romans used. What do you say, my lord?"

Rumon said, "Yes, indeed," while thinking that the matter was of scant interest, and trying to quell an uncomfortable feeling that the steps were not at all what the two had been discussing. But then, what else could it have been?

"Come breakfast with me, Rumon," she said softly, putting her hand on his arm. "There's been such a crowd here of late, I've scarce seen you at all."

The Earl laughed. "I perceive that I'm dismissed. Ah, would that *I* were a handsome young gallant! I'll remain here, Lady, and — take measurements."

She nodded without looking at Alfhere, and led the way up the private stairs to her chamber.

Merewyn was in the Bower, kneeling by a painted chest into which she was folding Alfrida's body linen, and sprinkling it with lavender buds. Her eyes widened when she saw Rumon, her hands shook; she spilled some of the lavender onto the rush-strewn floor.

"Lord Rumon and I will breakfast in my chamber," said Alfrida in a cold tone. "Tell a housecarl to bring up some of the spiced French wine, and a venison pasty."

Merewyn bowed and said nothing. Her wide pink mouth tightened.

"That girl —" said Alfrida entering her own chamber and indicating that Rumon should sit beside her on the bed. "How she has altered! Sulky, grudging of service, and she has phantasies. I begin to think she's gone daft. One can scarcely believe a word she says — when she *does* speak. I'm dismissing her. She can go to her aunt at Romsey — and good riddance."

Rumon swallowed. "I thought you were fond of Merewyn."

Alfrida shrugged delicately. "I suppose I was, until I discovered her real character. And she's turned rough. She yanks out my hair when she combs it — and look!" Alfrida in one quick gesture pulled her gown down to the waist, and turning, exhibited her slender white back. "See that bruise below the shoulder blade? I swear she pinched me last night!"

Rumon saw the bluish spot. He bent over and kissed it. "Poor darling," he said, and his hands went of themselves to cup the round breasts.

"Not now, dear —" She gave a husky little laugh. "The housecarl will be coming. Later we can bolt the door." She kissed him on the lips, and pulled her gown around her shoulders.

He drew back, his hands fell slowly. He looked at her, beseeching. "Jesu —" he whispered. "It's been so long — so long."

"I know," she said, nestling against him. "Wait only for an hour or so."

"I don't mean that —" he cried. "Yes, I *do*, but when can we tell them all that you will be mine forever? Today, when he returns from the hunt, couldn't we tell Edward that we will wed? For sure, he'll give his blessing."

Alfrida was silent a minute. Why not? she thought. This announcement would disarm all possible suspicion. Not that there was any suspicion now — except, perhaps, Merewyn, who was no longer of consequence as she was to be got rid of quickly. But later there might be suspicion — and if it attached to Rumon, would that be harmful? No. Besides a betrothal was not a marriage. Could be broken — most virtuously broken, if Rumon could be made to seem involved.

She slowly bent her lovely head. "At dinner," she agreed. "We'll tell Edward and the rest."

Sweat broke out on Rumon. He fell to his knees in front of her, putting his head on her lap, murmuring incoherent gratitude and endearments. He called her his angel, his white dove. He told her of the plans he had so often wistfully made for their future. Rescue from this paltry Castle. The building of a Castle worthy of her on his own lands, and while it was a-building they would travel to other countries. To Ireland, perhaps. Ethelred might go too, said Rumon. He knew how devoted she was to her son, who would profit by change and new companions. He told her how he had admired the saintlike way in which she had forgiven Edward's early slights, how he admired her goodness, and her tolerance even of Alfhere, yet he was sure her happiness would increase if they eschewed the intrigues either of the Court or the Monastic party — leave England at least for a while, adventure forth together in a dream of love.

He did not look up to Alfrida's face where the underlip had thrust out revealing the gleam of her lower teeth; he did not see the raised eyebrows, nor the curl of her nostrils, while she stroked his dark hair. Blessed Christ! she thought. *Ireland!* And rustication in the wilds of Somerset, as though Corfe weren't bad enough!

She spoke only once. "Rumon, have you the means for all these costly plans? Alas, I have but scant property and a poor widow's pension."

He brushed this aside. "The means will come, beloved. For now I can make full confession and go to Mass again, and God will help us. I shall give thanks to Him and He will help us."

Alfrida barely choked back a derisive sound. She had a very shrewd idea of Rumon's resources, yet for a moment — so eloquent was he — had wondered if she could possibly have been mistaken. It was apparent that she was not. St. Mary, what a fool he was! And she pushed his head from her lap with relief as the housecarl came in bearing food.

At noon, Rumon emerged from Corfe Castle, bound for his lodging in the village where he would don his most splendid clothes in readiness for the betrothal announcement to the King.

He crossed the drawbridge at the gate, and ran exultantly down the steep slope towards the swineherd's thatched hut which marked the boundary between Castle grounds and village. The early sun had vanished behind heavy brown clouds; there was snow-smell in the air, and Rumon's eager footsteps crunched on freezing grass beside the flinty path. Until she blocked his way, he did not notice Merewyn who came breathless from behind the swineherd's hut.

"Rumon!" she cried. "Rumon —" she faltered, seeing that his face was transfigured; no longer seeming thin, and older than his years, no longer sorrowful. Indeed he gave her a brilliant smile. "What are you doing here?" he asked, laughing. "Jumping out at folk like a bogle!"

"I wanted to say farewell. I leave this afternoon. There's a couple of the King's thanes returning to Winchester. They'll drop me at Romsey."

"Ah, I'm sorry for that," he said. "Then you'll not be here for the announcement of my betrothal."

She shrank against the hut's plank wall. "Your *what?*"

"My betrothal to the Lady Alfrida. We'll be married at Eastertide."

She put her hands to her chest and pressed hard against the sick thudding of her heart. "You're mad," she whispered. "Bewitched."

He threw his head back and frowned. "What's the matter with you! If you are my friend, as you've always pretended to be, you should rejoice."

She glanced up towards the Castle where a noisy dogfight was engaging a group of thanes, she looked down the village street where three ragged children were skipping over a leather thong. All their elders were at work. There was nobody near.

"Rumon, I *must* warn you," said Merewyn, her voice shaking. "She's evil. She means evil. I know it. I swear it." She crossed herself solemnly. "Escape whilst you can. Oh, dear Lord Jesus Christ, make Rumon believe me —" she added, half sobbing, while her voice slurred into the Cornish accent she had nearly conquered.

Outraged, furious, he glared at her a moment. Then he shook his head. "Poor child," he said. "She told me about you. I had forgotten since so much came later. Poor child, 'tis well for you you're going to the Abbess's care."

She drew in her breath, her pupils dilated to blackness in her frenzy of effort to reach through to him. "I'm going to my aunt, because I'm afraid to stay here, and because Lady Alfrida now hates me. Don't you *know* that there has been blood already on her hands. There will be more. Do you think it should be *mine* — or yours?"

Down Rumon's spine there went a chill; it induced fresh anger. "Bah!" he said. "You rave! Farewell, and may God cleanse your muddled wits."

"Listen to me!" she cried with desperate courage. "Alfhere is her lover. They conspire together . . . ah, you don't believe this either! Who do you think gave her the new white gown? The squirrel mantle? The gold enamel brooch — I forgot, she has not worn that when you were near!"

His hands raised as though to strike her. She flinched but stood still, pressing against the wooden wall.

His arms dropped. "You lie, Merewyn," he said hoarsely. "Even as she said you do. Now it is not for *your* sake I'm glad you're going but that SHE will no longer be threatened by an adder's forked tongue."

Merewyn sagged. Her nose grew pink, her chin trembled, tears welled down her pale cheeks. "If I swear to the truth by the Body of Our Blessed Lord, and tell you what I have heard, what I have seen . . ." She choked; dabbed at her blinding tears with her sleeve.

Into Rumon's mind there darted a curious irrelevance. He had never seen Alfrida weep. Aye, but of course he had. The noble grief for Edgar when he lay dying.

"Rumon!" Merewyn cried, clutching at his arm, "I pray you . . ."

"Enough," he said, shaking off her hand. "I'll *never* listen to your wicked lies." He turned and stalked down the village street, leaving her alone.

The Corfe Castle feast at dusk that afternoon was the gayest of all this Yuletide's festivities. The young King was in high spirits. He had speared a great boar in the forest — single-handed — and knew that his thanes were impressed by his courage. In fact, Godwin, the royal gleeman, made up a new song, extolling the King's feat, and sang it for them while the wassail bowl was passed up and down the High Table. And Edward was happy because — though he had much enjoyed his visit to Corfe — he was returning to Winchester on the morrow, and very soon Elgifu and her parents would come there too, and he might at least see her often during the Lenten period of waiting for their wedding.

When Rumon and Alfrida rose hand in hand, and kneeling before the King, asked his consent and blessing on their betrothal, Edward gave one of his rare, boyish laughs. "Why 't-tis an excellent idea!" he cried. "See how one m-marriage leads to another! M-my cousin Rumon and my Lady M-mother. Seems fitting! What do you say, Ethelred?" He turned to his young brother, who had already drunk a great deal of the strong spiced wine, and looked confused. His beautiful young face was flushed, his pale golden head drooped. "What-chyou mean?" he asked thickly. He tried to focus on Rumon and Alfrida who were both dressed in red — the bridal color.

Edward gave Ethelred a good-natured thwack on the shoulder. "Never m-mind, you little toper," he said smiling. "Your consent's not needed, and I freely give m-mine!"

A roar of congratulations surged around the Hall. Shouts of

"Wassail!" "Wassail!" and the answering "Drink heil!" "Drink heil!"

Rumon put his arm around Alfrida's waist; he kissed her on the lips, yet at the same time, without full awareness of it, he watched Alfhere. The Earl's shouts of congratulations were as fervent as anyone's. More than that, he leaped upon a bench and made a boisterous speech extolling the pleasures of the marriage bed, and wishing the new-affianced couple a lusty brood of progeny to carry on their august lines.

By midnight almost everyone was drunk. Gunnar, though staggering, helped his master and Ethelred up to bed. The thanes sprawled on the benches. Even the normally temperate Rumon had succumbed, and slept with his head on Alfrida's lap.

All the candles had guttered out, except the huge one — as big around as a neck — on which an approximation of the hours was marked with encircling red paint. It acted as the Castle clock, and burned down for twenty-four hours. Alfrida glanced at it, then dared at last to look towards Alfhere. He had drunk as much as any of them, but he had an iron head and never showed his liquor, and he sat with chin propped on fists, watching Alfrida, down the table from him. She had barely sipped the wassail, and alert for the safe moment, now made a cautious signal.

Rumon did not move as she eased his head down on the bench. "I'm going to the latrine," she murmured to him, in case there might be a remnant of consciousness. There was not.

She glided from behind the table and out of the door to the inner ward. Alfhere followed in a minute. Nobody else stirred in the whole besotted Castle.

The two conferred for some time. The next day Alfhere departed with the King and his company.

The winter weeks passed quickly for Rumon. He kept busy, riding, hawking and practicing archery. His intellectual interests returned. He entertained himself by making a new English

translation of Boethius, the Roman philosopher, lingering pleasurably on such statements as "Who can give law to lovers?
Love is a greater law to itself."

And he made up riddles to amuse Alfrida.

He saw her daily at the Castle, but there was no more carnal
intimacy between them. Rumon had gone back to Wareham
and made full confession to the priest at St. Mary's. He had been
absolved from his sins of fornication, having vowed that they
would not recur, and he found contentment and relief at being
once more enabled to take the Sacrament at Mass. After all he
and Alfrida had but to wait through Lent until their wedding
and the blessing of the Church on their fleshly union.

Alfrida agreed, as she did to everything he proposed during
this time. She looked docilely at the plans he drew for their
castle in Somerset. She listened to his descriptions of the wonders
of Ireland — descriptions Rumon had garnered from the monk
Finian at Glastonbury. She smiled at the riddles, particularly
one about a bookworm which ended, "And yet that stealthy
thief in the dark was never made the wiser by the words he
swallowed."

In March, past the middle of Lent it occurred to Rumon that
his beloved did not look well. She had grown thin, there were
shadows beneath the violet eyes, and at times she had a strained
anxious expression, almost as though she were waiting for something which did not come.

He taxed her gently with too much Lenten fasting; indeed
when he dined with her she ate almost nothing. She seemed
startled, but said that perhaps he was right. "Only I get so tired
of greens and salt fish. I believe I heard that off St. Aldhelm's
Head the mackerel are running. Something fresh would tempt
my palate. Could you arrange that?"

Rumon instantly said that he could. His chief housecarl, Leof,
had once been a fisherman on the Severn.

"Will you go with your servant, Rumon?" she asked softly.
"Make an expedition of it. Take Ethelred too, the boy wants a

change. I shall rest in bed a few days, for 'tis true I've not felt quite myself."

And so it was arranged. Alfrida retired to her chamber under the care of Lady Britta and Lady Walsiga — the fat, stupid wife of a Dorset thane who had been commandeered to replace Merewyn.

The fishing expedition was gone for three days. Ethelred was not only excessively bored, but he was afraid to put out to sea in the oval hide-bound coracles. He spent his time lolling in St. Aldhelm's Chapel, and badgering its solitary monk.

Rumon, on the contrary, enjoyed his days on that wild coast. The weather was good, overcast but not wet, there was little wind, and Rumon soon learned to paddle his skittish coracle, and even caught a couple of mackerel himself.

They returned with a dozen fish, carefully preserved in wet seaweed, and found that in their absence a visitor had arrived. This was Cild Aelfric, Alfhere's twenty-four-year-old son and heir. He had come, it seemed, to visit his poor sister, Britta, and break the tragic news to her that their mother, Godleva, had finally died.

All this Rumon was told after he proudly presented the fish to Alfrida, who received them and him radiantly. She had entirely recovered her health; he rejoiced to see her gay and so beautiful that afternoon at dinner. She wore the elaborate new white and gold dress — about which Rumon had never questioned her, having rejected all Merewyn's crazy talk. Alfrida had twined early primroses into a garland, and the flowers — little paler than her hair — added a youthful sweetness. They all dined greedily on the mackerel, and then Alfrida, having made seemly allusion to the sad reason for Cild Aelfric's visit, pressed him for more news. "We are so far off here, and I have heard nothing about the King, the Court or anyone, since they all left in January."

Cild Aelfric was physically very unlike his father. He was beardless, slight, weedy, and had a high somewhat girlish voice.

His mouse-colored hair hung lankly about his narrow ears. His stubby eyelashes were so light that one tended not to notice the cold shrewdness of the hazel eyes behind them. To the un-informed he appeared insignificant. Yet at nineteen he had won his honorary knightly title of "Cild" — or "Childe" by engi-neering a subtle plot for the massacre of four of his father's enemies. He possessed neither conscience nor fears. He paid lip service to the observance of religion only when it suited him, and was entirely free from Alfhere's occasional attacks of worry over hellfire and damnation.

"Not much news," he said, answering Alfrida. "Edward prepares for his wedding — and, oh yes, to be sure — there was that hocus-pocus at the Witan in Calne last week. Another 'miracle' for the Monastic party, which I believe impressed my father."

"What was the miracle?" asked Rumon slowly.

Aelfric shrugged. "I wasn't there, nor the King, but Dunstan was, had traveled all the way from Canterbury to force through a law returning the monasteries to the Benedictine rule. My father was furious. You can imagine what a row there was, stamping and shouting, and Dunstan was losing, as usual, when the floor gave way. Everybody but Dunstan fell down to the room below. One thane was killed, others hurt. My noble father sprained his ankle."

"What happened to the Archbishop?" said Rumon.

"Oh, he seems to have balanced himself on the one beam which didn't collapse. Pity he didn't fall with the rest, for the bishops were very quick to cry 'Miracle'!"

"Aye, of course," said Rumon dryly. "Like the speaking crucifix in Winchester Chapter House. Yet I cannot believe that Lord Dunstan knew how *that* was done, nor was party to *this*, which would moreover seem hard to arrange ahead of time."

"Oh —" interjected Alfrida, who was not interested in any happenings at Calne, and had been toying with her girdle clasp. "Surely, Rumon, you are not still siding with that wicked, meddlesome old man! You know how much trouble he always gave ME."

"I have hoped that he would solemnize our marriage," said Rumon, gravely.

Alfrida started; a violent flush covered her face and neck. Her underlip dropped, her eyes narrowed. She gave Rumon a malignant look, which he could not believe he had seen, since it vanished at once, as Cild Aelfric said in his high lisping voice, "Oh, I forgot to tell you. The King is coming back to Corfe next week. One of the royal archers reported a wild boar, big as a pony, with tusks two feet long, seen in the Purbeck Chase. The monster killed one of the forester's children. And Edward feels that though hunting for game is forbidden in Lent, the killing of a murderous beast is different."

Alfrida, who had already learned of this prospect from Cild Aelfric — and learned considerably more besides — sipped some wine, composed her face, and smiled. Rumon was slightly puzzled. He had heard of no huge dangerous boar ranging the royal preserve near Corfe. Such news usually got around. However, he was pleased to know that the young King would again be in the vicinity. He liked Edward, and knew that he was a good influence on Ethelred.

"When will the King be here?" Rumon asked. "He is coming to the Castle?"

"Oh, yes," said Aelfric. "He particularly wants to pay his respects to the Lady Alfrida; to you, Lord Rumon; and to his little brother." The young man's pale eyes exchanged a lightning glance with Alfrida. "One can't be quite certain of the day," he continued.

"I'll post a lookout in the tower," she said. "Be sure that we see Edward coming in time to give him proper welcome."

There was nothing in this natural statement to disquiet Rumon. And yet he felt a quiver of unease. There had been a strange note in her voice, a voice he had often likened to silver bells; surely it was ridiculous to think that the bells had jangled.

What's the matter with me? he thought, looking at her beautiful face beneath the innocent primrose garland.

For the next week, nothing else disquieted Rumon. True, Cild Aelfric stayed on at the Castle, averring that he too wanted to greet his King and hear about the boar hunt, but Rumon thought little about that. One could not be jealous of this young man whose tastes quite obviously did not run towards women; besides he was an entertaining addition to their sparse company. He had a fund of rather malicious anecdotes; he played chess with Alfrida — a game Rumon had never learned — he could play the viol, and sing with it in a thin tenor.

Monday, March 18th, was a day of high winds and intermittent sunshine. After a nearly sleepless night, Alfrida was awakened at dawn by Britta who came nervously mincing into the chamber carrying a posset of warm milk. "Your pardon, my lady," she said quickly to forestall annoyance, "but my brother wishes to speak with you — at once."

Alfrida curbed the angry rebuke on her lips, sat up slowly. "What about?" she said in a faint voice.

Britta shook her head. "I don't know, my lady." She sniffled, being afflicted by one of her colds. "Cild Aelfric never tells me anything."

Naturally not, you sickly, snuffling idiot, Alfrida thought. But Britta's total lack of curiosity, and her dullness of mind were assets.

"My chamber robe," Alfrida commanded. "And poke up the fire." Britta obeyed, wrapped her mistress in a loose gown of purple wool, ineffectually poked at the fire, and picked the ivory and gold comb off the table. Alfrida pushed it away. "Let be!" she said. "You're too clumsy. I'll do my hair later." For a moment she regretted the loss of Merewyn — Merewyn as she had been during the first years. "Let your brother come in," she said.

Cild Aelfric soon appeared and shut the heavy wooden door carefully behind him. He glanced indifferently at Alfrida's masses of tangled yellow hair, at her pale sharp early morning face, unsoftened by the usual tints and unguents. "It'll be to-day," he said.

She stiffened, her cheeks grew paler. "How do you know?"

"Messenger. Arrived an hour ago. One of my father's thanes, disguised as a woodcutter."

"Where *is* my lord Alfhere?" she asked, her voice faltering.

"With Edward in Great Wood, near the Drinking Barrow. Oddly enough —" said Cild Aelfric, quirking his eyebrows, "they've found no trace of the giant boar. And Edward being so near here is coming to Corfe today."

"How can we be sure he comes alone?" she whispered.

"My father has seen to that. A delay in following the King is easily arranged since every retainer accompanying Edward on this hunting expedition is in my father's pay. You may trust his wits — as well as his purse."

Alfrida breathed fast. Her old white cat stretched and gave a long drawn-out mew. She pulled it to her lap and began to stroke it violently, so that it struggled while her grip tightened. "I'm afraid —" she said beneath her breath. "Afraid — what if things go wrong?"

He made an exasperated sound. "They won't. We're making triply sure. You have Wulfgar posted in the tower, and he has his orders?" She nodded. "And you will have the welcome cup in readiness — what are you putting in it?"

"Nightshade," she murmured, her hands clenching in the white fur. He nodded. "I'll do the rest. The little matter of the stirrup — and this." He put his hand on a short silver-hilted dagger which hung from his belt. "There's a spot by the left shoulder blade which draws very little blood."

"But it must look like an accident!" she cried.

"It will. At least nobody will care to prove it otherwise. By the bye, what of Rumon? Best keep him out of the way. A sleeping draught, I imagine — not lethal of course — we might need him later. Give it to him as soon as he comes to the Castle this morning. Tell him he looks to be sickened with fever."

Her hands went limp on the cat, which fled. "I'm afraid —" she murmured again. "I see darkness ahead — darkness . . ."

"Christ, woman!" Aelfric caught her by the shoulders and shook her. "Isn't this what you've been planning for years? You've never shown cowardice before! You'll be well mated to my father, and isn't that what you want? Don't you wish to be Queen of England again, with far more power than you ever had under Edgar? Stop this maundering drivel, or I'll wield my considerable influence to see that you *don't* marry my father, and to keep Ethelred from the throne. Then off *you* go to Somerset or Ireland with your dear Rumon!"

"Never!" she said, raising her head. "I've come to hate the man. His stupid devotion sickens me. He makes me uncomfortable —" Her voice trailed off. She had almost said that Rumon made her feel unclean.

"Well then!" Cild Aelfric stepped back and gave his high-pitched laugh. "Get prepared, Lady, for we have much to do e'er nightfall."

When Rumon came up to the Castle later, Alfrida welcomed him charmingly, and inquired at once about his health. He replied that it was fine, but she thought otherwise and said she would prepare for him a little draught, which was certain to ward off the spring fevers. He was touched by her solicitude, and yet when she brought the draught and he tasted it and found it had an acrid musty tang, he surreptitiously poured it on the floor rushes — not wanting to hurt her feelings.

A man, he thought tenderly, must sometimes decide these things for himself. Women, even the best of them, were prone to fuss. Besides she seemed in more danger of a fever than he did.

Her eyes glittered. She was extremely restless, pacing up and down the Hall. She started when he spoke of the King's probable arrival — when would it be?

"How can one tell?" she replied, staring past him at the tapestried wall. "How can one ever tell the future. St. Mary, but it's cold in here!" she added angrily. "Can't those housecarls ever build a decent fire? And the wind blows so, wailing in the chimney like a demon. Jesu, how I hate this Castle!"

"You'll not be in it long," Rumon said. "And I assure you ours in Somerset'll be protected from the winds. I'll have it all built of stone, as they do in France. Much snugger."

"No doubt." She tried to smile, but her lips quivered, and she glanced towards the Hall door through which Wulfgar would come running from the watchtower. "Rumon," she said, wondering why he showed no signs of sleepiness — the draught she gave him had been laced with poppy juice — "Rumon, where is Ethelred? Shouldn't you be teaching him something?"

"Perhaps —" Rumon smiled. "At any rate I'll find him for you. My love, you seem distracted today, nervous."

" 'Tis the wind," she answered. "And the time of the moon which afflicts women."

"You should rest, then," he said. "I'll take Ethelred out riding."

"No! No!" she cried vehemently, for there must be no possible risk of his meeting Edward. "There's too much wind. March winds are dangerous. You must stay inside. Give the boy a writing lesson. In truth, he makes little progress."

"Ethelred has not a scholar's mind," said Rumon temperately. "But he improves in other ways — manners and disposition."

She was not listening to him, but to a sound she fancied she heard outside. Wulfgar descending the stairs? or Cild Aelfric who was also unobtrusively keeping watch through a slit window in the upper passage.

Rumon was conscious of her strained expression, of the tremor which rippled through her body. He pulled her carved wooden armchair nearer to the fire. "Sit down, my love," he said.

"Rest." There was no further sound from outside the Hall, so she obeyed him, and rested her primrose-garlanded head on the gilded chair back. "You're a good man, Rumon —" she said in a thin voice. "What a pity that goodness is not — always rewarded."

Rumon laughed, looking down at her fondly. "Oh, I think it may be," he said. He bent over and kissed her on the forehead, savoring, as always, her perfume — relieved to feel the forehead so cool under his lips.

This was the last time that he ever touched Alfrida.

The wind blew all day off the sea. It moaned down the chimneys and lifted bits of thatching from the roofs. But the sun continued to shine intermittently behind scudding white clouds. Little of the sunshine penetrated into Corfe Castle's great Hall, where Alfrida kept the shutters closed, being unable to bear the cold draughts. The Hall was lit by the fire, and by the huge candle which acted as clock.

At three, they all dined together — Alfrida, Rumon, Ethelred, Cild Aelfric, and the Ladies Britta and Walsiga. Everyone but Alfrida ate heartily of eggs, cheese, and bread downed with ale. Alfrida poked a bit of bread around her wooden trencher, then subsided into an apathy which worried Rumon, though Cild Aelfric made up for her silence by a spate of lewd jokes which soon had Ethelred — precocious enough in this area — howling with laughter.

Between jokes, Cild Aelfric excused himself from time to time, saying that he had caught cold in his bladder. Upon each return to the Hall, Alfrida looked up, then lowered her head again.

Once Cild Aelfric, profiting by Rumon's polite converse with the Lady Walsiga, whispered into Alfrida's ear. "Why isn't Rumon asleep?" "Don't know," she answered from the corner of her mouth. "I put in enough." "Where is it?" he hissed.

She slipped her hand into the pouch which hung at her girdle and brought out a small glass vial, nearly full of a brownish liquid.

Cild Aelfric took the vial, then turning to Rumon said, "We all seem rather dull today. Lord Rumon, we need music. Where is your harp?"

"Over there, hanging on the peg," said Rumon.

"Oh, play to us, my sweet," said Alfrida. "I pray you."

Rumon bowed, and walked across the Hall to get his harp. Cild Aelfric made a lightning movement, and poured the vial's liquid into Rumon's unfinished ale. The Ladies Britta and Walsiga noticed nothing, because at a signal from their mistress they were trailing out towards the Bower and their duties. Ethelred saw Cild Aelfric's motion and thought nothing of it, for he was pouting, gripped as usual by a single idea at a time.

"*I* don't want to hear Rumon play," he said. "I want another of Cild Aelfric's stories — like the monk in the cornfield with the blacksmith's lass."

Aelfric laughed his giggling peal. He pinched the boy on the cheek. "Hey, my pretty one — you're full young to be thinking of those games. But after Lord Rumon has played to us — something stirring about battle, perhaps? Then I promise you one more droll tale. My lord —" he bowed to Rumon, "wassail to you, as the ablest of bards!" He drank from his beaker, the others followed. Then as was customary, Rumon acknowledged the toast. "Drink heil," he said, smiling, and drained his beaker noting vaguely that the ale had an acrid taste. He turned to Alfrida. "If you like, dearest lady, I'll sing you something from my own country. I learned it long ago from a blind harper and it has to do with the voyage to Provence of the Three Saintes Maries, I always thought it charming and I've made a translation for you."

Alfrida inclined her head graciously.

Rumon tuned his harp, riffled a chord, and began a gay haunting song Englished into the unrhymed alliterative meters which pleased the Anglo-Saxon ear.

Stout was the ship   These holy folk
Did sail in   Over the swan-bath.
From that sad land   Where all
Had bided near   Their Loving Lord.
God's breath blew   The Boat upon a beach
There was Mary the maid;   Mary the mother
And Mary the Magdalene.   Martha too
And Maximin   And Sara, swart as soot —

Alfrida jerked up her head, and Rumon paused, for they all heard the sound of footsteps, running down the wooden stairs outside. "At last," said Cild Aelfric, beneath his breath, gripping Alfrida's arm. He ran to open the door and Wulfgar burst in, his broad stupid face alight.

"The King —" he said to Alfrida, "is riding up the Castle Hill."

"He's alone?" she said in a flat breathy voice.

"Alone, Lady. Not even one of his hounds did I see."

"I'll greet him at once," she said, taking a ready-filled silver cup from a shelf. Cild Aelfric had already disappeared down the private stairs, and Rumon naturally made to follow him.

"No!" she cried. "You stay here with Ethelred. It is my privilege to greet the King alone in my own Castle!"

Rumon hesitated. An odd languor was seeping through his body. A drowsiness. "My place is beside you when you greet the King," he said slowly, and was aghast by the face of naked fury she turned on him. "I *command* that you stay here!" she screamed, and holding the silver cup to her breasts, ran through the door slamming it after her.

Rumon stood paralyzed, stock-still on the rushes. Then he put his harp carefully down on a bench, and turned to look at Ethelred who was cowering, big-eyed, behind his mother's chair.

"Don't disobey her, Rumon — when she's like this," whispered the boy.

"When she's like this —" Rumon repeated in a dragging voice. Like this, the demon woman of his two dreams. Like Merewyn's warnings. "Evil coming." "Blood." "Fear" — "Danger" — the meaningless words. My head spins, I can't think. Why can't I think?

A voice spoke very clearly and quietly inside his mind. "Because you have been poisoned." The voice pierced through him like a spear. He jumped, and running to the brass basin of water for hand-washings, poured the greasy contents over his head. He sluiced his face, and sticking his finger down his throat, tried to vomit, but could not. He flung open the door, thinking even then that it was a mercy there was no way of barring it from the outside.

He ran down the private stairs, and stopped transfixed at a slit window which commanded the gate.

Edward, his fair head gleaming in the sunset rays, was sitting easily astride his gray stallion, and leaning down to accept the stirrup cup which Alfrida — all welcoming curtsies — was handing up to him.

Cild Aelfric stood upon the mounting block to the left and a trifle behind the King. Wulfgar stood on the horse's other side holding the bridle. Edward, smiling, took the cup from Alfrida, and began to drink.

"Stop!" Rumon shouted through the window. "Edward — don't drink!"

Edward heard the shout and looked around him, startled. At that moment Cild Aelfric and Wulfgar both sprang at the boy-king, who started to laugh, then quavered, "What are you trying to do, break my arm?"

Rumon saw a flash of steel in Cild Aelfric's hand, before half sobbing, panting, he raced down the remaining steps.

When Rumon reached the gate, Edward's horse had bolted. The panicked beast went thundering down the flinty slope, while the boy entangled by one stirrup bumped along face down over rocks and under the hoofs of the terrified stallion.

"Christ!" said Rumon. "Jesus Christ!" He started to run after the fleeing horse and its banging blood-spattered encum-

brance, but Wulfgar at a signal from Cild Aelfric grabbed
Rumon and pinioned his arms.

"You'll not catch up on foot, my dear Rumon," said Cild
Aelfric, inspecting one of his fingers which had been mashed
when he twisted the stirrup, "and unfortunately there are no
mounts immediately available. How could one foresee such a
deplorable accident? It must have been your shout that frightened the horse."

Rumon struggled against Wulfgar's burly grasp, though a
wave of nausea surged through him, and an overpowering weakness. He looked at Alfrida with blurring gaze. She stood frozen
by the mounting block, staring at the silver cup which had
dropped to the ground during the scuffle with Edward. The
fresh garland of primroses still crowned her golden head — and
not a petal quivered.

"You are accursed — woman! Accursed!" Rumon whispered,
striving to hold on to consciousness. "For the love of God, send
help to the King — it may not be too late!"

She did not move, she seemed not to hear. She continued to
stare down at the silver cup, and its spreading stain of spilled
wine.

Rumon gave an inarticulate moan, and slumped down between
Wulfgar's arms into blackness.

"Well — " said Cild Aelfric shrugging, "that poppy juice of
yours took long enough to work. Wulfgar, get someone to take
Lord Rumon to his lodgings, his churls can care for him —
though if he dies 'tis no great matter. Lady Alfrida — rouse
yourself, we've much more to do, and see yonder down by the
barrow here come my father and the King's straggling retainers.
We must prepare to break to them the shocking news — of the
runaway."

As she still did not move, he shook her shoulder. Her dazed
eyes rested on his impatient face. She turned slowly, and proceeded to climb the steps to the Hall, pausing on each one like
an old woman.

In the Hall, Ethelred was waiting, and playing with a hound puppy.

"Where's Edward?" he asked eagerly. "I want to show him Bela's new litter."

"I fear you can't," said Cild Aelfric. "There's been an accident. The stallion bolted and threw Edward. I'm sorry to tell you that he's dead."

Ethelred's pink cheeks grew white, his round eyes stared. "But he can't be! Edward could ride anything."

"He is dead," repeated Cild Aelfric. "And *you*, my pretty one, will shortly be King of England."

The boy shrank back. "I don't want to be —" he whispered. He put his grubby little hand to his mouth. "I want Edward." He began to sniffle. For the first time he looked at his mother. "What did you do to him, my lady — you've hurt Edward, I know you did —" he choked and began to sob.

Alfrida made a strange animal sound in her throat. Her body shook with a massive tremor, her lower teeth bared, her eyes became slits.

"You fool — you idiot brat — weeping there — you ingrate — 'twas done for you — Jesu, stop that sniveling!" She whirled and seized the nearest weapon she could see — the huge candle clock. She wrenched it from its spike, and rushing at Ethelred began to beat him on the head, the shoulders, with the massive flaming candle.

Ethelred screamed, trying to hide beneath the tables, the benches. Still she beat down senselessly, until the flame went out, and Cild Aelfric, momentarily stunned by the onslaught, grabbed her by the hair and jerked her head back. "Lady!" he cried. "If you act lik this, Ethelred will not be King of England. He'll end up in a tomb — like the other."

She dropped the huge candle which was broken in three pieces.

Her hands unclenched, they made a feeble pawing gesture in the air, then she fell down onto the rushes, where she lay prone, scarcely breathing. And it was thus that Earl Alfhere found her when he presently mounted the stairs and entered the Hall.

For over a month, Rumon lay very ill in his lodgings, cared for by Leof and his two other housecarls who often despaired of his life. Twice they summoned the village priest who came with the viaticum, but each time the young man's body continued to fight, though it had no help from Rumon's will. His mind seemed to have hidden itself behind a gray screen, through which neither memory nor awareness penetrated.

He vomited frequently, and for days could scarcely retain water — as though his body rejected the horrors of realization which his mind would not accept. Day by day he grew thinner and weaker, inertly staring up at the rafters while his servants tended him.

Nobody else came near him but the priest, and Rumon asked no questions of anyone.

On April 22nd, he at last had a visitor. There was soft fragrance in the spring day. Leof had opened the shutters to the sun, and a beam slanted across the chamber. Rumon gazed at the dancing motes of rust in the sunbeam with more attention than he had shown to anything in a long time. He swallowed some of the beef broth Leof brought him, and found strength to quell the immediate rise of nausea.

Soon there were sounds in the Hall outside his chamber. He heard Leof's peasant voice shrill with some sort of awed excitement, and then another voice — a man's which held a mixture of gentleness and command. The door was flung open, and a smallish black figure limped in. "My son —" it said. "My poor son — what a sorry pass you've come to!"

Rumon raised himself painfully from the straw-filled pillow. He saw the white locks, the ring on the gnarled hand which covered his. He saw the compassionate old eyes.

"My lord Dunstan —" he whispered in wonder.

"Yes, Rumon," said the Archbishop, signing the cross on Rumon's forehead. "I did not know that you were so ill until I came here to consult with Corfe's priest. Indeed I've heard nothing from you in years."

"True, my lord —" said Rumon vaguely after a moment. "At least I scarce remember — scarce remember —"

"Hm-hm —" said Dunstan, and sat down on a stool beside the bed. He sighed as he examined Rumon's gaunt face; the stubble of black beard; the bluish hollows around lackluster eyes. The old man knew from his long wisdom that this sickness of the body was but the outer stamp of soul-sickness, which must now be cured. He sent up a murmured prayer for guidance, and said, "My son — what do you remember of last March 18th, here at Corfe?"

Rumon sank back on the pillow, he made a feeble gesture — let his hand fall limp. He did not answer.

The Archbishop waited a moment, then banged the floor with his staff, calling, "Churl! Come here!" Leof ran in, tugging at his forelock and bowing.

"Have you strong mead?" asked Dunstan.

"Aye, m'lord —" said Leof. "Time and again I've give it to Master, but he allas pukes it up."

"He won't this time," said the old man firmly.

Dunstan himself raised Rumon's head, and held the cup of fermented honey until it was empty. He sat back and watched a faint color gradually tint Rumon's cheekbones.

"It is necessary that you *face* the pain," said Dunstan in the authoritative voice which no one ever disobeyed. "Necessary for your soul's sake. *What happened on March 18th?*"

"Blackness —" said Rumon with great effort. "Treachery — and the woman accursed."

"Ah-h —" whispered the Archbishop, sighing deeply. Treachery. Treachery and murder. He and Ethelwold had suspected this. But they had no proof. And now it was too late. Too late for England — Blessed Christ help us — thought the old man.

"I shall stay here tonight," he said to Rumon. "You will take the cup of mead with an egg beaten in it every hour. Tomorrow we shall talk again." He blessed Rumon, squeezed his hand and went out to the Hall to give Leof instructions.

Next day, Rumon was much stronger, the gray screen had nearly lifted from across his mind. And the knowledge of Dunstan's nearness had solaced him all night.

When Dunstan appeared, Rumon had been bathed and shaved. He sat upright in bed, his eyes had lost their emptiness. "What date is it, my lord?" he asked, with a feeble smile of greeting.

" 'Tis April 23rd, the Feast of Saint George; we must pray to him that he save England from its dragons of iniquity — O woeful woeful plight wherein Satan has plunged us!"

"Edward is — is dead?" asked Rumon, his voice almost steady.

The Archbishop crossed himself. "Yes. And Ethelred is King. I crowned him at Kingston a week ago. He was elected by the Witan. There was nothing else to do. Our land must have a king. And they wanted Edgar's son. His other son. A lad of twelve who will be under the thumb of Alfhere and his godless party, and of —" the Archbishop paused, looking intently at Rumon, wondering how far he might try the new strength. "And of his mother — who bewitched you."

Rumon put his hand over his mouth as bitter fluid rose in his throat. He retched, and the Archbishop struck him sharply on the arm. "It's *finished*, Rumon! You're not the first to be duped by the lure of woman-flesh. Our Blessed Lord knows that long ago, I too — but no matter. Shame, disgust, guilt — you have felt and *should* have done. Now repentance is enough. Presently we will pray together. First, however — Atheling of England — I wish to know what you saw on March 18th."

Rumon started at the title which Dunstan had never used to him. He understood that the Archbishop was invoking the English side of him, the blood line of the great Alfred, and its royal fortitude. He squared his shoulders and permitted the banished memory to return.

"There was certainly a plot," he said at last. "There were many straws in the wind which in my stupid blindness I would not notice. Even Merewyn — Merewyn — then she was neither daft nor a liar — Merewyn tried to warn me. My dreams warned me. My dreams warned me — twice."

"They often do," said Dunstan. "But go on."

"The woman —" He could not bring himself to say Alfrida's name. "She tried to poison me in the morning, or at least to befuddle me into sleep. Someone tried again in the afternoon, and eventually succeeded. Edward was hunting in Purbeck Chase, so they said. After a monstrous boar, nobody around here had heard of. He was daily expected at Corfe Castle. To pay his respects. Wulfgar — the woman's housecarl — was stationed in the watchtower. Cild Aelfric, Alfhere's son, had been visiting Corfe for a week — with sufficient excuse, or so I thought." Rumon paused, and drew a shaky breath. The old man murmured, "Go on, my son."

"That afternoon of March 18th I was playing and singing for them — a Provençal ballad — when Wulfgar told us the King approached alone. SHE rushed from the Hall with a cup of some liquid. Also Cild Aelfric. She would not let *me* go. She turned on me the face of a — a — maniac — a devil. But I went down the stairs, and through the window I saw her present the welcome cup to Edward as he sat on his gray stallion. He took it and I shouted a warning. I saw the gleam of a dagger in Cild Aelfric's hand. But when I got down to the gate, the stallion was bolting, dragging Edward by one stirrup, over rocks, over flints. I tried to run towards Edward, and was stopped by Wulfgar. This is all I know. Since then I have not cared — until now."

Dunstan was silent, thinking. After a while he said, "You do not *know* what was in the welcome cup given to Edward by the Lady Alfrida?"

"No, my lord."

"Are you sure you saw a dagger in Cild Aelfric's hand?"

"I thought so, and I know I saw a scuffle, and heard Edward cry out — 'What are you trying to do — break my arm?' "

"You did not see Cild Aelfric or Wulfgar entangling Edward's right foot in the stirrup, nor the blow on its rump which undoubtedly started the stallion's bolt down the hill?"

"No, my lord."

"Ah, they planned shrewdly," said Dunstan, clenching his staff, "And the devil aided them at every point. But they'll not enjoy the fruits of this murder for long. God will punish them. Already there have been miracles wrought by the martyred Edward."

"Miracles, my lord? Where is his body?"

"Entombed in St. Mary's church at Wareham, where I inspected it three days ago. Most of his bones were broken, his skull crushed in from the rocks over which he was dragged. The flesh is so much discolored by bruises and dried blood that it was impossible to be certain where a dagger wound might be, and yet I believe I saw such — in his back. Now I *am* sure, though THEY would deny it. But the miracles — these I heard from the priest here. He has suspicions, though dared hardly voice them even to me." Dunstan's old eyes filled. He rested his head on his hand.

"The miracles, my lord —" said Rumon, striving for something to blank out the thought of the young king's broken body.

"These —" said the old man, after a moment. "By report from the priest. The stallion stopped its wild flight after a mile or so at the bridge. Somebody — probably Wulfgar — was sent from the Castle to find out what happened. Edward's body was hastily hidden in the nearby cottage of an old blind woman, a pensioner of Lady Alfrida's. But that night, she claims that her hovel was filled with a supernatural glow. She was much afraid, yet in the morning found she had regained her sight. She went around Corfe babbling of this. Then they removed the body from her hovel, and stuffed it in a well, near Rempstone. At once the passersby noted a light around the well. They called the priest to investigate. He it was who found the body, and supervised its removal to a Christian burial at Wareham. By this time the putrefaction was advanced enough so that the dagger wound might not be seen. No doubt that was their plan.

"At Corfe Castle, the Lady Alfrida, Earl Alfhere and his son, all expressed great horror at the fearful accident, and ignorance of its cause. Little Ethelred seemed dazed, I hear, and scarcely spoke. They had the stallion killed as being the true culprit. It was so that the story reached me in Canterbury. I had grave doubts, so did Bishop Ethelwold, but it was not until I reached here that they have been confirmed."

"Where are they now? — The woman — and the rest?"

"At Winchester Palace. Where else? For Ethelred is King."

"He *shouldn't* be!" Rumon burst out. "My lord Dunstan, how *dared* you crown that baby-faced weakling, if you suspected murder?"

"I've told you," said the old man patiently. "Edward was dead no matter how, and Ethelred the natural heir, and elected by the Witan. But this reign will never prosper. There've been signs and portents enough, beginning when the wretched Ethelred defiled the font at his baptism, and then a blood-red meteor was seen all over England on the day of his Coronation."

"Will nobody avenge Edward!" Rumon cried wildly.

"Will *you*, Rumon?" asked the Archbishop in a sad level tone. "Would you assassinate Alfhere, Cild Aelfric, perhaps Ethelred? Would you assassinate Alfrida? Aye, think of it —" he said watching the young man's eye widen. "More murders would not restore Edward. Nor are you a man of violence. Also it is written, 'Vengeance is mine; I will repay, saith the Lord.'"

Rumon's head sunk on his chest. "Oh, wicked, miserable fool that I was. That I loved her, that I blasphemously likened her to the Blessed Mother of God, that over and over I let her dupe me — that I would not listen, nor look at what was plain to see — I might have warned Edward, had I not been so blinded by my filthy lust—" He beat his fist on his forehead, and gave a choked sob.

"Come now, my son," said Dunstan. "It is natural that you suffer. It is your penance, and I shall impose others, but you may not forever wallow in remorse. That too is a sin. What do you think of doing now, Rumon? You will surely leave this ill-omened Corfe."

Rumon lifted his hands, and let them fall on the blanket. "*I* don't know. I suppose so. Yes, I'll leave here. I hadn't thought."

"Shall you go to your own lands in Somerset?" pursued Dunstan. "Or have you still the urge to wander abroad?"

"No!" Rumon cried. His Somerset lands—wandering abroad—the plans he had made for these with Alfrida. *To* her, while she seemed to assent by her faint seductive smile, and all the time despising him, as he now knew.

"Then—" said Dunstan with decision, "you will return to the Vale of Avalon, to Glastonbury. You will climb the Tor daily for a month and pray in the chapel. You will also pray in the wattle church which Our Blessed Lord dedicated. That holy place will give you balm, and I expect that this time, God will inspire you to join our order."

"I cannot see why God should interest Himself in me," said Rumon, his head falling back on the pillow. "Nor you either, my lord."

Dunstan smiled, and pulled himself upright on his staff. "You are more love-worthy than you think, my poor son," he said.

chapter seven

Sunday, August 15, of the year of grace 980, was a day of high festival at Romsey Abbey in Hampshire. It was the Feast of the Blessed Virgin Mary's Assumption into Heaven. She was patroness of this Abbey and convent, and the ceremonies in Her honor, the processions, chantings and High Masses had lasted from dawn until the noon feast, which had included such rare and delicious items as rabbit pies and honey comfits. There had even been a roasted peacock (symbol of immortality) served in all the glory of his plumage.

At two o'clock of the hot sunny afternoon, Merewyn sat on a well curb at the foot of the cloister garden, next to Elfled, who had once been Queen Alfrida's despised Bower Lady.

Merewyn wore a plain blue wool gown. It had been given to her by her aunt, the Abbess Merwinna, who had shown much kindness to the girl ever since her desolate appearance at the Abbey portal three years ago, seeking asylum from the miseries of Corfe.

Merewyn was now a grown woman — she had entered her twenties, but the peaceful, ordered convent life, the absence of any emotional strains, had preserved her youthful zest. And in Merwinna she had found the mother she had so mistakenly sought in Alfrida. Except for the shameful, never quite conquered ache for Rumon, the girl had been busy and content.

At the moment, she might have been fourteen again as she slid from the well curb and crouched on the lawn, searching with absorption to find a lucky four-leaf clover. The curly tips of her thick braids swept the grass; the brilliant sun lit golden flamelets on her bare auburn head, while her sturdy fingers poked amongst the clover.

Her companion, Elfled, had a more productive occupation, although this was the Holiday recreation time and the Abbess permitted idleness for its brief period. But Elfled was a novice who would take the veil when Bishop Ethelwold made his next visitation, and she was very devout. Her small pale face bent over an altar cloth on which she was embroidering a St. Michael in red and gold. Her mousy hair was already cut short, and hidden under the gray novice's hood which topped her shapeless gray gown. Her needle made little plops through the sturdy linen, and she kept peering anxiously at St. Michael's halo which seemed a trifle askew.

Further down the garden, two of the nuns were caressing a pet lamb, which had been presented to the Abbey by a neighboring shepherd. Other black-robed figures walked sedately around the wooden cloisters, chatting together in demure tones.

"I can't *ever* find one," said Merewyn, referring to the four-leaf clover. She impatiently went to the border to pick a fat pink rose, then sat on the rim of the well beside Elfled and sniffed the fragrance.

"Well, perhaps you will some day," said Elfled, "and perhaps you'll start your novitiate. I *did* hope," she added, "that you and I would take our vows together. Since we first shared a bed in that vile woman's Bower — and you were so kind to me, we have been friends, Merewyn. I hate to lose you again."

Merewyn squeezed Elfled's bony knee affectionately, then,

frowning, sniffed at her flower. "We'll still see each other," she said. "You won't lose me."

"Ah, but you know very well it can't be the same," said El-fled, twining a gold thread through Michael's halo. "The Reverend Mother is strict about particular friendships, especially between a nun and a secular. Besides —" She paused, her rather beautiful gray eyes looked troubled. "I had one of my dreams about you, Merewyn, last night. You were not at Romsey. You were far, far away in a place of dark high mountains and ice. There was a man —" She paused again, lowered her lids and colored, adding in a whisper, "He had his arms around you — kisses." She bent close to the altar cloth.

"A man kissing me?" Instinctively, Merewyn thought of Rumon. She also thought of shameful dreams she herself had had. Dreams of passion which sent a melting sweetness through her body, the feel of a man's enfolding arms, of his weight upon her; often the man's eyes were Rumon's, sometimes she saw no face, felt only the delicious pressure of a man's naked body. The sorrow of loss when she awoke and the shame of the dreams were a secret misery.

"What sort of man?" Merewyn asked. Elfled's dreams were much respected; often they had foretold happenings in the convent — like Sister Dudda's death, like the disastrous flooding of the river Test two springs ago. Even the practical Abbess had been impressed by Elfled's dreams, as she was by the girl's rather bizarre mortifications — notably bathing in the Abbey fishpond even when it was iced over.

"The man," said Elfled, putting down her needle, "was huge, near as big as that Cornish giant of yours." She stopped and slowly took another stitch. "Oh," said Merewyn. Caw had been retrieved from Lydford by the Abbess after Merewyn's arrival at Romsey, and assigned to the Abbey Farm as general laborer. "Go on," Merewyn said to Elfled. "Is that all you saw of this dream man?"

Elfled answered hesitantly. "He had shaggy hair, the color of corn, a yellow beard — and he wore a bronze helmet."

"Oh, Elfled," said Merewyn, "I don't believe this dream. And they haven't *all* come true, dear."

"I think this is a true one," Elfled said sighing. "For when I awoke my cell was glowing with a violet light which comes from around my crucifix. This happens after TRUE dreams."

"Well," said Merewyn, shrugging. "I don't know any man like that, nor want to — the bronze helmet sounds like a *Viking!* Or at least I've heard that's what those beasts wear. And I don't want to leave Romsey, ever. Which means that I am at last almost sure that I *have* a vocation. Soon I'll tell Reverend Mother so."

Elfled looked up and smiled. "I hope my dream is wrong," she said gently. "It has been your feeling for Lord Rumon which held you back, hasn't it — since you refused Gunnar, and that Kentish thane."

Merewyn nodded slowly. "Rumon — I suppose so. A stupid, mule-headed passion, which he has never shared, and *I* can't quite stamp out."

"He did send you that letter," said Elfled.

"Aye —" Merewyn's freckles merged in a blush. For she had wrapped the letter in a green silk kerchief, which she kept hidden at the bottom of her chest under her one embroidered chemise. On feast days, she took the letter out, and painfully reread the distinctive black script. Her aunt was teaching Merewyn to read and write, but when the letter came, the girl's skill was not up to deciphering what Rumon had written. The Abbess read it to her.

It was addressed to "The Lady Merewyn — Boarder at Romsey Abbey." It came from Glastonbury, and contained a fervent apology. "Forgive me for the times in which I doubted you. Forgive, if you can, my insensate, my criminal behavior. England's tragedy is my punishment. No worse deed for the English was ever done than that was — since first they came to the land of Britain. Men — and a woman — murdered Edward, but God hath exalted him. Remember me in your prayers, I beseech. Romieux de Provence."

"Very proper sentiments" said the Abbess Merwinna solemnly as she handed the letter to Merewyn. "And God HAS exalted the martyred Edward. We should think on this when we pray for his soul."

Merewyn had often meditated upon the events of the year after the young king's assassination. She thought of them now as she sniffed the rose and watched Elfled's industrious needle.

At Romsey they had soon learned most of the facts from Bishop Ethelwold, who frequently rode here from nearby Winchester. He admired the Abbess Merwinna — her royal descent, her aristocratic composure, her devotion to God and the Benedictine Rule, her ability to regulate eighty-two nuns with the minimum of clashes. The austere, often sickly old Bishop found peace in the Abbess's immaculate whitewashed parlor, and solace for his many cares in consulting her able intelligence, and in keeping her abreast of events in the turbulent outside world.

Merewyn and a discreet nun or two were often present at these interviews, while sitting withdrawn by the window darning the convent's black wool habits and homespun shifts.

Thus it was that Merewyn heard of the rumors and confusion, and heard too that gradually the whole of England, from Cornwall to Northumbria, knew that murder had been done. But thanks to the criminals' shrewd manipulations of the rumors, few were quite sure what had happened.

One account had it that Edward had been set upon by thieves; another that he had been killed by a mad treacherous Dane. Those who whispered that it would be reasonable to find the culprits amongst those who profited by Edward's death, and how extraordinary it was that no steps were taken to avenge the foul deed — those shrewd ones confined themselves to whispers. For Ethelred was on the throne, and the country was ruled in all but name by Queen Alfrida (always popular with the masses) and by Alfhere — the terrifying Earl of Mercia. Even Dunstan held his peace, and had enjoined Bishop Ethelwold and others who knew the truth to do so. For Dunstan trusted in God's will — and his trust was justified.

After an unusually long absence, on Shrove Tuesday, March 4th, the year after Edward's death, the Romsey portress hurried to Merwinna's parlor to announce that Bishop Ethelwold and his attendant monks were riding down the Winchester road. The Abbess immediately summoned her prioress and allowed Merewyn, who was practicing writing, to remain — not only because of her fondness for the girl, but because she felt that Merewyn's inside knowledge, and forebodings of the crime entitled her to information.

And this time the Bishop was, indeed, full of tidings. After the Abbess, the prioress, and Merewyn had kissed his ring, he settled himself in the armchair and accepted a noggin of strong wine especially kept for him by the Abbess, who never touched spirits herself. He clasped together his blue-veined, emaciated hands and said, "Have you heard aught here, of what happened in February?"

Merwinna shook her head. "With the cold, and the ways so mired, we've had no visitors in weeks, my lord."

The Bishop nodded. It pleased him to impart outstanding news. He crossed himself solemnly. "God," he said, "has already begun the chastisement which man has feared to inflict!"

The Abbess folded her hands and waited. The prioress imitated her superior but Merewyn gazed eagerly at the Bishop, who continued in a low reverent voice.

Last autumn, he said, Alfhere had been stricken suddenly with a loathsome skin disease which appeared first upon his privy parts — an obvious sign of divine wrath at the Earl's notorious venery. And after that God smote at Alfhere's eyes. He suffered great pain in them; his sight dimmed. By Christmastide, so reduced and frightened had the reprobate Earl become that he had actually sought out Dunstan at Canterbury. The result of that meeting would soon be known throughout England. For in the middle of last February, eleven months after Edward's paltry burial at Wareham, Alfhere himself, with Dunstan beside him, led a ceremonial procession through muddy tracks and frozen fords to conduct Edward's body to the royal Abbey at Shaftesbury, and to a regal entombment there which lacked nothing of the honors accorded to his father, the great King Edgar.

Edward's broken body was placed in a silver casket, covered by a snowy-white embroidered pall worked by the nuns at Shaftesbury. It was conveyed in a chariot painted black and drawn by four black horses. The body was installed at the foot of the altar in the Abbey church. Dunstan and Bishop Ethelwold between them celebrated the Requiem Mass while Alfhere in black homespun robes — like an ordinary thane — knelt throughout the ceremony. He was observed to shudder at times and to press his hands against his swollen, painful, and half-blinded eyes.

"True repentance, do you think — my Lord Bishop?" asked Merwinna softly.

"I believe so, Reverend Mother. And even that pimply, perverted son of his, Cild Aelfric, prayed and sighed during the Mass."

"Did the little King not go to Shaftesbury to honor his poor brother?"

The Bishop shook his head. "Ethelred is suffering from a flux, so they said, and was too much weakened for the journey. I think myself he suffers only from fears."

Merewyn, forgetting the decorum her aunt had taught her, burst out, "And Lady Alfrida? The Queen Mother — did SHE go?"

"Child!" said the Abbess, frowning, but the Bishop was not annoyed. "She did *not* follow the procession to Shaftesbury," he answered the girl, who had subsided in embarrassment. "She tried to, but here again God gave a plain sign of her guilt. I did not see this myself, of course, but one of my monks told me of it. When the Queen mounted at Winchester Palace bound to join Edward's funeral cortege, her own palfrey, shivering as though in terror, braced its forelegs and would not budge, though the grooms whipped it and hauled on the bridle. I believe they tried another horse, which also refused to carry the Queen. Then she tried to set off on foot in the direction of her sainted victim, and swooned away at the West Gate. Upon my return to Winchester I found the whole town buzzing, and was told that the Lady herself was secluded in her Bower."

His listeners were silent. Not one of them doubted the tale. Merewyn's heart swelled with wonder — and with triumph too, at the thought of Alfrida's humiliation.

"I thought," said the Abbess, "that when she broke — or repudiated — her betrothal to Lord Rumon," she sent a glance toward her niece who winced, "she and the Earl of Mercia would be wed."

"Ah —" said the Bishop with a dry little laugh. "Lord Alfhere is in no condition of mind or body to wed. He has not even seen her since our return from Shaftesbury. And SHE, concerned at last for her own salvation — if indeed any be possible — is desperately planning to found nunneries. One perhaps at Amesbury, another certainly at Wherwell. They'll start building at Wherwell this summer."

The Abbess Merwinna stiffened. "Wherwell!" she cried. Her eyes flashed. "The village above here on our river Test?"

"Yes," said the Bishop, as startled as Merewyn was by the little Abbess's vehemence. "She owns property there and 'tis near where her first husband was — was slain by Edgar."

"Blessed Jesu —" whispered the Abbess. "Must that slut —" She paused mastering herself. "Must the Queen," she went on, "choose a place for the expiation of her crimes which will sully our river with all the ordure from her convent?"

"Oh," said the Bishop, distressed. "I see why you are upset, my lady Abbess, but you exaggerate the danger. Water purifies itself every — I forget how many yards — but certainly in a mile, of which there are several between here and Wherwell."

Merwinna bowed her head. "Forgive me," she said. "I am very foolish, my lord. It is because nothing earthly concerns me as does the welfare of Romsey. I'll do penance for my outburst."

"You need not, Reverend Mother," said Ethelwold, his withered lips smiling. "I absolve you. It is your anxious care for Romsey which makes it the jewel of nunneries in my diocese — nay, I might venture to say in all England."

Color ran through the Abbess's sallow cheeks. She rose slowly and knelt to kiss the Bishop's ring again.

Merewyn thought of this scene as she sat beside Elfled on the well curb, basking in the hazy sunlit peace. It was so warm as to be sultry, yet there were hints of autumn in the air. A bonfire and the smell of apples from the Abbey orchard; the pungency of thyme, sage, rosemary from the herb garden where the Infirmaress grew her medications. Roses too added their scent, those wonderful roses from countries far overseas — like Rumon's mysterious Provence, or so Bishop Ethelwold had told them, when he presented cuttings to Romsey. Besides these scents, which Merewyn's keen nose enjoyed, she detected a whiff of incense which still floated through the church's narrow windows — a reminder of High Mass this morning.

Merewyn watched a butterfly drift towards the shining pewter ribbon of the Test. Then she looked at the Abbey church and thought, as she often had, that it was like a huge gray mother cat, keeping a protective watch over all the little thatched convent buildings which surrounded it.

The church was venerable, and considered to be magnificent, with its long nave, its rounded apse, its chapels — all cunningly fashioned of alternating long and short stones, until the walls reached the lofty timbered roof. Few English churches were made of stone. This one had been built seventy years ago by

King Edward, the son of Alfred, for his holy daughter, St. Ethelfleda, whose gilt and silver shrine was one of the wonders of
Romsey. Though now, thanks to Bishop Ethelwold's generosity, Romsey contained a relic of such awe-inspiring sanctity
that pilgrims came almost daily to worship it.

This was a lock of the Blessed Virgin's hair. Several strands
of the sacred hair had been sent as a gift by Pope Benedict VII
to Dunstan in Canterbury. Dunstan then shared a portion with
Ethelwold for a shrine at Winchester, and the Bishop in turn
conveyed three of the precious hairs to Romsey which was dedicated to God's Mother. Merwinna thus was able to install on
the High Altar, below the elaborately carved stone Crucifixion,
a relic more impressive than any of the saints' bones, or even
splinters of the True Cross which other churches boasted. The
Abbess had the hair enclosed in a golden box, studded with crystals and moonstones, and often did she admonish herself, and
all her nuns against the grievous sin of pride.

The great iron bell began tolling for Vespers, and Elfled,
carefully folding her embroidery and tucking it in her pocket,
said, "You coming, Merewyn?"

Merewyn hesitated. As soon as she entered the novitiate,
she would be obliged to attend every service from Matins to
Compline, and gladly would she do so, of course, but this afternoon she felt too lazy for the unrequired discipline of joining the
nuns and novices in plain song, and she shook her head. "I'm
going to see if I can wheedle a peach from the farmer's wife."

"Oh, Merewyn!" Elfled was half amused, half reproachful.
"Sometimes I think gluttony is your besetting sin!"

"Well —" said Merewyn laughing, "I've had little chance to
try the other six deadly ones, and you wouldn't have me go to
Confession with nothing to say, would you?"

"Shame!" Elfled primmed her mouth, but her eyes twinkled.
She was fond of Merewyn though the girl sometimes shocked
her.

Elfled walked off to join the procession of black and gray-

robed figures who were filing into the church. Merewyn slid off
the well curb, and leaving the convent garden — or "Paradise"
as they called it — began to climb a stile over the hedgerow
which separated the Abbey precincts from the Abbey Manor
farmlands. She turned as she heard her name, and saw Sister
Herluva, the Infirmaress, standing in the cloister garth and making urgent gestures.

Merewyn ran back towards the nun. "What it is, Sister?"

"Our Reverend Mother," said Herluva panting — she was
portly and she had sought Merewyn all over the convent —
"Our Reverend Mother has had a fainting spell. I've given her
foxglove tincture, and it has helped," added the Infirmaress, who
was a renowned herbalist and skilled nurse. "I've put her to bed,
and she asks for you. She summons you to her lodgings at once."

Merewyn nodded, and sped past the Infirmaress. As she ran
she felt foreboding, which she at once denied. Aunt Merwinna
had had fainting spells before, usually at the end of Lent, when
her habit hung like a sack over her spare body. The Abbess
asked no self-denial of her nuns which she did not doubly inflict on herself. But this was not Lent, it was a High Feast Day.
It's the sultry weather, thought Merewyn, explaining her appre-
hension. Thunder in the air.

The portress peered through the grille in the entrance door
of the Abbess's lodgings, and greeted Merewyn with a worried
nod. "Something's amiss," she said, while her huge iron key
grated in the lock. "Not an hour ago, I let in a man in a mailed
sark, and helmet, his face covered wi' a metal nose mask."

"Why did you let him in?"

"He'd a paper wi' writing on it for Reverend Mother, and
she told me to let him in. Then she had her fainting spell, and
one o' the servants got Sister Herluva."

"Is the man still in there?"

The portress shrugged. "He's not come out."

Merewyn, puzzled but scarcely disturbed — the Abbess received many visitors of all kinds — walked through the parlor

and knocked at the door of the inner cell. The Abbess was lying on her wooden cot, propped high by pillows filled with wood shavings. Each fold of her black habit was in place, her wimple and veil framed her pale face with their usual precision. Her eyes were very grave. "Come in, child," she said.

"Are you all right?" cried the girl, running to the cot, and taking Merwinna's hand.

"Quite recovered," said the Abbess, scornful of her own weakness. "But I want you to hear of a matter so shocking — and so preposterous — that I can hardly credit it. Gunnar!" she added, raising her voice.

Merewyn looked around in astonishment. Homespun curtains screened off the Abbess's private chapel from the cell. Through the curtains, Gunnar, Thored's son, appeared. Merewyn gaped at him.

She had always seen the young Danish thane dressed as a courtier, in mantles and tunics and cross-gartered stockings scarcely less splendid than his erstwhile master's — King Edward and Martyr. Today Gunnar wore a coat of chain mail, a conical brass helmet with a hinged brass fighting mask pushed up. There were leather greaves on his shins, an immense scabbard hung from his belt, and a round wood and bronze shield painted with a black raven was fastened to his left forearm. He had grown a brown beard, which aged him. Strangest of all was the expression of his hazel eyes which had always gazed at her with hurt devotion — even two years ago when she had finally and impatiently refused the marriage proposals he proffered through Merewyn's guardian — the Abbess.

There was no devotion now in Gunnar's eyes. They were cold, unswerving, and topped by a scowl. "It is," he said to Merewyn, "for the reason that I *once* luffed you that I come here today. "Also," he added with a grating laugh, "for the reason that I vas *once* — a Christian."

Merewyn gasped. The Abbess made a sound and clasped

her hands over her crucifix, but she spoke quietly. "You are no longer a Christian, Gunnar?"

"Vy should I be?" he cried. "My King, for whom I vould haf died, vas a Christian, did this help him? Those who killed him are Christians. Should I be one vith *them?* My father, Thored, my mother, Hilde, they are Christians — so meek — so mild — that do you know vat they are doing!" He lifted his bearded chin, and spat on the floor of the chapel.

"What are they doing?" said the Abbess in the same controlled tone.

"Elgifu!" shouted Gunnar. "My sister! Who vas to marry Edvard, who luffed her! They are giving her to Ethelred. To ETHELRED, for whom Edvard vas murdered, they make her ved that pretty little milksop — that coward — and for vy? So that my father, Thored, gets his earldom in the North, so that my mother may be mother to a Queen of England. England stinks of treachery and Christians. So I am no longer English, and I am no longer Christian!"

"And if you are not," said the Abbess, her eyes fixed on the angry young face, "what are you, Gunnar?"

"I am a Norseman," he said, proudly touching the raven on his shield. "I am the loyal servant of Thor and Odin. England shall soon see which gods are most powerful. You shall see it here, tonight — or at dawn perhaps."

There was a silence. Merewyn, uncomprehending, saw her aunt's face quiver, and take on new pallor. The girl turned on Gunnar furiously. "What nonsense is this!" she cried. "No wonder I wouldn't marry you. Always I felt the taint of your Danish blood, always I must have guessed how shallow was your faith. And now you come here dressed — dressed up as some sort of warrior — to frighten women. To threaten them!"

"No, Merewyn," said the Abbess. "Gunnar came to warn us."

"Ja!" he agreed violently. "And if *they* knew I vas so soft they'd split my brainpan vith a battle axe!"

"Who would?" whispered the girl.

"The Jomsburg Vikings," said Gunnar with relish. "And I haf joined them at Southampton."

"Southampton?" repeated Merewyn blankly. Southampton was the harbor down the Test, less than eight miles from Romsey.

"Vikings in Southampton?" she said. "What are they doing there? Why, I've not heard of any in all my lifetime. The raid on Padstow which killed my father was twenty-one years ago."

"True," said Gunnar, shrugging. "For all those years England vas strong. Now she is not. And our young chief Sweyn is shrewd. He is the son of the Danish King Harald Bluetooth — who is now *my* King. Sweyn too vas baptized once. He like me is disgusted vit a religion fit only for silly vomen and puling monks. He worships Thor, the Thunderer — as I do," said Gunnar, making the hammer sign of Thor.

Merewyn shrank, her heart thumping. It still seemed unreal, ludicrous that this arrogant Viking could be the dull courteous Gunnar whom she had so disdained. Nor had she quite grasped the meaning of what he was saying.

The Abbess, however, had, and she no longer felt the first shock of Gunnar's revelations which had caused her to swoon. She saw that the young man was growing restless, that the impulse which had brought him here was waning. She forced herself to smile at him, for she needed more knowledge of the danger.

"Gunnar," she said, "where did these — Vikings — come from on Friday? You told me they landed Friday?"

"They sailed from Normandy," he answered after a moment. "The Norsemen rule Normandy. They are our cousins."

"How many are at Southampton?"

"Seven shiploads. Four hundred and twenty men."

"And what do they want?"

"Plunder — slaves, gold and vomen — the destruction of the false god's temples. Last night they burned the little monastery of St. Michael — they killed the priests and monks, but got little plunder. Sweyn has heard of Romsey, how rich you are, your gold shrines and relics, your silver plate, and he knows that some of the nuns vill be young enough to appease the lust long voyages have incited in his men. So he vill come here."

The Abbess's face showed nothing, though her hands shook and she hid them in her habit. "You came to warn us, what do you propose that we do?"

Gunnar scowled harder. He did regret coming to Romsey, and inwardly vowed that never again would he yield to weakling sentiments. "You could escape perhaps —" he said coldly. "Hide in the voods."

"And what would happen to my Abbey? Even if it is possible for all my nuns and our servants to hide indefinitely in the forest?"

"Your Abbey and all the convent vill be burned, of course," said Gunnar. "After Sweyn has removed the treasure, vich I know is too heavy for you to take in time."

The Abbess thought of St. Ethelfleda's gilded shrine which weighed half a ton. She thought of the reliquary which contained the Blessed Virgin's hair. It was cemented deep into the altar. She thought of the two riding horses which the Abbey possessed, and on the manor farm there were a team of oxen and a wagon. That was all. She thought of her Abbey church in flames, gutted by fire, its timbered roof a heap of ashes in the nave; and of the dozen convent buildings, from Refectory to Chapter House to Dorters, all wooden, all thatched — and all destroyed. She thought of the two old nuns lying in the Infirmary, both paralyzed.

The Abbess arose slowly from her cot. She stood straight and proud before Gunnar, holding out towards him her crucifix. "By this Holy Cross in which you once believed, I exhort you, Gunnar, to dissuade your chief from harming Romsey!"

The young man shook his head. "I could not stop Sweyn, even if I vished to, I haf sworn to be his man, and pledged it with my blood." Gunnar pointed to a fresh cut on his wrist. "Even this varning I should not haf given." He glanced at Merewyn, who was beginning to understand and had turned as pale as the Abbess. "From now on," said Gunnar, "ve are enemies. I am an enemy of *all* the English."

"We're not English, my Lady Aunt and I," said Merewyn. "We're Cornish, we are of the line of Arthur —" She did not know what she hoped to gain by this statement.

Gunnar laughed his contempt. "Cornvall is in *England*," he said. "And let King Arthur's ghost protect you if it can!"

"No!" cried the Abbess, as Gunnar pushed roughly past her towards the door. "God will protect us. God and Our Lord's Blessed Mother. They have prevailed many times before against the heathen, and they will prevail now!"

Gunnar strode out, his scabbard clanking on his chain-mail tunic. He went through the parlor and shouted to the portress to unlock the door.

For a second Merewyn and the Abbess stood rooted, then the girl sat down on the cot and hid her face in her hands. "I don't believe it! Gunnar's lying, or gone mad!"

The Abbess shook her head. "We've little time! Merewyn, get the prioress! And we must remove the sick nuns from the Infirmary — in the farm oxcart — alert all the others, give them their choice."

"Choice!" repeated Merewyn, staring at her aunt's resolute face.

"Yes. Those who wish — whose faith is not strong enough — may try to hide in the forest."

"But what will *you* do, Reverend Mother!"

Into the Abbess's dark eyes came a look of exaltation. "I shall pray at the High Altar in our church," she said softly. "Pray

that Our Blessed Lord will work a miracle. Get the prioress,
my child! Run!"

During the next hours of confusion, Merewyn had no time
to feel fear. Most of the nuns were incredulous, after the pior-
ess had summoned them to the Chapter House, and told them of
Gunnar's warning. Not one of the sisters, even the oldest, had
any knowledge of violence, let alone of Vikings, whose menace
in this southern part of England belonged entirely to the days of
King Alfred nearly a hundred years ago. Nor did the prioress —
a wispy Kentish lady — possess the Abbess's authority. Consequently after the prioress had announced to them the danger in
the words dictated by the Abbess, the nuns fluttered around outside the Chapter House, some exclaiming, a few weeping, many
openly scornful of so absurd a threat. Ever and again one of
them would slip into the church, longing to question the Abbess.
But none dared disobey what they knew were her orders, nor
dared disturb that small motionless black figure which was kneeling on the altar steps, the hidden face upturned towards the
Blessed Virgin's relic, and the stone Crucifixion.

Merewyn obeyed her aunt; for the second time that day
she started towards the Abbey Farm. But now dusk was
gathering, the sun had dipped behind Stanbridge Woods, though
the breathless heat had scarcely abated. Merewyn scrambled
over the stile near the thatched farm buildings, and saw her serf,
Caw, pitching hay into the barn.

She ran to him and put her hand on his arm. "Yoke!" she
said to him in Cornish, pointing first at the oxen, then at their
yoke which leaned against the wall. "Yoke the oxen, hitch them
to the wagon!"

"Yoke — oxen?" he repeated in his thick stumbling voice.
The little black eyes showed his bewilderment, but they also
showed a spark of pleasure at seeing Merewyn, who spoke to
him in the only language he really understood, and to whom he
knew he belonged.

"Aye! Aye!" she cried, pushing his enormous hairy hands down onto the yoke. The farmer appeared at the barn door, followed by his eldest son — Bodo — a sharp, inquisitive lad of eleven.

"Wot be ye doing here, wi'me oxen?" said the farmer angrily to Merewyn. "T' Lady Abbess can't want 'em terday. 'Tis a Feast."

"I know," said Merewyn. "But we're all in fearful danger. There's seven shiploads of Vikings landed in Southampton."

"A likely tale! Ye be dodders, m'girl," he said, thrusting out his lower lip. "Go back to the women."

The farmer was heated with ale as well as the weather, or he would not have been rude to the Abbess's niece, and the real owner of the useful Caw — though the farmer mostly forgot that the giant Cornishman was not his own serf.

Merewyn raised her chin, and cried, "Farmer! — There are four hundred and twenty enemies in Southampton — and they'll be here tonight, to burn us all, or kill us all — and rape those they wish to. The Reverend Mother commandeers the oxen and the wagon, so that the two bedridden sisters in the Infirmary may be carried to hiding." She tried to speak with conviction, but doubt crept back as she heard her own words. What could possibly disturb the fragrant stillness of the summer evening, except the drowsy hum of bees around their skep, and the rhythmic munching of the oxen? *Gunnar is mad*, she thought. *I know him better than Aunt Merwinna does; only madness would explain the change in him.*

"The Lady Abbess *ordered* the oxen," she said feebly. "We can't disobey her."

"Bullshit!" The farmer swung on his heel. "Ye may tell her ladyship I'll not work m' beasts on Sunday, for a female whim — Naow wot ails thee?" He broke off addressing his son who was tugging at his arm.

"Look, dad!" cried young Bodo, his weasel face quivering with excitement. "Look yonder!" He pointed south to the patch of sky between the farmhouse and the barn. The sky was red — a sinister orange red which glowed through the trees and high above them.

"St. Mary!" muttered the farmer. He ran behind his house for a better view. Merewyn stood staring at the red sky, while her breathing checked, then raced. She turned violently back to Caw, crying, "Yoke those oxen!" And she shoved him.

The farmer came back slowly, his face had lost its truculence, he looked as bewildered as Caw, whose labors at goading and hauling the oxen under the yoke he did not stop. "Must be the whole o' Sou'ampton afire," he said dully. "Wot'll us do?"

"They'll be *here* next," said Merewyn. "You can hide, I suppose, or you can fight. Pull up that wagon!"

The farmer obeyed her in a daze. "I've naught ter fight with," he said. "Bar me mattock an' scythe."

"Bodo," said Merewyn. "You're a nimble lad, and I'm sure you know every part of ground hereabouts. Run and see where they've got to. Don't let them see you!"

" 'Course not!" cried the boy eagerly. "I'll spy on 'em — an' be back in a wink. I'm to go to the Abbey after?"

"Yes," she said. "Report to us there."

Bodo pelted off towards the glowing sky.

Merewyn clenched her hands and waited until the oxen were hitched, and the wagon started trundling down the rutted road, while Caw sluggishly prodded the beasts. "Oh hurry!" cried Merewyn in a frenzy. "I must get back and warn the others!"

"I'll tak' over," said the farmer, yanking the goad from Caw.

"But what about your wife, and the baby?" she cried. "Go tell them to hide." She did not wait to see what happened.

She sped back over the fields and the stile, across the gardens to the cloister, where the nuns were still milling about and murmuring. She saw Elfled and ran to her. "It's true!" she cried. "At least Southampton's on fire. You can see it from the farm."

As she spoke there came a distant rumble of thunder. The nuns gaped at Merewyn, they turned in bewilderment towards the prioress who let out a mew of dismay. "What'll we do?" she whimpered. "We must ask Reverend Mother!"

"She's already *told* you what to do!" cried Merewyn. "You may run and hide in Stanbridge Woods, or you may stay to help her with your prayers."

"Run . . ." somebody quavered. "Hide . . ." said another voice. Panic spread through them as the whispers grew, rustling like wind through the elms. "Run and hide . . ." "Run and hide . . ."

One of the novices began the flight. The prioress gathered up her black skirts and followed. Then the nuns moved as one terrified body, streaking through the cloister gate towards the Mill Bridge over the Test, and beyond into the darkness of the forest.

In a moment there were but three women left standing by the Chapter House — Merewyn, Elfled, and Herluva, the Infirmaress. "I see you got the oxcart, my dear," said the latter calmly, nodding towards the Infirmary door where Caw and the farmer were halting the oxen. "I'll help put my poor old charges into it; send them off, then join Reverend Mother in the church."

"And I also," said Elfled through dry lips. There was sweat on her narrow forehead, but her eyes and voice were steady. "You'd best flee too, Merewyn. You've not trained to prayer as we are." She reached up and kissed her friend on the cheek. "God be with you." Elfled turned and slipped into the church.

Merewyn hesitated. Her heart hammered against her ribs, her muscles were tensed for flight, and yet she could not run to the forest after the others. Not leave her aunt like that. Not betray the royal blood they shared. Let those *English* women scurry off like started hares, she thought, but my Lady Aunt and I are British; and see too — there's little Elfled. She has not even kinship with King Arthur to give her courage, yet she stays. Though Elfled had never suffered from this kind of danger. She had never had a mother with a withered arm, a scarred thigh, and the intermittent light of madness in the desolate eyes; Elfled had never had to imagine a father with his skull split open by a Norse battle-axe.

And still Merewyn stood trembling in the cloister. She saw the oxen start off with their loaded wagon, accompanied by Caw and the farmer who prodded the great beasts into a shambling lope. The wagon rumbled over the wooden bridge towards the forest, while the noise of the clumsy wooden wheels was echoed by another growl of thunder from the south — where surely the sky was redder — and surely now she could smell smoke.

Herluva came waddling back from the Infirmary, and in the gloom bumped against Merewyn. "Why, my dear!" she said, peering. "You still here? Why don't you go with them?" She pointed towards the disappearing oxcart.

"Listen!" said Merewyn, not moving. "Listen!"

The Infirmaress paused but her ears were not keen enough to hear what Merewyn meant. A distant rhythmic howling or roaring, like wild beasts, like demons — like nothing the girl had ever heard, and yet she knew the sounds for battle cries. "They're coming nearer," said Merewyn. "The fires are nearer too!"

Lady Herluva took her by the arm. "I hear nothing but thunder," she said. "Come into the church. 'Tis never wise to brave a thunderstorm."

"Is it wise to let us be slaughtered?" Merewyn gasped.

"Blessed Jesu!" snapped the Infirmaress, forcibly propelling the girl along the cloister. "You can die but once. And if this happens at prayer in a sanctuary, your road to heaven will be that much shorter." She opened the church's little convent door, and pushed Merewyn inside.

The church was lit only by the four wax altar candles. Between and below them, a small erect black figure knelt as motionless as it had been two hours ago. Even the wavering of the candlelight on the stone Crucifixion — its angels, its figures of the Blessed Virgin and St. John, its Roman soldiers, and the impaled Central Figure, seemed not to flicker over the Abbess. She was as still as a tree trunk, as an ebony post.

Merewyn's knees could carry her no longer. She sank onto a rough bench which had been placed in the nave for sickly parishioners.

She clasped her hands, and tried to pray.

"Merciful Mother of God — Ave Maria ora pro nobis — Our Saviour — Pater Noster — St. Michael — St. Petroc — St. Gundred where I went to help my mother — yet it *didn't* help. O Blessed Christ —" she began again, but her invocations jangled in her head. In her heart was panic, her ears strained for sounds from outside. She tried to concentrate on the three praying women. Elfled and Herluva were kneeling together in the choir, many paces behind the Abbess. They were not uncannily still like their Superior. From them came murmurs while Elfled rocked slowly back and forth, and the stout Infirmaress leaned often against a choir stall to ease her rheumatic knees.

We'll be trapped in here, Merewyn thought. They'll come first to the church for the treasure. She looked toward the altar above the motionless black head. The gold and jewels of the Blessed Virgin's relinquary sparkled in the candlelight. Will they come by boat, she thought. Up Southampton Water and into the Test? Or along the banks? Oh, where is Bodo? Perhaps they caught him. She had an instant image of the boy — his head split in two, the spurting mess of blood and brains. Stop it! she cried to herself, forcing desperate concentration on the altar.

Merewyn jumped at a sound like the crackle of tearing linen, then a stupendous thunderclap while the church was lit by white brilliance. Elfled and Herluva also started. Elfled grabbed for the Infirmaress's hand. But the Abbess never moved.

The thunderstorm! Merewyn thought in fresh panic. The heathen god Thor was the Thunderer. Gunnar said so. They've called on their gods to help destroy us. And what can *we*

simpletons do? Praying to that sorrowful Woman up there, to
that Man, already dead, limp on the Cross, having begged His
God in vain to spare Him. Blasphemy! The accusation seemed
to hurtle around her amongst a new explosion of thunder, and
another blinding flash throughout the church.

I can't stand this, she thought. She glanced at the west door.
It was not even barred, but if it were — 420 berserk men could
have broken it down in a trice. Were they outside yet — surrounding the church? She could hear nothing but a cataract of
rain on the wooden roof.

The altar candles had burned down and were guttering. Oh,
but we can't wait here in the dark! Desperate for any action,
Merewyn ran to the little sacristy, where she groped until her
fingers found the box of candles. She took four and hurried to
the altar. She genuflected, and sidled around the motionless black
figure on the steps. As she replaced the candles, she looked into
the Abbess's face. It was luminous and blank as a pearl. The
wide dark eyes, upturned towards the Crucifixion, never flick-
ered, nor seemed aware of Merewyn. From the eyes streamed
power, almost it might be command directed towards the Figure
on the Cross.

A calming awe fell over Merewyn. She walked slowly down
into the choir and knelt near Elfled, who received her with a
tiny nod, then went on murmuring her prayers. Merewyn
echoed them as best she could. She had ceased to think. Drowsiness, a sense of lull, enfolded her like a feather bed.

The rattle of the rain gradually softened to a whisper. Thunder rumbled ever farther off to the north, then vanished. The
fresh candles burned down to half their length. Time went by.
Merewyn vaguely observed that the slits of sky through the
windows were brightening.

She began again with Elfled, whose voice had grown nearly
inaudible and who was trembling from giddiness. "Libera nos,
quaesumus, Domine, ab omnibus malis —"

Herluva also had weakened; no longer able to endure the pain in her legs, she rested her bulk on a stool, though her head was devoutly bowed as she recited the *Agnus Dei*. But from the black figure on the altar steps there was still no sound. The three women in the choir had joined in another Pater Noster, when they heard a shout outside. They stiffened, sucking in their breaths. Herluva crossed herself, the others followed.

They saw the west door thrown open, letting in some morning light.

Transfixed they watched, but all that came through the door was a small boy, crying, "Sisters! Sisters! I couldna find ye!"

"Bodo!" cried Merewyn. "What news?" Her voice cracked and she put her hand to her throat.

"They've gone!" said the boy triumphantly, coming into the choir. "Them Viking pirates has sailed away in their snake ships, bound for the sea."

"How do you know?" demanded Herluva.

" 'Cause I watched 'em, that's why. They was at the head o' Sou'ampton Water, guzzling an' burning an' hollering fit to wake the dead. Then the storm come. I was right near 'em, I'd shinnied up an oak, an' could see fine." Bodo tossed his head, exceedingly pleased with his exploit. "Oh, they was coming here all right. I heard 'em saying, 'Romsey, Romsey —' an' they don't speak very different from us, I could sense some o' their meaning."

"Yes. Yes. But why did they leave?" said Herluva. "Hurry up, lad!"

"Thunderstorm," he said. " 'Twas fearful bad down there, an' the chief's boat was struck by lightning. It hit the mast an' splintered it an' killed one o' the crew who was still aboard."

"The thunderstorm," repeated Merewyn in a dazed voice. "Thor is god of thunder."

"That's wot they kept screeching, Lady. 'Thor! Thor!' an' they'd make signs wi' their fingers like we do fur the Cross, an' they'd run about and jabber something like 'Ill luck.' Sounded so ter me."

"You're sure *all* the shiploads left?" said Herluva.

"Aye, Lady. All seven o' 'em. They towed the chief's ship. Cast a rope around its prow, an' horrid ugly them prows are too, carved an' painted like grinning monsters — snakes maybe or dragons."

"But what if they came back . . ." whispered Elfled, far more frightened now that Bodo's report had made the threat real.

"They won't," said Merewyn with certainty. "Not when they think Thor hurled a thunderbolt to show his anger, not when a man was killed by Thor's hammer." She had no idea how she knew this, her speech had spurted forth from some deep atavistic well, of which she had no inkling.

The two women and Bodo stared at her, but the Infirmaress at once recalled herself. "Then we are saved," she said quietly. "Thanks be to God and His Son, to the Blessed Virgin — and —" she gestured towards the kneeling figure — "to our Holy Abbess, who is surely bound for sainthood."

Herluva walked to the altar steps, and put a gentle hand on the black shoulder. "We are saved, Reverend Mother," she said. "The danger is gone. You must rest now."

The Abbess seemed not to hear. The two girls watched with awe from the choir. "There's a light around her," Elfled whispered. "Not from the candles — can you see it?"

Merewyn shook her head. Her eyes blurred. So the Christian prayers had won. The True God had won, and used the false god as his instrument. But the real warrior had fought in that dedicated little body up there, with the unremitting force of faith and invocation which had conquered evil.

Herluva spoke again, and this time she was heard. The Abbess swayed, then fell forward, arms outstretched on the altar step.

"Help me carry her!" cried the Infirmaress. The girls and Bodo rushed forward. "She dead?" asked Bodo curiously, as they maneuvered the limp body through the church door to the convent.

"No!" Herluva snapped. "But her heart is very feeble, and I pray she'll have the strength to recover from this night."

They bedded the Abbess in her own cell, while Herluva hurried to get the foxglove tincture from the Infirmary. Merewyn and Elfled chafed the thin bloodless hands, after loosening the linen wimple around the Abbess's face and throat.

Herluva came back and added other ministrations, but so slow was the Abbess's return to consciousness that soon all three women were weeping.

"Bodo!" called Herluva to the parlor where the boy was amusing himself by making a whistle out of an oat straw. "Can you find the priest?"

"No, Lady," he answered with a snicker. "Leastways he wasn't in his house, I went there after I couldn't find nobody i' the convent."

"He ran to the forest with the others," said Elfled. "I saw him."

"The *coward!*" cried Merewyn, furious with fear that not only would she lose her beloved aunt, but that there might even not be time for the last rites.

The Abbess suddenly opened her eyes which rested upon Merewyn's anguished face. "Hush, child," she said. She breathed more deeply as her feeble gaze traveled to Herluva, then Elfled. "Are you the only ones who stayed with me?" she asked in a tone of remote interest, almost amusement. Their silence answered her.

"I shall not need the priest just yet," she said. "I wish to see all my household together again, and stronger in faith than they were before. Merewyn," she added. The girl knelt down and kissed her aunt's hand. "I think I could relish a noggin of our Bishop's special wine. 'Tis no longer a feast day — yet I think I would relish it."

chapter eight

THE ABBESS slowly regained strength. She was able to preside
in the Chapter House, and to hold private interviews with each
of her contrite awe-struck nuns. Herluva saw to it that everyone
heard of the Abbess's heroism, and many took on voluntary
penances for their desertion — though the Abbess imposed none.
She spoke to them only of faith, and devotion.

In October Bishop Ethelwold visited them, and Elfled with
four other novices took the final vows. Shortly afterward Merewyn asked to be accepted into the novitiate. She was startled
when her aunt demurred. "I don't think you are ready yet,
child," she said gently. "I've seen no signs of true vocation.
Gratitude or affection for me is not a sufficient motive."

This interview took place in the Abbess's parlor, at the hour
of Merewyn's writing lesson. She was copying an English
translation of the "Regularis Concordia" or "Monastic Agreement of the Monks and Nuns of the English Nation." This was
an extremely detailed document written by Dunstan and Ethelwold for the uniform regulation under Benedictine rule of all
the country's convents. It specified the prayers, procedures, and
ceremonies to be observed on each day of the year. Merewyn

in her copying had at last reached the rule for Easter Sunday. The joyous ceremonies decreed for that day filled her with excitement — the Cross which had been hidden in the Easter Sepulcher since Friday now returned to the altar loaded with lilies; the three nuns weeping. They represented the three Marys; the nun who represented the angel was sitting in the empty sepulcher. Then came the triumphant announcement of the Resurrection, and the shouts of "Alleluia, Resurrexit Dominus!" All these Merewyn had, of course, seen from the congregation but never understood as she did while copying the instructions, and it was her strong desire to act — some day — in the glorious pageantry herself; it moved her to announce her decision to the Abbess.

"Nor," went on Merwinna, smiling as she inspected the parchment and her niece's blotted writing, "is the enjoyment of the little drama we play at Easter a sign of true vocation. If I thought so — and I have given the matter many prayers — I would certainly not make a request of you which precludes your entering the novitiate at present."

"Request — of ME?" said Merewyn, — "Oh, Reverend Mother, you know I'd do anything for you, but I am, *am* disappointed that you don't think I have a vocation. Certainly I've no wish to marry, or even live outside Romsey. I want to be near you, and Elfled."

Merwinna put her hand on the girl's shoulder and searched deep in the upturned blue-green eyes. "I think you are made to wed," said the Abbess slowly, "that the natural desires of your body are strong, that you are made to be a mother, and that if Lord Rumon should want you for his wife, you would forget all about Romsey."

Merewyn blushed; her gaze faltered from her aunt's. "He never will," she said, cleansing her goose quill on a scrap of linen and then thrusting the pen into a noggin full of river sand.

"Perhaps not," said the Abbess, thinking of Bishop Ethelwold's recent remarks about Rumon, whom he heard of through Dunstan. "Yet in all this time since he went back to Glastonbury, Lord Rumon has neither married nor taken orders. And the letter he wrote you showed interest. However —" added the Abbess hastily, chiding herself for unconsidered speech, "whatever happens is God's will, and has naught to do with my request, which is a personal one, for which my conscience pricks a little."

Merewyn stared at her aunt, whose face had lost its serenity and whose bluish lips were parted to ease the rapid breathing.

The Abbess sank down in her chair and gazed at the embers of the small fire she had recently permitted herself, since her hands and feet were always chilled. The November gloaming was lit only by Merewyn's working candle.

"I shan't be with you long," stated Merwinna. "No, dear child," she said, raising her hand to still Merewyn's shocked protest. "It's true, and I'm ready to go — may God be merciful to my sins, and may He permit me to continue praying for Romsey's welfare. They will bury me here, wherever the newly elected Abbess may think fit in the church, but — " She paused. Whom *would* they elect to replace her? The prioress probably, though Herluva would be a better choice. There would be bickerings and jealousies alas. "I've been thinking of Cornwall. My childhood home. Lately many memories of Padstow have come to me in the night. The river Camel and its golden sands, flowing past Tre-Uther on its way to the sea. That sea of blue and emerald — much like your eyes, my dear. The sound of the sea beating over against the rocky cliffs — the beds of sea pinks behind those cliffs, how we romped in them, running, tumbling — boisterous as puppies, Uther, my brother — and later another lad."

"Another lad?" repeated Merewyn, trying to imagine her aunt as a romping girl.

The Abbess rested her chin on her hand, still gazing at the embers. "Another lad," she said quietly in Cornish. "One who made me a garland of sea pinks and the white sandwort, I loved him."

"What happened?" whispered Merewyn, as her aunt seemed to have stopped speaking.

"My father —" said the Abbess, coming back from memories, "always vain of his royal blood, thought the lad unworthy to wed into the line of Arthur; he planned for me a marriage with the old lord of Bodmin, but God had other plans — for which I thank Him daily. My father died suddenly before the marriage settlements had even been broached, and Uther, who inherited of course, would force me to nothing against my will. Ah, my brother was a good man . . ."

"*My father!*" said Merewyn, her eyes alight. "But then you could have married the lad?"

"He was drowned," said the Abbess. "One fearful night of storm when he was crossing the Camel in his curragh, bound for Tre-Uther and me."

The girl silently put her hand on the black-covered knee. Grief, she thought, and love loss, she had never thought her aunt touched by these. But then she had never thought of the Abbess as young.

"He was buried in St. Petroc's churchyard," continued Merwinna in a faraway musing voice to which the Cornish lilt added cadence. "Yet it is not for that reason — I'm sure it is not for that, nor even that all our family are buried there — that I make my request of you, Merewyn."

The request. The girl had forgotten the request.

"In St. Petroc's one morning I was praying —" said the Abbess. "I cannot describe what happened, I think it wrong to describe holy things, but I know God called me, and then I knew that I would never be the bride of any man," her voice dropped, and she added very low — "Only the Bride of Christ."

A thrill tingled down Merewyn's spine. This was TRUE vocation, and she saw how superficial had been her own impulse.

"When I am dead," continued Merwinna whose voice gained strength, "I ask of you, my child, to undertake a journey back to Padstow — with my heart." She smiled a little as Merewyn started. "With my heart," she repeated. "I wish it buried in St. Petroc's, so that some part of my earthly body shall be near those once dear to me, but principally as a thank offering to St. Petroc and his church where I dedicated my life to God.

"Now," said the Abbess briskly in English seeing the girl's tearful surprise, "we must be practical. I'm aware that when I'm gone, you'll be very much alone. Nor, naturally, by the rules of our order, do I have property to leave you. I do however possess one valuable brooch given to me personally by King Edgar. It is kept in the sacristy. I have consulted about this with the Bishop, and he feels that the money from the sale of this jewel may very properly be given to you, since I am your only relation, and that the expenses of the journey actually constitute those of a pilgrimage."

"Oh, Reverend Mother —" whispered Merewyn. "It hurts me to have you talk like this. Sister Herluva can make you well — and all our prayers too."

"No," said the Abbess impatiently. "My body is worn out, and I do not wish to stay. Listen, please, to the rest of my instructions. You will take Caw with you, and since England is not the safe ordered place it was under Edgar, the Bishop will lend you one of his brawniest housecarls as well."

She paused for breath, fighting a nauseating wave of blackness. It passed, and she went on. "I would like you to go to Glastonbury on your way west, pray for me at the tomb of our ancestor, King Arthur, and — she added quietly, "if Lord Rumon is still there, I would approve of your seeing him."

The girl gathered herself in tight. "Dear Reverend Mother —" she said, "you have hopes for me, where I have none."

"I cannot —" said the Abbess with sudden force, "think that a man like Lord Rumon could find you unpleasing; he was only beglamoured — by — the Devil and that lady who is again our queen. I am chary of praise, as you know — but you *are* comely." She looked at the tendrils of auburn hair, the wide sea-colored eyes and was puzzled, as she had not remembered to be for years, by Merewyn's total lack of resemblance to her parents. "Comely enough," she went on. "You have intelligence, a warm heart; AND high birth, which I believe would have an influence on Lord Rumon, as I believe that your sad lack of fortune would *not* affect him. You both have modest ambitions, it seems."

Merewyn was startled and excited by the remarkable things her aunt was saying. It was so unlike the Abbess to be personal, so unlike her to actually be encouraging thoughts of pursuing Rumon.

The Abbess read the girl's mind, and sighed, not entirely easy in her conscience because it was the strong motherly affection she bore the girl — the fears for her wordly future, which had moved her to abandon her usual aloofness. And earthly love, earthly concerns, must never be excessive. They interfered with pure spiritual devotion. "Ah well —" she said quickly, "you are in God's hands, my child, and must listen ever to HIS voice — not mine."

That was the last private conversation Merewyn ever held with the Abbess, who had another fainting spell that night, and who thereafter never again found enough strength to leave her cell. Herluva and other nursing nuns were in constant attendance, and they managed for some months to keep life in the fading body which at last became swollen with dropsy. Merwinna never complained, she lay in a shadowy half-land, aroused only by the priest's or Bishop Ethelwold's arrival with the Blessed Sacrament.

The end came at last in the rainy dawn of May 13. The Abbess spoke aloud and exultantly, "In manus tuas Domine," and ceased her long struggle for breath.

During the next days of mourning, the gentle spring rain dripped down as steadily as did the nuns' tears — and Merewyn's. They all knew their loss, nor needed the Bishop's eulogy to remind them of the heroism which had saved their Abbey and also shortened Merwinna's life. Already they spoke of her as *Saint* Merwinna, and planned a tomb as gorgeous as St. Ethelfleda's.

After the Requiem Mass, all the sisterhood gathered in the Chapter House to begin the balloting which would end by electing a new Abbess. And Bishop Ethelwold summoned Merewyn to the guest lodgings where he was installed.

He greeted the girl solemnly, and pointed to a small bronze box, which lay on a strip of white linen. "You know what that is, I suppose, my daughter? The Reverend Mother told me she had informed you of her wishes."

"Yes, my lord," said Merewyn kneeling to kiss his ring. Then she rose and crossed herself, looking sadly at the small box. She had no more tears left to shed, and the sharpest grief had passed.

"I've made the arrangements for your journey to Cornwall, and though the ways will be muddy after this rain, still I believe not impassable, and I think you should start tomorrow."

"Yes, my lord," she said. She was eager to go. The convent now seemed empty, dull — and though she was not of them she could not help noticing the little whispering plots amongst the sisterhood, the disunity and factions, none of which would be resolved until a new abbess was elected — if then.

"Here," said the Bishop, tendering a leather pouch, "is the silver for your expenses. I have defrayed them myself and in return taken King Edgar's brooch, which I shall have embedded in our shrine at Winchester. My reliable housecarl, Goda, will accompany you and your serf, that should be sufficient protection, even for a young woman."

"Thank you, my lord," said Merewyn. "I shall do everything commanded by you, and my dear aunt — but where shall I go on my return?"

The Bishop hesitated. He knew that the Abbess had hoped the girl's future might be assured by Rumon, but he was not sanguine, since by all accounts that young man was half a monk already; moreover he did not share Dunstan's indulgence towards Rumon's behavior in general. For that matter, he had to lash his weary mind, his sense of duty to a royal ward, into feeling much interest in Merewyn's welfare. Either a suitable husband must be found for her — difficult without a dowry — or she would enter a convent. It was simple enough, but the responsibility was a nuisance. "Report to me at Winchester when you return," he said. "You may lodge in the nunnery at the new Minster, until your future is decided." He picked up the bronze box, blessed it and gave it to Merewyn. "God be with you," he said with finality, and stalked off to pray in the chapel about really important matters, such as the management of the rebellious members of the Witan, who were constantly bullying Ethelred into refusing new land grants to the monasteries.

The weather was clear at last when Merewyn set off next morning on her long journey. Her only regret was the farewell with Elfled, who kissed her at the convent portal and lingered some time watching and waving until Merewyn's little company crossed the river Test and turned west towards Salisbury.

The Bishop had done his full duty by Merewyn. He had provided her with a saddled horse — a small gentle bay mare, who had no liking for speed; consequently the two men on foot easily kept up with her. The Bishop had armed both Caw and Goda. They had knives strapped to their belts, and rugged blackthorn staffs which would act as cudgels if need be. Goda was a big man, near six feet high, but he was dwarfed by the enormous Caw, whose sluggish wits had finally understood that he was going home with his mistress, and was as excited as his dim emotions would permit.

Goda was older than the other two, somewhere near thirty. He was nimble, intelligent, and devoted to the Bishop, simply because custom had decreed that he be the Bishop's housecarl, as had Goda's father before him. He was an ugly brownish man, scarred across the face in a drunken brawl with one of Earl

Alfhere's housecarls. He left a woman and six children behind in Winchester, nor thought about them at all.

Merewyn wore her green wool mantle and hood, which she soon slipped down around her waist as the laggard sun made up for the past week by brilliant warmth. The saddlebag strapped behind her carried her few possessions: a comb, a shift, another gown, and — wrapped in white linen — the bronze box containing Merwinna's heart. The pouch full of silver hung at her girdle, and gave her a new feeling of importance.

Never before had she been in full charge of any enterprise, except that long past and useless trip to St. Gundred's Well, when she had met Rumon.

The mare and the men sloshed along the muddy roads, which were rapidly drying; thrushes and blackbirds caroled from the tender-leafed trees on either side, the air was fragrant from crabapple blossoms and wayside violets. Merewyn, with an uprush of hope, allowed herself to think of Rumon. Of all her meetings with him from that first moment by the Camel River. I loved him at once, she thought. There have been these miserable years between, but they're gone. Soon I'll see him again. Aunt Merwinna thought that this time he'll not be indifferent to me. I'm no longer a child, and I *am* comely — other men think so. She lifted her chin and smiled faintly, aware that Goda's eyes held respectful admiration.

"How lovely it is," she said impulsively, "to be on a journey through the Maytime! Surely Heaven can't be more beautiful!"

"Aye, Lady," answered Goda politely, looking at the mud which encrusted his leather shoes and sturdy bare legs, and wondering when they would come upon a decent alehouse — surely there would be one this side of Salisbury.

"How soon do you think we can reach Glastonbury?" asked Merewyn whose exuberance demanded speech. Response from Caw was naturally impossible. He shambled along like a patient mastiff, his eyes on the road.

"Three days wi' luck, mebbe a bit over," said Goda who had never been west of Winchester, but had prepared himself for this jaunt by consultation with a West Countryman in the Bishop's household.

"Ah well —" said Merewyn dreamily, looking at thousands of bluebells below an oaken copse, "it matters not, we'll reach the Isle of Avalon in God's own time."

"Isle of Avalon?" said Goda frowning; he didn't like his plans disrupted. "What's that, lady? My Lord Bishop said naught about any Avalon, an' he told me where we're to go."

" 'Tis what some call Glastonbury," said Merewyn laughing. "It was a fairy island once, I think, where everyone was happy. At least so my mother used to tell me, and that's why they buried my forefather — King Arthur — there with his queen."

"To be sure —" said Goda, relieved. He had never heard of any King Arthur, but he knew that his charge had some kind of royal blood, the Bishop had said so. *"There's* an alehouse, lady," he added, pointing to a thatched hut, with a bush hung above the door. "We better quench our thirst. I'm dry as straw."

Merewyn made no objection; she dismounted; gave Goda a silver penny and waited contentedly in the sunshine outside the malodorous hut.

The fine weather held, and their journey progressed without incidents. Nobody molested them. The few travelers they met were either perfectly indifferent local thanes riding out to inspect their lands, or drovers herding cattle to the nearest market. Merewyn spent two nights in monastic guesthouses, where her proffered payment was refused. Goda and Caw slept in haymows.

On May 27th, Merewyn and her escorts set out from Pilton, having spent the night on a farm — there were no monasteries to be found nearby — and breakfasted heartily on rye bread and the yellow cheddar cheese which was the district's specialty. It had rained in the night, and the marshy land grew even wetter as they descended from the slopes of the Mendips. Often the mare was in water up to her hocks, while Goda and Caw splashed along doggedly.

Even though her gown and feet were soon wet, Merewyn did not mind. The sun was out, and she was enchanted by the Mendip Hills which appeared to her as veritable mountains.

Then she looked ahead over the shimmer of grassy marsh and cried with such force that the mare started, "Oh, there it is! It must be!" And she pointed. "The Isle of Avalon!"

Caw looked up obediently, and Goda stared at the high round hill to the West. "Looks like a upended green bowl wi' a stump stuck on top," Goda said. "Wot's so good about that, lady?"

What, indeed? Merewyn thought. Yet her first sight of the Tor had given her goose pimples. Was it because her mother had told her that long long ago before even the Romans came there had been worship on top of that hill? The supplanted folk of her own race — the Celts — had worshiped there, ever searching for the magic door through which the fortunate dead might pass into a blessed abode where there were no storms, diseases, or sorrow. Breaca had heard these things from Uther who had traveled much, and little Merewyn had listened eagerly to her mother.

In any case the Tor exerted on her now a mysterious attraction. She watched it all the time as they approached, and saw that what had seemed to be a stump was actually a stone tower, surmounted by a cross.

Just as the ground began to rise, there were tremendous splashings on the road behind them, and the whicker of a horse. Goda instantly whirled around, his hand on his knife hilt. "Beware!" he said to Caw, who had been taught this word and at once brandished his cudgel menacingly.

There was a cavalcade behind them; four well-mounted horsemen and a string of pack mules. Goda's hand relaxed as he saw that the leader was a Benedictine monk. The other three men were dressed in colored mantles, cross-gartered hose, and embroidered caps — obviously of the upper classes.

"Greetings in Christ," said the monk, surveying Merewyn's party with astonishment. "Ye've naught to fear from us. Must that — monstrous gossoon keep flaying about with his staff? He'll do someone harm."

"Stop it, Caw!" commanded Merewyn in Cornish. "*No* danger!" Her giant serf lowered his staff, and the monk laughed. " 'Tis a mountain o' protection ye got *there*, I'm thinking," he said, his shrewd green eyes twinkling. "Ye're bound for Glaston loike the rest of us, no doubt?"

"Yes, Father," said Merewyn. "Is it far now?"

"Glory be to St. Michael," said the monk, bowing towards the chapel on top of the Tor. "It is not. Ye on a pilgrimage, my daughter? *They* are." He indicated his companions, and surveyed Merewyn curiously. It was rare indeed that women made this pilgrimage — not unless they had dreadful sins to expiate. Moreover, oddly enough her command to her serf had been made in recognizable Celtic. "We'll ride along together," he said. "I know the paths hereabouts loike the back o' me hand. And ye might go astray t'other side o' the Tor."

Merewyn agreed, and readily told her mission, although omitting mention of Rumon. In return she discovered that this was Brother Finian, the Irish subprior of Glastonbury, that he had been in Canterbury to consult with Archbishop Dunstan, who had delegated him to guide back these three foreign pilgrims. Two were French and one was Frisian; they spoke little English. All three were merchants. "And I'm thinking," said Finian with a shrug, "that they've come to England not so much for the good of their souls but wi' an eye to trade." He indicated the pack mules. "They'll be off to London, once they've prayed and been shriven here."

"I didn't know Glastonbury was so great a shrine," said Merewyn.

"Second only to Rome, m'daughter," said Finian in his sprightly way, "an' some of us, loike the Archbishop and me, would say second to none, what with our Blessed Lord coming

here as a lad, and dedicating the little old church Himself to
His Holy Mother."

"I see," said Merewyn, and again a thrill went through her.
"I didn't know Our Blessed Lord came here," she whispered.

"Och, but He did, as a boy with His uncle — that would be
Joseph of Arimathea who was a merchant, loike those behind us
now. The Holy Grail is here too, m'daughter," added Finian
with sudden solemnity, "but *that* no mortal eye is pure enough
to look on, ye can only see the blood-red water which runs from
the chalice's secret hiding place."

Merewyn was too much awed for speech.

They circled the Tor's base, and Merewyn watched the chapel
on top, while an odd elation grew in her. That tower was a
finger pointing to heaven, pointing upward to bliss. In this
sacred place nothing could happen except good. Her anticipa-
tion deepened and mingling with it a sharper yearning for
Rumon, almost a fever to see him.

Wattle huts and some wooden buildings now lined the road.

"There's the Abbey," said Brother Finian, pointing to a great
stone church ahead. Merewyn scarcely glanced at it. "Reverend
Father," she said abruptly, her hands trembling on the reins,
"Lord Rumon — the King's cousin, Lord Rumon — he is here,
isn't he?"

Finian raised his eyebrows, noting the sudden color in the
girl's face. Now what was this? Obviously there was more to
the colleen's visit than a pious pilgrimage and wish to pray at her
ancestor's grave. "He was here when I left for Canterbury," he
said cautiously. "Ye wish to see Lord Rumon?"

"Yes," she said, dropping her eyes. "I wish to very much."

"Then no doubt ye may," said Finian briskly. "Rumon is
ever courteous, — but he's got scant use for women. Once
bitten, twice shy, and he still does penance for that wretched
affair at Corfe. He'll be a priest yet. What do ye want o' him?"
added Finian in a sterner tone. He was fond of Rumon, and had
been glad to see the young man's gradual immersement into the

monastery's activities. Rumon, though as yet only a lay brother, was superior to any of the clerical monks in the Scriptorium. He had made a gem of gold illumination on the first pages of the Leofric Missal; he had designed a silver chalice, of which even Dunstan approved. He had composed a new and very moving tune for the Te Deum, which he accompanied on his harp. His daily devotions shamed those of many a monk. If ever a man seemed called by God, this was *he*, and yet — though Finian thought, the flesh was subdued — he could not ignore a restlessness, a lack of resolution in Rumon. Finian looked with new attention at Merewyn.

A pleasing and buxom young woman — aye. He noted the full bust, the wide tender-set mouth, the earnest eyes of a color you didn't see every day in the week. He couldn't see much of her hair; it was properly covered by the hood of her gown, but the hair seemed to be red. She reminded him of a lass or two in Connemara — fisher girls, peasants — as Finian had once been himself. What could she possibly have to do with the aristocratic and disillusioned Rumon, who moreover — during many a conversation about the past — had never mentioned her.

"What do ye want of Lord Rumon?" he repeated more sharply.

She lifted her chin, and spoke with dignity he had not expected. "I cannot see why that should concern *you*, Brother Finian."

The little monk was taken aback and then he laughed. "I see ye've got spirit, and perhaps ye may be roight." He pointed with a knuckly finger. "Yon's the guesthouse. We've few females here, but the cook'll look after you."

So Merewyn was allotted a small plain room in the guesthouse which stood outside the Abbey gates. The three foreign merchants were also lodged there. No special provision was made for Goda and Caw, nor did they expect any, but they were allowed to sleep on the floor in the kitchen, and eat scraps hospitably provided by the fat old woman who cooked. Before he left to enter the Abbey precincts and report to his Abbot, Finian's face twisted quizzically and he said with a shrug, "I'll tell Lord Rumon you're here. No doubt he'll be assisting at None this hour, but ye could see him outside later."

"Thank you," she said. "I shall be praying at King Arthur's grave. Where is it?"

" 'Tween two pyramids, south of the Abbey in the monks' churchyard, 'tis marked. But my child," he added kindly, "ye'd do better to pray in the little old wattle church which God built. 'Twould be more efficacious indeed. Arthur's not a saint."

"He's my ancestor," she said, "and that of the Abbess Merwinna whose heart I'm carrying to the homeland of Arthur. I'll pray to the others too, you may be sure."

"Ye moight try St. Bridget," said Finian chuckling. "We've several of her relics, and I suspect that yours is a womanish petition which a female might lend a readier ear to than a man."

Finian blessed Merewyn rapidly, and scurried off towards the Abbey as the great bell began ringing for the service.

Merewyn went to her room and gazed out for some moments through a tiny glassless window at the Tor. She could see the top of the dark green hill with its odd ridges running round and round it; she could see the tower, of course, but the message it had held for her earlier seeped away, giving place to uneasiness.

The Tor, in the bright noonlit sky, no longer seemed a friend. What *am* I praying for, she thought — why do I want to see Rumon?

She dismissed these uncomfortable questions, with the help of action. She went down to the kitchen, where Goda and Caw were devouring pork trotters, smiled at them vaguely, and asked for a jug of hot water, which the cook provided. She took it to her room, and washed herself thoroughly then doused herself with lavender essence from a small lead vial. She combed and rebraided her hair.

Her gown was sweaty and mud-spattered. With some reluctance she donned her other gown — the yellow silk one given her by Alfrida, so long ago. Her aunt's common sense had insisted that Merewyn keep Alfrida's gifts, which included the green mantle and the brooch. Hatred of the donor was no excuse for repudiating such valuable assets.

Embroidered silk, and velvet and a brooch were not in Merwinna's power to give her niece, "but as long as you are in the world, my child, there will be times when you must dress suitably according to your rank."

Yes, this was certainly such a time, and perhaps one which the Abbess had foreseen. Nor was there any real fear that Rumon would recognize the gown and be reminded of Alfrida. "I don't think he ever actually saw me at all in those years," she said aloud. "My blessed Aunt, pray for me that it is different now." She crossed herself, and taking the little bronze box, wrapped in its linen, held it tight to her chest. Her breath was uneven, her mouth dry as she left the guesthouse and entered the Abbey gates.

The sound of chanting came through the church windows; she skirted the western end, vaguely noting the littleness of the old church, made of wattle and daub, thatched with reeds; and on entering the monk's cemetery, she easily found two small pyramids, and a flat carved stone between them. Of the Latin inscription she could make out "Arturus Rex."

She pressed the bronze box tighter to her breast and knelt down by the slab. Her prayers for the dead rapidly gave way to a feeling of communication. She could almost see King Arthur standing beside her, and his shadowy Queen too, could feel him smiling at her and welcoming her as his beloved descendant.

It was thus that Rumon saw her as he emerged from the Abbey, reluctantly yielding to Finian's information. He stopped some feet behind her, and said "Doux Jésu" under his breath. There she was, looking very pretty, praying for King Arthur with whom she had no connection whatsoever. It was pathetic, exasperating, and positively no concern of his. She was a reminder of all he wanted most to forget — of the agonizing, despicable time with Alfrida. But she must be greeted, of course. Finian said that she particularly wanted to see him.

Rumon cleared his throat, and Merewyn turned around. She got up and looked at him quietly, startled by the changes in him. He wore the lay brother's brown homespun habit, whereas he had always been so richly dressed. His black hair was cut shorter, his face was leaner and paler than she remembered. Nor did he seem as tall, the dark, large, reflective eyes were about on a level with her own.

"Good day, Merewyn," he said smiling and with constraint. "I am distressed to hear of the reason for your journey — the Abbess's death — may she rest in heavenly peace."

"Thank you," said the girl in a small voice. She noted the constraint, and that after the first moment Rumon looked beyond her towards the Abbot's lodging. So he was *not* glad to see her, there was still the barrier he had always erected. Nothing had changed.

But it had, and Merewyn's interpretations were wrong. Rumon, suddenly, and to his dismay, found the girl appealing, and realized that he had never forgotten her, despite the years of silence. For he had dreamed of her several times — dreams scarcely acknowledged to himself, and hastily dismissed. They had been dreams of tenderness and companionship, and once a dream of marriage. Preposterous!

"You wanted to see me?" he asked abruptly. "You have some special reason. Come, we can sit on the bench near the Abbot's kitchen, it's not forbidden to women." He quickly crossed the cemetery and Merewyn followed. They sat down, and he turned slightly away from her.

"Do I need a special reason for wishing to greet an old friend?" She spoke as coolly as he did, though her heart was sore.

He noted the traces of Cornish in her voice, and that despite the fact that this time she seemed very clean, and smelled of lavender, there was still an earthiness about her, an overpowering essence of crude womanhood. And what is she, after all, he thought, but the bastard of a pirate and an illiterate half-mad peasant woman.

"How long do you intend stopping in Glaston?" he asked.

She stiffened. "I believe I shall leave tomorrow."

"So *soon?*" he cried involuntarily, dismayed to find that he did not want her to go. He added quickly, "I mean you'll not have time to see the place properly — pray at the shrines — and you really should climb the Tor."

She was silent, staring at a little blue speedwell which grew near her foot.

"The moon's near full tonight," said Rumon. "I'll guide you up the Tor after Compline if you like, the place has a particular feeling at night — one can see the Isle of Avalon as it used to be."

"It is not here anymore, Avalon?" said Merewyn, puzzled by Rumon's sudden offer — uncertain what to say.

"I don't *know!*" he cried with vehemence. "At least *I* can't find it here. For me this is not the island of the blest, where all is beauty, all is peace. Though Finian says that there *is* such an island in the West." He frowned, having half forgotten Merewyn, and went on to voice his doubts. "Ah, I can live here like a cabbage, sink myself into the chants, the devotions, I can illuminate manuscripts, and play the harp, I can talk to Brother Finian, I can do penance for my part in — in Edward's murder. But I do not find peace."

Both were startled by this outburst.

Poor Rumon, thought Merewyn, faintly aware that pity had crept in to her long obstinate love. He seemed diminished, flattened out, and yet a few minutes before, he had been the composed autocratic figure of her memories, despite the hideous lay brother's habit.

"I shall be glad to climb the Tor tonight," she said. "I have always heard that there is magic there — from the long ago."

Merewyn spent the rest of the day praying in the "old" church, offering pennies at the various shrines in the magnificent new one. All this she did in a daze, even when she went back to Arthur's tomb and offered it a garland of wild flowers which she had made. She supped at the guesthouse, and afterwards in the twilight Rumon appeared to fetch her. He was dressed again as a nobleman — gold-embroidered tunic, red velvet mantle, the atheling's gold circlet on his head. They greeted each other politely and set off upon the road to Weary-All Hill. Two of the French merchants accompanied them, after asking ceremonious permission, and one of them — a man from Calais — was delighted to find a sort of compatriot in Rumon. At least "le prince," though coming from faraway Provence, could speak French, and seemed to be a person of importance.

The man from Calais bombarded him with questions. Was this really such an efficacious shrine? Would this long tiresome climb to the tower of St. Michael surely add virtue to the hard pilgrimage to a dreary little spot in the middle of no place? When he got to London would the discomforts of this journey influence the London merchants in his favor? What sort of people were the English anyway?

Rumon replied as briefly as possible. He was increasingly conscious of Merewyn, walking sturdily and at a few paces withdrawn from the men.

The May night was balmy, and everyone was sweating as they left the ridge and began the actual climb of the Tor on a track well-worn by footsteps throughout countless centuries. Black clouds drifted across the moon, whose intermittent brightness gave Merewyn an eerie feeling. Light and shadow, light and shadow, — was this perhaps the meaning of everything?

Her thoughts were not formulated, they drifted through her

mind like the clouds, and always she was conscious that just above was the stumpy dark tower.

One must reach it — Rumon had said so — but why? Because of the wooden cross on top? But why must one do what Rumon said? What is Rumon? A barefoot lay brother this morning, an aristocrat tonight. And now speaking an incomprehensible language to the merchant. I want to be free, she thought, I want to be ME, Merewyn. These thoughts had never come to her before.

They reached the tower at last. The man from Calais sat down on a stone and said, "Oof, I'm winded."

"I've the key," said Rumon producing a large iron bar with crude flanges. "There'll be candles inside — and flint and tinder."

"Mais oui," said the man from Calais, wiping his forehead on his sleeve. "Having come this far we must pray to St. Michel, I suppose."

Rumon unlocked the great battered door. But the flint was nowhere to be found. There was no means of lighting the candles, and the tower remained in chilly darkness.

"Eh bien," said the man from Calais. "St. Michel is indifferent to us. Me, I wish now to get *down* that hill — le plus tôt possible."

His companion agreed, and they started off.

Rumon looked at Merewyn. "You will linger a moment?" he asked diffidently, for her silence and the mysterious beauty which the night lent her, both upset him.

She inclined her head. "It is strong up here," she said. "Not St. Michael — the others from the old time. I doubt that *they* are gentle."

Rumon thought this a strange speech, but it also made him see Merewyn in a new light. The quiverings of desire long denied began to tingle.

They sat down on the stone where the Frenchman had, and saw the glimmer of water all around Glastonbury below them;

not only the sheet of the great Meare, but a myriad of rivulets, marshes, and ponds, shining silver and enclosing what was once the island.

"Merewyn —" said Rumon after a moment. He put his hand over hers. She let hers lie quiescent, and looked at Rumon's hand — thin, white, nervous, and barely bigger than her own.

"Yes . . . ?" she said, turning her face up towards the moon.

"I want you, Merewyn," he whispered, and was appalled by his own words. He threw his arms around her, and kissed her on the cheeks and then fervently on the mouth. A part of her leaped to respond. Had she not yearned for this so desperately? Yet part of her drew back. He felt the withdrawal and at once released her. "I have thought sometimes that you wanted *me*," he said, in a gruff biting tone.

She gazed out over the silver and black landscape. "I always did," she said puzzled and remote. "It is because of you that I refused offers of marriage — that I did not enter the novitiate at Romsey. Now you seem of a sudden to lust for me. That is interesting. But it is not enough. Not *my* dream, nor the wish of my Aunt Merwinna. A woman of my birth must not be tumbled by stealth on a grassy bank."

"A woman of *your* birth —" Rumon spoke through clenched teeth, and swallowed down the rest he would say. He was angry with her, and angrier with himself. "Is it *marriage* that you had in mind?"

She flinched from the contempt, but spoke staunchly. "And why not? Except for my lack of dowry, and even this may be somewhat remedied when I get to Tre-Uther. Its sale should bring in some money."

"*Money!*" he repeated. "Do you think a few silver pennies from that ramshackle hovel you lived in could possibly matter to me! I am Romieux de Provence, an Atheling of England, both Alfred and Charlemagne were my forefathers. Do you think I'd sully my line by begetting sons of ignoble birth?"

She gasped, and jumped to her feet. "How *dare* you!" she

cried trembling. "How dare you speak to me like that! As if I were a peasant, a serf. King Edgar thought me a fit wife for anyone in the kingdom! He said so — so did the Archbishop. But *you* — I suppose only queens are fit to mate with you — lewd fornicating queens!"

Rumon shrank from her rage, while his own vanished. She looked like a pagan goddess, like the statue of the angry Juno which he had seen in Arles. There was also pathos in her trembling voice, a wild hurt that he recognized. "Tell her," a voice urged him, "tell her." But he could not. He could not augment the furious hurt he had already dealt.

"I'm sorry, Merewyn," he said feebly. "I shouldn't have spoken as I did. But I think marriage is not for me."

"Ha!" she said, not softened. "Marriage with *Alfrida* was glorious enough for you. She would have made you miserable — but then I wonder what does *not* make you miserable? And I who loved you, aye, I loved you, for this you cared nothing. Shall I tell you something, Rumon — if you had forced me just now, even in lust, I would have given myself. But you drew away; hot and cold, hot and cold — light and shadow like this evening on the Tor."

The wind had begun to blow harder, and it seemed to her that in its whistle there were voices, harsh yet haunting voices, and that they were speaking to her. Her mantle flapped around her, a strand of hair blew across her face.

Rumon's heart began pounding. He stood up and clenched her arm. "I've dreamed of you —" he said half inaudibly; the wind carried his voice away around the dark tower. "You said you loved me — is it finished? We can go in and lie down in the tower, where we'll be sheltered. Merewyn —"

She shook his hand off her arm. "That's *enough!*" she cried. And turning, she began to run down the path, holding her mantle close, guided mostly by instinct, off the Tor, onto the ridge, and thus down Weary-All Hill, until she reached the town and her lodging. She told the porter that nobody, absolutely *nobody* was to be admitted who asked for her. She drank a large tankard of mead in the kitchen where Caw and Goda were snoring. She went to bed and slept without dreams.

Rumon sat for a long while on the Tor. When he descended, he walked slowly, his head bent and there was a stinging in his eyes.

Merewyn aroused her servants and left Glastonbury at three in the dawn light, thus missing Rumon who had spent a sleepless night pacing the floor, unable to think or pray; battered by storms of incoherent emotions, none of them pleasant. Again and again he relived the feel of the soft pink mouth beneath his, then felt the shock of her recoil. Over and over he struggled against his desire for her, knowing well to what depths of shame and crime lust had brought him in the past. He knew that his desire for Merewyn was nothing like what he had felt for Alfrida. For Merewyn he felt love. When the bells rang out for Prime, he could stand his turmoil no longer. He MUST see her, though what he wanted to say, he did not know. He ran across the precincts and through the gate to her lodging.

Why, the Lady Merewyn and her servants had been gone these two hours, said the yawning porter, and before that she'd left orders not to admit anyone who might call on her. Not ANYONE.

Rumon pulled a penny from his purse, and pushed it into the dirty broken-nailed hand. "Which way did they go?"

"I wasn't watching, my lord. That way belike —" he waved vaguely toward the west, "though wi' so many tracks flooded now, no telling where they'd get through. Regular mizzy-maze getting outa here that direction."

"Yes," said Rumon after a moment. Two hours' start. And if he did find her — what then? She clearly had not wanted to see him again.

He walked back to the Abbey, to the Refectory where — Prime being over — the brethren were breaking their fast. Here he saw Finian, and was reminded of the day's exciting event which he had totally forgotten. The Archbishop was arriving. Dunstan would be here by Vespers at the latest.

"And he'll be sorry to see ye looking so queasy," said Finian cocking an eyebrow at Rumon. "Always takes an interest in ye, does his lordship. That young woman unsettle ye?"

Rumon did not answer, and his friend gazed at him curiously. "A comely, spirited lass," he said. "An' it might be the Devil sent her to tempt ye. Old Nick he has many a trick up his scarlet sleeve — though by St. Bridget, I'd say this was a good lass."

"She is," said Rumon beneath his breath. "She *is.*"

"Ah —" said Finian. "Well, whatever it is, ye can tell his lordship all about it. He's a wise old man — is the Archbishop."

Rumon said nothing. He went off to don his lay brother's habit, and to the amazement of the monks detailed for duty in the vegetable garden that day, he insisted upon seizing a spade and helping dig the new bean bed. Lord Rumon was never one for manual labor, and the brothers thought his rather frantic digging most peculiar.

Dunstan duly arrived that afternoon, and his litter was set down before the Abbot's lodging. Abbot Segegar came rushing out, followed by the Prior and by Finian, and other ranking officials of the monastery. They all knelt to kiss the amethyst ring, and then helped the Archbishop emerge from his leather-curtained litter.

He had grown frailer since his last visitation to Glastonbury; his white tonsure was sparser; he had lost all his teeth but his cheeks were pink, and his voice as mellow as ever.

" 'Tis ever good to return," he said looking around the beloved Abbey. "I see you've a new carved door to the chapel — and *there's* a fine stand of early peas." He waved towards the vegetable garden, then peered more closely. "Surely that's not Lord Rumon wielding a spade! Come here and greet me, my son!" he called.

Rumon slowly obeyed, murmured apology for his tardiness, but he did not meet Dunstan's probing eyes, and the old man saw that there was something amiss. "Come to my chamber, immediately after Vespers," said the Archbishop, and turned to precede the Abbot into his lodgings for an hour of questioning, consultation and report.

Rumon later reluctantly presented himself as he had been told, and found that Dunstan was alone, meditatively sipping mead, and glancing over the list of novices the Abbot had given him.

"Well," said the old man smiling, "since when have you taken to rough work? You must save your hands for the crafts at which they are so skilled. Or was it some penance?"

"Perhaps, my lord," said Rumon, and clamped his mouth shut. He could see the Tor through the open window behind Dunstan's chair, and he stared at it. His dark eyes were glum.

Dunstan pushed aside the parchment, folded his hands in his sleeves and considered Rumon, who had never before been so curt or shown so little affection. "Sit down, my son," said Dunstan. "I can see you're troubled. I insist that you tell me what it is."

"My troubles could scarce interest you *again*, my lord; there must be plenty of far worthier men in this monastery who need to unburden themselves."

"No doubt," said Dunstan dryly. "And they shall have opportunity either by interviews or in the confessional. At the moment I wish to hear from *you*."

Rumon sat down on the extreme edge of a stool and continued to look beyond the mitred head towards the Tor.

The Archbishop had dealt with hundreds of recalcitrants before this but there were few of whom he had been so fond. Yet, why, he thought, should I be astonished at any human behavior? Oh, Blessed Christ, he thought wearily, it must be a woman again — but surely not *that* woman who was known to be moping in Winchester, or quarreling with Ethelred, and —

by reports Dunstan received — ailing with a skin disease much like Lord Alfhere's.

"Rumon," said the Archbishop quietly, "I have always looked upon you as a son. I always remember you in my prayers. I observe with sadness that again you are not on the list of applicants for the novitiate. Let that pass."

As Rumon said nothing, and continued to gaze at the Tor, Dunstan continued in a neutral voice. "Did I understand from Brother Finian that you've had a visitor? In fact, the Lady Merewyn?"

The young man's start, and sharp intake of breath were answer enough. Dunstan sighed and nodded slowly. "So is that good reason for you to look tormented?"

Rumon clenched his hands and whirled around on the stool. "I desire her!" he said fiercely. "By God, I love her!"

"Well —" said Dunstan raising his grizzled brows. "Is that such a tragedy? I believe that she has always loved *you*. It seems that it is not God's will that you become a monk now, and if so 'tis better to wed. Our Blessed Lord has said so. St. Paul has said so. *I* said so to you, long ago, here in Glastonbury. This girl of high birth — in these latter years most carefully trained by her aunt —"

Rumon jumped to his feet, interrupting Dunstan with vehemence. "The Abbess of Romsey was NOT her aunt!"

"Not her aunt . . . ?" the Archbishop repeated, frowning. "What is this nonsense?"

Rumon threw back his shoulders and confronted the old man. "Shall I break a vow I took?" he asked with a mixture of defiance and anxiety. "A sacred vow to a dying woman. I swore by the Cross, and kissed her crucifix. Shall I break a vow, my lord?"

Dunstan took a sip of mead. "That is a difficult matter to answer," he said slowly, "but I am inclined to think that you have already broken it when you said that the Abbess Merwinna was not Merewyn's aunt, and I also think there is little sin in telling ME this secret, which I shall treat as though you were in the confessional."

"Very well, my lord," said Rumon in a rush. "Merewyn has no drop of Arthur's blood — nor Uther's. She was sired by a chance-come Viking raider, whose name nobody knows."

"Ah — h," said Dunstan on a long breath. He shook his head. "Poor child, poor child . . . Now tell me exactly how you know this, Rumon."

Rumon, full of relief, quickly described the actual events at Padstow eight years ago, the interview with Poldu the prior — the pitiful confirmation given by Breaca.

"I see," said Dunstan at the end. "This is indeed distressing. Especially for a man of your pride. From the worldly viewpoint, it *is* most distressing. But search yourself, Rumon. If Merewyn were what she thinks she is, would you then wish to wed her?"

"I *would!* cried Rumon from his heart. "Of late I've even dreamed she was my wife."

"Uhm-m —" said the Archbishop, and was silent a long time before he spoke.

"Many things are shown to us in dreams. She is an excellent and Christian girl, no matter what her birth. I understand how THAT deters you, for arrogance, Rumon, and an excessive squeamishness are faults of yours. But since you have at last come to appreciate Merewyn, I think you should marry her. After all, nobody in England but you and me will know the facts. This is not a sinful deception, it is the very spirit of the vow you took to Breaca, and were rewarded by a vision, were you not?"

"Yes," said Rumon, "but no visions have been granted me in years. My lord —" he added, his eyes grew brilliant, his face suddenly young and eager, "then you really think I should wed her? But she's gone. She was very angry with me. She may not want me anymore."

"Follow her," said Dunstan. "And find out. Aye, and you

shall have a mission to Padstow which accords very well with my plans. Reports on that deplorable priory there are most unsatisfactory, and the Bishop of Crediton is lax and won't bestir himself. I shall send you with Brother Finian to make a personal inspection. I believe that reprobate Poldu is still prior, but even this is unclear. You will be able to travel faster than Merewyn, and will soon catch up with her. At any rate you must forestall any contact between her and the priory."

Rumon nodded joyfully. "Danger that Poldu would tell her what he told me? — though I don't think Merewyn would believe him. She was too much impressed by her mother's hatred of those monks and their 'lies.' "

"So now you look happy —" said Dunstan smiling. It pleased him to bestow happiness, of which there was so little on this earth. God's will, of course — and suffering for sins was man's lot — but surely Rumon had expiated his sins by now, and human love was acceptable in God's sight. There were some who could not truly understand divine love, or worship, without the aid of human love. They went into an arid state of outward conformity — and nothing more. As Rumon had.

"Pray in the Old Church, my son," said Dunstan. "Pray that Our Blessed Lady will smile upon your mission."

Rumon and Brother Finian set out the following dawn for the West. They rode on exceptionally fleet and sturdy horses — Rumon's own stallion, and the Abbot of Glastonbury's best gelding.

Rumon was dressed according to his rank, but Dunstan who supervised every detail, had ordered that he wear beneath his tunic a suit of very fine chain mail, and that he carry a dagger as well as a sword. The country in general had grown lawless since King Edgar's death, moreover there were rumors of a Viking raid near Bristol. As for Finian, he could not of course bear arms, but he had a formidable eating knife in his saddlebag, and his black habit should protect him in all Christian places.

Rumon obeyed Dunstan only from courtesy. He had no thought of danger, in fact now that he permitted himself to, he thought only of Merewyn, and enjoyed a feeling of certainty that despite her head start of a day, they would very soon find her.

As the two men left Street and began trotting along a causeway, Rumon burst into a Provençal love song. The Irish monk laughed.

"I'm wondering would these merry spirits be entirely from the hope o' seeing your young woman, or maybe part from the journey itself — which pleasure I share wi' ye."

Rumon smiled. "It *is* good to be headed west again. Since my childhood, I've had a yearning towards the west, and visions of a magic place out there in the pathless sea or beyond it. It was foolish of me."

"I'm not so sure," said Finian slapping a horsefly off his gelding's neck. "Have ye not read St. Brendan's 'Navigatio'? We've a copy at Glastonbury. He set out from Ireland for the Isle of the Blest, and found many marvels on the way."

"Yes," said Rumon laughing. "*Too* marvelous! Like lighting a fire on the back of that friendly whale who kindly appeared each Easter so that Brendan and his monks might dine on top of him."

Finian snorted. "There's naught impossible to the real saint, remember that, especially an Irish one! And 'tis not only Brendan who voyaged out to wonderful lands. Our Culdees have gone westward ever westward for centuries, fleeing from those Norse heathen, until they reached a country beyond the sea — may God have preserved them."

"How do you know this?" asked Rumon, interested and skeptical.

"Sure and how does a body know anything? 'Tis handed down from father to son, and so on backwards through the years. The priest who taught me in Connemara, he knew much about the wanderings o' the poor Culdees. Moreover if ye have 'the sight' and many have it in Ireland, ye'll know things wi'out the need o' being told."

Rumon digested this in silence, half agreeing.

"What exactly are Culdees?" he asked.

"Celi De, 'Servants o' God,' a sect we had in Ireland, white monks who felt called to become hermits in the dark unknown lands, but they were men o' peace. I'm bound to admit they left Ireland, because o' certain disagreements. That was a long time ago, m' son, in the time o' me great-great-grandfather, I believe."

"I see," said Rumon. "Well, unless they actually found that Blessed Island, there'll be nothing left of them in this world now."

"Loikely not," said Finian shrugging. "I spy a fine shade tree yonder, me belly's growling, and I wish to sample the bread 'n' cheese the Cellarer sent wi' us."

On the third day they crossed Dartmoor by the usual western trackway, the remains of the Roman road — having suffered several delays and annoyances. Finian's gelding went lame from a sharp stone wedged in its hoof, nor was cured until they found a smithy at Exeter. Then Dartmoor treated them to one of its sudden mists; they lost the increasingly muddy track and had to wait until the mist lifted. Then the bridge over the West Dart had crumbled during the winter, the river was in spate and the horses seemed as incapable of swimming it as were their riders. They searched a long way upstream before they managed to struggle through a ford.

They were a weary hungry pair when they finally got to Tavistock in the dusk, and heard the Abbey bell ringing for Compline.

"Ha, 'tis a welcome sight," said Finian of the large new Abbey, which had recently been finished by Lord Ordulf — Alfrida's brother. Ordulf, Devonshire's richest nobleman, had skimped neither time nor money in finishing the Abbey as his dead father, Earl Ordgar, had wished. The church, the separate bell tower, and all the monastic dependencies were unusually large — built from massive oaken timbers, painted white. This shining whiteness gave the whole Abbey an effect of light and purity, and startled Rumon pleasurably. " 'Tis like the floating City of God," he said. " 'Tis like no Abbey I've ever seen." He felt a flash of kinship with this Abbey, of serenity he had never known at Glastonbury. He listened to the mellowness of the bell, which mingled with the rushing gurgle of the Tavy as they crossed the bridge, and because all his inner thoughts were now centered on Merewyn, he at once decided that he would find her here, at the guesthouse.

Inquiries along the way had produced no news of her, but despite their own delays, she could scarcely have come further than this — the only logical stop on the way into Cornwall.

"We'll find her here," he said exultantly to Finian. "I'm sure of it."

The emotion in Rumon's voice caused the monk to give him a quizzical glance. "I hope so, m'son," he said, "and I observe that ye've really fallen in love wi' her at last. M'self — shall be glad o' meat, drink and a bed. But then our wants are different."

They entered the cluster of white buildings, and Finian presented their credentials to the porter. It turned out that Lord Ordulf was here, that indeed — though he was not in orders — he acted more or less as Abbot for his foundation. An irregularity which Finian noted as something to be reported to the Archbishop; though there were precedents.

Both were invited to sup with Lord Ordulf and they were directed to the hostel.

The hosteller, a pleasant, apple-cheeked young monk named Lyfing, greeted them warmly, said he was glad to see someone from the outer world, and at once produced bread and beer for them. Finian murmured a blessing and downed the beer.

Rumon, however, stared at Brother Lyfing, and said slowly, "Have you had *no* guests lately? Hasn't a young woman come here with two servants?"

"Haven't seen a woman in months," said Lyfing cheerfully. "Barring his lordship's Lady Albina, and it was last Yuletide she paid us a visit. Why would women be traveling through? There's naught beyond here but Cornwall."

"This one was *going* into Cornwall," said Rumon, and his voice dragged. "I'm trying to find her, and I was sure she'd come through here. How else could she go?"

"I don't know, my lord," said the young monk. "This is the only good way west, but she might not know about Tavistock — or indeed she might be lost on the moor. The Devil has raised more mists than usual this spring."

Finian was cutting off a slice of bread with his own knife, but he looked up and said to Rumon, "Did ye not tell me that when ye two came from Cornwall years ago, ye went to Lydford? She'd know that. Could she've gone back there?"

"To be sure, she might!" cried Rumon, clutching again at hope. "We never came near Tavistock before. We went straight from Lydford to Bath. She must have gone there." He refused to consider the possibility of Merewyn lost on the moors. Or the possibility that he might not find her nearby. With each delay his love grew more compelling.

"His reverend lordship would know if the lady went to Lydford," said the young monk. "He was back there at the castle yesterday."

But when they got to the Abbot's lodgings, and were kindly received by Ordulf, Rumon was again disappointed.

The huge blond Thane was fifty now and had grown very stout. He sat them down at once to a supper of capons, roast beef, and wine; he asked a few desultory questions about their journey; he was eager to talk about Tavistock, and proud of his achievements here; but he knew nothing of Merewyn whom he had some difficulty in remembering. "She wasn't at Lydford yesterday," he said, signaling to his table carl for more wine. "I'd've heard at once. She'd go to the castle of course."

"Yes-s —" said Rumon, for where else in Lydford would she

go for hospitality? It never occurred to him that Lydford
Castle's connection with Alfrida — whom Merewyn had first
met there — might be a deterrent. And so unreal now seemed
his own passion for Alfrida that this meeting with her brother
did not disturb him. He thought only of finding Merewyn.

"It could be —" he said, "that traveling as slowly as she must,
she has not yet arrived. We've somehow passed her."

"Indeed," agreed Ordulf, gnawing gustily on a capon thigh.
"There've been mists on the moor. You'd better wait a day or
so. I'll send a churl to Lydford Gate, in case she comes there,
and it'll be my pleasure to keep you two here as guests, case
she comes *here*. Are you not surprised at the fineness of my
Abbey?" he asked, reverting to his favorite topic, and dismissing
this boring chase after a woman. For Ordulf, the hot pursuit of
any woman was long past. He was contented enough with his
lethargic wife, Lady Albina — when he saw her. Life outside of
Devon, and particularly Tavistock, never captured his interest.
He knew, of course, that Lord Rumon — this dark intense young
man — had once been embroiled with Alfrida, who had thrown
him over when in some way best forgotten young Ethelred
ascended the throne. Well, all that was far away and finished.
Ordulf did not concern himself with the behavior of his ambitious sister, nor even of his nephew young Ethelred. It was
agreeable to be uncle to the King, no doubt, but neither he nor
Albina bestirred themselves to go to Court. The overlordship
of Devonshire; the reeveship of Cornwall — which he never
visited — these were public duties enough. For the rest, eating,
drinking, occasional hospitality and the ownership of this Abbey,
as his father had envisioned it, satisfied him.

"Och, and 'tis a splendid Abbey, m'lord," said Finian as
Rumon did not speak. " 'Tis dedicated to Our Saviour, an' His
Blessed Virgin Mother, isn't it? Sure, it must've been Our Lady
Herself inspired ye to paint it white. Ye must be touched wi'
grace."

Ordulf nodded, his mild blue eyes shining. "My father was.

It was his idea. Took tons of whitewash too. But wait'll you see the inside of the church. We've pictures on the walls — angels, saints, the Holy Family as big as life. I sent clear to Rome for a painter fellow who could do 'em."

Ordulf continued to talk about his Abbey, while Rumon struggled with indecision. Was Merewyn really behind them? Should they lose further time by waiting, in case she weren't? Why should he have a sudden foreboding of disaster when he had been so confident two hours ago? "Have you sent your man to Lydford, my lord?" he suddenly interrupted the ponderous catalogue of Tavistock's attractions and the precious relics enshrined beneath the altar.

"To Lydford?" said Ordulf gaping. "What man? What for?"

"To see if the Lady Merewyn has come there." Rumon tightened his jaw. "Never mind, I'll go myself. Pray give me a guide."

Ordulf slowly adjusted his mind to this request, and found it erratic. "But 'twill be deep night when you get there," he objected. "Eight miles or more. You can go in the morning."

Finian chuckled, his sharp gaze on Rumon's flushed, anxious face. "Let him go, m'lord. I've oft observed ye can't argue wi' a man in love. They've no more sense than puppies. I'll keep a look-out at the hostel here," he added smiling to Rumon, "but remember, there's no cause for this mad haste. A day or two won't matter either way."

These sage words echoed in Rumon's head as he galloped along the trackway north, accompanied by a carl of Ordulf's who grumbled and cursed as loud as he dared. It was indeed dark when they got to Lydford, and Rumon made himself thoroughly unpopular by immediately starting inquiries from householders who had long since retired. Had anyone seen a young woman and two servants? Nobody had. Nor had they at the castle when the sleepy porter finally succumbed to a bribe and disturbed the slumbers of Lady Albina.

"You mean the girl descended from that old British King who

was here some years ago?" she asked, yawning and clutching a purple gown around her ample figure. "Whatever made you think she'd be here?"

Whatever indeed? thought Rumon suddenly aware of the folly of this trip. He apologized to Lady Albina, accepted a bench in the Hall for two hours' sleep, then prodded up his outraged guide for the journey back to Tavistock. He arrived there at six, while the thrushes sang and the dew lay glistening on the lavish Abbey gardens. He heard the monks chanting Prime inside the church, and entered. After he did so he had two separate and vivid impressions.

The first was that Merewyn was there. He thought he saw her kneeling at one corner of the south transept, her face upturned to the High Altar. She looked older, thinner than when he had seen her last on the Tor, she was garbed in something dark green and he felt that she had suffered. He stared for a moment, his heart melting with relief, love, pity. Then the figure rose and resolved itself into a black-cowled monk.

Rumon blinked and knelt down hard on the prie-dieu. Am I going mad? he thought. I was *sure* that was Merewyn. Am I bewitched? He shivered, aware that he felt very odd, as another impression seized on him. The beauty of the church itself. The walls sparkled with color, fresh, vivid and at that moment to Rumon magical as well. He gazed at the fresco of Our Lady. She was garlanded with roses, her blue gown was translucent. She seemed to smile and beckon. The other figures grouped along the walls, and the Calvary over the altar all pulsated with life. Then his eyes were drawn upward to a silver dove with crystal eyes. It hung by plaited flaxen threads two feet in front of the High Altar. It hovered there swaying gently in the breeze which came through the open windows, and from its outstretched wings there radiated a benediction. This is where I belong, Rumon thought. He bowed his head, and at once the mystical feeling vanished. He looked up and saw a large, well proportioned church with well-drawn frescoes and an expensive silver emblem of the Holy Ghost strung overhead. How had that oxlike Ordulf even with money, luck, and a high degree of filial piety managed to achieve so much? Well, the ways of Providence were inscrutable — and actually this wooden Abbey, impressive as it was, could not hold a candle to Dunstan's stone creation at Glastonbury.

Rumon hurried out of the church and to the hostel, where there was no news of Merewyn.

All the remnants of exaltation vanished. He discovered that he was bone-weary, but he had emerged from the marshes of indecision. "We'll travel on today," he said to Finian. "Either wait for her at Padstow or find her there."

"As ye loike, m'lord," said Finian sighing. "I'm comfortable here, but've long since learned that comfort is seldom the Lord's wish for us. So off into Corn'll, and may St. Christopher keep an eye on us — *and* your young lady," he added as an afterthought. "By the bye — there's been rumor of another Viking raid on the Avon. Brother Lyfing heard it from a Somerset trader, who came here wi' venison last night for the Abbey — poached n' doubt."

Rumon shrugged. "The Norse pirates have come and gone for a century, like bleeding comets, like crop failures, like the plague — but all of these pass."

Finian screwed up his long-lipped ugly face, one that sometimes reminded Rumon of the intelligent ape the Lord of Les Baux had kept for his own amusement in Provence.

"Everything mortal *does* pass," Finian said solemnly, "but ye may find someday that there's something *beyond* mortal worth fighting for, even it might be — the love o' a woman. Which I've never known, excepting for me ould mother in Connemara. Ye're a restless man, m'lord, an' I pray for ye. For ye're not all o' a piece. Ye want this woman now. Whilst back ye wanted another woman. An' all the time beneath, ye've a hankering for Avalon."

"Avalon?" said Rumon, astonished and a bit annoyed at the tone of criticism. "What do *you* mean by Avalon?"

" 'Tir nan og' the Irish call it — 'tis all the same. The fairy islands o' the Blest. We've talked o' them before. I'm something drunk, m'son. Lord Ordulf's wine is good an' I had a flagon to breakfast wi' him. Well — never mind this now. I must go to the West — 'tis the Lord Archbishop's orders. An' ye're on fire to go. So we go. God alone knows what 'ill come o' it."

chapter nine

Rumon and Finian entered Cornwall at Launceton, since there was no southern way to cross the river Tamar, which was in spate like the Tavy, nor could a horse ferry be found. At Launceton there was a bridge. There was also the Castle Inn which Rumon remembered well from his previous journey with Merewyn. And here at last, Rumon got news of her. As he ate he spied the same long-nosed silversmith they had met eight years ago. Rumon approached the man, greeted him, offered another flagon of ale and hopefully asked his question in Cornish — or at least the approximation to Cornish which he could remember.

"To be sure," said the silversmith, appreciatively guzzling his drink. "There was a woman through here two days ago, and now you remind me, I suppose she was the girl with you before. *I* never thought of it, but I remember *you*. You were going to King Edward's Court at Lydford." The silversmith sighed. "By St. Neot, I wish we had Edgar back."

"Yes," said Rumon, "but what of the woman?"

"Oh, she didn't linger, just long enough for her and the giant serf and another man to eat and drink. Great hurry she was in,

like she was running away from something. The Sawsnach complained she kept 'em walking all day and most the night. I
couldn't understand him well, but I gathered he had to do her
orders. Good looking wench," added the silversmith reflec-
tively, "though I like 'em darker and smaller myself."

Rumon, elated, went back to Finian. "Only two days ahead
of us and we've barely two more till Padstow. She'll be there
all right."

"No doubt," said the monk, and belched crossly. The Cornish pasty he had just sampled was loaded with rancid grease.
"Must have iron stomachs down here," he said, but Rumon was
already outside telling the ostler to saddle the horses.

From then on they made good time. The tracks were dry on
Bodmin Moor, and Rumon waved a jubilant hand towards the
hill called Brown Willy, thinking how recently Merewyn must
have passed by here, and that she must have remembered how
they had once seen it together, while HE remembered the delicate
pressure of her arms around his waist as she had ridden pillion
behind him. Yet at the time he had scarcely noticed that. How
strange; when now he so longed for her nearness. What a senseless young gawk I was, he thought.

The late afternoon sun was still bright when they came to the
broad estuary of the Camel River, and looked down it northward towards the sea. There seemed to be a bluish haze ahead
of them; Finian pulled up his gelding, frowned and sniffed the
air. "Smells like smoke," he said.

Rumon shrugged. "Somebody's lit a bonfire. What's the
date? They've a lot of pagan customs here. Light fires, dance the
old dances with a hobbyhorse, jump over wishing wells . . ."

Finian gave a snort. "Dare say they do. But as near as I can
figure, it's Tuesday, June second, which doesn't celebrate any
Christian event I know of. — Now, what 'ld THAT be?" He
pointed to a thicket where something moved, and two dark eyes
peered out. " 'Tis a child," he said. "Come here, little one!"

But the child would not move until Rumon spoke to her in

Cornish. Then a frightened small girl emerged gingerly. "Are you *more* of them?" she whispered, hanging on to a branch and staring from the monk to Rumon who said, "What's the matter?"

She pointed down the Camel and gabbled something, whereupon Rumon flinched.

"What's she saying?" cried Finian. "It sounds like trouble — like 'anken,' we've much the same word in Ireland."

"It *is* trouble, I think," said Rumon. Spurring his stallion he galloped ahead down the river road.

Finian followed, while the little girl scampered back into the thicket.

The acrid smell of smoke grew stronger as they neared Tre-Uther, and soon they came upon the site of the house. The thatch had fallen down amongst the slates, and still smoldered. "Merewyn!" Rumon cried, though he could see that there was nobody in or near the burned house. "I suppose the thatch caught fire," he said to Finian, as calmly as he could. "She'll have taken refuge in the village, or even the monastery."

"I hope so, my son," said Finian, and crossed himself. "There's more smoke ahead. I'm beginning to wonder has there been a Viking raid."

"Impossible!" cried Rumon with the fury of fear. "Don't be a fool!"

"There was one before."

"Twenty and more years ago!" Rumon cried.

They continued towards the village and looking below saw several heaps of smoking rubble, and no sign of life. "The church," said Rumon. "The church is granite, it wouldn't burn, they must be there."

They turned up the hill towards the church of St. Petroc. The horses had been increasingly restive, and as they neared the churchyard Rumon's stallion reared, nearly unseating its rider, then stood trembling, while the gelding balked.

They soon saw why. There were two bodies lying beside the road. One was Caw, his cudgel and knife still clenched in his hands. Rumon knew the gigantic figure for Caw, even though the skull was split down to the hairy black chin. A cloud of gnats circled the mess of bloody brains. The other man had not been treated so roughly, though he lay in a red pool which oozed from a chest wound. He still made gurgling sounds. Rumon, so horrified that he trembled like his stallion, recognized the Bishop of Winchester's badge on the man's sleeve.

Finian jumped off his horse, which promptly bolted, and kneeling by Goda, held up his crucifix and began prayers for the dying. The glazed eyes responded for a moment. "I did me best," he gasped, and tried to kiss the crucifix Finian held to the gray lips.

Rumon had already slid off his stallion, which streaked down the road after the gelding. "Merewyn! The Lady Merewyn, where *is* she?" Rumon cried. But there was no reply. Goda gave a last gasp; his eyeballs rolled upward. He was still.

"Doux Jésu, Doux Jésu," Rumon whispered over and over, staring down at the second corpse.

Finian closed the eyelids, murmured a prayer, then said firmly, "Now we'll go to the church, and mind ye, m'lord, whatever we find'll be God's Will. *Come*," he added, taking Rumon's arm. "Have ye never before seen a man die? I've seen hundreds."

"Not like this," said Rumon. "Not like this . . ."

"Don't brood on it." Finian propelled Rumon up the hill. "Plenty o' martyrs've died loike this, an' loike that other poor lad," he indicated Caw. " 'Twill shorten their purgatory, I don't say they were martyrs f'r the faith exactly, but they did die doing their duty, and that's heavily counted in their favor." He continued to talk in a calm, reasonable voice, though he noted that there was more smoke far up the hill where he guessed that the monastery had been, and he tried to ignore the question of Merewyn, for if she too were found with her skull split he suspected what would happen to Lord Rumon. Madness. That sensitive artistic mind would never keep its balance under such horror. May Our Lord have mercy —thought Finian — and there's nobody in the church either. The carved wooden door had been wrenched from its hinges and carried off. Sunlight flooded through the door hole, and one could see that there was nothing inside. Except the bare altar.

The monk and Rumon walked in silently. The latter was still shaking as though he had an ague, while Finian clenched his hand around his crucifix.

"Look!" said Finian pointing to the floor, where a small square stone had obviously been moved. On it was scratched a crude "Merwinna." "She got the heart buried," said Finian, "anyway." Rumon stared down at the stone.

"But there is someone here!" Finian cried with forced heartiness and pointed to a fat white shape which was hunched on a tombstone in the cemetery. "At least he's alive." For the figure was rocking back and forth, its queerly tonsured head held in its hands.

Rumon looked and said in a thin voice, "It's Poldu, the prior."

"Ah —" said Finian. He walked over to the rocking figure and put a gentle hand on the grayish-white cloth shoulder. "Are ye hurt, Brother?"

Poldu started, he shrank, and then seeing the black-robed Benedictine, he moaned and began sobbing. "They took m'silver ring, 'n' m'gold brooch."

"Werra, werra —" said Finian soothingly. "Those cursed horses've bolted wi' the saddlebags or I could give ye a drop to calm ye down. We can see ye've had bad times. An' I begin to wonder do ye understand the English tongue?" For Poldu's ashen, sweating moon-face was a frightened blank. "Can you get this better?" continued Finian in Celtic. After a moment the prior nodded.

"Lord Rumon, come here!" said Finian sharply. "Betwixt the two of us, we can foind out what's happened."

Rumon stiffened and squared his shoulders. His trembling

stopped. "Yes," he said, and turning to Poldu, added in halting Cornish, "Have you seen the woman Merewyn from Tre-Uther? Is she dead?"

Poldu shook his head. "She wasn't when they took her away in their longship, and it's because o' her that *I'm* alive. Don't know who else is." He pointed his fat hand back towards the monastery. "They slaughtered and burned everywhere. I've been here since yestermorn when they spared me."

"What happened?" said Finian and sat down on another gravestone. Rumon remained standing, his arms folded tight against his chest; there were swirls of blackness in his brain which he ignored with a violent effort.

It must have been about dawn when they came, Poldu said. Nobody saw the Viking ship sail down the harbor, over the sandbar. But they saw it later: its carved snaky prow and stem, the solid flanking of round shields along the gunwhales and the great red striped sail with the black raven on it. Must have been fifty men aboard, and they landed near Tre-Uther because they burned that first, whooping and yelling. Couldn't've got much loot from there, and Merewyn escaped up the road with her two servants, the Vikings hot after her. Poldu didn't know what happened to the servants, but the young woman tried to take refuge in the church. They soon found her and because the chief — a great red-bearded fellow — obviously took a fancy to her, she was bound and thrown on the grass in the cemetery while they ravaged the church, putting everything they got from it aboard their ship, including the silver reliquary which contained some of St. Petroc's bones. "They burned the village," said Poldu, "and then they went for the monastery. I remembered the raid years ago, and ran for the same tree I'd been up then. But I couldn't get up it now. They soon caught me."

Rumon held himself very still, while Finian shook his head. "And then —" he said.

"They bound me and threw me in the churchyard near that

girl, yammering about a special sacrifice to Thor. Some of those devils were from Ireland, an' I could understand them a little."

Poldu went on to say that Merewyn never made a sound as she lay with thonged ankles and wrists in the cemetery, but that he, Poldu, knew of course who she was. She had come to the monastery upon her arrival, and requested someone to officiate at the burial of her aunt's heart in the church. Poldu had not bothered to do this himself, had sent a young monk who didn't know her story — but they all had a good laugh later in the Refectory about the appearance from England of Breaca's bastard. However, as Merewyn lay bound in the churchyard and despite the terror of his own fate, Poldu had felt sorry for her. After burning the monastery, the chief and his men had returned to the churchyard. They had kicked Poldu, guffawing at his fatness and two of them rolling him like a tub between them. By then Poldu had recognized the captain in his horned helmet; he seemed scarcely older than when he had come before, but he had a lumpy purple scar across his cheek, which Poldu had seen clearly from his tree — and saw now.

This red-bearded leader went to Merewyn, and untied her ankles. There was no doubt what he had in mind. She gave a low hoarse scream and began to kick as hard as she could. The red-bearded man laughed and his men laughed. Then Poldu spoke up in a desperate shout.

"And so, you Norse fiend — you would rape your own daughter?"

The majority did not understand, but the Irish Vikings did. They cried in warning, "Ketil, Ketil!" which seemed to be the leader's name.

Ketil, who was already on top of Merewyn, looked up much astonished. He stared around and came over to Poldu, jabbering something and waving his battle-axe.

Poldu, though expecting the axe to finish him any moment, saw indecision in the scarred face, scented reprieve and repeated, *"Your daughter.* You were here twenty years or so ago. You raped Breaca, the little dark woman at Tre-Uther, and you murdered her husband that very day. He'd not been home in four months. This woman is *your* child."

Ketil lowered the axe; he turned to the Irish-speaking Vikings and demanded to know what the prior had said. His men shifted uneasily, they stared at the ground, but two of them translated. Ketil went back to Merewyn who had gone limp as grass. He examined her carefully. Poldu had lifted himself on one elbow to see what was happening. Her eyes were staring blindly at the sky. Ketil gazed into them for a moment. He said something like "My mother" in a startled voice. He yanked down her bodice and examined her skin. He pulled loose from its long braid one half of her hair, and held the strands against his own beard. The hair mingled with his beard, darker, finer, but of the same reddish hue. His men drew around, murmuring and watching. One of them — a big young fellow with a beard like ripe corn — said something, and Ketil listened. After a moment he nodded. It was odd, said Poldu, to see the change in all their faces which had been hideous with blood lust and jeering laughter. They became grave, thoughtful. They all drew aside near the church and conferred. Ketil spoke for some time pointing down to Tre-Uther and nodding again.

Then he spoke to the yellow-beard, and gave a command. The young man picked up Merewyn and slung her over his shoulder, but gently, as though she were a valuable burden. As she still remained completely limp, the young man transferred her to his arms, and ran down towards the ship.

Ketil, the chief, came over to Poldu and himself untied the prior's wrists and ankles. He said something in his heathen tongue, and made a solemn though mocking salute. Then he led his men out of the churchyard. As soon as he dared, Poldu got up, and saw the great dragon ship sailing down the estuary towards the sea.

Then Poldu collasped. The fear he had not quite felt earlier overwhelmed him. His legs turned to water. He could not move and he had stayed in the churchyard.

When Poldu finished his account, his jowls quivered. He looked at his two appalled listeners and whimpered, "I'm thirsty."

Rumon paid no attention. He drew a long harsh breath and said, "My Merewyn, my poor love. So now she knows. I suppose she *knows*."

Finian looked around at the young man who stood with clenched hands, staring into the distance. "Knows what?" said Finian, anxiously inspecting Rumon for signs of extreme disturbance. "What d'ye mean?"

Rumon gave the monk a perfectly lucid, sad look. "Didn't you understand what the prior said?"

"Some o' it. That the red-beard raider, Ketil, was her father. Ye don't believe those vapors — do ye? This poor prior's maundering."

"No," said Rumon. "It *is* the truth. I've known it over eight years. And do you think they would have spared Poldu, if in his own way Ketil had not been grateful that Poldu stopped him from vile incest?"

"Ye amaze me," said Finian, screwing up his face as he digested this. So the Lady Merewyn was actually a Viking's brat, and unless matters were more sinister for her than Poldu's account would indicate, she would not be harmed. All very bad, Finian thought, but there were more pressing things to be considered. "We must see what's happened at the monastery," said Finian.

Rumon did not hear him. He continued to gaze down the estuary towards the open sea. "I shall go after her. It is my fault that this happened. Had I not insulted her at Glastonbury, had I not been such a vacillating fool then and earlier — ah, I see it now. I'll find her this time, may Our Blessed Lord protect her, and I'll bring her back to what she and I both want."

Finian opened his mouth to protest, to point out the difficulties of this pursuit — where would Rumon find a boat in the deserted village? How would he know where to go? But Finian did not protest. Rumon's tone convinced him. This was a man who had found a purpose at last. And all was in God's hands. No doubt it was God's wish that a Christian girl be rescued from the heathen murderers. If such a miracle could happen.

"Well, may all the saints help ye," he said, "and in the meantime," he took Poldu's fat arm and dragged him to his feet, "there's much to be done now."

The next morning Finian stood on the Padstow beach waving goodbye to Rumon, who had certainly so far received evidence of divine favor. A large fishing coracle had come back to Padstow at dawn. When the four fishmen saw what had happened to their village, they scarcely needed Rumon's money to persuade them to set out again. They were mad with grief and the lust for vengeful action — any action. Nobody would listen to Finian's tentative warnings. That even granted they could find the Viking ship, or catch up to her, what could five men do against the fifty aboard?

That was not the plan, Rumon said, with an icy determination Finian had never seen him show. He had been conferring with the ablest of the fishermen: one Colan, who had often been to Ireland and knew the christianized Norse settlements at Dublin, Cobh, and Limerick. This raid, said Colan, was obviously instigated by Vikings from the far Northern Seas who had persuaded some of their Norse-Irish kin to join them. They would undoubtedly return to Limerick for provisions and barter. There was a famous Icelandic merchant at Limerick, Rafn by name, who played both ends against the middle very cannily. For silver he would do anything. And he could certainly raise an Irish force from the surrounding countryside to overcome these Viking murderers.

"So — Brother Finian," Rumon had said in the same controlled way, "my plan to rescue Merewyn is not as foolish as you think."

Finian said no more. He saw many uncertainties in this expedition. He wondered if Rumon — notably averse to violence — realized what such a battle could mean if it did happen. Yet if the young man had divine guidance . . . ?

So he had shriven Rumon and celebrated Mass in the empty church and bidden him Godspeed.

And there went Rumon in the coracle, a proud diminishing figure in his velvet mantle, the favorable southeasterly wind blowing into the one lugsail while the fishermen paddled.

Finian returned wearily to Poldu and the ruined monastery. There were seven corpses to be decently buried, including Merewyn's two servants. But it might have been worse. Since Ketil had started his raid at Tre-Uther, the clamor had given warning in time for some escapes.

One by one they straggled in from hiding — four monks, ten of the villagers. They had no homes left; many of their precious pigs had been thrown on board — and other valuables such as wooden doors, fishing tackle, cheeses, casks of ale, and, of course, the ornaments from the monastery and church. But *they* were alive.

Poldu seemed in a stupor. He drank water without protest. He ate the new peas one of his monks put before him, and did nothing else but sleep. Yet Poldu was amongst the lucky ones. His wife had died some years ago, and his son was on a visit to Truro, and had escaped the whole disaster.

Finian took charge. He buried the dead in the churchyard. He assured the wailing bereaved ones that the Blessed Lord Jesus would take these slaughtered lambs directly to his bosom. He forebore to express any displeasure at the ridiculous state of the so-called monastery — at the long-forbidden type of ear-to-ear tonsure exhibited by the monks, at their dirty white robes, at the two young women who returned from hiding and obviously belonged — as wives or not — to the monks.

When all was in order he walked around the ruined village, and even as far as the blackened shell of Tre-Uther. He came back and roused the somnolent Poldu.

"Bestir yourself, Brother!" he said. "You're leaving here."

It was some time before he made the prior understand, though Finian spoke in slow measured Celtic. Then Poldu raised frightened objections.

"I've the authority," said Finian, "invested in me by Lord Dunstan, the Archbishop o' Canterbury, to whom — though you seem not to know it — you owe every obedience. Here's the parchment to show it."

Poldu gaped at the vellum document which he could not read. "THAT Viking ship'll probably never return," continued Finian. "But I understand this is the only dacent harbor within a hundred miles. Some other band of heathen may decide to try here, an' you've no means o' protection at all. I shall lead you, your monks, and the villagers who wish to, as far inland as Bodmin anyway. There they've a monastery with a prior who obeys the Benedictine rule, and you shall join them."

So Finian on his recaptured gelding and Poldu on Rumon's stallion headed a weeping procession away from devastated Padstow. Finian settled the little flock in Bodmin before he set off wearily on his own journey back to Glastonbury. He found that he missed Rumon, and worried about his safety — for which there was no recourse but prayers.

Rumon and his fishermen reached the mouth of the river Shannon on the sixth day after leaving Padstow. All had been favorable. The Irish sea was calm, and the coracle skimmed over the ripples with a following southeasterly breeze. They had been parched and starved until they touched the Irish coast past Cobh. There the fisherfolk welcomed them with food and drink and sped them on their way, having refused Rumon's offer to pay for their hospitality.

These Irish all hated the Norsemen who had gradually en-

trenched themselves into parts of their proud island, and they
wept with sympathy at the tale of the Padstow raid.

It was drizzling when the coracle entered the Shannon. Rumon, exhilarated by the hope that this time he would find Merewyn, scarcely felt the wet, and stood up to see where might be
a Viking ship.

Colan, the able skipper, reproved him. "Crouch down!" he
cried. "Put that sealskin over yer shoulders! If they saw ye in
that red mantle anyone'd know we wasn't an ordinary fishing
boat. We must reach port wi'out their noting us."

Rumon started, then humbly obeyed, hiding under the sealskin. He felt lightheaded. His belly gnawed. The cooked pil-
chards they had put aboard near Cobh were scanty fare. The
barley cakes were finished, and the cask of ale.

They continued quickly up the Shannon on a flood tide. They
reached the first wooden quay at Limerick before the turn, and
drew the coracle under the wharf. They emerged cautiously
onto the shingle, and looked up the harbor. There were a dozen
ships in port, some at anchor, some provisioning at a dock.
"There's three Norse ones," said Colan, after peering a moment.
"Yon —" he pointed, "will be from the Orkneys, I know her.
There's a Dane, I think, at the dock. T'other one, I can't tell, —
but they're all traders, not fighting ships, and none big enough
for all the men ye said was aboard." He looked at Rumon.

"She must be here," said Rumon on a long breath. "Up the
river perhaps?"

Colan shrugged. "Might be — best thing is to find Rafn, he'll
know."

They walked into Limerick — a town of muddy streets lined
with thatched cottages and dominated by a high gabled church.
Six days had cooled Colan's fever for revenge. He and his men
had consulted during the voyage and realized that they had not
waited long enough in Padstow to see who might have escaped
the slaughter. They had set out again in obedience to this black-
browed foreigner's command — and silver. There was that, to

be sure — Lord Rumon had promised them each a piece of silver. But if they did not find the particular Viking ship this young man was after? Would he pay? Aye, he would — Colan thought. They were five against one. And even I, alone, could best him. Colan looked contemptuously at the slender fine-boned man who had been seasick on the voyage though the sea was calm as milk, and who talked very little, though when he did, it was either about this woman he'd lost, or to say prayers. Neither topic befitted a man.

"Rafn's house," Colan grunted, pointing to a stone mansion which commanded both rivers — the Shannon and the Abbey. "And there's his wharf, and a trader beside it."

Rumon could see this for himself, and he also felt the unfriendly change in Colan. Rumon lifted his chin and eyed the Padstow fisherman sternly. "You will be paid," he said. "No matter what happens. I've given you my word, nor have ever broken a promise in my life. Wait here. I'll talk to Rafn alone."

Colan found himself bowing assent. His crew uncertainly copied him. They all muttered amongst themselves as Rumon banged his sword hilt on the Limerick merchant's door.

The door was opened at once by a tall fair-haired woman with bright gray eyes and an elaborate gold necklace. She stared a moment; murmured something and stood aside while motioning Rumon to come in. He entered the Hall where a stout middle-aged man was bent over a table transcribing figures by the light of a whale-oil lamp. The man put down his goose-quill pen, and studied Rumon. "What do you want?" he said in Irish.

Rumon started to reply in the same language, but Rafn gave a chuckle. "Is it perhaps that English would be better?" he asked. "I have all the tongues, even the Frankish, I need them in my business, which is that of being the best merchant in the whole Christian world. I see you're Christian." He stabbed the pen towards Rumon's crucifix.

"Yes, I prefer English," said Rumon. "I've heard that you're a famous trader. And that you know everything which happens in Limerick, and many other places too."

"Very true," said Rafn, examining the young man's crucifix — gold; the red velvet mantle, spotted but of good quality; the bulge under the linen shirt which probably indicated a money pouch. "Gudrun!" he called. His wife appeared from the shadow of a doorway where she had been listening. Rafn gave a rapid command, and the tall fair-haired woman reappeared with bread, roast lamb, and two silver mugs.

"Drink!" said Rafn. "Skoul! This is the best Frankish wine. Now you must say 'Skoul' to me before we do business."

"Skoul . . ." said Rumon, and sipped warily. But the wine was excellent. The best he had tasted since his days at King Edgar's Court. It restored his strength. He drank deep and ate a hunk of bread. "I am searching," he said, "for a Viking ship, striped sail with a raven on it, about fifty men aboard, and at least one captive. The chief is a big red-beard called Ketil."

"Ah . . ." said Rafn. His faded blue eyes narrowed as he re-inspected Rumon. "That would be the *Bylgja*. She put in here — Ketil had several little items of trade for me — mere trifles." Rafn glanced towards the great strongbox in the corner of his hall where Poldu's brooch and ring and the silver relics from St. Petroc's reposed. "The *Bylgja* sailed yestermorn," he added, leaning back in his chair and tapping his pudgy fingers.

"She's gone . . ." said Rumon after a moment. "She *can't* be gone yet. It *can't* be. Doux Jésu, WHERE has she gone?" He bowed his head and stared at the lush Turkey rug which covered the floor planks.

"To Iceland, of course," said Rafn brisky. "My own home, though naturally I regret its heathen state — good Christian that I am."

"Iceland," Rumon repeated. He had barely heard that there was such a place, somewhere in the far frozen North. "Ultima Thule — the end of the world, had not Pytheas said so, or was it Pliny?"

"May I —" inquired Rafn in a neutral tone, "ask why you are so interested and apparently upset by the destination of the *Bylgja?*"

"There was a woman on board — captured in Cornwall by those pirates." Rumon continued to stare at the rug.

"Ah-ha —" said the merchant. "Your woman?"

Rumon raised his hands and let them fall on his knees. "Yes," he said. "My woman." He looked up suddenly. "Could it be that she *escaped* here?" His somber eyes lit with hope.

Rafn beckoned his wife to replenish the mugs. "You ask many questions, sir," he said, "I think some —" His voice trailed off.

Rumon put his hand down his shirt and extracted a coin from the pouch. He handed the money silently over to Rafn, who tucked it in a recess of his mantle. "Ketil," he said pleasantly, "had two women aboard, but since one was a thrall — an Irish serf captured not far from here — I suppose it is the other one you want to know about. A red-haired handsome girl. She stayed here with my Gudrun while the ship was at dock. We treated her well, but *she* acted daft. Never spoke once. Not a word. I don't even know her name, but Ketil said she was his daughter. How then could she be YOUR woman?"

Rumon was silent. The futility of explanation overwhelmed him.

"She didn't try to escape," continued Rafn. "She lay like a log in the box bed, saying nothing, eating and drinking a bit when Gudrun made her. She didn't even weep, as many captives do. I've seen quite a few go through here," said Rafn, then checked himself. "To be sure, I deplore these heathen raids, but business has nothing to do with religion."

As Rumon still did not move, Rafn continued. "One of Ketil's crew, a brawny lad called Sigurd — I believe he's Ketil's foster son — he came twice a day to see the young woman. He even brought her a little gilded brooch he had picked up someplace. But she wouldn't speak to him either. I thought they had cut her tongue out, but Gudrun looked one night when the girl was asleep, and she still had her tongue."

"She never spoke," said Rumon. He bowed his head on his hands, feeling in his own fibers the shock and despair which Merewyn must have felt. The helplessness. She had seen her two servants murdered. She had fled to the church as a sanctuary. Here she had been nearly raped by Ketil. And then, worst of all perhaps, she had heard Poldu's warning. And she had known at last the falsehood on which her whole life had been based. Now she knows what I meant by my insults on the Tor, he thought, my brutal behavior, and she thinks I deserted her. She doesn't know that I love her and have followed her. My sinful pride has ruined her. He clapped his fist on his chest and whispered savagely, "Mea culpa."

Rafn stared, recognizing a phrase of self-blame from the Christian rites in which he joined when it seemed expedient.

"What is it exactly that you want?" he asked, eying the bulge of the money pouch. "I've told you all I can."

"I want to follow her, to find her." Rumon spoke in the same agonized whisper.

The merchant considered this, and shrugged. Young men — he thought. Yet long ago, had he not himself wanted Gudrun very badly? Enough to kill for her. It seemed very long ago, and other interests had naturally supervened. "So you want to follow the lady?" Rafn said "the lady" in a respectful voice, because though she might or might not be Ketil-Redbeard's daughter, it was obvious from the dress, speech, and demeanor of this young man that the whole affair had to do with the highborn. Rafn had experience of those — in Norway, Frisia, and even here amongst the Irish.

"I want to find her," Rumon repeated. He cut himself a slab of lamb and gulped it down. He finished his wine.

The merchant watched and made a decision. "It's not impossible, sir," he said. "Not impossible to find the lady — after a few days' sail, of course. Maybe a week. Ari Marson will set out tomorrow for Iceland. He's returning with some timber they've commissioned, mostly oak which of course they can't get there. Nor for that matter, many trees bigger than a shrub. There used to be pine, in my childhood, but I understand that's mostly been cut down."

"Where is Ari Marson?" Rumon interrupted. "I'll go with him."

Rafn inclined his head. "For a certain recompense, sir — and you may trust me to be fair — I'll arrange this matter for you. Tonight I offer you the box bed. And may Odin help you to a lucky voyage — though of course no good Christian would call on those false half-gods. I only jest."

Rumon was not listening. He was swamped by tiredness and relief. A few more days, and this time he would find Merewyn — in Ultima Thule, the faraway land on the edge of the world.

Rumon sailed from Limerick when the tide turned next morning. He had paid off his Padstow crew and was pleased by their cordial waves from Rafn's wharf as Ari Marson's ship glided down the Shannon. Rumon had slept dreamlessly for seven hours in the box bed, yet been aware that Merewyn's warm body had lain there so recently. He felt her thoughts near to him, and was certain that by now she knew that he was coming to her. Had not Finian said that there were ways of knowing things without ordinary means? And it was true. He sensed it. God would protect her, and she would be waiting for him.

Ari's trading ship was roomy, yet crowded from the load of timber aboard: the chickens which ran about wildly; and the pigs; and casks of ale. There was a brazier amidships for cooking. And the twenty-man crew slept where and how they could. But Rumon, who had paid well for his passage, was given a pallet in the quarter-decked bow, and the privacy of a wool blanket hanging around it. The ship's name was *Thorgerd* — for Ari's fat, sharp-tongued Icelandic wife. Not that Ari was sentimental about his wife. She was much older than he was.

But she had given him three sons, and some recognition was customary.

Ari was thirty-five — sturdy and well made, like his ship which had been built in Norway and was so limber that her oaken strakes could yield and weave through any buffeting. Ari's massive, yellow-fuzzed hand clutched the steering oar with certainty as his blue eyes squinted ahead down the river, or at the mast where his men had hauled up the great square sail. The sail had originally been painted in a neat red latticed pattern, but many a voyage had faded it to an orange blur. There were no embellishments on Ari's ship, no painted ravens, no carved dragon prow, no rows of gaudy round shields along the gunwhales — these features belonged to the Viking ships, the raiders who might plunder, murder, and burn as much as they liked for all Ari cared. He preferred a peaceable way of life, and was content with modest profit from his cargos.

There was a small wooden image of Thor and his hammer pegged inside the prow, because this too was customary, but Ari had never invoked it, nor often called on Aegir, God of the Sea, to quiet his nine turbulent daughters — the waves. Ari was a cautious skipper, and storms he had met he weathered without supernatural aid.

That this routine summer voyage between Ireland and Iceland was to be an extraordinary adventure, and change Ari's life forever, naturally never occurred to him.

They sailed comfortably out of the river Shannon. They rounded Loop Head into the Atlantic. Ari, with a casual squint at the sun, steered north by northwest. In two hours the sun turned a dirty red, and then disappeared behind dark scudding clouds. The wind and the waves came up fast. The wind blew directly from the north. The sail flapped violently, then swiveled as far around as the lines would let it. Despite Ari's struggle to keep on course, the ship veered south and wallowed in the troughs. They shipped water, the chickens squawked, the pigs squealed, and the crew began to bail with their leather buckets.

" 'Tis only a squall," shouted Ari to his second in command, an able young Icelander named Jorund. "We'll row 'till it's over."

"Can't, Master," shouted Jorund. "Couldn't get all the oars in without swamping us. Besides we need bailers."

Ari considered a moment. The row of oar holes beneath the gunwhales were each closed by small sliding panels, through which green water would pour if they were opened. The oars were mostly used anyway for coastal waters and fjords. In the ocean Ari depended on his sail, with which he could sometimes beat into the wind. Not this time. The wind from the north strengthened to a gale.

Ari grunted and bawled out orders to lower the sail while he clenched the tiller of the great steering oar. "Four oars to be put out on either side to act as a sea anchor," he shouted. "Fourteen men to bail; see that the cargo of timber doesn't shift, and lash down everything you can!" Then Ari tried to keep his ship steady across the mounting waves while they hurtled south, ever south.

Too bad, he thought, without much concern. It'll take us a day or so longer after this blows off. But there was food and ale enough aboard. Ari always saw to that.

By next morning the wind had hardly slackened, yet a rain like icy needles stung their faces. A rain from the north, mixed with sleet. Ari gave the tiller to Jorund while he went forward to rest for a while under the quarterdeck. Here he found Rumon, whom he had forgotten. "Bit of a blow outside," said Ari, seizing a hunk of bread and cheese. The old Norse was very like English and Rumon usually understood these Icelanders.

"We're being blown away from Iceland?" Rumon asked. He was pale and composed. He had been seasick in the night, but he was not now. He was thinking of Merewyn, wondering if her ship had been caught by the same storm.

"Oh, we'll get there," said Ari. "I'm a lucky man and I always bring my cargo in."

He looked aft towards Jorund at the steering oar and saw something beyond him in the ocean. A greenish-white crest bobbing in the waves. Iceberg, Ari thought, a calf. But I've *never* seen them so far south. The iceberg drifted out of sight, and the wind howled louder.

A tremendous following wave crested and then crashed over the stern, drenching Jorund, whose steering oar was wrenched from its socket while he clung to it desperately as long as he could. The whole ship was awash, the tethered pigs half drowned, and three chickens floated away in the sea, their squawks rapidly stilled.

"We will consider —" said Ari in a loud reassuring voice, "that the fowls are a sacrifice to Aegir, who will now be appeased."

His men nodded. The rowers held their oars as steady as possible, the others at once started bailing. There was a slight lull. The *Thorgerd* skimmed southward with the waves. Ari sloshed back to the stern and said to young Jorund whose face was glistening wet, "The steering oar's gone? Aye, I see it is. We'll fit in the other when we can. In the meantime there's nothing to do but go where Aegir's fierce daughters send us, until they tire of the sport."

"And where will they send us, Master?" said Jorund, who had made quite a reputation as a skald — or bard — during the long black winters at home in Iceland. It was thus that he had won his pretty wife, Katla, whom he loved.

> Where will the nine daughters waft us — over the
> wild widow-maker
> The white horses are galloping — would they waft
> us to Valhalla?

"*We* are not warriors," said Ari, who had scant use for poetry. "And I think only warriors are taken to Valhalla. Go forward and eat, Jorund." He scanned the sky. The freezing rain had dwindled, but the wind whistled faster around them. "You might rub a little ale on Thor," he said. "For Aegir seems not yet appeased, and my father always told me that Thor was more powerful than any god, even Odin."

The days and nights blurred for Rumon. There was a time in which the air grew warmer around them, times when the sun came out, and dried them, and seaweed floated past them. The wind dropped, and Ari raised the sail, but the blurred orange canvas slatted feebly, for there came a dead and oily calm, while great westbound swells rolled beneath the ship. She floated over them easily. Now all the men rowed, but they made little progress. They also fished and caught two dolphins which were devoured down to the bones. The new steering oar was fitted. Constantly Ari tried to steer north, navigating by the few days in which sun and stars came out. Later they killed the last pig and the remaining chickens — eating them raw, since there was no means of cooking. The brazier had been carried away by an assaulting wave.

One day the air grew colder again, the skies blackened and the northeast wind began to blow. Ari ordered that the useless sail be lowered. He looked up at the sky and ordered that the rowers cease. "It is fate," he said. "If we are doomed by the Norns to fall over the edge of the world, then we must go. For I don't know where we are."

Rumon, who had been taking his full share of the rowing to relieve one or another of the crew, looked down at his thin, blistered hands. One of the blisters was bleeding on the oar.

So, he thought. We don't know where we are, and I don't know where Merewyn is either. He still thought of Merewyn, though she had receded during these days of hour-to-hour survival. He had drunk pig blood as greedily as the rest of them. And when Ari Marson ordered the last keg of ale broached, he was as excited as they were. But it was the last keg.

"We have aboard —" continued Ari in his flat, emotionless

voice, "a foreigner. I know that he has done his best, but I feel
he is unlucky. I have always before had a lucky ship. This
foreigner is a Christian. That means he worships that helpless
god who was nailed on a tree, killed by his own race. Perhaps
it is because we carry this passenger that Thor and Aegir are
angry with us. I suggest we throw him overboard as a sacrifice."

Some of the crew murmured agreement, not all — for they
knew that Rumon had paid for his passage — and not Jorund
who was by nature sympathetic and had taken a liking to Rumon.

"Master —" said Jorund, looking squarely at Ari, "there may
be truth in what you say, but we are Icelanders and stick to
bargains. I propose that we give the foreigner's god a chance.
Let the foreigner pray aloud to his god, and give him a day
or so more to see whether there is any result."

Rumon understood most of both speeches, and his heart
thudded. I was nearly drowned once, he thought; is it to be
complete this time? And he realized that though he had said a
few prayers during this long ordeal, they had been perfunctory.
Nothing had seemed important except that constant physical
battle against the sea — and hunger. "The helpless god nailed
to a tree" seemed as shadowy to him, as it did to the Icelanders,
who were all looking at him expectantly.

"I'll try," he said. Then he stood.

He took off his golden crucifix, and held it up in his right
hand while he steadied himself on the gunwale with his left. He
began in a voice which faltered at first and startled the crew, for
he spoke in Latin, the first words which came to him. "Kyrie
eleison. Christe eleison . . . Quia tu es, Deus fortitudo mea:
quare me repulisti?" As he went on his voice gathered power and
became as compelling as ever Dunstan's was. It could be heard
above the wind. Nobody knew the strange language, but it
impressed Ari. There might be strong runes in such an incanta-

tion and there was dignity in the thin figure whose dark eyes gradually became fixed as he gazed on the golden cross he held up before them.

Rumon prayed for half an hour, when the wind grew wilder and a wave broke over the stern. They all sprang as usual to the bailing buckets and Ari remarked that the foreigner's god certainly wasn't helping yet. However, being a reasonable man, he would wait a day or two as Jorund had asked. Though even if they ever got a favorable wind, he did not see how they could reach Iceland without provisions. A day and night passed, while the northeaster kept blowing. Though this storm was not as violent as the one off the coast of Ireland, neither sail nor oars could beat against it.

By the following morning, Rumon was given black looks by the crew. Everyone was starving, and the ale — though rationed by Ari — was gone. "Throw him overboard," somebody muttered, and a growling chorus echoed it. Ari nodded and sighed. While he raised his hand in the gesture which would have finished Rumon, Jorund suddenly cried, "Wait! Look!" They looked, and overhead there were sea gulls mewing while they circled the ship.

"Ah . . ." said Ari, staring at the gulls. "Is it possible?" He then ordered the smallest and lightest of the crew to swarm up the mast. The youth came down, red with excitement. "There is land, Master," he stammered, pointing to the west. "Far off — I see trees."

Ari wrinkled his weatherbeaten forehead. "So? Then put up the sail and we will also *row* for land."

The crew ran to obey. "Land . . ." they shouted. "Land-ho!" and some of them stared at Rumon in a frightened way. For what land could be here? Was this foreigner a wizard? Had he made his god invent a phantasm?

In two hours they all knew that the land was real. They passed salt marshes and there were forests ahead of them. The sweet smell of white pine and wildflowers drifted out, since the sea wind ceased to blow. There was also a fjord, or possibly a river ahead. They pulled onward, while Ari, tasting the water at intervals, announced that it was getting less salty. So it *was* a river. The men cheered. Soon Ari said that he thought they might risk drinking, and a bucketful was dipped out and passed around.

Unused as they were to drinking water, all were grateful. It grew hot as the forested banks closed in, and the sun glared down. Food next, Ari thought, but what and how? This was a vast wilderness of a kind he had never seen. He looked with awe at the crowding trees, recognizing pine and birch, but there were many others. Amongst trees there must be wild beasts to eat, and to make valuable pelts for barter. If indeed the silent land was inhabited by anything — except birds. The sea gulls followed them, and in the forest he could see flashes of yellow and blue amongst the branches. The birds might be edible, if there were means of snaring them. At least we'll go ashore, thought Ari, and see what we find. He was about to give that order when Rumon, who had been standing in the bow, gave a startled shout and gestured.

Ari looked ahead; the rowers lifted their oars and turned. As they reached a bend they saw a patch of cleared earth near the water's edge. On it grew many tasseled green plants, and a profusion of golden fruit, almost as round and big as shields, running along vines. There were people working in the plot, prodding at the dirt beneath the green plants, gathering the golden fruit. The distant figures might be women, since they all had long hair and shifts.

Ari approached cautiously, and noted, drawn up on the bank, a slender birch-bark craft of a shape new to him.

"Ho!" he shouted. "Vinur! Vinur!" — which meant friend.

The work party turned, dropping their implements and fruit. From the ship you could see them gaping, and their hesitancy.

They moved close together. Ari and his crew waved, making open-handed signs of peace. At length one figure came down the bank as the ship drew nearer.

It was an elderly man; hair shaven back behind the ears, as had been Poldu's, and grizzled strands hanging below his shoulders. On his long buckskin shift a large black Celtic cross had been embroidered with porcupine quills. He made the sign of the cross in the air, then watched in silence as Ari's crew expertly moored the ship, winding one line around a large tree and letting down the anchor.

By the three Saintes Maries, Rumon thought, staring at the man, can this be a Christian? And he looks white, not like the others. At least his little eyes seemed light, and his skin far paler than his three co-laborers, who *were* women. You could see their sagging breasts outlined. They all had brown faces painted with red stripes on the cheeks.

Ari let loose a flood of Norse, explaining that they needed food. That they had no idea where they were. That they implored help, which would be paid for.

The man continued to stare at them and shrugged.

Rumon leaned over the bow. "Christe eleison —" he called tentatively, and held up his crucifix.

The man started, and touched the black cross on his shift. "Per omnia saecula saeculorum," he said in a deep guttural tone.

Then Rumon was sure. Finian's stories came back to him. Of the Irish monks who had fled ever and again before the Vikings to different unknown lands beyond the seas.

"Culdee?" called Rumon.

The man nodded, while eying Rumon narrowly. He again made the sign of the cross in the air. Rumon did the same.

Ari, Jorund, and the crew watched this interchange with awe. For it did seem that the foreigner's god had accomplished something. They all waited for Rumon to speak.

"Where are we?" he asked in Celtic.

The man knit his brows; the accent was strange to him, but

as Rumon repeated, he caught the meaning. "Great Ireland," he said waving his arms in a wide circle, "and country of the Merrimacs." He pointed to the Indian women who were whispering in the field.

"Culdees live here too?" asked Rumon.

The man nodded, pointing to the north. "We live in the old caves," he said. "From whence comes this big ship?" He indicated the *Thorgerd*.

"Blown across the seas many days — weeks — " answered Rumon, suddenly wondering how long they had been on the endless voyage. Weeks, certainly. How many?

"Food!" Ari interrupted, banging his stomach and pointing to his mouth. "Tell him we must have food." And he jumped ashore.

The old man looked at the ravenous crew who were all coming ashore, and made a wary gesture of assent. "There is plenty of food in this land," he said. "Always plenty. Follow."

He led them around the planted patches and up a hill into the forest where they presently came upon an Indian village where a fire was blazing under a spitted deer. The Indian women tagged along after, tittering behind their fingers at these big light-haired men who stumbled up the trail as though they had never been on land.

Other women and several children emerged shyly from the long bark-covered tribal house as *Thorgerd's* shipload approached. One of the women squeaked and ducked into the shelter. The children stood solemnly watching, their shiny jet eyes round with wonder. The Culdee said something in their language, and two young boys went off running into the forest. The women obeyed the other command. They cut hunks from the roast meat and gave them to the pale-face newcomers, who gulped avidly. Another woman brought a stack of flat corn cakes which had been baked on hot stones. Still others brought pottery vessels full of water.

The Culdee said yet something else, and the women offered to

Rumon the deer's liver tendered with great ceremony. They knelt before him as they held pieces of the delicacy out on long wooden spits.

Ari, at first too hungry to care, then noticed this special attention with annoyance. "It's true," he said to Rumon, "that your god seems to have saved us so far, but you might tell that old man that *I* am master of the ship."

"As you like," said Rumon, and complied.

The Culdee gave Ari a long hard stare. "Norsemen?" he asked Rumon, who nodded. "Heathen?" Rumon shrugged assent.

"They captured you?" said the old man.

Rumon said no, that these were not Viking raiders.

"Pah!" said the Culdee and spat in the direction of Ari. "They're all the same. 'Tis from the like of them our grandfathers fled. We were men of peace, and in peace we have lived here, undisturbed. But the memory of our persecutions has been handed down. And Papa Padraic will know how to handle this."

There was definite menace in the Culdee's speech, and no mistaking the tone.

Ari looked up from his meat and frowned. What danger could there be, from an old man and a lot of women? Skraelings, he thought, savages. He had never seen any like these, though the Norsemen called all primitive people "skraelings," and he had seen some on a voyage to Lapland. He looked around at his crew. Their sole weapons consisted of their cutting knives. Though there were a couple of spears and a harpoon aboard. Surely enough to terrorize this bunch, if need be. Yet Ari had no wish to fight. He wanted to repair his ship; provision it; and set sail again for Iceland, his cargo enriched by pelts. And being a reasonable man, he thought, as he always had, of barter. Yet what was there on the ship which would attract this odd lot of folk? Not the carefully cherished timber. Money then. He had a pouch of silver which included Rumon's fare.

"We can pay, you know," said Ari. "Tell the old man that," he commanded Rumon. "Silver. We wish to pay for his hospitality. To stay here some days, — or whenever the wind is with us — to put food and water on board. And we will give him money in return."

Rumon, whom a full stomach was making sleepy, yawned and translated.

The old Culdee listened. He looked with contempt at Ari. "What is money? What use to us? I've never seen any, though my grandfather used to speak of it as the Devil's lure. You are heathen, and shall be dealt with by Papa Padraic."

"He doesn't know what money is," said Rumon to Ari, who frowned again, then started as his eye was caught by a girl skraeling. She walked slowly out of the long bark house and gazed at *Thorgerd's* crew in amazement. She wore a shell-embroidered buckskin apron around her middle, but her breasts were bare. They were full, uptilted; her small nipples were like wild strawberries. Her skin had the sheen of copper. Her neck was a long, graceful column, her small head delicately poised on top. Her glossy black plaits hung to her small waist so slender that a man's big hands could encircle it. She had no paint on her cheeks, only a round red mark on her forehead which seemed to enhance her luminous dark eyes — very large, like a doe's. There was a hush. They all looked at the girl. The crew stopped eating. The old Culdee stepped forward and made a slight bow. He spoke in rapid Algonquin, obviously explaining this invasion.

The girl — she might have been sixteen — held herself with dignity while she gazed into the faces of the light-haired men. Some of them simpered and others made smacking noises. Her liquid eyes did not rest long on Rumon, they returned to Ari Marson. Ari flushed and felt tingles up his back, such as he had never felt before. Of its own accord, his great calloused hand went out to her. She did not touch it, but she nodded gravely.

"Who is this girl?" Rumon said to the Culdee.

"Norumbega, daughter to Chief Hoksic who is hunting —

but not for long." The old man spoke with sardonic relish. He glanced behind him at the forest. He cocked his head as though listening.

There's danger here, thought Rumon, of what kind he did not know. But like the crew who lolled on the grassy earth, he was stuffed, logy, and disinclined for action. The everlasting motion of the ship still rocked in his head.

In a moment Jorund came up to Rumon and spoke behind his hand. "I don't like it," he said. "Something's brewing. I've spoken to Ari, but he is bemused. He keeps gaping at that naked girl. We should get back to the ship. I've already sent young Olaf to guard her. Your god has put an enchantment on most of us."

"Perhaps this is Avalon — the Island of the Blessed," said Rumon dreamily. "I've always heard of it, yearned to reach it, though I never thought it would be like this."

"I don't know *what* this place is," said Jorund tartly, inspired by none of the poetic strain which had made him a skald, "but I see a great many skraelings closing in on us." His intelligent young face tightened.

It was true. From the fringe of great trees surrounding the village, there were scores of red-painted men stepping towards them. They each had bows and arrows ready notched, except two who were twirling dried stag bladders suspended from sticks and filled with something which made a fearsome rattle.

The crew stared around blankly. Ari kept his gaze on Norumbega who had seated herself on a tree stump where she looked regal.

"Do they mean to kill us?" cried Rumon to the Culdee.

"That depends —" said the old man. "Not *you*. You're a Christian. But —" His grimy veined hand gestured towards the north. Rumon saw a strange procession filing through the forest. They were light-skinned men, about a dozen of them. They wore long, bleached robes, all had Celtic crosses made of quills on their chests. They were led by a bearded oldster. He carried a banner with quill embroidery on it. He had an iron knife of an antique pattern in his other hand. He was tonsured across from ear to ear.

"Papa Padraic —" said the first Culdee in a tone of reverence, and made a deprecatory gesture while explaining to his superior that all these men were Viking heathen, but he had not thought it right to refuse the hospitality they asked for. Moreover, there was a Christian aboard the vessel. One who knew the Mass, and had a gold crucifix.

Father Padraic listened. He was ancient, nothing surprised him anymore; yet his wits were still keen, and he remembered his father's tales of the old world — the brutality and treachery of the pagan Norse. "So," he said. "Here they are. No doubt St. Padraic sent them. They shall all be baptized — forcibly if need be." He turned and spoke in Algonquin to the ring of Indian warriors, whose ranks were being gradually increased as others silently came from the forest.

Chief Hoksic went forward to join the Culdees. He was unmistakably the chief since he had eagle feathers in his topknot, and five necklaces of purple wampum, and his breechclout had been dyed red and yellow. Moreover, he gestured to Norumbega who at once brought a feather mantle from the longhouse. He donned the mantle.

Rumon watched, slightly dazed, particularly when Father Padraic and the chief each crossed themselves, and grunted, as though a pact had been agreed on.

Ari watched Norumbega.

Jorund and the rest of the crew watched the circle of skraelings, their flint-tipped arrows notched and ready in the drawn bows.

"Go on! March!" commanded Father Padraic to the Icelanders. His gesture made the words clear. The crew, already on their feet, muttered uneasily and looked to Ari for guidance. He withrew his gaze from the beautiful brown girl, and said to Rumon, "What is it they want?"

"To make Christians of you," answered Rumon, seized with a hysterical desire to laugh. "That or death, I think."

Ari was puzzled, but he certainly understood the words "Christian" and "death."

He looked at the threatening circle — must be fifty of them now. He looked at the girl who gave him a small beseeching smile, while pointing up the hill behind her.

Ari shrugged and spoke to his men. "We had better do as they wish. We're not warriors, and I see no other plan."

Thus it was that Ari, Jorund, and eighteen of *Thorgerd*'s crew were herded some miles north to a place of upright stones and caves and tiny beehive huts. In the midst of these was a small Y-shaped stone chapel, near a well half filled with shiny crystals and a wooden cross erected by its brink.

In this well, amongst the standing stones and fallen stones, all of *Thorgerd*'s crew were docilely made into Christians by Father Padraic, who poured a jarful of water over each Icelander while intoning the Latin words with gusto.

Rumon, the Culdees, and many Indians watched. The latter group had all submitted to this rite, mostly as babies, and the chief had decided that whatever all the water-pouring was, it made good magic for the tribe; nor did Manitou, the great Algonquin god, seem to object. Food was plentiful; no disaster had assailed the Merrimacs during the many years since these bearded men with crosses had come to live near them. Besides, Hoksic respected the Culdees, for they were not afraid of this place of stones, where one could smell ancient blood, and which his tribe always avoided by night.

After the baptism, Father Padraic said Mass in the tiny Y-chapel which could not begin to hold them all, so the others stood or knelt outside near a large grooved stone while a Culdee lay inside the chapel on a stone bench and repeated each phrase through a hole which made his voice resound like a bull's in the quiet air.

It was part of the magic; so were the little pieces of corncake passed to everyone after Father Padraic had tinkled a bell made of a thin pottery jar hit by the iron knife.

Rumon accepted the "Host" reverently, but while it was still on his tongue, the peculiarity of the situation overcame him and he choked, trying to strangle another surge of wild laughter. Avalon! he thought. These dirty old Culdees, these savages, and now a new-made bunch of Icelandic Christians who hadn't the vaguest idea what Christianity meant. And the whole place stank — there were piles of ordure outside many caves. Some of the rock formations looked like heathen dolmens from the Druid days — such as he had seen in Brittany, and on the trip to Cornwall. And *that*, he thought, looking at the man-sized stone shaped like a gravy platter with a runnel around the edge, was certainly used once for human sacrifice — even if it wasn't any more. How soon could they get away? Surely now that *Thorgerd*'s crew had been baptized, these extraordinary natives would be helpful.

He soon found out how wrong he was.

After the Mass was over, everyone went to a tree-shaded Council Ring outside the weird cluster of higgledy-piggledy rocks. Chief Hoksic seated himself on a long maple slab with Father Padraic beside him. And they conferred.

Norumbega, her doe eyes glistening, went and stood near Ari Marson who looked, Rumon thought, as besotted and pleased as ever a man could.

Did I look like that when Alfrida wanted me? Rumon thought with repugnance. It seemed so long ago. It had happened to a different man. And now there was Merewyn. Where was Merewyn? And where am I? Amongst the Merrimacs and Culdees in an unknown wilderness across the sea.

He no longer wished to laugh.

Father Padraic addressed his monks and Rumon. There was an hour of laborious, hesitant translations before Rumon really knew what the chief and the priest had decreed.

They were delighted with the huge ship which had been sent

them, by God — called either Manitou or Jesus, it didn't matter. Hoksic had already had her dismasted — nobody understood the sail anyway. But they could row. And such a ship would be the wonder of the Merrimac country. Would do them all great honor. The sailor, Olaf — who had been left on guard by Ari — had defended the ship and had been brained by a tomahawk. Father Padraic regretted this violence but the man was after all only a heathen, not having been summoned to the baptism. Rumon — here Father Padraic bowed slightly towards him — and *Thorgerd's* crew might found a community not far away; they would be given food until they learned how to get it for themselves. They would also be given Indian women to sleep with and work for them. There were plenty of women in the tribe. All would be agreeable. Hoksic, from past experience and that of his father, had learned that men of different races could live together pleasantly. Moreover, the tribe would be strengthened by the birth of many babies.

Here Norumbega said something shyly to Hoksic, who raised and lowered his hand, then made a perfunctory sign of the cross.

"My daughter wishes THAT man," he said, pointing to Ari, "and I will give her to him, since he is the chief of these strangers."

Norumbega moved closer to Ari, who put his arm around her, and chuckled joyfully when she nestled against him.

Rumon gasped. He sprang towards Ari, shouting, "You dolt, you fool! You're mad! Don't you understand what they're doing? They've got your ship, and they mean to keep it. They want us to stay here forever — make babies for their tribe. What about your wife, your home, your sons, your ship? How can you stand there like a grinning idiot?"

Ari waved him away tolerantly. "It's good here," he said. "I'm a lucky man. And now I bow to *your* god, since he brought us here."

The watchful circle, seeing the way things were going, made

approving noises and looked with amusement at Rumon, whose anger drained out leaving despair.

He wandered away from the Council Ring towards the acres of stones. Nobody stopped him. Nor did they stop Jorund who followed. When Rumon got to the avenue of what looked like menhirs, Jorund came up to him. The young Icelander was flushed, his blue eyes wary. "Careful —" he said. "We must bide our time. I've no more wish to stay here than you. Nor has most of the crew. But we must plan and wait. Do you agree?"

Rumon bowed his head. "How long?" he said in a whisper. "Blessed Lord — how long must we stay here?"

Jorund shrugged. "That depends upon Thor, Odin, or this new god you believe in. Take one of the women skraelings to your bed —" Rumon made a gesture of disgust. "Well, nor do I want to, for I love my Katla, yet to sleep with those —" he gestured towards the Indian village, "is nothing, and will please the skraelings, and the old men with crosses. They'll be off guard."

"I don't want any woman but Merewyn," said Rumon. He watched a mosquito land on his arm and bite; when he swatted it he looked down at the drop of blood.

"I *think* there will be no bloodshed," said Jorund with a mixture of understanding and sarcasm. "I do not like it myself, but —" The young man threw back his head, and began to chant in his "skald" voice a poem to which he was suddenly inspired:

> Sometimes *should* spill . . . the scarlet safeguard.
> We are tormented thralls . . . In this terrain of trolls.
> Our leader lost in lechery . . . She-skraeling has seduced.
> We must find freedom . . . Across Aegir's whale-way.

"Yes," said Rumon. "It's a good poem, Jorund."

chapter ten

On a May afternoon in the year 984, Merewyn sat on a bench outside her homestead at Langarfoss, near the Borgarfjord in western Iceland. She was enjoying the bursts of brilliant sunlight as she pulled wool from a mass beside her and expertly twirled long threads on a spindle. Her little boy, Orm, crooned to himself as he played some game of digging holes amongst the new scanty grass.

Orm was fifteen months old, yet already manly, she thought, and so like his father — Sigurd. Orm's curls were golden, he had great blue, serious eyes. She loved him dearly, as she had come — in time — to love Sigurd. And her home. Though at first, this country of ice, snow, boiling waters, and never a real tree had frightened her.

For a while everything had frightened her. She had been nearly mad in those early days. Afraid to speak, almost afraid to move. Frozen, she was then, like the glacier behind to the west on Snaefellsnes. And always wondering what they would do to her. She had hated Ketil-Redbeard, her father, never allowing herself to admit that he *was* her father. But she knew it now, and he had been kind to her; not even forcing her into immediate marriage with Sigurd who asked for her. They had all been patient with her daft state which she could barely remember.

She looked up as a flock of purple snipe flew from the south over her head. That was good luck if they passed from the south, and they were soon followed by four singing swans — MORE good luck! She had learned these things from Sigurd's widowed mother, Asgerd, who had despised Merewyn until the birth of little Orm, when her midwifery had saved the baby. Asgerd had quarreled with Sigurd, furious that he should marry a foreign captive, and Ketil's bastard to boot. Matters improved when Ketil adopted Merewyn as his daughter before the local assembly, or Thing, gave her a dowry and proclaimed her his heir, for he had no other living children. Ketil's wife and two sons had all died together of a spotted lung-rot, while he was out a-viking, some years ago. This sorrowful happening, as Merewyn now knew, had increased his fondness for her. Also she much resembled Ketil's long-dead mother. He often remarked on it.

Merewyn twirled her spindle, and her gaze went as usual towards the beauty of the Hafnarfell Mountains directly in front of her. They loomed up across Borgarfjord, and were all snow-capped, with white snow threads trickling down them like a fringe. Vaguely amused for a moment, she remembered how exciting she had thought the little Mendips in England. But she seldom lingered on thoughts of England, where she had suffered so much.

The Hafnarfells were inhabited only by trolls, and the ptarmigan which brave lads sometimes went there to snare. One of the peaks was triangular like a farmhouse gable. She liked to watch it turn rose-violet under the slanting rays of the late-night sun. So did the river Langa turn pink as it meandered down below the mountains to join the bay called Borgarfjord.

Smiling, she watched Orm make another hole and pack it carefully with stunted bits of grass. The singing swans had gone, but there were many other comfortable noises in the clear sharp air. A bird said "Tiki, tiki" in a pert way; the lambs bleated as they frolicked on the new pasturage, while the shaggy little horses in the shed snickered occasionally.

OUR sheep, OUR horses, she thought, and the sow about to farrow, and the cow whose milk Orm drank, since her own milk was lessening.

Sigurd has done quite well, she thought tenderly, as a bondi — a farmer. He leased this homestead from Thorstein Egilson, the great chief of Borg. Sigurd was even now in Borg, unless he had had to sail his fishing boat as far as Reykjavik to find the best price for their fleeces. Surely he was happy. He had soon consented to her pleas that he go no more a-viking. Her father had also, but not willingly. Ketil had said with gloom that he was getting a bit old for fighting and raiding and that skilled crews were hard to find. Moreover, he had suffered bad dreams which might be a portent. In the dreams all the foreigners he had killed stood on high rocks jabbering and throwing blood clots at him. One must not disregard dreams.

On the other hand, said Ketil, he was not pleased to be sitting home all summer, carving on bits of wood, or counting sheep. That he did not know what the Norns had yet in store for him, but he hoped it was more interesting than now.

Ketil lived with Sigurd and Merewyn in the homestead. And as she thought about him he wandered outside towards her.

Ketil was over fifty now, a straight-backed powerful man. There were streaks of gray in his hair and beard; the old cheek scar had pulled his right lower eyelid down a bit, and a leg wound made him limp at times; but otherwise he had few signs of age.

He said "Dottir" politely to Merewyn, then picked up his grandson, whom he bounced up and down quite roughly, but they both enjoyed it. Orm squealed with excitement.

"I wonder has Sigurd got a good price for the fleeces," said Ketil, dandling the child. "But it's getting harder. Too hard. Winter of iron we had this year. The miserable sheep can scarce

yet find anything to browse. And there'll be snow again soon,"
he added peevishly. "Baula is frowning."

Merewyn glanced towards Baula, a conical mountain to the
north now half hidden by misty clouds. She sighed patiently,
and twirled her spindle. "Father —" she said. "I was sitting here
in the sun, thinking how content we all are, that soon perhaps
Sigurd may *buy* this homestead for us, and that next month we
will travel to the Althing. It'll be pleasant to see so many people
from all over Iceland. They say it's very gay with music and
dancing and the skalds making a special poem at the door to
each booth."

Ketil grunted and put Orm down. He looked at Merewyn
with tolerant affection. "Women," he said. "They think of
gossip, gaiety, handsome young skalds. We men have graver
matters on our minds at the Althing. But you're a good wench,
and have earned a little change."

He remembered how unhappy she had been during her first
months here. And that because of her pregnancy and then last
year Orm's birth she had never been included in the annual
journey to Thingvellir where the Icelanders met in Council and
decided matters relating to the country. It was a time for the
Law-speaker to assert his mind, though the humblest bondi, or
yeoman, could speak up if he chose. It was also a time for family
outings, for meeting folk from Reykjavik, from the northern
fjords, the eastern, the southern, and even the little Vestmann
Islands.

"You've become a true Icelander, dottir," he said. He never
called her "Merewyn." It seemed to him outlandish, and a
reminder of an unconsidered moment of which he was not
ashamed, precisely. But there was a faint discomfort about the
circumstances which had given her birth, and a stronger one
from that moment in St. Petroc's churchyard when he had
wanted to rape her. Whole thing best forgotten. She was his
daughter and publicly recognized. She was happily married to
a good man. She had a fine son. And that was that.

Ketil picked up a pine slab which leaned in readiness against the turf wall, and continued the carving of interlaced vines which he had started on some days ago. The slab when finished would back the High Seat in the Hall which he shared with Sigurd. It would have runes on it to enhance its meaningful beauty. It would be finer than the elaborate doorposts brought from Norway, as fine as anything Thorstein Egilson owned, thought Ketil and made a "Tcha!" sound through his teeth.

He did not like Thorstein, from whom Sigurd leased this homestead. Thorstein was chief of all the Borg district. He officiated as "godi" or priest in the Temple to Thor he had near his house. He was called Thorstein the White because his hair was so flaxen, and he was generally thought to be handsome, though no equal in distinction to his famous father, Egil Skallagrimson. Ketil considered Thorstein a high-stomached and mincing fellow, like his cold-eyed wife, Jofrid.

Thorstein had never been a-viking. What did he know of real danger, of the sea's thrill, of the berserker excitement of raids! All Thorstein could do was squabble with his neighbors, and assert his authority. And how did Thorstein get all this authority and lands? Entirely because his old father Egil had moved south and given them over.

Ketil made an angry sound and threw down the half-carved slab. "Dottir," he said, "I'm going to walk to the naust — see how my ship is."

Merewyn smiled, and said, "No doubt, since you do almost every day." As he started off down the road towards Borg, she realized again how discontented her father was especially when May came around, the time he used to go off raiding. The "nausts" were literally nests, or shedded cradles, where ships were kept safe for the winter. But Ketil's great longship — the dragon ship which had carried her to Iceland — had not been out for three years. It lay idle.

Sigurd on his short coastal trips used a small fishing boat with a clumsy woolen sail. If, she thought, Father would only sell his great ship! — Thorstein had even asked him to — then we could buy our homestead. No longer be tenants. She sighed. Ketil would not sell. He would rather let the *Bylgja* rot there in the naust, than have her broken up for timber as Thorstein certainly would do.

The sky changed, as it constantly did. Vivid silver-rimmed clouds scudded closer together, patches of blue between grew fainter and Baula, which could be at times, a golden pyramid, was now cloaked in gray. She listened a moment for the sound of Langarfoss — the cataract up the river, and could plainly hear its purring roar as the north wind began to blow.

Merewyn put down her spindle and gathered up Orm. "Come, little heart," she said to the baby. "It grows cold, and is time for something to warm you."

She carried Orm into the homestead, her housewife's keys jingling from her girdle. Keys to the storerooms, and lofts, and the special one for the bed-closet where she and Sigurd slept in privacy. She felt a glow, thinking of all the nights in the box bed with Sigurd. The strength of his arms around her, the feel of his golden beard on her mouth, on her breasts. The feel of that other thing — the pleasure maker, the life-giver — on her thighs — and later, when she and he were one — the power and excitement and the bliss, up to the moment when he went limp against her, and lay quiet, his big head on her shoulder, sleeping so soon, but contented, she knew, while she murmured the love words he had taught her — "Elsknan min, elsknan min," which in English meant "my beloved." Ah, would he but come back this night, she thought, and was immediately brought to the present by the untidy state of the Hall and the exasperated discovery that the central fire was nearly out and there was nothing cooking in the cauldron.

Most family activities took place in the "stofa" or Hall, which had a long central hearth, and was raftered and lined with wood, though the outer walls were of turf. There was a smoke hole in the ceiling, and four square windows gave sufficient light in summer, and kept out the winds, for they were filled with hardened, almost transparent membrane made from the afterbirth of cows. Along the walls ran benches and trestle tables. In the center nearest the hearth was the dual High Seat. Above that hung Ketil's great sword, which he called "Bloodletter" and had inherited from his grandfather, as he also had inherited the posts which guarded the door and were carved with vines, swastikas, and little figures representing the gods. The doorposts and the sword had been brought from Norway. Ketil's and Sigurd's battle-axes also hung on the wall, but nobody except Ketil ever looked at them. And when he did he sighed heavily.

Merewyn was proud of her Hall, which was unusually large since the homestead had been built for one of the mighty Egilson family. Now she saw only the clutter of unwashed wooden plates and the dying state of the fire. She looked around for Brigid, the thrall they had brought with them from Ireland, and found the young woman crouched on a stool, idly flicking maggots off a hunk of putrescent lamb.

"Brigid!" cried Merewyn, and added in Celtic, "That meat stinks. It was not well smoked. I *told* you to give it to the pig! And why are you not preparing our meal?"

Brigid looked around. Her dull, flat face became as lively as it ever did. She had scarcely learned a word of Norse, and was thankful that her mistress's speech was always intelligible.

"I didn't think," said Brigid. "I've a bellyache."

Merewyn put Orm down on the hearth, safely away from the embers. She looked at her handmaiden, who was dressed in the rough gray vadmal all slaves wore. Beneath the stupid face, the thick neck, the pendulous breasts, there was a swelling which she had not noticed before.

"You're with child?" said Merewyn. "Or have you the bloat?"

"I dunno," said Brigid after a moment, and flicked off another maggot. Her stringy black hair fell forward on her shoulders, and she grabbed her middle with both hands. She moaned.

"You *must* know," said Merewyn sharply, "if you have lain in the grass with some man, or —" She added, remembering that if this was pregnancy, it must have happened during winter, "Have you lain in the straw?"

"Och — aye, mistress," said Brigid, astonished by the question. "Often wi' all of 'em — Cormac, Einer, Grim, and that thrall — can't say his name — one of Thorstein Egilson's shepherds."

"Blessed St. Mary!" cried Merewyn. All their menservants plus one of Thorstein's. And she felt shame for having been so caught up in her own happiness that she had not better regulated her household. She had a sudden memory of her Aunt Merwinna, and the strict, vigilant rule she kept over many women. While here at Langarfoss homestead in Iceland, there was but one stupid woman for her to rule.

Brigid, seeing her mistress frown, gave another moan, while a glint appeared in her eyes. "You was a thrall yourself, mistress —" she said. "You was captured like I was. But you got luck. You got wed to a bondi. I've a bellyache," she added.

Merewyn's annoyance was silenced by justice. It was true that she had also been a thrall, and had been lucky thereafter. Cormac! she thought — we could handfast her to Cormac, who was also an Irish captive. No doubt Brigid would prefer him picked as legal father to her child.

In the meantime, though Merewyn had scant knowledge of midwifery, something must be done. Brigid's moans seemed genuine.

"How many months," she asked, "since you've had your courses?"

Brigid looked up dumbly. This feat of memory was beyond her. "I dunno," she said. "Och, aye — mebbe 'twas at Yuletide, for I had a bloodstain on m' kirtle before the feast."

Probably five months gone then, Merewyn thought, feeling helpless. "Well," she said, "you must lie down. I'm sure of *that*. Into the straw with you!"

She helped Brigid up the ladder which led to the loft above

the loom room where the woman slept, and she took Orm with her since he must at this age be kept an eye on.

Brigid subsided at once, her moans lessened. She went to sleep.

Merewyn returned to the Hall, poked up the fire, filled the cauldron with good smoked lamb and water, then sat down to nurse Orm. While he tugged at her breasts, she had anxious thoughts, and she said a prayer for Brigid, the first prayer she had said in ages. She had not lost her faith exactly; it was there underneath, but it was hard to remember private observances when there was no church to go to, and both Sigurd and Ketil thought Christianity negligible, fit only for silly women — not worth talking about.

But she was concerned for Brigid. She knew that a baby born before its time meant danger, and she wished very much that there were someone to send for Asgerd, her mother-in-law, who lived ten miles away on the White River with her sister.

She went up to look at Brigid, who was sweating and groaning now, though still half asleep, and there was blood on the straw. "Holy Blessed Virgin," Merewyn whispered. "From thy great mercy, help this poor woman. Or tell me, Lady, how to help her."

When she came down again, Ketil was back, and cross at first because the lamb was not ready. She explained, and he shrugged.

"If the babe comes living, it must be exposed, of course, for it will be no good to us. On the other hand, it'd be a pity to lose even so stupid a thrall as I have given you."

Brigid had been part of Merewyn's dowry from her father.

"Exposed," repeated Merewyn faintly. This custom of leaving unwanted babies on a hillside until nature dispatched them was one she had heard of with a trembling revulsion.

"However," said Ketil, munching on a slab of dried codfish, "Asgerd's skill might save the mother, and I shall take two horses and fetch her."

"Thank you, Father," said Merewyn gravely.

Ketil returned with Asgerd when the May night sun had lowered behind the Hafnarfell mountains, but there was still light. By this time Merewyn was frantic. She had locked Orm into the bed-closet; told him to behave himself and go to sleep. She had raced up and down to the loft, bringing their precious mead for Brigid to drink, bringing hot cloths to put on the convulsed belly, turning under the fouled bedstraw.

She was so much relieved to see her mother-in-law that she kissed her on the cheek. Asgerd looked amused. "Well, well —" she said. "What a to-do about a lewd thrall! You should have always locked her bed loft every night and kept the key. However, I suppose I must see how matters are going." She calmly ate some boiled smoked lamb, which was now cooked, drank mead, and hoisted herself up to the loft, grunting a bit, for she was portly.

Merewyn followed with a whale-oil lamp, and watched as her mother-in-law examined Brigid first on the belly and then inside.

Soon Brigid gave a screech, followed by a long sigh.

"Hold the light closer," said Asgerd to Merewyn. "Ah, there it is, and you'll not have to expose it for it's already dead. Only a girl, anyway. Now I shall try to save your thrall. She has lost much blood."

"She might die?" Merewyn whispered. When Asgerd nodded, Merewyn tried desperately to think of Christian prayers for the dying. Those that the priest and Bishop Ethelwold had used for Merwinna. She made the sign of the cross and did her best. Brigid seemed not to listen. Certainly Asgerd did not. She watched her patient carefully, and when the tiny afterbirth slithered out, she grabbed for Brigid's now flaccid belly, and squeezed hard on the womb beneath the flesh.

An hour passed. Asgerd gave Merewyn various orders — a stool to raise the woman's hips — hot water to cleanse her — more mead to strengthen her. Get rid of that unfinished infant. Bury it in the midden pile. All those orders Merewyn obeyed, and said a prayer for the scarce-formed little creature she buried.

It would go into limbo, had it been a Christian, wouldn't it? Yet it had never breathed, nor been baptized. Where then would it go? She did not know, but when Asgerd finally came down into the Hall, saying "I think she'll do now, but that woman is not rightly made to bear children, and I think her —" she darted a cold look at Ketil, who was sipping from his drinking horn and waiting to be fed, "a very poor thrall to be the chief part of a dowry."

Whereupon Merewyn burst into tears.

Both Ketil and Asgerd stared at her. "Thunders of Thor!" cried Ketil waving his knife with a hunk of smoked lamb on it. "What ails *you*, dottir? The wench is saved, and though I think Asgerd's remark discourteous, we must remember that she has put herself out considerably to be of help — and we thank her."

"I know," said Merewyn, wiping her eyes on her cloak. " 'Tis not that. At least . . ." She trailed off, unable to explain how the many differences between this home and England had suddenly overwhelmed her. And that if Brigid had died — she knew no sure means of easing, either physically or spiritually, the passing of the poor thing. "I wish Sigurd was here," she said very low.

Asgerd gave a reluctant chuckle, and winked at Ketil. The two were for once united in a common thought. Unreason; tears; longings for a husband who was only on a few days' trip; young wives acted this way when they were breeding. At least daft, half-foreign and base-born wives might, thought Asgerd with sudden anger, which she did not see as jealousy. She had accepted Merewyn, she could even admit that the girl had a certain comeliness — if one liked dark red hair and freckles and those greenish eyes — but she would never understand why Sigurd had turned down many a handsome, well-dowered maiden in the district for this one.

"I expect," said Asgerd pursing her mouth, "that you have some place prepared where I may sleep the rest of the night?"

"Oh, to be sure," said Merewyn flushing. Hospitality was the first law, but she had forgotten everything in the turmoil of Brigid's plight. "I must warm the eiderdowns." She ran to the other bed-closet — the one for guests. It, like her own, like Ketil's, opened off the Hall. The guest closet was dank and chill. The piled eiderdown quilts gave out a musty smell, for Brigid had not aired them in weeks. *I* should have seen to this, Merewyn thought, conscious of her mother-in-law's disdainful sniff.

While Merewyn hauled the eiderdowns near the fire and spread them on benches, she heard the sound of voices outside, and amongst them unmistakeably Sigurd's.

"Oh, thank you, Blessed Lord," she whispered, and ran to the door. She saw her husband, and their three menservants behind him. Under the silvery midnight sky, Sigurd caught her up in his arms and kissed her many times. "Still not abed, elsknan min?" he asked without surprise. In winter everyone slept a lot — not much in summer. "Have you food for hungry men?"

"I think so." She tried to remember what was left in the cauldron. "Dried fish, and skyr anyway — your mother's here."

"My mother?"

She explained breathlessly, thinking all the time how big and strong, yet tender, Sigurd was, and how his blond hair curled a little over his ears, and that his short beard and mustache smelled of the sea spray, and that they would lie together tonight.

They walked into the Hall, and Sigurd made the proper greetings to Ketil and Asgerd. Then he went to their own bed-closet to see Orm; upon finding him fast asleep, Sigurd did not disturb the little boy. He touched him gently on the head, then shut the door.

When he came back, Merewyn had a plateful of food ready for him. The menservants were clustered as usual at the end of the forty-foot Hall, and she fed them too.

"What price for the fleeces?" asked Ketil, as soon as Sigurd had swallowed a few mouthfuls.

The young man sighed. "Not good. Though I finally went

to Reykjavik, but there was a trader in from Norway with a load
of live sheep, big fat ones, and that was all anyone wanted
much."

"Tcha!" said Ketil, scowling. "This is a poor business you
have here, and the profits from farming get worse yearly."

"We've had a couple of bad winters," said Sigurd slowly.

Asgerd's sharp glance went from Ketil's face to that of her
son. "You both did much better when you went a-viking!" she
snorted, and turned the eiderdowns which Merewyn had forgotten.

Ketil slammed down his empty drinking horn. "Asgerd
speaks the truth!" He got up and stalked around the fire,
frowning.

Merewyn drew herself in, tight and anxious. She looked
towards her husband and whispered, "Sigurd, you *promised*,
you swore to me you wouldn't."

Nobody heard her, even Sigurd, yet because there was love
between them, he knew what she was thinking. And though
much taken up with his own concerns, he had understanding of
his wife, and her natural horror of Viking raids.

"Ketil Ketilson, my foster father — " he said formally, because he wanted to penetrate the mead-anger he saw rising in
the older man. "Though I had scant luck in Reykjavik, yet I
heard news which may be of interest to you. To *us*. Your kinsman, Erik the Red, is back from his exile. He has spent these
years as an outlaw, exploring an uninhabited land he found to
the west of us. He likes it much, and so much wants to go back
there with colonists that he will give anyone who joins up
square miles of this rich land. The climate is very mild, and the
grass high and thick. He has named the place *Greenland*."

Ketil's attention was indeed caught. He came over to Sigurd,
and said, "Repeat what you heard! *Erik* is back?"

Sigurd nodded. "And will be at the Althing next month
looking for colonists."

"He will *give* away miles of rich land?"

"So they said. And he has already established some homestead for himself up a pretty little fjord in that Greenland."

"What nonsense you talk," cried Asgerd rounding on her son. "I can see where you're tending, and think you've lost your wits. Is Erik Thorvaldson, the outlaw, a man to trust? A man to lead anyone anywhere? He was exiled from Norway, exiled from Iceland for murders, and —"

"Asgerd Orsmdottir!" interrupted Ketil, while his face scar grew purple. "Remember you speak of my kinsman! And he has done no murders — only man-slayings. A very different matter in which *honor* is involved." The two older people confronted each other angrily, and Merewyn felt immediate sympathy for her father and husband, no matter what it was they were discussing. She wasn't entirely sure.

Sigurd, who hated bickering, downed his hornful of ale and said quietly, "My mother — these are men's affairs, and nothing is decided. We must wait for the Althing. In the meantime, I wish bed — with my wife. And am sure you need yours, after the long ride and the care I know you've given to Brigid. All this will wait until later." He stood up, put his arm around Merewyn, and said, "Good night."

Asgerd stayed several days, as was customary, and Merewyn was grateful for the expert, offhand care she gave Brigid who quickly recovered.

Sigurd and Ketil had many a private talk together, especially when they shared the High Seat at meals, but the two women who sat on the Cross Bench at the end under a gable could not be sure what the men were saying, though Asgerd strained her ears to listen. Merewyn did not pry, even alone in bed with Sigurd, with whom she had such happy nights of kisses and deeper pleasure that she scarcely thought of anything else. And everyone was preparing for the journey to the Althing, except Asgerd, who said sourly that such expensive junketings were not for her, and she was anxious to get home to her sister; to a household *properly* run, where the clabbered milk called "skyr" was always tasty, and there was abundance of such delicacies as fried whale blubber, raw shark, and pig's liver; where the *four* woman thralls were efficient, and the eiderdowns aired daily — not in haphazard fashion.

Merewyn received these criticisms in guilty silence, and tried to do better, aware that in Asgerd's eyes — and alas in that of others too — this was a shamefully impoverished household, and that it was partly her own fault since she had stopped her husband and father from their yearly Viking raids.

On June 5th, Asgerd finally left Langarfoss. Sigurd had gone up the Langa River in search of a strayed ewe, Ketil had stalked off to inspect his ship as usual, and had taken tools with him. It was again a brilliant blue day, with high white puffy clouds, everchanging, and the golden pyramid of Baula Mountain looking near enough to touch.

Merewyn waved goodbye to Asgerd who bobbed along on one of their horses, escorted by Cormac, the Irish thrall. Merewyn sighed relief, and went to the loom room, where she straightened out Brigid's clumsy weaving. She entered the Hall, and turned the spitted hindquarter of a lamb which was roasting over the fire. She sniffed the aroma happily. Fresh meat for a change, but she'd have to smoke the forequarters for the journey to the Althing. And it was such a skinny lamb, the only one Sigurd had dared to spare from the flock. Still, thought Merewyn, determined to be hopeful, the sheep will soon fatten up in the summer pastures, and Sigurd did well at fishing. They had a surplus of drying codfish, enough to sell to the dalesmen, or barter for hay. Even for linen to make me a new headdress, she thought.

She picked up Orm and carried him outside, settling herself on the bench with her wool and spindle. Spinning and weaving *at least* I do well. She glanced down the road to Borg where Asgerd had vanished earlier, then put her spindle down in

astonishment. There were two men on horseback coming towards Langarfoss.

"Blessed St. Mary, not guests!" she murmured, at once concerned about the amount of lamb she was roasting. Would it
stretch?

She squinted hard and still did not recognize the men. One
was bearded and dressed like an Icelander. The other was not,
though there seemed something familiar about the tilt of his
head and the way he wore his mantle fastened on the left
shoulder. The shaggy mounts were certainly Icelandic.

As they drew near, the one who had no beard waved his arm.
She returned a decorous salute and walked down the homestead
path to make the proper greetings. Orm trotted behind her.

At the gate, both men dismounted and the beardless one
hurried towards her. "Merewyn —" he said in a choked voice.
"Oh, Merewyn — my dear."

She stood rooted, her hand on the gate, staring at the dark,
thin face, its eyes on a level with hers. Her spine prickled. A
ghost! Or a troll playing tricks. They did that. Asgerd said so.
Could change themselves into any shape they wished to. She
whirled around and snatched up Orm, held him tight against
her while backing off. She made the sign of the cross.

"No, dear —" said Rumon smiling sadly. "It is really I. We
came as quickly as we could, or I would have warned you."

"You came as quickly as you could —" she repeated in a daze,
no welcome in her sea-green eyes which had darkened with fear.
She stepped farther back, still clutching Orm, who began to
whimper.

"May I come in?" asked Rumon gently. "I and my friend,
Jorund Helgison, we have traveled a long way together."

Merewyn did not move, but her heart thumped. She saw the
glint of the gold crucifix at his neck, she recognized the long-
forgotten English voice, and its aristocratic intonation — the
inflection she had once tried so hard to copy when he first taught

her English. "Enter," she said very low. She put Orm down. He quieted, gaping at the strangers.

She led the two men silently back to her house. On the threshold, she turned. Hospitality demanded that she take them in to the Hall, fetch a washbasin and rag for cleansing, food and ale, but she could not speak the necessary invitation. Her tongue had gone dry in her mouth, and she could make it say nothing but a thick questioning sound.

Rumon drew a sharp breath. He had expected to astonish her mightily, but he had also expected to see more than dismay in her eyes once she knew him. "Yes," he said. "It's been a long time since we saw each other last on the Tor at Glastonbury, and I've been searching for you ever since."

"I do not believe that," she said flatly. Her arms stretched out across the door as though to guard her home. A cloud drifted by, and the clear sunlight fell on her. She had defiant beauty as she stood there; the tips of her long auburn braids were tucked under her girdle from which dangled a bunch of keys, her freckles were almost gone, her whole body was thinner and seemed taller than it used to, while her mouth — which he had so angrily kissed while they were on the Tor — had parted to show her perfect rows of teeth, but not in a smile.

Jorund, seeing that matters were not going as they had expected, and that Rumon, with whom he had endured so much danger, was at a loss, came forward and said politely, "Merewyn Ketilsdottir — can you not give us welcome? We have come very far and would like to rest our horses. Is it too much to ask?"

Quick red flowed up her neck. She turned to the Icelander, who had a good face and steady blue eyes like Sigurd's. "To be sure you may. You are welcome at Langarfoss. Sigurd will be glad for company."

"Sigurd?" said Rumon.

"My husband," she answered proudly.

"You are not then a thrall?" said Jorund who understood the situation far better than did Rumon.

"Certainly not! My father claimed me as his daughter and heiress at the Thing. Then I married Sigurd in the Borg temple."

Rumon recoiled, staring at her. "Marriage!" he cried. "You call that marriage, Merewyn! You who are Christian, who lived at Romsey Abbey, with your saintly Aunt Merwinna!"

Merewyn's eyes gleamed. She drew herself up even straighter. "I am married to Sigurd," she said in a furious voice he had never thought her capable of. "And I suppose you'll say next that *he,*" she pointed to little Orm, "is not my true-born son!"

As the two confronted each other, Jorund, who was hungry and more nervous of this outcome than he had been of anything since he had maneuvered the stealing of their ship in that faraway land across the ocean, now intervened. "Whatever you two wish to talk about can wait, I suppose," he said. "When does your husband return?" He looked at Merewyn.

"I don't know," she answered vehemently. "He is searching for a ewe. You shall eat. And I'll find Grim to care for the horses."

She left the two men in the smoky Hall, flew to tell Brigid to attend to the visitors, flew to the field where Grim was plowing. She gave instructions. And all the time she thought, What is he *doing* here? What *has* he been doing all these years? Oh, why am I forced to remember a life that is finished?

She came back to the Hall, where Brigid had presented the basin of water, the towel. The men were sitting on the guest bench next the High Seat. Jorund knew the proper place. Merewyn brought them each a mug of ale, then said, "The lamb is cooked, I believe. You shall shortly have some."

Rumon cleared his throat, and said quietly, "It is Friday, Merewyn. And that day as I have often told Jorund — who has been baptized a Christian — is the day when we mourn the Crucifixion of Our Lord by fasting. Have you fish, perhaps?"

Merewyn inclined her head. "I'm sorry. I did not think and

Friday, even in English, is named for the Norse goddess Frigg. The way I live now is not yours, Lord Rumon," she said defiantly.

"So it seems," said Rumon, "and that much has happened since I saw you last."

Merewyn silently went to fetch dried codfish. The men ate, then Jorund said, "The lamb smells good, and I'm hungry for meat. Out of gratitude to Rumon's powerful god, I shall take none, yet hope there may be a bite left tomorrow, if your husband will allow us to stay that long."

She murmured something and retired to the women's Cross Bench. There was a long uncomfortable silence. It was broken by the return of Ketil, who was delighted to see guests.

Jorund made discreet explanations, of which Ketil grasped but two things. "Ah!" he cried, gulping down his ale and gnawing at a lamb chop. "I know who you are, Jorund Helgison! I even entertained your father once, when he was up north in Haukadale. I had my own homestead and family there then," he added bitterly. "But never mind that — what is fated must befall — and tell me of *your* voyages! Did I understand that you went a-viking in the west, to a place nobody knows?"

"No," said Jorund smiling. "It was not quite like that."

"Tell then!" Ketil cried. "Tell me how it was? Did you get much booty? Did you have many battles?"

Jorund looked from Rumon to Merewyn. Both were utterly still. He said, "Ketil, may your daughter draw near and hear this account? I think it will interest her."

"To be sure! Dottir, come up with me on the High Seat!"

This unusual honor meant that Ketil was in great spirits, and Merewyn did not dare disobey, nor really wanted to. Curiosity was not the least of the emotions she felt. She climbed to the dais and joined her father.

Jorund launched into his narration. He said nothing about the reason that Rumon had become a passenger aboard the *Thorgerd*, bound for Iceland from Limerick, but he described their captain

— Ari Marson — and their shipload. Then he described the fearful storm which had blown up from the north, and how their steering oar had gone.

"Bad, bad —" said Ketil tugging at his beard. "This happened only once to me — you must have angered Aegir — but go on!"

Jorund agreed that Aegir and his nine daughters were indeed angry. That he had made a poem about it.

"You are a skald?" asked Ketil eagerly. "And can you also tell a saga?"

Jorund modestly answered that he did have talent along these lines.

Ketil was entranced. "You will entertain us later, when Sigurd has come home," he cried. "You will stay with us several days, I hope — but in the meantime, what of the voyage!"

Jorund continued. He told of the weeks and weeks they had been blown to the west, of the calms and the fogs and then renewed winds. Of the thirst, hunger, and despair on board. Then he glanced at Rumon, who was staring down at the table. "There were those on the ship who thought our bad luck might arise from this passenger who is a foreigner and a Christian."

"Indeed," said Ketil, with contempt, drawing together his bushy eyebrows. "*I* would have thought him bad luck, but then on the *Bylgja* I would never have had such a passenger in the first place. *I* was not a trader. But go on!"

Jorund, speaking in the same even voice, said that Rumon had prayed aloud to his god, and that there had been an answer. They had sighted land.

"Land?" said Ketil. "What land? Where were you?"

"I don't know," Jorund said. "It is far, far to the west, where we always thought the sea dropped off into Hel."

"And it doesn't?"

Jorund shook his head. "There were rivers and forests and living people there. Skraelings, and also some papas whose forefathers had been Irish. Those had come long before and *they* called the country Great Ireland."

Ketil looked above his head to his sword, the "Bloodletter," then to the battle-axes. "Did you kill them?" he asked with relish.

Rumon clenched his hands, his bowed head fell lower, and Merewyn could not help noticing that he had grown pale. She returned her gaze to the smoky beams across the Hall.

"We only killed the skraeling who was guarding *Thorgerd* the night we took it back. I think Rumon knows exactly how long that was after our landing. He notched sticks for every day."

"Nearly three years have passed," said Rumon in a thin voice.

Three years of living amongst the savages and the half-breed Celtic monks, of abortive secret plans, of searching for their ship, which was hid most cannily when the skraelings were not rowing it on long coastal expeditions. Three years of longing for this woman who sat there so coldly on the High Seat next to her fierce Viking father.

"You were prisoners?" said Ketil, shaking his head in distress.

"Yes, and no." Jorund smiled. "They treated us well, made us part of the tribe, but they knew we couldn't escape without our ship. And the old chief Hoksic never quite trusted us enough to let us near the *Thorgerd*. Then Hoksic died. During the mourning period their vigilance relaxed, and Rumon here discovered where the ship was hidden eight miles away up a creek. We escaped in her two nights later while the skraelings were having a powwow and the monks were chanting around their Y-shaped chapel in the Place of Stones. Each lot thought we were with the other."

"Ah, what a wondrous thing!" Ketil cried. "I always heard that Ari Marson was a lucky man, and how proud he must feel of making this incredible voyage home at last!"

There was a pause, then Jorund said, "Ari Marson did not come with us, nor did two other members of the crew."

"What?" cried Ketil. "They were dead then?"

Jorund showed embarrassment. This disgraceful explanation for the nonappearance of Ari he had already had to tell several times since the *Thorgerd* had finally achieved home port at Reykjavik two weeks ago. Even his loving wife Katla after transports of joy — for she had of course believed him lost — had condemned the dishonor of Ari's behavior.

"Well, what then happened?" Ketil demanded. "An Icelandic captain never deserts his ship, and for my part I don't see why Ari did not fight long before, no matter if you *were* outnumbered and killed."

"Rumon would not let us," said Jorund. "The Christian god hates bloodshed."

"Tcha!" said Ketil. "Those Christians I've seen are always a white-livered bunch. But Ari shouldn't have listened to this foreigner."

"Ari did not *want* to leave," said Jorund reluctantly. "He married Norumbega, the chief's daughter, and is bewitched by her. Most of us took women — not Rumon," he added, glancing from the stony profile at his side up to Merewyn's wide, fixed eyes.

Ketil gave an impatient roar. "Women, naturally! 'Tis what all men enjoy in foreign places. What has that to do with Ari's leaving on his ship? Besides he *has* a wife, I believe, waiting here in Iceland."

Jorund flushed, feeling himself in deep waters. "We were all made Christians of," he said. "Ari and Norumbega were wed by Christian rites in the chapel at the Place of Stones."

Ketil exploded with a furious noise. Merewyn drew herself in tight and small. Yes, she thought, in truly Christian eyes I am not married to Sigurd. She hardly listened to Jorund's remaining account.

The voyage home had been remarkably easy, westerly winds had sped them all the way, for which Jorund — at the steering oar — gave thanks to the Blessed Lord Jesus, as Rumon had

taught him. They had a stout deerskin sail, sewed tightly together with thongs by one of the crew's women, who had no
idea what the thing was for. They had been able to ship enough
maize and venison for the voyage, and had filled casks with water
as they fled down the Merrimac River. The sixteen men on
board had not suffered much. They had landed, and gone to visit
Jorund's nearby home for a while, taken horses, and traveled
three more days to Borg. Many in the south knew that Ketil-
Redbeard, the once famous sea king, lived in the Borg district.
Inquiry at Thorstein Egilson's great homestead directed them to
Langarfoss. And here they were.

Ketil nodded, pleased by the tale which was interesting as a
saga, though there were no good fights, and Ari Marson had
certainly disgraced himself.

But now a new thought struck Ketil. WHY had the young
men traveled up to Langarfoss? Surely not to tell of their adventures, nor even to look upon an old retired Viking. "You have
some business to discuss with Sigurd Hrutson, my son-in-law?"
he asked, suddenly remembering that Sigurd had recently been
in Reykjavik, and wondering if this visit were about the great
news of Greenland. "You've met Sigurd?"

"No," said Jorund swallowing. Nothing was going as they
had planned — he and Rumon — during the years on the Merrimac, and during the voyage home. They had expected to find
Merewyn confined somewhere as a miserable thrall, possibly
sold by now to some other bondi.

Rumon, who still had a pouchful of money on him, had
expected to buy her freedom and return to England with her,
where she would become his wife. All was to be tranquil and
orderly — a matter of a few days to arrange — and now Jorund
perceived that there were serious complications, including the
young woman's manner.

"Well," said Ketil sharply, annoyed by everyone's silence, "so
you've not met Sigurd, and I am, to be sure, delighted to have
you as guests, but I don't understand why you honored us."

Rumon lifted his head, and looked straight up at Merewyn. "We came here so that I might find your daughter," he said.

Ketil's jaw dropped, and the ensuing spark in his blue eyes made Jorund glance nervously towards the battle-axes which were rusty, and the great sword, which was not — since it was frequently rubbed with whale oil.

"And why did you want to find my daughter?" Ketil rose from his seat and towered over them.

Rumon also got up, his dark gaze was somber. "Because she once loved me, and I love her now and have tried to reach her since before the day you captured her at Padstow, in Cornwall."

Ketil took this in gradually, and heard Merewyn make a strangled sound. Ketil sat down. "*Love!*" he snorted. He turned to Merewyn. "What is all this nonsense about, dottir? Did you know this man?"

"Yes," she said, staring at the rafters across the Hall. "He is a prince in England, an atheling — and there was a time when —for a long time —" She stopped. In the shadow of the beams across the Hall, she saw pictures — of King Edgar's Coronation at Bath, where she sat by her Aunt Merwinna and watched Rumon; of a lane in Corfe when she had pleaded with him; of the night on the Tor when he had kissed her so disdainfully, and said that he could not marry a low-born creature. And yet he had followed her, it seemed, to the end of the world and back.

"Do you mean that he dishonored you?" Ketil cried. He leapt on the seat to grab down "Bloodletter." "You were not a virgin when you went to Sigurd? This is for *Sigurd* to avenge! We shall have a holmgang —" He ran his finger down the sword blade.

"No, Father —" She put her hand on Ketil's. "I was not dishonored and I was a virgin when I came to Sigurd. There's no reason for a duel."

She shut her eyes, so that there might be no more pictures forming in the smoke across the Hall.

There was another silence, during which Rumon sat down;

Ketil tested the sword point, scowling; and Jorund was about to make a tactful offer of a saga, or edda, or even an original poem when Orm, who had been trailing Brigid at her sluggish household chores, gave out a happy cry of "Papa!"

Sigurd walked in. He already knew that they had visitors since he had talked to Grim, and seen the strange horses. But as he greeted Jorund and Rumon cordially, it occured to him that his wife and Ketil, together on the High Seat, were both looking odd, and that there was something uncomfortable in the air.

"I found the ewe," he said, taking his place beside Ketil as Merewyn vacated it. "Doubtless *you* gentlemen are not poor farmers, and don't know how important this is." He looked from Jorund to Rumon, puzzled by them, waiting politely for explanations. Merewyn brought him food.

He was yet more puzzled as Merewyn, handing up the wooden plateful of meat and the drinking horn, suddenly whispered to him, "Sigurd, I love you."

He stared a moment at her flushed face, her trembling lips. "What ails you, elsknan min," said Sigurd, picking up Orm who had swarmed up to the High Seat and was trying to climb on his father's leg. "Here, son — you shall have a bone to suck."

"You may well ask what ails my daughter!" cried Ketil. "And I don't feel like mincing matters. This Christian foreigner," he stabbed his eating knife toward Rumon, "says he has been after her for three years, and finally tracked her to Langarfoss."

"Oh?" said Sigurd. "Indeed?" He lifted Orm down off his knee and folded his arms. "Are you from England?" he said evenly to Rumon.

"Yes." Rumon turned his head, forced to look up towards the huge blond fellow whose bright blue eyes were expressionless.

"You knew my wife in England?"

"Yes," said Rumon through his teeth, and sprang to his feet, so that he need not look upward at these Vikings who had abducted Merewyn, and done so many murders. "She's *not* your wife!" he cried. "Heathen folderol before an idol doesn't make her your wife!"

"Rumon!" murmured Jorund anxiously. "Be careful" — for the dark blood had rushed up into his friend's face, and the look he gave Sigurd was one of hatred. Jorund had never seen that look on Rumon, and he marveled what jealousy could do.

Ketil growled, but Sigurd's steady eyes remained coldly appraising. "Since *you* consider Merewyn to be only my concubine," he said, "what do you propose? That we fight for her?"

Merewyn, who stood by the Cross Bench, gasped and cried, "No!"

Jorund interrupted hastily. "We are both unarmed, Sigurd, and we are your guests," at which Ketil laughed and said, "True, so we must go out of Langarfoss, have a proper holmgang observing, of course, our Icelandic rules." He rubbed "Bloodletter" gleefully, knowing that with Sigurd wielding it, that slight, dark foreigner would never stand a chance, no matter what sword *he* could find.

"Not so fast, Ketil," said Sigurd. "The Englishman has not answered my question, and I see that it upsets him. I think that fighting is not what he wants."

"It isn't," cried Jorund jumping up beside his friend. "His religion is against violence, he himself has a horror of it. We came here in good faith, and after many hardships, having no idea that Merewyn was anything but a thrall — and if Rumon still continues to think her so — I do *not*."

Sigurd spoke after a moment. "I see, and shall prove to you that my wife is not a thrall. Come here, Merewyn."

She walked unsteadily to the base of the High Seat. "You never told me about this man to whom you must have given some encouragement. Did you love him?"

Merewyn lifted her chin, and answered slowly, "I have never talked about my life before — before that day in Padstow, nor wished to mention this man whom I did love once, and who I thought repudiated me."

Rumon glanced at her, and made a sound in his throat. "I was a haughty fool," he said. "Do not three years of trying to find you prove my penitence?"

All three Icelanders were astonished by his speech, which sounded abject, not the way one handled women. Ketil was annoyed, for the prospects of a rousing duel were obviously lessening. Jorund was half ashamed for his friend, remembering how Rumon had wept in the Merrimac country when they murdered the skraeling who was guarding their ship. Into Sigurd's eyes there came a quizzical light, for this was, after all, no worthy rival to consider. And he laughed, saying with assurance to Merewyn, "And do you still love this man, who will not even fight for you?"

"No," she said. "I love *you*, Sigurd. And I think that Rumon will always be wanting what he cannot find, and that if he finds what he thought he wanted he will be disappointed. As he is now." She tried to smile, but tears came into her eyes, and she retreated to the Cross Bench.

"Tcha!" said Ketil. "What a pother about nothing! Thor and Odin be thanked, dottir, that you were never close to this man."

No, I was never close to him, she thought, nor ever could be after having belonged to Sigurd. But she felt pity and gratitude. For he had kept the secret of her true paternity all these years that she had been so childishly proud of "descent" from King Arthur. And having in some strange way come at last to love her, he had tried his best to reach her. No woman could be entirely unmoved by that. "I'm sorry, Rumon," she said, slowly. "Have you at least found Avalon, the Island of the Blest?"

"No," said Rumon, after a moment. "Nor do I know where else to search." His voice like his words held such a bleak futility that the Icelanders, though in varying degree contemptuous, nevertheless recognized sympathetically something of the melancholy which often afflicted themselves in the long black wintertime.

"Well," said Ketil, returning "Bloodletter" regretfully to its pegs. "No use being dismal, and since Jorund is a skald, perhaps he'll amuse us with a poem about the adventures of the *Thorgerd?*"

Jorund hesitated. He felt deeply for his friend, and tried to respect his refusal to fight for Merewyn, even though he did not quite understand it. "No poem has come to me," he said slowly, "nor even a drapa in honor of our hosts, but I can remember, I think, the saga of 'Ragnar Lodbrok,' will that do?"

Ketil and Sigurd assented heartily. Merewyn sat tight and withdrawn on the Cross Bench.

chapter eleven

A FORTNIGHT after Rumon's visit, the little cavalcade from Langarfoss approached Thingvellir — the wide plain east of Reykjavik, where the Althing was held annually.

Ketil led the group, and had made himself as fine as possible. He wore his old horned helmet, brightly polished, as befitted a Viking chief, and "Bloodletter" had a new leather scabbard. The sword dangled against the horse's left flank — its thumpings often caused the beast to shy — but no matter; Ketil was dressed according to his erstwhile rank. He had even produced a bracelet with gold bosses which had been left him by his father.

Sigurd followed along the winding lava road, and was not as dressy as Ketil. Sigurd wore his conical brass helmet, from which the nosepiece had long been removed, a red jerkin and mantle of foreign weave picked up years ago on some raid, but no jewelry. Orm was tied to Sigurd's pommel, clinging to the horse's rough mane, but his father was gratified to see that the child scarcely needed these precautions. Orm was by nature fearless, and had instinctive balance.

Merewyn followed her men. She wore the green dress and

mantle she had been captured in at Padstow, and which was still her best clothing. She had on her new folded linen headdress, and her mantle was held by the silver-gilt brooch Sigurd had given her in Limerick three years ago. She knew that they were a presentable lot, and need not be shamed, but they could not compete with the rich bondis and chieftains whom they had seen on the way.

Grim, their ablest thrall, ended the procession. One could hardly appear at the Althing without *some* servant. Brigid and the other two men had been left home to care for the live stock; in any case there were no more horses for them to ride.

During the trip Merewyn had seen many marvels. In the Bay of Whales two of the monsters had been towed in and were being flensed. After that came boiling springs, and a geyser. Then there were piled masses of black lava which Ketil at least could identify as images of giants, trolls, or even the gods — Thor with his hammer, Odin and his ravens, and Freyr, the obscene little god of fertility. There were beautiful flowers to be seen sometimes, a purple drift of arctic fireweed, the modest angelica, and there were streams all silvery with salmon — which they caught and ate. Above and behind all these was the stark magnificence of snowy mountains, volcanoes, and glaciers, under the changing clouds.

The interest of the three-day journey had eased the pain and unrest Merewyn felt, most unwillingly, after Rumon's departure with Jorund.

While the visit lasted, she had been numb, remote, listening absently to Jorund's chanted sagas, never speaking to Rumon except for the barest civilities. Then at night in the box bed she had clung to Sigurd, showing a passion which had amused as well as delighted him.

"So come now, my heart," he said once. "You will exhaust even *me*, and you don't need to prove so hard your love. I don't doubt it, and also know that that foreigner could never satisfy you in the way a man does a woman."

Which was true. She also thought so. Yet, once, on the last morning she had not been able to avoid Rumon's sorrowing, reproachful look. Nor to avoid answering when he said, "Merewyn, I am going back to England, and I had thought to take you with me. As it is, have you no message for anyone there?"

She said, "No," angrily, to which he returned, "I will pray for you nonetheless."

And after Rumon left, making stiffly courteous farewells, she had watched him disappear down the road to Borg, then fled to Langarfoss — the waterfall. She crouched on its brink, listening to its roar, and watched the tumbling snow waters through a sudden mist of anguish.

Then she had turned capricious towards Sigurd, no longer eager for his embrace, refusing him on pretexts which he accepted because he thought her with child. Though she was not. A dismaying fact. She longed for another child, and was sad to be so slow at conceiving one.

During that miserable week, she had her first quarrel with Sigurd. It had to do with Christianity and was incoherent on Merewyn's side. She said that she had heard Jorund say there was an Irish missionary priest in Reykjavik, so they must go there to see him on the way to the Althing, that Sigurd should be baptized, and then they could be married properly. Sigurd, patient at first, finally got angry at her unreason. He said that he had stopped going a-viking for love of her, but there were limits to any man's tolerance. That he believed in the gods of his fathers, and certainly had no interest in a god who turned men into weak timid women, and the whole subject was ridiculous.

Whereupon she slapped him, and his immediate retaliatory blow was so violent that it threw her head against the wall; lights exploded behind her eyes and her cheek puffed up scarlet.

She tottered from bed and went into the Hall, where she sobbed away the long gray-lit hours. Sigurd remained snoring in the bed-closet.

In the morning, Ketil came in wanting his breakfast, and laughed when he saw her swollen cheek and half-closed eye. " 'Twas high time for that, dottir," he said. "I wonder Sigurd did not do it sooner. You and your mingy Christian suitor were enough to try any man, though I must say —" Ketil took a long draft of ale, and judged fairly, "I did not see you give the foreigner any encouragement, and Jorund the skald much pleased us with his sagas. We'll forget the whole business."

So it was. Neither Sigurd nor Merewyn referred to their quarrel, and by the time they left for the Althing, Merewyn's cheek and painful emotions had alike subsided. They did not go to Reykjavik.

Now they plodded along the rough lava trail, which wound monotonously, and was shut in by hillocks. Merewyn began to wonder what could possibly be attractive about the valley they called Thingvellir — whenever they reached it. Occasionally in view ahead of them was the huge company following Thorstein Egilson, their landlord. You could just see Thorstein's moon-white head in the vanguard of his household — his children, retainers, and thralls — and the golden tissue headdress of Jofrid, Thorstein's haughty wife.

Ketil grumbled every time he caught a glimpse of Thorstein's party and once said to Sigurd, "That *man* — thinks himself so grand because he's rich — through no doing of his own. I'm glad I brought "Bloodletter.""

"I trust, Ketil," said Sigurd in the deferential yet firm tone he often used with his father-in-law, "that there could never be a use for your sword here at the Althing. We have no feuds with anyone, and we are not barbarians."

Merewyn heard these speeches and was struck by Sigurd's answer, "We are not barbarians." Yet they had plundered, raped, murdered, both of them, and back in England she with all the nuns had prayed to God that He deliver them from the fury of the Norsemen. That was during the terrible night at Romsey Abbey when Southampton was attacked. Yet, she thought, trying to puzzle it out, these people have a code, a system of honor, and they live up to their code which concerns only themselves. It was respect for their laws which brought them to the Althing each year to listen while the Law-speaker recited what had been decreed, and made them arbitrate quarrels and apportion punishment according to Icelandic rule.

And I am one of them, she thought. My father, my husband, my son they are Icelanders — so am I. "Not entirely," said an unwelcome voice in her head, "and aren't you *Christian?*"

Sigurd turned suddenly in his saddle and cried triumphantly, "There is the Logberg, now we're almost in Thingvellir. Come here, wife, and look!"

Merewyn gladly turned her horse. The "Logberg" or Law-speaker's rock was not particularly impressive, but the view beyond it was. Below the basalt cliff, Thingvellir's grassy plain stretched out for miles on either side of the shimmering river Oxara. There was a big lake to the south. The placid lake, the largest in Iceland, combined with the mountain-girdled valley to make a tranquil scene, unusual in this rugged land of fire and ice. The tranquility was scarcely disturbed by the distant bustle of many little figures, all erecting temporary shelters far below.

"We must hurry," said Ketil, also looking down at Thingvellir, "or there'll be no decent place to build our booth. That Thorstein," he added angrily, "of course has his own booths which are kept from year to year, and in the very best site."

"We are not great folk, Ketil," said Sigurd quietly. "We'll have to make do with what we can."

Actually, when they had descended to Thingvellir, they found a pleasant location on the brink of the river, because they were early; many from the north and east fjords, a seventeen-day journey away, had not yet arrived. Sigurd and Grim built a shelter of birch saplings, and covered it with a huge canvas which was always carefully stored for the annual trip. The canvas, made of hemp and picked up years ago on some raid, had been repaired and well oiled by Merewyn and Brigid. It would keep out the rain, should any come. But the sky was blue above the white clouds.

Orm, wild with excitement, raced up and down to other booths, where he was made welcome. Merewyn followed, smiling; though a trifle daunted by the gold bracelets, brooches, and hair dangles exhibited by many women, she refused to let anything discourage the holiday mood.

Sigurd went off to Thorstein's permanent turf and stone encampment, to pay the traditional respect to Borg's chief, but Ketil did not go. He had a more important matter in mind.

He did not even dismount, but trotted here and there along the valley, greeting old friends, accepting drinks, and inquiring at all the booths if anyone knew whether Erik the Red had arrived. Nobody knew.

It was evening before Ketil spied Erik, riding down the trail off the cliff, followed by a score of men and women, which included Erik's sedate wife, Thiodild, and his three young sons, Thorwald, Thorstein, and Leif. The slanting sun rays picked out Erik's beard and hair, which were as fiery as Ketil's once had been. The latter let out a war whoop, and galloped to meet Erik. "Glad to see you, kinsman!" he bellowed. "Glad you're back, and none the worse I see from your time as outlaw."

Erik grinned, and recognized Ketil by a hearty arm clasp. "So you still go a-viking?" he asked, noting the sea king's war helmet, the chain-mail shirt, the sword.

"Nay!" said Ketil. "Tcha! But I still have my ship."

"So . . .?" Erik's hazel eyes sharpened. "The *Bylgja?* Well, ride along with me until we set up our booths. We've many things to talk of."

Erik Thorvaldson, nicknamed "The Red," was a shrewd man, and had often been a violent one, for which he had suffered in both Norway and Iceland, because he had slain Norsemen, not foreigners. But the slayings had been deemed affairs of honor, and in Iceland had incurred only the punishment of three years exile. He was now in his forties, younger than Ketil, and was overpowered by a new enthusiasm.

During his outlawry Erik had sailed west to a land once sighted by Gunnbjorn Krakuson and had reached it in summer, when there had been a green border around a towering central ice cap. The landscape seemed not unlike Iceland, or even the west coast of Norway — his birthplace — for which Erik retained a nostalgic memory. The best thing about this new land was that there was nobody on it. Here a man could be free from autocratic kings in Norway, or from code and law and jealousy in Iceland. The discoverer of this new land might make his *own* laws. Erik, during the summers of sailing up and down various fjords, and exploring the terrain, had become enchanted with the idea of settling the unknown country with a picked bunch of men and their families.

There were certainly some in Iceland now who were as discontented as their forebears had been with Norway when Ingolf Arnarson first came to Reykjavik over a hundred years ago. And in Iceland now, the habitable land was all taken up. So in Greenland (as Erik slyly named it, determinedly ignoring the perpetual icecap and the long white winters) there would be room — on the southwestern coast — for all those who might join his kingdom.

In Ketil, Erik found a very willing ear. They talked long together that night, which was no night since the glow remained in the western sky, and there was singing, and the plucking of harps all around them from the other booths.

Ketil was completely won when he found that he might have a whole fjord and its surrounding country to himself, and name it Ketilsfjord. Miles of land as well as the water — which would give him twice as much property as Thorstein Egilson owned, more than twice, said Erik, *far* more — and that then he, and Ketil, and the others who came would be chieftains on a scale never thought of in Iceland. Ketil was dazzled.

The Althing, once convened, plodded along its usual way.

The Law-speaker stood on the Logberg, and recited the law through a horn megaphone every day. The people gathered on the plain below and listened. The principal chiefs of Iceland constituted a legislature. Important quarrels were judged; disputed property lines examined; there were two duels held on Oxara's island. A hotly contested divorce between a beautiful young woman and a stingy old bondi was ratified in favor of the girl. A new-made heir from the distant East Coast was exiled because there were grave suspicions that he had hastened his father's end.

When business was over, there was gaiety — the people sang and danced and drank and went visiting.

Merewyn enjoyed herself. She made friends amongst the women in nearby booths. They sat together, cooking, sewing, and watching their babies, while no rain fell, and the guardian mountains all around reinforced the scene of peaceful order.

After the customary two weeks, everyone left Thingvellir, and Merewyn had not ridden two miles up the cliff before she heard the words which altered her life again. "So now I have decided, Sigurd," boomed Ketil, "and we will leave early next summer, as soon as the ice breaks up."

Merewyn listened tensely for Sigurd's hesitating answer. "I'm not sure — can it be wise . . .?"

Ketil snorted. "*Wise!* What a question to ask of *me!* Have you forgotten our voyages on the *Bylgja?* You never questioned my commands then. Have you forgotten that you are not only my foster-son but my son-in-law, and I am head of the family?"

"I've not forgotten," said Sigurd, "but I talked with Erik myself, you know, and am not altogether satisfied with his descriptions of Greenland. He is not precise as to the amount of arable land, or even grazing land, and when I asked him what sort of trees grew there, he waved that paw of his airily and said, 'Oh, all kinds . . .' which I think astonishing if the place is as far north as he says."

Ketil swiveled so abruptly in his saddle that his horse jumped. "Do you suggest, Sigurd Hrutson, that my kinsman is a fool? Or that I am? That the hundred men who have already agreed to go with Erik are fools? Oh, very well — you may stay at Langarfoss slaving for that Thorstein Egilson, you may keep my poor daughter in a miserable state where she has not even a bracelet or second brooch to wear — you may raise my grandson like a pauper — but I shall ready the *Bylgja* and shall find plenty of brave adventurous men to go with me. And you may rot at Langarfoss, for all I care!"

"Father . . ." whispered Merewyn. She had never before seen her two men really angry at each other, and Sigurd was also angry, she could tell by the outjutting of his golden beard.

They all rode for many miles in silence, then Sigurd spoke in a harsh voice. "I shall consider the matter of our going to Greenland very carefully, Ketil. I assure you I don't *enjoy* slaving on another man's land."

Whereupon Merewyn's heart sank. Intuition told her that they would all go to Greenland, a place of which she knew nothing except from gossip amongst the rich bondi wives she had met at Thingvellir.

Erik the Red, they said scoffing, a troublemaker always, unsettling folk with harebrained schemes. Well, if he wanted to live in some other place, let him, and good riddance. Iceland could do without him. Then some one of the ladies would remember that Merewyn was kin to Erik through her father, and would tactfully change the subject. They had all been kind and a bit patronizing to Merewyn, but they liked her, and she had liked the companionship of other women, which was denied her at Langarfoss. You could hardly count Brigid.

If we do go to this Greenland, she thought, it'll be because the Norns have decided our fate. Nor did it occur to her that once she would have put the same concept in very different words. "It is God's Will."

* * *

The Icelandic winter came early, and brought great hardship. A griping bowel sickness attacked everybody but Ketil, who remained healthy and even jaunty, as he continually talked of Greenland, and struggled often through snowdrifts and ice hummocks to tinker with the *Bylgja*. One of the horses died, and they ate it because provisions were low. Merewyn had only a momentary qualm as she ate the horsemeat, which was considered in England to be a revolting heathen practice.

By March the hay was gone, and Sigurd was forced to go to Borg and "borrow" hay from Thorstein Egilson, who complied contemptuously. "You may take this as a gift," said Thorstein, "for you obviously have no means of paying, and I do not like my tenants to suffer. But I must say that you seem unlucky as a farmer." He inclined his flaxen head and pursed his lips.

"Doubtless," said Sigurd, "you could find much better tenants for Langarfoss homestead?"

"Doubtless and easily," said Thorstein, while Jofrid, his wife, made a derisive noise from the background.

"Then you will be relieved of us in the spring," said Sigurd, who finally made up his mind at that moment. "We are going to Greenland with Erik Thorvaldson."

"Are you indeed?" said Thorstein, shrugging. "As you like — Sigurd. I've nothing against you, there is no bad blood between us, but I cannot regret your leaving, for I'm thinking that my son Skuli shall farm at Langarfoss, he is about old enough to marry, and this would keep another homestead in the family."

"So it would," said Sigurd, and he felt for his landlord, who sat there like a rich white complacent slug, some of the rage which Ketil so often expressed. Yet this was unreasonable. Thorstein had been generous in giving them hay and he returned a just part of the yearly rent which had been paid in advance last October as usual. This silver enabled Ketil and Sigurd to outfit the *Bylgja* properly, and there was scant difficulty in getting a crew. The Greenland fever had spread rapidly through Central Western Iceland. Erik saw to that. Even in winter he made

tireless recruiting trips from his homestead in Haukadale, down
to the Borg district and around the shores of the Breidafjord.

By early June, twenty-five ships were ready to sail from the
western fjords. Erik was to meet his flotilla of colonists off
Snaefellsnes, and thereafter guide them to Greenland. A matter
of four or five days' sail only, said Erik. Nothing to it. Why,
Greenland was much nearer than Ireland, or the Orkneys, or
Norway where they had almost all gone at one time or another.
It was only Norse stubbornness which made them sail back east
for years, said Erik, when all the time there was this rich wonderful country, just waiting there to make everyone's fortune.
By spring, Erik had excited his colonists with such visions of
lush grass, flowery meadows, forest, and dimpling fjords
crammed with fish that he believed all this himself. And he excited them with the idea of importance, too. They would be
like — yes — earls, rich and landed as Norwegian jarls had ever
been in the old country.

On the appointed day, Merewyn looked her last at Langarfoss homestead and turned with her household down the road
to Borg, where the ship was waiting. She listened for the sound
of the waterfall, she looked north at the golden cone of Baula
Mountain, and at the Hafnarfell range across the fjord. It was a
beautiful, warm day. The marshy hillocks were dotted with
tiny pink flowers, birds twittered. A flock of singing swans
rushed northward overhead. "Farewell —" she said to them,
and to the turf farmhouse where she had known happiness, very
often. And lately a new happiness, for she was at last pregnant.
Two months. This babe, she thought, would be born in Greenland, and she pictured herself suckling it in the shade of a great
and leafy oak, like the ones in the forest near Romsey. And
there would be more time for Orm to play outdoors in Greenland than he had so far had. One would not be forever huddled
around a fire during nine months of dark winter. Nor would
there be constant struggle to get enough food. They might even
grow barley and wheat — Ketil said so, and Sigurd had bought

pecks of seed in Reykjavik, off a Norwegian trader. *Good* bread, she thought — and *butter*. They were taking the cow with them and knew that amongst the ships there was a fine young bull. No more begging Thorstein for the use of his bull. No more begging anyone for anything. Her enthusiasm for the move to Greenland had greatly increased after she discovered that Sigurd wished to go.

They arrived at the creek where the *Bylgja* was docked and already provisioned. Ketil supervised the boarding, shouting orders, cursing some of the young men who had enlisted as crew — a swaggering but efficient Ketil in his war helmet, a chieftain again — a sea-king.

Merewyn thought the *Bylgja* very large, when she went on board. There was room for the tethered cow, the three horses, four ewes, and all their possessions. Though the longship was narrow, having been built for war, she had a surprising capacity, and Ketil had only taken twelve men instead of the sixty he had once shipped.

Merewyn, Orm, and Brigid had straw pallets in the prow. The three men thralls would supplement the crew. They had to go wherever their master took them, but they were pleased with this venture and by the coming change in Sigurd's status, for they had often been jeered at by other Borg thralls for belonging to such a lowly man that he did not even own the land he farmed.

The *Bylgja* sported her curly dragonheads at prow and stern. They were fearsome red-tongued beasts, repainted by Ketil. One never knew whether the land spirits of a country would be intimidated or annoyed by these monsters, and certainly when approaching places like Norway, it was wise to remove them — but Ketil had wanted his beloved ship to lack none of its former trimmings. Though the row of war shields along the gunwhales was not practicable. Easily make new shields, said Ketil, when they had settled in Greenland. And weapons of any kind were not of great importance, since there were no inhabitants.

He had of course brought "Bloodletter," sundry spears and knives, but he left the rusty battle-axes behind. During all the arrangements for their move he had been reasonable and forethinking. Sigurd admired his wisdom as much as he had in their old days of raiding.

The *Bylgja* had a great new striped canvas sail, ordered from Norway, and the canvas tent they used at the Althing could be fitted to cover the prow.

They rowed, then sailed out of the creek into Borgafjord, then along the south coast of Snaefellsnes. "Look, my heart —" said Merewyn to Orm — "there is the glacier which your Grandma Asgerd says has been guarding us while we lived at Langarfoss."

Orm obediently squinted at the high glistening ice peaks. "Ice too where we're going?" he inquired. He spoke plainly now.

"Oh, no," said Merewyn, "at least maybe only a little. There'll be lots of green — trees, bushes, grass, and you can make a garden! Oh, Orm, maybe we can grow roses. You've no idea how wonderful they smell! We'll have more fun than you can think of — Orm! That *bucket* is for what you're doing. Remember that on shipboard. Your grandfather wishes everything kept very clean!"

Orm obeyed and used the bucket. Then he went to sleep on a pile of eiderdowns they had brought.

They rounded Snaefellsnes, and Brigid began to be sick into the bucket, but nobody else was, and there was an eager expectancy aboard. Particularly when they sighted other ships bound for Greenland, and saw Erik's big trader, waiting, the distinguishing little red pennant on the masthead.

Ketil steered close enough to exchange shouts and gestures with their leader, from which he gathered that they would wait for five more ships to appear, then sail west following Erik.

"AND," said Ketil to Sigurd, "it'll be hard to stay *behind* that tub. Tcha! There isn't a decent ship here, except the *Bylgja*." Sigurd on the whole agreed. The other ships were traders and cutters. Nobody else had a long sleek serpentine warship like the *Bylgja*. His desire to brave the open sea again almost equaled Ketil's.

It developed months later that the five ships they awaited had started out from Breidafjord, and had lost heart — at least the skippers and their families did. They had turned back to home ports.

Sometime in the sunlit evening Erik gave the signal which meant they would wait no longer, and must start out. So they did. On each ship a sail was raised, there were halfhearted cheers, and fluttering hands waved back towards Iceland.

At first all twenty of the fleet were in sight of each other, and the *Bylgja* — steered by either Ketil or Sigurd — continually, as Ketil prophesied, threatened to overtake Erik's ship; which would have been a breach of propriety.

By the third day it grew very cold, and they threaded their way amongst pack ice. Merewyn lay quiet with Orm in a nest of eiderdowns. Brigid retched dolefully into the bucket as the north wind raised sizable waves.

The next morning they saw agitation on Erik's ship — wavings, pointing gestures. They looked ahead and saw a great expanse of bluish ice high in the air.

"That couldn't be Greenland," said Sigurd in a flat tone.

"Erik told us," answered Ketil, unperturbed, "that the first landfall would be icy. I think he called that glacier Blausark. One must sail around the south and west to reach the green."

"I did not understand that there *were* glaciers," said Sigurd. "We have plenty of those in Iceland."

Ketil did not answer, because some trailing misty wisps suddenly coalesced into fog, and Erik's ship disappeared. So did the ships behind the *Bylgja*.

"The horn —" said Ketil calmly to Sigurd. "Blow it with all your strength. Break out the rowers. Get the sail down, and keep a sharp watch in the bow. I haven't —" added Ketil with relish, "seen a fog as thick as this since we were off the Orkneys eight years ago, wasn't it?"

Sigurd, who was obeying orders, as he always used to, did not wait to hear this reminiscence. He blew the ram horn at intervals, and was relieved to hear answering horns ahead and behind him, though the blasts were distorted and it was hard to be sure where they came from.

Greenland — he thought. What has Ketil got us into? Or Erik? But he was too much occupied for speculation, especially as he heard wailing in the bow. At a moment between blowing the foghorn, and nudging aside the drifting ice with an oar, he stuck his head under the canvas tent. It was very cold. He noted that Brigid's teeth were chattering, though she was wrapped in an eiderdown, and she was making frightened noises as well. Merewyn, however, in a cocoon with Orm, turned up large inquiring eyes, and smiled a tremulous welcome.

"It's fog, of course," she said. "I can smell it, as I often did at Padstow, and then the horn."

"It's fog," he answered. "And should lift soon. Lie quiet there my wife, take care of Orm and the other one in your belly."

She nodded. "I will — but have we far to go?"

"Round a cape — the tip of this Greenland," said Sigurd with more assurance than he felt. "Try to sleep."

Merewyn would gladly have obeyed, but Orm began to whimper with hunger, and her breasts were completely dry since the new baby had started. She looked with resignation at Brigid who was crouched over the bucket. So Merewyn got up, clutching her cloak tight around her, and fumbled aft through the drifting fog to the tethered cow which was mooing in the same hopeless way that Brigid was. She took a bailing bucket and managed to extract a little milk from the cow. But the cow would soon be dry.

The crew, having nothing to do but rest their oars and push

off ice, had taken to chanting. They sang old Norse ballads and exchanged jokes. In the midst of the fog it was noisy on board, what with Sigurd blowing the horn, the singing, and moos from the cow, bleats from the sheep, and occasional barked commands from Ketil at the steering oar.

Nevertheless, after drinking the milk, Merewyn and Orm dozed. Brigid also became quiet, and at her mistress's invitation, lay down with them.

Then Merewyn had a dream. It began with a forest, a huge forest of elm, oak, beech, and bluebells growing beneath. There was holly too, scarlet berries on the glossy leaves, ready for the Christmas season. The bluebells changed to daffodils, thousands of cream and golden cups. Then there was a garden, like Romsey but not quite like it, for even Romsey had not had so many pink scented roses, nor jasmine. Then Elfled swam into the dream and looking at Merewyn with sorrow she said, "How very far you've gone, dear friend . . . why didn't you take Rumon?"

"How could I?" Merewyn retorted angrily, while the figure of Elfled wavered and became the Abbess Merwinna. "But I as much as told you to," said Merwinna. "Who would want Rumon when there is Sigurd?" Merewyn answered. "But he's a *heathen*," said the Elfled-Merwinna — and Merewyn woke up as a calf iceberg grated against the *Bylgja* and the whole longship shuddered.

The fog lifted at what would have been dawn if the sun had ever really disappeared. Erik's ship was now visible ahead of them, and some others behind. Ketil raised his sail and followed Erik.

It was true that once they had passed the cape, and turned further to the west, the fierce north winds stopped blowing and they saw green. It was the green of long grasses near the shore, one could even see little flowers amongst the grass, but *no* trees — except a few birches even more dwarfed than they had been in Iceland.

"Where's the forest, Mother?" asked Orm. She had taught him this word, and what a forest was. She looked at the black-rocked fjords filled with pack ice, at the strip of green around the edges, at the great stark snow-threaded mountains, and the towering cap of ice over all the land.

"I don't know," she said. "I thought there would certainly be pine." Bleak, desolate, mountainous, cold. What sort of place had they come to? For this they had left at least an adequate living in Iceland, and here everything must be started fresh. How?

Sigurd shared her dismay, but Ketil's enthusiasm had not abated. He was pleased that they had brought the ship through fog and ice; he was pleased that at the entrance to a fjord, Erik veered his ship around for conference and shouted, "Well done, my kinsman — and you might like *this* fjord for your own." He gestured widely; " 'Ketilsfjord' it shall be, and one of the most desirable — being southward. But now we must all go up to MY fjord, to Brattalid where I built a shelter last summer. It will be *my* home, and not far from you if you want this one. Barely a day's sail or ride. We shall be neighbors, and yet we shall each rejoice in our independence."

"Very good, Erik," said Ketil.

One by one the ships straggled into Erik's fjord, and anchored in the cove which Erik had selected for his homesite. His house had held up well during the past winter. Erik, having nothing else to do until he sailed back to Iceland, had piled many stones and cut much turf, and reinforced the roof with little birches. It was snug enough inside, and would — with crowding — hold a hundred people.

"Welcome!" Erik shouted as each boatload came ashore. "Welcome! You are now in Greenland, and must drink with me to our venture!"

There was little response. Nobody had expected Greenland to look like this.

Erik's wife, Thiodild, went around pouring ale, her lips sternly compressed, her pale lank hair untidy under the ceremonial gold-threaded coif she had immediately donned when they landed. She was the chief's wife, the queen, as it were, of this company, and would do her duty, come what might, but her disappointment could not be hidden. Her young sons, however, were in wild spirits. Leif and Thorstein romped through the grass, where all the cattle they had brought with them were soon grazing.

Twenty-five ships had started on the venture, fourteen eventually arrived at Brattalid, and of the eleven missing ones, some had turned back but others were never heard of again. They had sunk then? Nobody knew. Or perhaps, said Merewyn, consulting Sigurd, some of those ships had been blown like Ari Marson's to that faraway land across the sea where Rumon and Jorund had been.

"Perhaps —" said Sigurd, who had no time for any thoughts but the immediate settling of his family.

He and Ketil sailed the *Bylgja* around south into Ketilsfjord. They found a site on a little vik or creek near the entrance to the fjord. There was a big black crag which would keep the arctic winds off.

There were acres of grass, and some of what Ketil's determined eyes decided was arable land, as well. "An ideal place," he kept saying, "much can be grown here, the cattle will flourish, I'm sure — and as for the fish in my fjord — which will be yours some day, Sigurd — why, they are as plentiful as midges, and nobody to dispute our right to them!"

"There is no wood," said Sigurd, in a quiet voice.

"Tcha!" cried Ketil. "Plenty of stones and there's turf to burn, until we start regular voyages to fetch timber, or maybe we'll go west to that forest Jorund told us of. With a good ship, one can do anything."

Sigurd said no more, and indeed Ketil's optimism infected his crew members. They had come along partly for the adventure, and also because they all had had trouble in Iceland, one way or another, but now three of them decided to stay on Ketilsfjord for this winter. The other men drifted back to Brattalid to see what was going on, and what land grants they might get. Two of them expected to bring wives from Iceland later. From Ketilsfjord to Erik's headquarters was only a day's ride around between the tips of the fjords and the edge of the icecap, and it might be even quicker by water.

Merewyn, Brigid, and Orm slept on the ship until their homestead was built; nor was it long a-building for there were eight men working, Ketil, Sigurd, their three serfs, and the three members of the crew who had elected to stay with them.

By mid-July they were well ensconced at Ketilvik, the name they gave their new home. It was, to be sure, not nearly so fine as Langarfoss, but it had a long hall, with the High Seat they had brought, and the carved Norwegian doorposts which Ketil cherished almost as much as "Bloodletter." There was an alcove, for Merewyn and Sigurd, temporarily screened off by canvas until they could get more wood for a wall, and there were raised benches made of turf and stone for the others to sleep on in the Hall. There was a storeroom and a barn.

Ketil was jubilant on the day that Merewyn moved from the ship. "Well, dottir," he said. "Not so bad, eh? And all our own. No rent to pay to anyone! We must invite the neighbours to a feast. Invite Erik himself! This is as good, though not as big, as that house he built at Brattalid."

Merewyn, four months pregnant, and struggling to find places for the household goods they had brought, heaved a sigh. "I promised Orm that there would be forests — and roses," she said, "and with *what* could we give a feast?" They had been living on fresh-caught fish, and seal, the latter so tame that it took a man but a moment to spear one. She was sick of both foods, and longed for bread. The white bread she had dreamed of — so foolishly. She had not needed Sigurd to tell her that no wheat would grow here.

"Oh, we'll slaughter a sheep or two," said Ketil, "and they're fattening nicely."

That was true. The sheep and the cow and the horses were growing sleek as they browsed the long grass. They also chewed up the few tiny shoots which might have developed into birches.

"But in winter, Father . . ." she began, and stopped because he was ticking off on his fingers the settlers who would be invited to Ketilsfjord. " — Hjerolf, Einar, Thorbjorn, Snorri, Hrafn — and Erik the Red, of course. All the families in the Eastern Settlement."

Father, she wanted to say, don't you see that this is worse than Iceland, that though we have shelter, already in July it's cold, that there is nothing here but the rough grass and that towering mountain of gray ice behind us, and I hate the noise of seals barking where I imagined I might have a garden. Don't you see that Sigurd is not content, or guess that even alone with me he has grown silent, and does not seek my arms?

"A-ha," said Ketil with satisfaction, having finished his list of guests. "We'll have a fine gathering — like the old days in Iceland — nay — better than that, like the feastings we had when I was a boy in Norway. My father was most hospitable."

Inside Merewyn something snapped. She flung down the load of eiderdowns she had been carrying. "You stupid old man!" she cried. "Why did you ever leave Norway, if you liked it so? And why have you made us leave Iceland? Because of pride, because of killings? Ah yes, killings — plenty of those — you murdered Uther, who I always thought was my father, and Blessed Jesu — I wish he had been!"

Ketil stared at her in astonishment. He saw only an angry young woman who reminded him of his mother when she was in a temper, and the temper became them both. Merewyn looked quite beautiful: her tall body stiff as a spear.

"Dottir, dottir —" said Ketil. He turned to Brigid who was staring dumbly around the Hall. Ketil clapped her roughly on the shoulder. "Here, you take care of your mistress. Fetch her some ale!"

Brigid never understood Ketil's speech, and she was afraid of him. She gripped her knuckly chapped hands, and looked help-lessly at Merewyn.

"Bring ale," said Merewyn in Celtic, "and we will drink together to this beautiful home, and this charming country to which Ketil Ketilson, my father, has brought us — for what else can we do?"

"As you say, mistress," said Brigid, pleased by the thought of a drink, and she scuttled away.

It was then that Merewyn felt the baby in her womb, like a little message, like a fluttering of butterflies. Butterflies. Shall I ever see them again! Violet, and gold, and scarlet, or even pale blue were butterflies, flitting over a scented English garden until dusk came, and then you saw the great white moths, and presently at Romsey one often heard the nightingales.

She thought of the pink rose she had held and sniffed so rapturously on the day the Vikings raided Southampton. She thought of what happened later and of Merwinna's heroism, praying — praying — before the altar in Romsey Abbey. She shivered. Despite a feeble peat fire on the long central hearth, the Hall was cold. A new wind was blowing down off the ice cap. It did not actually enter the house except around the doors, for no windows had been cut. There were as yet no cow-birth membranes with which to cover windows and let in light. But the damp cold seeped through — and it was still only July.

"I HATE this place," she cried to Ketil. "I won't stay here. I won't have my baby here!" One could jump into those freezing waters out there amongst the seals, and very soon there'd be no more struggle.

Ketil — as perturbed as he ever had been by a woman — drew his reddish brows together, and opened the front door. He shouted for Sigurd, who was supervising the last stores to be taken off the *Bylgja*.

Sigurd arrived frowning, and at Ketil's helpless gesture went to Merewyn. "What is it, wife?" he said. She gave him a despairing look. He put his arms around her, and kissed her. He kissed her on the mouth, and she wilted against him. "I can't *stand* this —" she moaned.

Sigurd grabbed her arms and shook her. "You can —" he said. "You have endured much, and will endure Greenland, because *I* say so. This is no time for a man to think of love-making nor have I thought of it for a while. Too much else to do. But there is love between us, and you must do your part. Half of you is Norse, and I think the other half is not lacking in strength. So drink that ale Brigid keeps trying to offer you, and keep quiet, Merewyn."

She bowed her head against his sweaty leather jerkin. "Yes, Sigurd," she whispered.

Ketil's housewarming feast duly took place in August. Though it had been postponed, for there was a week of fog, but then it cleared at last into sunlight. It grew almost warm. And the ships sailed up the big fjord into the vik which was quite large enough to harbor them near the homestead.

Just before the feast, Sigurd had a piece of luck and speared a walrus which had been floating down the fjord on an ice floe. Riches, indeed! Not only the beast's flesh and blubber, and the oil it gave for the lamps, but its tusks! The ivory was worth its weight in silver, and could be sold in any European market. Even kings bought ivory from walrus tusks. They had it carved and set it gold. They used it for their baubles, their chessmen, their caskets and reliquaries. The other source of good ivory — elephant tusks — was scarcely known, or obtainable out of Africa.

Merewyn, whose spirits had been low, could not help feeling gayer as all their guests arrived, and were most polite in praising the new homestead, and in extolling Sigurd's luck with the walrus. And it was pleasant to feel important, and to chat with the other wives of whom four had accompanied their husbands to Ketilvik. There were children too for Orm to play with. Einar had brought his little boy; Snorri Thorbrandson had a girl

of six, and then, of course, there were Erik the Red's lads, Thorstein, Thorwald, and Leif. Erik's wife, Thiodild, had not come.
She had a pain in her chest, said Erik, also there was so much to
do at their Brattalid homestead. But he brought with him his
bastard daughter — Freydis, for whom Merewyn felt an instant
and uncanny dislike. Why do I? Merewyn thought, trying to
be fair, and knowing that Freydis's situation was much like her
own. Freydis had been born of a foreign woman in the Orkneys,
and later recognized and taken into the family by Erik because
he had no other daughters. Also Freydis was very young, fourteen maybe — Erik could not remember — but she looked older.
She was big, full-breasted, and strident. She talked a lot in a
grating, deep voice. She had some pimples on her heavy face,
and her wiry, red hair was chopped off short below the ears . . .
an eccentricity which puzzled Merewyn. But these were not the
peculiarities which made for antipathy. It was the look in the
girl's yellowish eyes, a look both bold and sly, and something
else which Merewyn felt as not human. A cat look, was it? Or
like a dog at the convent who had gone mad and bitten a stable
boy who thereafter died in agony.

Yet Erik acted fond of his daughter, and nobody else seemed
to think her odd. Freydis was well-mannered and praised the
homestead and the feast louder than anybody.

After serving the men, the women sat on the Cross Bench to
one side of the Hall and now Merewyn discovered a friend.
Not only a friend, but nearest neighbor, which delighted them
both. This young woman was Astrid, the second wife of a
plump and kindly man called Herjolf, who had settled himself
on the next fjord below Ketil's and was building his homestead
on a sheltered cape, naturally called "Herjolf's Ness." There
was not a man in the company who did not feel pride in owning
and naming such large tracts of land for himself. The women,
more imaginative, wondered about the coming winter, but they
too were merry as they downed their wooden beakers full of
Ketil's imported mead.

Astrid was pretty and high-born — from one of the best families in Iceland. She had curly blond hair, and a sweet smile, and she also was pregnant. "We'll help each other when the time comes, won't we —" she asked Merewyn, an imploring smile in the mild blue eyes. "You've had one, and will know what to do, and at home I have watched two births with my mother. Also you'll have this one before I do. You can teach me, please."

"To be sure," said Merewyn valiantly, ignoring her own doubts. "And on horseback I think we're only a few miles apart. We'll visit often."

They talked together until some of the men began snoring on the benches.

Merewyn learned that Astrid was quite fond of her stout middle-aged bridegroom, who was always good to her. And that by his first wife he had a son, whom Astrid had never seen, since Bjarne had left last year on a trading ship to Norway. But, said Astrid, Bjarne would probably turn up here before the winter set in, because he always tried to winter with his father.

"But won't he look for Herjolf in Iceland?" asked Merewyn, thinking how far away *that* place already seemed.

"No doubt," said Astrid, "but they'll tell him where we've gone, and Bjarne's a great sailor, his father says."

Merewyn sighed and yawned, dismissing Bjarne, and very glad that Sigurd had neither previous children nor bastards for her to raise.

She looked up at Sigurd, as he sat beside Ketil on the High Seat, and saw that he was patiently enduring Ketil's spate of anecdotes about the days they went a-viking — the raids, the plunder. But when Ketil, who was drunk, said something about Padstow and the rich booty in Cornwall, Sigurd said "NAY!" in an angry shout, which even awoke one of the snorers.

Ketil was startled. His bloodshot eyes turned to Sigurd. "What's the matter with *you?*"

"From Cornwall, Ketil Ketilson, you got your daughter, and I my wife," said Sigurd. "And that's enough about it!"

Merewyn's throat choked up as Ketil looked bewildered. "Tcha!" he said, but feebly, and began to drum on the table. "Where's the mead? Somebody fill my horn, and I'll show you how well I can still down it at one quaff.".

Astrid put her hand on Merewyn's. "Your husband loves you," she said. "For this you are lucky, but you must have suffered much."

Merewyn returned the hand's pressure, and after a moment she said, "I am lucky to have found a friend — there's been nobody since Elfled at Romsey Abbey — oh, so long ago. And perhaps Rumon —" she added in a whisper.

Astrid did not understand, but she leaned her shoulder against Merewyn's and the sympathy comforted them both, until Merewyn suddenly stiffened and said, "That Freydis! Why does she stare so at us? Those yellow eyes — what do they mean?"

When Astrid looked down the Cross Bench, Freydis was noisily sucking on whale blubber and staring only at the fire. "Merevyn —" said Astrid gently, stumbling over the name, "you are tired, I think, and should lie down. Come, I'll help you into bed."

Fortunately winter was late that year, the first real blizzard not until September. By that time, everyone on Greenland had built snug turf homesteads. Even those in the Western Settlement, where some had gone to find property for themselves after the lands and fjords to the south were all given out by Erik, who called his particular district of cronies and relatives "The Eastern Settlement." But Erik at Brattalid, up Eriksfjord, remained the chief and leader of both colonies. Though there were many who grumbled, or railed privately at Erik as daylight shrank and freezing winds blew harder off the ice cap. There were many in the two settlements who vowed to sail home as soon in the spring as might be possible. Yet still there were others, like Ketil, who valued independence, who said that this was not much worse than Iceland, and the walrus tusks — others besides

Sigurd had now speared walruses — could be bartered for what they needed once they could get a cargo to Norway. Also there was talk about sailing west, where there were trees, and rivers, and greater warmth.

Before the snows became too heavy, or the fjords too much packed with ice, many of the neighbors came to Ketilvik, and speculated on the tale they heard from Ketil or Sigurd. The story of Ari Marson's inadvertent discovery of a fair land out there to the west. Of how he had not wished to leave it.

Ketil was always glad to entertain his guests with the account Jorund had given him at Langarfoss. He never mentioned Rumon, but said only that there was another returned voyager who gave corroboration.

Of all those who listened, young Leif Erikson was the most impressed. "I shall go there someday," he said, his blue eyes alight, "once I'm able to get hold of a ship, and —" he added sighing, "old enough to skipper it properly." Leif chafed at being only fifteen, and at his father's many restrictions. He resented his father, but was fond of his mother, Thiodild, whom he resembled — the same determined mouth and chestnut hair. He longed for adventure, for a change which Greenland did not provide. At Brattalid, in the temple dedicated to Thor, Leif often invoked that god, and had even once sacrificed a seal there, pouring the blood down over Thor's hammer. The purpose of the sacrifice was not entirely clear to Leif, except that he wanted to grow up fast, to find a ship somehow, to get away from Greenland.

Even beneath the bath of seal's blood, the carved wooden statue gave no quiver. The god did not answer. Leif stared at the pools of congealing blood on the turf floor, and was discouraged. He thought of his brothers, Thorwald and Thorstein; they each had the god's name combined with theirs, and would thereby surely get more results. He felt anger at his father who had named him Leif.

There was no anger at Ketilvik twenty miles to the south of

Brattalid, but there was melancholy, a plodding boredom from being shut up in the house during the ever darkening days, and for Merewyn a fear that she tried not to recognize. She must be somewhere in the last week of pregnancy.

Her body was distorted, her soul despondent. She dragged around, trying feebly to regulate Brigid whom she knew vaguely to be sleeping with the crewmen in the straw loft. It didn't matter. At least it kept Brigid from keening all the time, as she had at first.

For Merewyn there were but two comforts. One was the warm solid feel of Sigurd's rump against hers at night, and the other was Astrid. The two young women had visited each other whenever the weather made it possible, but now as Yuletide neared and great drifts hid the way between their houses, they had not been able to meet for a fortnight. Merewyn was reduced to Brigid's company, and she missed Astrid deeply.

One morning in mid-December — nobody was quite sure which day it was, though Ketil kept a sort of calendar notched on a beam — Merewyn, in bed with Sigurd, suddenly gave a muffled cry and grabbed her back. "It hurts —" she said. "The baby is coming."

Sigurd awoke, and heard her whimper like a small wounded beast. "Elsknan min," he said. "What is it?"

"The baby's coming," she repeated. "Oh Sigurd, I'm frightened. There was much trouble last time with Orm, but your mother helped. And I feel there's trouble now. I don't know — I had a dream, a bad dream — that Freydis was squinting at me with her yellow eyes . . . and over her head a cap of ice was forming, and I was so afraid."

"Quiet, wife —" said Sigurd, patting her on the shoulder. "Hush! I'll get Brigid."

"*Brigid!*" cried Merewyn on a wail. "She's useless. I want Astrid!" She gasped as another pain gripped her back, then receded.

Sigurd was dismayed. Merewyn had been pregnant so long,

even back in Iceland, and he had known that the birthing moment would come, but never thought much about it. Those things happened as they would, and when Orm was born his mother had managed the whole thing. Certainly Merewyn should have a woman with her, someone of brighter wits than Brigid. He thought of Erik the Red's wife, Thiodild, but she was too far away. He thought of other matrons on the nearer fjords, but they weren't the ones Merewyn had asked for and they too were further off. "I'll try to fetch Astrid," he said, "but it'll take some hours."

"No, no —" she cried, "Don't leave me! Send my father! Send one of the men. Don't leave me!"

"Ketil or the men," said Sigurd, his voice sharp with sudden fear, "could not find their way to Herjolf's Ness as I could. The path we made this summer is under snowdrifts as high as my middle, but *I* know it well."

"Oh, Blessed Jesu, Blessed Virgin," whispered Merewyn — who was too deep in her fear to heed him, "help me, for I think I shall die!"

"You won't die," said Sigurd really alarmed. "What's the matter with you? I heard that Einar's daughter had a baby last week on Einarsfjord. Women are always having babies."

She gave a bubbling moan, and clasped her hands again to her back. "Don't leave me," she said. "I want Astrid."

Sigurd, frowning, got up and put on his outdoor clothes. He went to rouse Ketil, who was annoyed at being wakened.

Sigurd explained, and Ketil said angrily, "What a fuss! Women should have babies without a fuss. I'm ashamed of my dottir."

"Women don't usually give birth on *Greenland* without other women to help," said Sigurd, looking straight in the eyes of his father-in-law.

"It's that foreign blood of hers — that weakling mother," said Ketil.

"*You* made that —" said Sigurd. "And it's not the time to

mention it. Merewyn is suffering, and she must have women with her — even by Icelandic Law. She wants me near her too. And Brigid is no help, though I shall now call her. If Merewyn or the baby dies, you'd feel sad — wouldn't you, Ketil Ketilson?"

After a moment of thought, Ketil agreed. "I would," he said.

In the end, Ketil took two of the crewmen and went around to Herjolf's Ness by small boat. He said he'd rather dodge the ice floes than wallow through snowdrifts, and he could make a boat go anywhere. Sigurd agreed with misgivings, and since their own home vik was frozen solid, helped carry the little sloop to the fjord.

"She'll have had the child by the time we get back and all this bother for nothing," were Ketil's last grumpy words as he and the men rowed away. It was still dark and two seal-oil lamps glimmered at bow and stern.

Sigurd thought this likely, but he did remember that Orm's birthing had taken a very long time, a day and a night at least, until Asgerd, his mother, produced some dark liquid from her pouch and made Merewyn drink it.

He went back to look at his wife in the bed-closet and found her asleep. She roused a little, and gave him a vague trembling smile. "The pains have stopped," she murmured. "Are they getting Astrid?" He nodded and she sighed. "*You* stayed with me, my heart —" she whispered, holding her hand out to him. Before he could grasp it, she was asleep again.

In the Hall he found Brigid stomping aimlessly about, and yawning.

"Gather snow to boil water," said Sigurd. "Keep the fire up, and have you linen cloths?" These had been needed at Orm's birth, though he wasn't sure why. Brigid wasn't either, but under Sigurd's intent and worried gaze she obeyed.

Merewyn slept quietly for hours while the short December day brightened and then vanished again. After his evening meal, Sigurd went to see her, and found her awake, her face flushed, her dilated pupils staring at the birch rafters. "The pains are beginning once more," she said. "Our baby wants to be born, but then again it does not. There is something strange about our baby. That Freydis has done something — because Freydis is a bad woman, and she hates me because I have you, and she hates women too."

"Nonsense, wife!" said Sigurd vigorously. "Freydis Eriksdottir hasn't seen you in months."

"Freydis —" said Merewyn dreamily, though pausing to wince, and go limp after a moment, "is a shape-changer. She has often come here to Ketilvik, I know. As the fierce white bear you saw running away one day, and there was the white fox too."

Sigurd could find nothing to say. His mother believed in shape-changers, all Norsemen did, as they believed in giants and trolls, and the gods. The age-old Asa faith.

"I hear something outside," he said with relief. "Perhaps they've brought Astrid." He patted her shoulder, and went out to see.

It was indeed Ketil, with Astrid, who was in her sixth month of pregnancy, and looked half frozen, but she gave Sigurd a gentle, worried smile, and said, "How is she?"

"About the same as when Ketil left for you," said Sigurd. "And no words will tell my gratitude to you. You show your noble Icelandic blood. I had wondered if you'd come."

"And don't think the trips were easy!" put in Ketil. "We stove a hole in the bow — ice — and if it weren't for my well-known prowess at sea —"

"True, Foster-father, and we're glad you were lucky. Astrid, warm yourself, then do what you can for Merewyn, for she is acting strange."

Sigurd beckoned to Brigid, who reluctantly brought a cup of the almost finished mead for Astrid.

As Astrid went into the bed-closet, Merewyn was writhing; sweat on her forehead, tears on her cheeks. "Thanks to God and the Virgin Mary!" she said when she saw her friend, "because you are good, and they told me — Aunt Merwinna always told me that good was stronger than evil. They don't believe that here, the Norsemen — I forgot you are one — Astrid, will you hold my hand?"

Astrid sat on a stool beside the bed, holding Merewyn's hand while two more hours went by. Then Merewyn gave a scream, and the baby came.

It was a girl, with fuzzy red hair all over its little squashed head.

The baby cried at once, which Astrid knew to be a good sign. She tied the cord off with a leather thong, waited for the afterbirth and cleansed Merewyn. Brigid, goggle-eyed, stood by and did what she was told.

Then Astrid, who knew all the customs of her country, wrapped the baby in the linen cloths and an eiderdown. She carried it to the Hall and put it on the floor near Sigurd. "There is your girl-child," she said. And waited. This was the moment for the father to accept a baby as his, and also to decide whether it should live or not.

"My daughter —" said Sigurd, looking down at the mewling little thing in the eiderdown. He picked the baby up in his arms, suddenly afraid of its tininess. "This is my child," said Sigurd formally, addressing Ketil, Astrid, and the assembled thralls and crewmen. "I acknowledge her, and she shall be called Thora, and be under Thor's protection."

Ketil made a grunt of approval; Astrid smiled, and the others gave a small cheer.

The baby was "water-sprinkled" by her father three days later, while Merewyn lay on a bench in the Hall, watching. It was like a Christian baptism, she thought, except there was no priest. And the Norsemen, she knew by now, had for hundreds of years been "water-sprinkling" the babies they did not expose to death on a mountainside. Nevertheless, and though she was recovering fast with Astrid's help, a dreadful uneasiness came over her. She raised herself on an elbow, and said, "Sigurd! I beg you, I want 'Mary' joined to the 'Thora' — please — it'll be better — you've been so good to me — be good now."

Ketil said "Tcha!" but Sigurd shrugged. "Very well," he said to the baby, "your name is Thora Mary Sigurdsdottir, and may you be a happy, lucky one, my child."

At very nearly the moment in which the baby was water-sprinkled, two thousand miles away in England at Glastonbury, the Archbishop Dunstan ordained Rumon as a monk in the Holy Catholic and Apostolic Church.

While Rumon took his vows, as he prostrated himself before the altar, he could not entirely control his thoughts. They raced through his mind. So I've done it at last. So may I find the love of God. And I've had no success with the love of women. That thing with Alfrida, with Merewyn, they are past forever. So I am no longer in or of the world. I am a Benedictine monk now — Chastity, Poverty, and Obedience. The first two aren't hard anymore, and the last — if it's Dunstan I must obey — I can do. And so this is the end of the search, for the Islands to the west — for Avalon, which I have never found. So this is the way it is, and I must be a new man when I leave this altar.

When he walked solemnly out of the Glastonbury Church and looked up at the Tor, tears came into his eyes, and he bowed his head beneath the black cowl.

chapter twelve

In June of the year 1000, there was a great commotion in Greenland. As soon as Leif's ship was sighted down the fjord, messengers were sent by Erik the Red to the Eastern and Western settlements, inviting everybody to a feast in honor of his son Leif, who was returning from Norway where he had been wondrously well treated by the King — Olaf Trygvason. This news had come from an Icelandic fishing boat which was already anchored at Gothaab in the Western Settlement.

Merewyn sat on a bench outside when Erik's breathless messenger arrived. Astrid was with her on a visit, which much relieved Erik's servant, since now he need not go farther south to Herjolf's Ness to deliver that particular invitation.

Merewyn offered the man refreshment, and turned him over to Brigid, who had grown fat as a tub and quite deaf through the years, but could always be depended on to welcome strange men.

"So Leif is back," said Merewyn to her friend. "How glad my Orm will be, he always admired Leif, and has missed him these two years of absence, though to be sure, Leif is so much older."

"Orm is a fine lad, Merevyn," said Astrid in her gentle voice. "I hope my Helgi will be as fine."

The two women were twirling their spindles — the first step in the making of Greenland woolens for which there had developed a foreign market. The annual trader from Norway now carried back several Greenland products besides walrus tusks and sealskins.

This sitting in the sunlight outside the homestead was like the time at Langarfoss in Iceland, so long ago, Merewyn thought. And yet, nothing else was like. Here were no beautiful mountains to look at, only black hills, and frozen sedge, and the shadow of the all-pervading gray ice cap. And there were many other differences. At Langarfoss, Orm had been a baby, and now he was nearly eighteen, big and strong as Sigurd. Ketil had been there too at Langarfoss. My poor father, she thought. Ketil had spent many months dying from some dreadful pain in his middle. Sometimes he'd be out of his mind, and run around the Hall brandishing "Bloodletter," completely berserker, while he fought imaginary battles and shouted the old Viking war whoops. Then only Sigurd could manage him.

Once during Ketil's illness, Sigurd sent for a seeress, who lived near Brattalid. Her name was Thorbjorg, and she was much respected for her ability to predict the future. She came to Ketilvik, and was elaborately dressed, since all who consulted her gave gifts.

She wore a blue cloak embroidered with tiny pearls, glass beads about her neck, and had on a black lambskin hood which she refused to remove, nor would she take off her gloves which were made of white catskin. Around her waist was a belt of touchwood, from which hung a big pouch containing the charms she needed to help her prophesy. She ate nothing of the dinner they offered her except a seal's heart. Then when they had finished, she asked Merewyn if she knew the "Varthlokur" chant.

Merewyn said "No," anxiously, but added that if Thorbjorg would repeat it, she would echo each line, for it seemed that two

or more women must do the magic chant if the spirits were to
come.

They were very quiet in the Hall when Thorbjorg began her
spells. Ketil dozed in the High Seat — it was one of his quiet
days. Orm was out fishing, but Thora's wide-eyed gaze was
rigidly fastened on the seeress.

Merewyn recited the chant in rote, while she and Sigurd
watched the mysterious procedures with Thorbjorg's staff, her
knife, and sundry small shriveled objects from her pouch.

At last Thorbjorg said, staring into the peat-fire smoke,
"Some things are clear. Ketil is not mad, he is dying. And you,
Sigurd, will prosper for a few years, I cannot say how long.
But for your wife, I see big changes someday. She will voyage
far — far — she will not die on Greenland." There was a pause,
and Merewyn asked, "Orm?" on a sharp breath.

"Your son? He is not here. People must be here, or I see
nothing. For this child," she pointed to Thora, "there is some
danger ahead — yet she will not die on Greenland."

That was all they got from Thorbjorg, who was rewarded
with a beautiful black sealskin and shortly left because she had
been summoned to another homestead.

At the end Ketil insisted on boarding the *Bylgja* though the
ship was still wintering in her naust. He died on the *Bylgja*
giving phantom orders to sail, and vomiting blood between each
order.

They buried him behind the homestead, and laid "Bloodletter"
beside him, with his favorite knife, and his horned war helmet,
and his own slaughtered horse.

Another change was Thora. Merewyn glanced at her with
the anxious love and pity she had felt for the child ever since it
had become plain that Thora was not right. Thora now was
crouched over the new grass, yanking it up and piling it, just as
little Orm had done at Langarfoss. But Thora would be fifteen
at Yuletide. She was red-haired and very pretty, yet there was

blankness in her dark blue eyes, and she had never quite learned to talk. Merewyn understood her, but it was hard for others to do so. When Thora did speak it was mostly in a language of her own, a prattling, which seemed to please her for she often giggled as at some secret joke. She was sweet-tempered except at the times when she wanted her mother to feed her, and petulantly pushed away a dish of meat or skyr. She wet her bed most nights, though by day Merewyn had trained her to use the outdoors privy, or the iron chamber pot when the weather was too fierce.

"Thora," said Merewyn speaking half to herself and half to Astrid, "is very much as Orm was when we came here. She will always be a small child, I fear."

Astrid also sighed. "It must be that the trolls got at her, after her birth."

"Trolls!" said Merewyn impatiently. "It was that Freydis. She has the evil eye, and I'm afraid of her. Do you know that she stopped here last month, with that puny little husband of hers, and she spent a lot of time with Thora, stroking the child's arm, squeezing her. And once when I came back from the larder, I found that woman kissing Thora."

Astrid looked up and said quietly, "What's so wrong with that?"

"That Thora liked this attention. And that when I sent off Freydis and her husband — believe me as soon as Sigurd would let me — I found that there were bruises all over Thora's arm, and a tooth-cut on her lower lip. And then Thora made me understand that she wanted to follow Freydis. She cried for her."

"Oh . . ." said Astrid, her mild eyes startled and full of sympathy. "Then you should perhaps not take her to Erik's feast, since, of course, Freydis will be there."

"Sigurd wouldn't let me leave her behind. He's so fond of her, and refuses to admit that she is — well . . . and he always thought my hatred of Freydis was silly. And he wouldn't let *me* refuse

to go. This is Erik the Red's first feast in two years, and it would
be a grievous insult if I refused it. He is still our chief. And I
wish," she added passionately "we had never come to Greenland.
It was all poor Ketil's doing. God rest his soul."

"Perhaps," said Astrid, always striving to comfort, "the
Valkyries took Ketil up to Valhalla, where he may drink and
fight forever. He'd be happy."

"Does Valhalla receive any man who didn't die in battle?"
asked Merewyn uncertainly.

Astrid was skeptical, but she said, "Sometimes, I'm sure, and
Ketil was in many a battle, earlier."

"Yes," said Merewyn, tightening her lips. There was the
"battle" of Padstow against peaceable and defenseless people.
That battle in which Uther and others had been killed, Breaca
raped and maimed. Another "battle" at Padstow with killings,
and *my* capture later. And similar battles, like the ones in Ireland
which had brought them Brigid and Cormac as thralls.

"Oh, why do men want to fight, and kill, and conquer — and
roam!" she cried, thinking of Orm who was restless, and had
picked a fight with Thorstein Erikson purely for the fun of it.
Even Sigurd was restless. He was planning a voyage to Norway
this summer on the *Bylgja* which he had, of course, inherited
from Ketil. And he would take Orm with him.

There was always love when she thought of Sigurd, but the
wild heyday of their passion was over. They had been married
— what was it? Eighteen, nineteen years. "And we are no
longer young," said Merewyn aloud, knowing that Astrid would
placidly follow any remarks her friend made.

Astrid smiled. "You *look* young, Merevyn," she said. So
much hair, and you've kept your figure, and your teeth. Me
not. Too many babies, I suppose."

Startled out of her own preoccupation, Merewyn inspected
her friend. Astrid had grown dumpy; her yellow braids had
dwindled to wisps; her sweet smile was marred by the loss of
several front teeth. Her husband had pulled the teeth out for

her when the pain grew too bad. And Astrid had borne four children after Helgi who was nearly Thora's age. At each birth Merewyn had been with her friend, and finally learned something of midwifery. The support the two women gave each other had been a precious thing to both of them.

"How is Bjarne?" asked Merewyn, referring to Astrid's stepson.

"Sailing again very soon, though I suppose he'll wait for Erik's feast. The Eriksons are always so eager to hear what Bjarne can tell them of the countries he saw to the west, though it is to Bjarne's shame that he didn't land anywhere, and as you know, when he went to Norway, they blamed him quite a bit for not having explored. But then," said Astrid, "Bjarne is not an inquisitive man, and he was anxious to reach his father before winter set in. He's a good son."

"No doubt somebody *will* go off to explore those places now," said Merewyn, thinking of Jorund — and Rumon. "My father always wanted to, and there are *trees* there," she sighed. "I've heard nothing about England in years, but Leif must have brought news. Ah yes, I'm *eager* for the feast," she said with a youthful laugh. "And you will help me guard my poor Thora from Freydis!"

Erik the Red's feast was lavish, and attended by all the families from the settlements who were well enough to get to Brattalid. It seemed that there was much sickness in the Western Settlement. Many grew fiery hot and then freezing cold, they had headaches and they sweated and had painful bellies which became covered with red spots. A few had died. Thorbjorg, the seeress, had been sent for, and after her incantations said that the sickness came from a crew member named Arne, who was off a fishing boat which had put into Gothaab. This seemed like nonsense to everybody, for Arne was a jolly, likable lad, who was gladly received in the homesteads, not only for his amusing tales of the southern voyage he had recently taken, but because he helped with the milking, and the carving of meat at whatever house he visited. The women doted on him, especially girls. How could he have anything to do with the sickness?

When pressed, Thorbjorg said that though Arne was healthy himself, and meant no harm, he seemed to give sickness to others.

It was generally felt that Thorbjorg was losing her powers, particularly when she said that the sickness would spread to Brattalid if anybody went down to Erik's feast. And that she, herself, would not attend the feast. This was ridiculous.

The news of illness in the upper settlement would have distressed Erik more if he had not been inflicted with a much greater catastrophe.

Leif had no sooner landed and greeted his parents than he presented commands from the Norwegian King, Olaf Trygvason. King Olaf commanded that all the Greenlanders were immediately to be baptized as Christians; Leif had a black-robed priest with him, brought for the purpose. Leif and his crew had already been baptized in Norway. Iceland, said Leif, would certainly vote for the new religion at the Althing this year, for there were many priests there now, and everybody knew how unhealthy for trade it would be to disobey the Norwegian King who had himself been converted somewhere in England.

Erik was at first incredulous, dazed. His bloodshot eyes popped and he tugged at his red beard. "I don't understand you, Leif," he muttered. "What has that Christ to do with us Greenlanders?"

"Christ is the only begotten Son of the ONE TRUE GOD," said Leif. "Those gods we have worshiped — Thor, Odin, and the rest — are bad. King Olaf has convinced me of that. We will tear down the unholy temples, and build Christian churches."

"Tear down my temple to Thor . . ." repeated Erik in a wheezy voice, and heard his wife, Thiodild, give a murmur of assent.

Rage spurted through Erik, and he turned on Leif. "How dare you come to me with this trash! How dare you tell me what to do! *I* am the Chief of Greenland! Get that man out of here!" He pointed a shaking forefinger at the silent black-robed priest who stood just behind Leif.

"I can't and I won't, Father," said Leif.

Erik quivered. He turned purple, he lunged forward, and hit his son a powerful blow on the face. Then he spat at the priest.

Leif staggered. He put his hand to his nose, which was knocked askew and began to bleed. The priest wiped the spittle off his habit and put a calming hand on Leif's shoulder.

Leif gritted his teeth. "If you were not my father, and old, I'd kill you for that."

Erik looked around, and saw his son, Thorvald, watching. "Help me," he said to Thorvald, "up to the High Seat, which is mine, and always *will* be in this land of mine."

Thorvald, who was Erik's favorite, hauled his father up to the High Seat where Erik slumped down, clenching his fists, and glowering.

At Thiodild's gesture, a servant brought ale to Erik, but his wife did not go near him. Instead she brought moss to staunch the blood pouring from Leif's nose, and she said to the priest, "You may baptize *me*, sir, at once. I've long been discontented with the old gods, and wish to worship a new one, if he is powerful, as I have heard he is."

"He *is* powerful, madam," said the priest, who was called Father Frederic, and had been born in Saxony; ordained at Bremen; and subsequently sent north to attend the newly baptized King Olaf in Norway. The priest was a short, stolid man, who would — as his superiors knew — do his duty even in this barbarous Greenland. He was a man who lived calmly, without thinking of the past or worrying about the future. The scene between father and son he accepted as part of the necessities involved when one Christianized a country. It occurred to him that it was fortunate that the chief's wife appeared to be willing to lead the vanguard, but also he longed for his dinner, since it was not a fast day. He thought of roast pig, and was soon gratified.

The quarrel between Erik and Leif took place before most of the guests had arrived. But the sultry atmosphere at Brattalid was apparent to all.

Erik sat on the High Seat, and muttered. He greeted his guests with sulky grunts, occasionally saying, "Had I known Leif's treachery, there'd have been no welcome feast."

Merewyn and her family arrived with Astrid's just after the episode. They were courteously greeted by Thiodild, who conducted the women to the Cross Bench beneath the gable. Ale was poured, huge pieces of roast pig handed out, but Merewyn was so mystified by what she saw that she could not eat. What was a priest doing here? He was certainly some sort of priest, with those black robes, silver crucifix, and tonsure. And why was Leif Erikson, his face all bloody, his nose crooked, sitting beside the priest at the very bottom of the benches, instead of up on the High Seat with his father who did nothing but glare.

"What *can* have been happening?" she said to Astrid, who shook her head and concentrated on trying to chew the succulent roast pork with her remaining teeth. But Thiodild heard. She got up, and leaning across two other women, said "Leif has become a Christian. King Olaf wants us all to be Christians, as is happening in Iceland now, Leif says. I do not mind, the old gods are dying, weak, but my husband is much displeased. I believe that *you*, Merevyn Ketilsdotrir, are a Christian?"

Merewyn flushed. Her heart gave a thump. "I was," she answered with difficulty. "Of course I was. I am . . . but Sigurd and Ketil they jeered, and for years I haven't thought . . ."

"So —" said Thiodild, fixing her sharp eyes on Merewyn. She raised her voice because she wished all the women to hear. "So now we will *think*. We will be baptized. I shall build a church which is where I believe Christians confess their sins; and regularly have something called a Mass; and do not pour blood around. Their God does not want it. He is too powerful for that. I heard this from an Irish monk long ago in Iceland, and thought then it was a good religion. You have a goddess too, don't you?" Thiodild looked at Merewyn.

"No," said Merewyn, on a gasp. "At least there is a woman one can pray to — the Blessed Virgin Mary, the Mother of Christ."

"Ah —" said Thiodild. "None of my prayers to Freya or Frigg have been answered. I feel that this goddess you speak of will do better."

"You must have instruction from the priest," said Merewyn, who could find nothing else to say, and it was then she discovered that Freydis had somehow moved next to Thora, and was fondling the girl's breasts, while Thora's eyelids dropped in what seemed to be dreamy satisfaction.

Merewyn gripped Astrid. "Look!" She got up from the bench, and going to Thora, said. "I'm off to the privy, dear, and am sure you need to. *Come on!*"

Freydis gave Merewyn a baleful glance, then shrugged. Thora was rebellious. She shook her head and leaned against Freydis who laughed.

"Come with me!" cried Merewyn, taking her daughter by the shoulders and swiveling her around.

"Nay, nay," said Thora, resisting while Freydis laughed again. Thora was as big as her mother, and might have won in a scuffle, which would be the most embarrassing thing Merewyn could think of, at this feast, and with Sigurd watching from across the Hall.

Astrid intervened. She squeezed down between the bench and the table, also making excuses about the privy. "Listen, Thora —" she said to the vacant eyes, the pretty face. "I've a bit of honeycomb with me. When you come back, you shall have it."

"Honeycomb —" Thora repeated, giggling. She licked her lips. Smiling, she went outside with Merewyn. When they returned, Astrid had taken the seat beside Freydis who was sullenly eating. Merewyn and Thora sat together, while Thora sucked happily on the honeycomb. Thora seldom had such a treat, for all sweets must be imported.

Erik's feast lasted longer than the habitual three days, because there was so much to discuss.

Leif, despite a painfully swollen nose, managed to make several speeches extolling the virtues of Christianity. From these speeches and those of Father Frederic, the company gathered that there were many advantages to being a Christian. When they died, all the good people went up to a place called Heaven, women too, and to get there you didn't have to die in battle or even be good all your life, you could repent at the last moment, and all your sins would be forgiven. Also the Lord Jesus Christ was loving and tender. He was like a shepherd counting and cherishing each one of his flock, and especially fond of the lambs, or children, in the flock.

This news appealed to the women. Erik, however, who listened angrily, now raised his head and said, "That god's a milksop." To Merewyn's dismay Sigurd spoke up. "I agree with you, Erik, and have always thought so. And what is this baptism Leif talks of but our own water-sprinkling? I see no difference, and forbid my son or daughter to have it done. For my wife, it is too late, she was made a Christian as a baby, and much good *that* did her! She was never happy until she came to Iceland."

"Oh, Sigurd . . ." Merewyn whispered, but had neither the courage nor the certainty to demur. For there had been little happiness in her early life — the miserable anxious years with her mother; the torment of loving Rumon and seeing him wanting nobody but Alfrida; the wretched times with Alfrida, while foreseeing the murder of Edward which she was powerless to prevent. Then Romsey convent. That had been better, but neither lucky nor happy; she had always been an outsider, and starved, she now knew, for the love of a man — found at last in Sigurd, her pagan husband.

She looked up as Father Frederic spoke again in his flat quiet voice. He was quite accustomed to all the arguments the Norse heathen brought out, and hardly listened to them.

"Luck and Happiness," he said, "are not important in this life. Our Lord Jesus Christ assures us of them later in the Kingdom of Heaven. But as a worldly thought, I will point out to you that your subsistence here depends upon trade with Norway and Iceland, that King Olaf Trygvason has sent us here, Leif and me, to make Christians of you, and will cut you off from all supplies if he finds that you refuse. Do you think Thor or Odin can help you then?"

This material consideration, which had already convinced Iceland, convinced almost all the men present. The women were already won. Thiodild gave orders for the immediate building of her church, ignoring Erik's growling protests, and she moved out of the bed she shared with him that night.

Christianity was not the only topic of conversation at Erik's feast. There was concern about the mysterious sickness in the Western Settlement, for two wives who had come to Brattalid began to ail. They had headaches and chills. They dragged listlessly around, and neither would sit on the Cross Bench. They did not want to eat. They wanted to get home as soon as their men would let them.

The men were in no hurry. For Leif had offered them a project far more interesting than illness or Christianity. He wanted to buy Bjarne Herjolfson's ship, hire some of the crew who had been with Bjarne on that voyage to the West when he had not landed, and go to see what was really there.

Bjarne, at first protesting that he must set off for Iceland as usual, gave in rapidly when he found what Leif was willing to pay for the ship. Leif was rich, in Norway the King had given him sumptuous gifts, and Bjarne decided that Leif's offer was worthwhile. So there was to be an expedition starting in a couple of weeks. Leif had no trouble finding an eager crew, and to that lad's intense excitement he invited Orm to join them.

"So . . ." said Sigurd ruefully to Merewyn as they were riding home. "Our son is wild to go with Leif. I think I must let him. But the boy has forgotten, or doesn't care, that he was to ship with me on the *Bylgja*."

"Orm is very young and adventurous," said Merewyn without expression. She liked neither plan. She was tired. During these days she and Astrid had guarded Thora as best they could. Even so there had been one bad moment when Thora slipped out of bed in response to a low throaty call. Merewyn awoke instantly and followed her daughter into the sunny evening. She had no trouble finding her, for she heard little laughs and shrieks from behind the cow byre. Thora was naked, except for her woolen night shift, and Freydis, huge and malevolent, had pulled up the shift, and was doing something between the girl's legs, while she pricked her on the breasts with a little knife.

"You devil!" cried Merewyn. "Leave my child alone!" She ran for Freydis, and jumped at her so hard that the woman fell down. Merewyn wrenched the knife from her hand, and held it trembling while she mastered the desire to cut down on that broad square face, to slash the yellow eyes.

"Mama —" said Thora, her mouth hanging open. "Mama, we was playing a good game." Merewyn took her by the arm and propelled her back to bed.

Merewyn had not told Sigurd of this episode. She would when they got home. She would have to make him realize, or admit, that Thora was a baby in a woman's body, and that Freydis was dangerous. But he was already unhappy over Orm's defection, and besides he did not look well. His face was drawn, his movements much slower than usual, as he guided the old horse. Thora rode with Merewyn on the mare which fortunately had foaled three times in Greenland. They had prospered in a way, as Thorbjorg had foretold. Their livestock multiplied, and Sigurd bartered walrus tusks, narwhal horns, and seal hides for luxuries which came in on the Norwegian trader or Icelandic fishing boats.

"Wife," said Sigurd when they reached Ketilvik, "I think I'll lie down. I've a headache, or at least a pain in my head such as I never had since a battle in Dublin years ago with Ketil."

"Go to bed then — elsknan min," she said quietly. "I'll bring you ale, and a cold cloth for your head."

She was not alarmed then, but she became so as the days went by and Sigurd showed no wish to get out of bed. He had chills at times, sometimes his body felt very hot. She was sponging him once when she noticed that his belly was covered with rosy spots, and wondered what they could be.

Brigid, when told to, shared the nursing. There was always soiled moss or straw to dispose of for the sick man's bowels ran like water. Merewyn occasionally got some sleep on the Cross Bench, since Sigurd was so restless he preferred to have their bed alone.

In a week, Orm came home, exuberant with plans for Leif's voyage of discovery to the west. Orm was full of news. Leif had indeed bought Bjarne's ship and hired seven of his crew. They had all been tinkering with the ship, and outfitting her. Orm, the youngest member of the crew, had been much flattered that Leif consulted him at times, saying that though he knew the boy had made only fishing trips himself, yet the blood of great sailors was in him.

Orm had come home to say farewell, and pick up his gear. They would all set out next Thursday, which was Thor's day and lucky.

"Were there many baptisms after we left?" asked Merewyn faintly.

"Oh, quite a few, I think," said Orm, bored with anything which had nothing to do with the expedition. "Leif scarcely paid attention, we are so busy with plans. The priest did all that."

"I wish you would, Orm —" said Merewyn, stirring a seal-meat stew, and looking at her son.

"Would what? Oh, you mean this Christian stuff? Father doesn't like it. He said so."

Merewyn bowed her head. "Orm, your father is very ill. I'm worried. He may have caught the sickness they have in the Western Settlement. And he's distressed that you are going with Leif instead of on the *Bylgja*."

"Oh," said Orm, his neck flushing. "I didn't think. But to go with *Leif* —" He trailed off.

"Yes, I know," said Merewyn. This was her restless, handsome son, who must exactly resemble his father as Sigurd was years ago, when Sigurd first went a-viking. But on the other hand the expedition with Leif was different. It was an adventure into the unknown, and perhaps there would be no rape and murder involved. Perhaps no trading either. It was not like a Viking voyage. And Leif was a Christian — she reminded herself of that. He had been baptized. So he would take care of her son, and get him baptized perhaps.

When Orm went to visit his father in the bed-closet, even his youthful unawareness was shattered. Sigurd's face was gray and pinched, he continually muttered something one could not understand. He plucked at the eiderdown and had made a hole in it.

"Father —" said Orm. As Sigurd went on babbling, he repeated, "Father!"

Sigurd came slowly back into the world. His heavy eyelids lifted and focused on Orm. "My son —" he said. "I'm dying."

"*No!*" cried Orm with a shiver. "You're strong. You've always been Sigurd the Strong!"

"No more —" Sigurd whispered, then gathered himself to say, "When I am gone, you must take care of your mother and your little sister. You will take them on the *Bylgja* away from here. The gods don't like Greenland. They do not wish us to be here. You will be head of the family now."

"Father . . ." said Orm helplessly, frightened by the look of the man on the bed. "You will not die, and I want to go with Leif," but he spoke so low that Sigurd did not hear him.

"I command this," said Sigurd. "Give me your hand."

Orm clasped his father's hand.

"Greenland was never the place for us," said Sigurd after a moment. "Nor will Norsemen endure here very long. There are evil spirits coming down from the ice cap. During these last days I've seen them. The white wolf with yellow eyes, she stalks my Thora. She hates my wife. I did not know before. Take your mother and sister away. Swear it! You must not go with Leif. Swear it!"

Orm swallowed three times, anxious to get rid of the burning hand which clung to his. "I swear —" he said in a feeble voice.

"Louder!" said Sigurd, raising on his elbow. "Swear by Thor and Odin, that when I am dead, you will take our womenfolk away."

"I swear by Thor and Odin," said Orm miserably after a moment.

"Swear by this new god too, that Jesus Christ —" said Sigurd. "Your mother believes in Him. And one can never be quite sure."

"By Jesus Christ," said Orm, his lips trembling, "and since Leif also believes in Him, perhaps He *is* a stronger god."

"Make Thor's hammer sign to seal the oath," said Sigurd, gasping and putting his hand on his belly. "I've noticed that it is very like the sign the Christians make. Thor and Christ must understand each other."

Frightened by the wild look in his father's eyes, Orm made with his thumb the hammer sign of Thor — down, up — and across.

Sigurd slumped back on the bed. "There is a strange feel in my belly," he said in a high plaintive voice. "Get your mother."

* * *

Sigurd died on the following day.

Even though Astrid came to Merewyn, the new-made widow was so numb that she could neither weep nor talk. Nor would she go near the bed-closet she had once shared with Sigurd. She lay on a bench in the Hall, gazing into the fire, unable to eat.

At last prodded by Astrid, who was most lovingly worried, Merewyn appeared at Sigurd's burial behind the homestead, and even counted out the assets which would make for Orm's "Ardval" or inheritance feast. A pig to be slaughtered, two lambs, maybe three — what did it matter — and there was silver enough to buy mead from the Norwegian trader which had put in to Brattalid.

Orm sailed in their small boat to fetch the mead, and was very serious on his return home.

He found Merewyn, Thora, and Astrid sitting in the Hall. It was snowing outside, not the great winter blizzards, but a drizzling snow which hissed on the roof.

Orm looked at his mother, at Astrid and at Thora who was happily playing with a mound of pebbles — arranging them and scattering them over the hearth.

"Leif sailed yesterday to find those lands to the west," said Orm, climbing to the High Seat — which was now his — and waiting for Brigid to bring him ale.

Merewyn looked up, she drew in her breath. "Leif sailed?"

"Indeed, and I'm glad I happened to be there. The nearest I'll come to going."

"But you *were* going with Leif," said Merewyn.

"I was once, I'm not. How could I leave here before my Ardval?"

"Nay," said Astrid quickly. "How could you! You're the family chief now."

"And," said Orm solemnly, "I swore to my father before he died that I would take my mother and sister off Greenland on the *Bylgja* — which is *mine* now." He tossed his fair locks, looking proud. "Mother, where would you like to go? If we sell our thralls, we'll have plenty of silver to hire a good crew. Erik the Red has a servant who would even pay something for Brigid as a wife."

"May heaven help him, whoever he is," said Merewyn with the first smile they had seen. "But since women are so scarce here . . . and everything else is scarce —"

"You want to go back to Iceland?" asked Astrid, glad that her friend was talking again.

"No," said Merewyn. "England. I want trees, and the soft summer air. I'm homesick." She said this in a faintly startled voice and spoke no more. The sleet hissed on the roof.

Astrid spoke to Orm. "At Brattalid, what was Leif's departure like?"

"Nothing special," answered Orm. "We all waved farewell — oh yes, Leif had properly asked his father to go with him, but Erik has been in a bad mood ever since that priest came and Thiodild is building a church. He did not want to sail with Leif, and managed to fall off his horse and hurt himself. Which he said was a sign that he should not leave Greenland. So he didn't go."

"Ah, yes," said Astrid, shaking her head. "Poor old Erik tries to rule his 'kingdom' here, but he cannot rule his wife or sons anymore. Nor," she added on a sigh, "can he rule death." She glanced at Merewyn.

"There've been several more deaths," said Orm cheerfully, "in the Western Settlement, and even at Brattalid — from the sickness."

"Death —" said Merewyn suddenly. "Everywhere is death — it took my Sigurd."

"We can sail in a week," Orm said. He missed his father but he no longer sorrowed for being unable to go with Leif. The ownership of the *Bylgja* excited him. And the voyage to England did too, now his mother had requested it. He had no doubts of his ability to skipper the ship, he had explored every inch of her from his childhood on, and had learned seamanship since he could toddle from both Ketil and Sigurd.

"The sooner the better," said Merewyn, glancing at Thora who had tired of her pebble game, and was standing by the window, her hand cupped around her ear, a delighted look on her face as though she could hear something they could not.

"It will be sad without you, Merevyn," said Astrid with another sigh. "But I know that for you it is better to leave here. And I have my husband and children." She got up and kissed Merewyn on the cheek. "I'll help you get ready," she added, "and you must not spend too much on Orm's Ardval — you will need many supplies on board the *Bylgja* to get to England. That is a long way, I think."

"It *is!*" cried Orm, jubilantly. "Farther away than where Leif's trying to go. I'm sure of that."

Merewyn looked at her young son. What it is to be eighteen, and so confident! Sigurd was once like that.

At the memory of Sigurd there came a kind of bleeding and weeping inside. She got up violently and went to Thora who was trying to make a bunch of moss stick on the head of a little wooden puppet Astrid had brought her.

"That's not the way, dear," she said. "I'll lend you one of my pins, and then the hair will stay on."

Thora relinquished the puppet, and looked up at her mother. "Thora wants Freydis," she said plaintively. "She'll come?"

Merewyn flinched and turned to Astrid. "My friend," she said, "will you help me start packing our chests, NOW?"

It was the middle of September when the *Bylgja* neared England. She had been about two months at sea and except for occasional adverse winds, one storm, and the discovery of a small mysterious leak in the bow, the voyage was uneventful. The leak was just behind the carved image of Thor, long ago placed there by Ketil. They caulked the leak with a wad of tarred canvas, and could not understand why each morning the canvas had fallen out and seawater was trickling in. Merewyn first guessed the cause of this, and stayed awake watching. Yes, it was Thora, who dug out the caulking, and crooned happily as she dabbled her fingers in the water.

"No, Thora!" cried Merewyn, slapping the girl's hand. "Don't do that! Orm would be angry!"

"Orm not my father —" said Thora. "Where's my father?" She began to cry. Merewyn, with a heavy heart and no answer, soothed the child by nursery rhymes and lullabies. After that she put Thora in a different place in the prow, and stayed alert for any movement.

During the voyage, Orm had been greatly helped in navigation by an old English-born seaman called John. John had often traveled as crew from various ports in England to Iceland. He had gone on to Greenland because his half-Icelandic son wished to better himself. But the son had recently died of the sickness in the Western Settlement. John wished to come home. He was stooped and little, his hair was gray, his mouth toothless, his cheeks netted with purple veins. Orm had been reluctant to take him on but now he was glad. Old John could read the stars, he could smell a coming storm, and like a swallow or a sea gull, he always knew which way to steer for where he wanted.

One day when they were becalmed and had broken out the oarsmen, John, normally taciturn, said to Merewyn, "We're driftin' south around the tip o' Ireland. Ye didn't want to land at Padstow, did ye?"

"No!" Merewyn gave a shudder.

"Wasn't sure —" said John, chomping with sharp old gums on a bit of pork crackle. "Folk get a hankering to get back where they was born. I do m'self, though 'twas only a hovel half the size o' this ship."

"You were born in our west country, weren't you?" asked Merewyn, keeping an eye on Thora who distracted the oarsmen by tripping back and forth between them and making little sounds. Thora was certainly very pretty; her red hair sprang in curls around her small innocent face; her breasts and hips were womanly; some of the crew gave her lecherous looks, but there was no real danger — no privacy except under the women's tent in the prow; besides, Orm kept as stern an eye on his men as ever Ketil or Sigurd did.

"I was born nearabouts Bristol, ma'am," John said. "Bristol's a fair port 'n' we better head fur it. Up the river Severn. Once there I can start ye all on your way."

"Start us on our way?" Merewyn repeated. Where to? She had thought only of reaching England. For all the weeks she had scarcely thought of anything but the needs of life at sea, of caring for Thora, and of admiring Orm when he left the steering oar and came forward to ask how she did.

Suddenly, and for the first time in months, she thought of Rumon. When she found Rumon, he would tell her what to do. She felt comfort when she thought of Rumon.

"Glastonbury . . . ?" she said to John. "It's in the west country, would it be near this Bristol you say we should land in?"

Old John pulled another piece of crackle from the grilled pig. "Glaston's near enough to Bristol," he agreed. "Wouldn't take much more'n a day to get there over the Mendip Hills."

Merewyn laughed, and the old man looked at her inquiringly. "I remember," she said, "when the Mendips seemed so — so enormous to me, but since then I've known great mountains in Iceland and Greenland. Hills now are enough."

"Fur me too," said John. " 'Tis because we're gettin' on, though ye're so much younger, ma'am. Ah —" His hunched body stiffened, and he licked his forefinger to hold it in the air. "Winds blowing up from the west, we'll make do wi' that. It'll help us." He went aft to speak to Orm.

Ten days later they had managed to get up the Severn, and enter the Avon. "Here's Bristol," announced old John with satisfaction. "The best port in the west country, wouldn't wonder was it better than London."

Everyone looked at the collection of thatched huts, the few stone buildings, and the spire of a church. There were many wooden docks and the Avon was alive with little coracles.

As they came into the town, a woman on shore gave a piercing wail, and began to run. Others gathered on the bank and began to point at the *Bylgja*. They too ran away. In a few minutes the church bell began ringing frantically.

Merewyn went aft to Orm. "They think we're a Viking raider," she said. "Lower the sail, and take off those dragons on the prow and stern."

Orm looked rebellious. He liked the *Bylgja* with all her panoply.

"You have to dock," said Merewyn quietly. "We're leaking and we've run out of drink, even water. Do you want them to kill us?"

She indicated a growing mass of men on the bank, all with bows and arrows and spears.

"We'll fight them," said Orm. "How *dare* they keep us from landing!"

Merewyn did not argue with him — he looked much like Ketil at the moment. She pulled off the white linen coif she had saved for the arrival, and waved it violently. She said to Thora, "Stand here beside me! Wait — first run forward and get your night shift — then wave that!"

The girl obeyed, and rapidly rejoined her mother.

The men on the bank seemed uncertain. One arrow whizzed harmlessly above Orm's head. Merewyn and Thora waved their garments.

Old John came up, and said to Orm, "Yonder quay is empty — steer for that, young master, I'll speak to them." As the *Bylgja* came close to shore, John shouted across the water. "Wot a way to greet fellow countrymen who're coming home! We expected a better welcome!"

A crowd of armed men had now reached the dock, towards which they saw the *Bylgja* heading. They milled about and conferred, while watching the two women waving their peace signals. Several of the men on shore suspected a trick. In the last ten years there had been constant Viking raids, and a constant paying-off by King Ethelred to stop them.

The men of Bristol, as in many another port, were ashamed. They were eager to fight.

The *Bylgja* edged towards the empty dock, someone let loose another arrow which struck an oarsman on the arm. Merewyn felt Thora trembling beside her, and straightening up very tall, she cupped her hands and called to a man in a rich blue tunic, garnished with gold, who had gold bracelets and a sword that glittered on his hip. "Are you an earl," she called, "or thane? You seem so by your dress."

The man nodded. "I am a thane." He said something quieting to another citizen who was aiming a spear. The thane came forward.

"You see," continued Merewyn, buoyed by a strength she had never used before, "we are peaceable. We have no shields along our gunwales. We have no real weapons. We've sailed from Greenland *only* to get home. We ask *only* that you let us land, for we are sorely athirst."

The thane, whose name was Odo, had a broad honest face, and he was perplexed. He fingered his sword hilt, and knit his bushy flaxen brows.

"Let's kill them, my lord," cried a male voice from the crowd. "We could get 'em all from here."

Odo made a dismissive gesture. "Wait!" He called to Merewyn, "Who *are* you? And where is this Greenland you claim to have left?"

Merewyn thought fast. One could not explain Greenland. "I am the Lady Merewyn —" she called back. "I was born down there in Cornwall. I served many years as waiting lady to Queen Alfrida. I am a Christian, and the descendant of King Arthur whom you well know here."

This last remark came without volition. It spoke itself.

Odo was impressed. "You come from the line of Arthur?"

"Yes," said Merewyn. "That's why I was favored at King Edgar's court and waited on the Queen until poor little King Edward's death. Then I went to a convent — Romsey. Have you heard of it?"

Odo shook his head and bowed. He revered the memory of the heroic Arthur, as did everyone in the west country.

"Who's *that?*" he asked, pointing at Orm, who was gripping the steering oar as though he would like to break it and scowling ferociously.

"That is my son," said Merewyn. "His father is dead. He has brought us home. Me and my daughter." She put her arm around Thora, who stared across the water with blank frightened eyes.

Odo slowly digested this information, and decided that the handsome woman was telling the truth. At least that though this looked like a Viking raider, yet none of the crew seemed threatening.

"The women may come ashore," he said. "Everyone else on the ship is to stay there for now, under guard." The men of Bristol grumbled assent, and aimed in readiness either their arrows or their spears towards the *Bylgja*.

Merewyn and Thora scrambled aft to climb on the gunwhale to the dock. "Mother," Orm hissed angrily, as she passed him. "That's not *true* what you said about Arthur. You're of Ketil's blood!"

"Shut up!" she answered from the side of her mouth. "Do you want us all murdered?"

Orm was confused and humiliated. He had never seen her look like this before, like Frigg, the angry goddess, flashing-eyed. He did not want her to intercede for him. He wanted to fight. To leap ashore with his crew and die in honorable battle if need be. But though the berserker frenzy rose in him, and though each of his crew had an axe, he gave no order. It was the sight of Thora which deterred him. The girl was clinging to their mother and sobbing.

Old John also deterred him. "Now look'ee, young master," said John, putting his gnarled hand on Orm's arm. "We've not come all this way fur a bloody brawl. Ye make one move, an' all them spears and arrows will be in us like stuck pigs. I'd like to see m'old home at Pucklechurch afore I die. Let yer mother handle this. She's one can do it."

Orm compressed his lips between the silky gold of his new mustache and beard. He sat fuming and silent at the steering oar, while his mother and Thora were greeted by Odo, then disappeared into the muttering crowd.

Merewyn did indeed know how to handle Odo. She had met many like him during her time at the English Court. She flattered him a little, yet was always faintly condescending as befitted her role of aristocrat. She told him truthfully, though vaguely, of her capture at Padstow. Odo remembered hearing of that raid when he was a youth. His wife, who was a mousy little thing, listened avidly, and sniffled sympathy for Merewyn.

Soon Merewyn and Thora were offered a bed in the Thane's own manor house, which was luxurious, timber-built, and remarkably warm. There were trees all over the manor. Great big oaks, elms, beeches.

Merewyn stared at the trees and sighed with pleasure. "Look, Thora —" she said to the girl, who was now silent and bewildered. "We're home — and over there is a rose garden. Do you see the beautiful roses?"

"Roses," Thora repeated carefully.

"Oh, my dear heart —" whispered Merewyn, kissing the girl. "All will go well for us now — you'll see."

All went very well at Bristol. That night Orm and the crew were permitted to land. The Thane ordered the townspeople to provide sleeping places for the crew, and his orders were obeyed though many of the households were suspicious and resentful. Their worries receded by morning, for the various crewmen behaved gratefully. Old John at once found a man he had known in childhood, and they spent half the night reminiscing and drinking. The news of this spread rapidly, and the townsfolk decided that the Thane was right. This ship at the dock might look Viking, but there were English people aboard, there was even a great lady who was a granddaughter (it soon became a granddaughter) of an old-time king whom the bards sung about on twilit evenings.

Orm kept a rotating guard on his beloved ship, but after three days of the Thane's hospitality, and of enjoying the soft, fragrant English countryside, and the bountiful food and drink Odo's household gave him, he was not so truculent.

At last he approached Merewyn thoughtfully. "What is it you want now, Mother?" he asked. And added, "I should say 'My Lady,' I suppose. They all do."

Merewyn considered her son, and answered, "Sell the *Bylgja*. Odo himself wants to buy her, then we'll have plenty of money for our needs."

Orm started. "Sell the *Bylgja!* Mother, you're mad. I never thought you'd act like this!"

"The ship has served her purpose," said Merewyn inflexibly. "And I never want to see her again."

"I DO," cried Orm though daunted by the look in his mother's sea-green eyes. "She's *mine!* What else have I from Ketil and my father, though you seem to have forgot them both!"

"There are times," said Merewyn, "when it is wise to forget the past, yet I do remind you that you swore to Sigurd that you would care for Thora and me. I have plans for you, Orm. You can be a great man here in England — a thane at least. Do you want to go back to the barren cold and the sicknesses of Greenland? Remember our dark smoky little house at Ketilvik, then look at this." She indicated the tapestried walls of Odo's manor, the cushioned benches, the flagons of wine and mead in silver ewers, always in readiness on the tables. She pointed to the wooden floor which was strewn with rushes and thyme and gave out fragrance.

"How could you make a great man of me, Mother?" said Orm uncertainly. Merewyn immediately thought, with Rumon's help; but she said instead, "I've known King Ethelred since he was a child. I know Court life. Queen Alfrida is no friend to me, but I understand from Odo that she has retired to her convent at Wherwell, and is ill. Ethelred's wife is from the Danelaw up north, and will not mind that my two children have Norse blood. This I cannot hide, though it seems Ethelred is terrified of the Vikings. He is a weak man, and I think I can manage him."

"As the Lady Merewyn of royal British descent?" asked Orm after a moment, torn between sarcasm and awe.

"Just so," said Merewyn coldly.

Orm bit his lips.

During all the years he could remember, he had never seen his mother anything but quiet, and anxious to please his father. Now she expected to live a lie. One he did not understand. Nobody had ever spoken about Merewyn's youth, or the circumstances of her capture at Padstow. But she was certainly Ketil's daughter. It was through the mother then — that Cornish grandmother of his who was never mentioned. He was puzzled, and his anger drained away.

"As you like, Mother," he said haltingly. "I'll sell the *Bylgja* and we will do as you wish. For now. But I don't understand."

Merewyn gave him a smile. "I don't either. Since I've been on English soil, I feel very different. May our Lord Jesus Christ help us. And *you*, Orm, shall be baptized. Thora too."

"Thora — perhaps," said her son. "Me NEVER! My father forbade it."

Merewyn turned away. Sigurd — his memory brought pain. They had loved each other so passionately for years until it dwindled on that accursed Greenland. And where was Sigurd now? Where could a heathen be? I'll pray for him, she thought. There was a chapel on the manor. She had gone to Mass each day since their arrival. But she had not yet prayed for either Ketil or Sigurd. She had not thought of her former life, her prayers had all been for the future, for the success of her plans. For reinstatement at Court which would help Orm to a thaneship, and for Thora who would surely grow up at last in this gentle country. Especially since Freydis was left so far away that her disgusting spells could not work.

Every now and then amongst her prayers, there floated an image of Rumon as she had last seen him at Langarfoss. She dimly realized that she thought a great deal about Rumon. It never occurred to her that she might not find him. And sometimes, in the middle of the night, she bitterly regretted the way they had parted in Iceland. And once she dreamed that she and Rumon were married.

chapter thirteen

Odo, the Bristol thane, paid generously for the *Bylgja*. And in exchange for the narwhal horn they had brought (the horn was a renowned aphrodisiac and supposed to be off a unicorn) he gave them two sturdy horses. Merewyn negotiated these barters and managed deftly to evade Odo's lust to bed her. She said that it was the time of the month when such a thing could not take place, and when he turned his attentions to Thora, she said that the girl had a secret malady, which might be catching. Odo was alarmed, and solaced himself with one of the maids.

He bore no resentment. He was pleased to have entertained some members of the Royal Court, however remote *that* was — nobody in Bristol knew where the Court was at the moment — and he enjoined Merewyn to tell King Ethelred of how well she and her family had been treated at his Manor.

Merewyn smilingly agreed; and they left Bristol in a haze of good will.

Now that the *Bylgja* was definitely gone, Orm felt for his mother considerable admiration. She had certainly managed to get more money than he had dreamed existed. He had a pouchful of silver under his tunic and Merewyn another pouch concealed beneath her skirt. Orm knew that the successful transactions were due to her authority and tact. Nor had he ever thought of her as a desirable woman before. But he had not missed the glint in Odo's eyes. So she still had charm for men. How extraordinary in a mother! He was now aware that she was slender, that there was no gray in her abundant reddish hair, and that her eyes were of a beautiful color. As for Thora — if she were not his foolish baby sister — would he not think her very appealing?

Thoughts like these had never come to him in Greenland. He was astonished by them. As they rode up over the Mendips, he even dismounted and walked so that the women's horse might be relieved of double load.

As he walked he steadied Thora in the saddle, for she tended to sway off balance. It occurred to Orm that Thora was not like the few other girls he had known on Greenland. His heartbeat quickened at the thought of girls. There seemed to be many of them here, he saw dairy maids peeping out from barns; he spied a pink-cheeked beauty herding home a dozen cows. He wanted to linger, for she gave him a provocative smile.

"No, Orm," said his mother. "You'll find plenty of that later. We must get on to Glastonbury."

"What's that queer-looking thing?" Orm asked. He pointed up the Tor to St. Michael's stone tower. I've never seen anything like it."

"Of course you haven't," she answered sharply. "You've never known anything but ice, and mean little heathen homesteads standing in barren plots. It'll be different now."

Long ago she had felt this same excitement upon nearing Glastonbury. She had wanted to find Rumon then, and that was what she wanted now.

At the hostel they were received with suspicion by the young monk in charge. They were, he felt, a peculiar threesome. They wore no crosses, brought no luggage or servants, and the young man spoke English with a strange accent, while the girl did not speak at all. Accustomed as Glastonbury was to foreign pilgrims, still it was wise, considering the recent Viking invasions, and the country's fear of more invasions, to ask for credentials before receiving anybody in the hostel.

Merewyn deftly handled the monk as she had handled Odo. She rummaged in her memory and brought out the name of the hospitaler who had received her years ago, then of the cook. The monk had heard of neither, but it finally developed that a kitchen boy, now middle-aged, remembered Merewyn. He said he did so because she was of royal blood, and had been in such a hurry to depart that he had had to feed her servants at three in the morning.

Once they were assured of beds in the hostel, Merewyn set off with Orm and Thora to seek an interview with the new Abbot of Glastonbury. She had never tried to approach his predecessor on her other visit, long ago.

As they passed the church towards the Abbot's palatial lodging, she paused by the grave of King Arthur, and looked down at it silently, her eyebrows drawn together in a frown. Her children paused too, though Thora, staring around, gave a chuckle of delight as she saw the Abbot's garden.

"Ro-ses," she said, "smell good."

"Yes, dear, yes," answered Merewyn. "Orm — no matter what I say, you must show no surprise. In fact it is proper for you to stand back against the wall with Thora, but first kneel and kiss the Abbot's ring."

"Why, Mother?" said Orm. "Why should I kiss any man's ring?"

"A mark of respect. Do as I tell you." Her voice trembled, and he realized that she was nervous. He grunted, and followed her sulkily to the porter's gate of the Abbot's lodging. He listened with amazement, while Merewyn explained their visit to the porter who stuck his cowled head against a grille.

She was a poor widow, said Merewyn, who had been captured by the Vikings and forcibly held in Ireland at Limerick with her children. The English all knew about the Norse in Ireland.

(They would not know about Iceland, nor did she want them to.) But, she continued to the porter, she would not have requested an interview with the Abbot, who must hear plenty of sad stories, except that she was royal, and anxious to have advice from so great a man as the Abbot Beorhted. She had learned the new Abbot's name at the hostel.

"You mean," said the flat Somerset voice of the monk through the grille, "you was captured by them dreadful Danes, ma'am?"

"Yes," answered Merewyn fiercely.

Behind her Orm stiffened. Even during the few days he had been in England, he had discovered that the English made no distinction amongst the Norsemen. They called them all "Danes." Orm knew little about the Danes, except that they were also Northern men. In Greenland he had heard tales from returned sailors, about the people who went a-viking from Denmark, Sweden, Norway, and even farther south, from a place called Jomsburg. But these were all vague names to Orm. He knew his real heritage and could recite the list of his ancestors. Both Ketil and Sigurd had whiled away many a black winter night by teaching him that. His stock came from Greenland, before that Iceland, and farther back was Norway. He had learned the genealogy they taught him by heart, as he had learned some of the eddas and sagas, and thought maybe of being a skald himself one day. But had thought also of being a sea king on the *Bylgja* as Ketil had been, Ketil who was his grandfather. Why, then, did his mother tell all these lies?

He understood better when they were finally received in the Abbot's parlor.

The Abbot Beorhted was a small, suave man who looked rather like a well-fed squirrel. His little dark eyes were shrewd — one did not become head of the most famous English Abbey without shrewdness. He wore a gold pectoral cross, studded with gems, and on his plump forefinger was an amethyst ring which he held out for the supplicants to kiss, quite as though he were a bishop, which was his next goal.

Merewyn knelt and kissed the ring, then glared at Orm, who made an indecisive gesture over the ring. But Thora copied her mother, giggling, for she thought this a fine game.

"Sit down, my lady," said the Abbot warily. "The porter says you have royal blood, but have also had great misfortunes. What can I do for you?" Charity, of course he thought. All three were dressed almost like thralls — patched and faded clothes, wrinkled white coif on the woman's head, a trumpery gilt brooch to hold her stained mantle. The boy had a sword, to be sure, and a bracelet with gold bosses on it, but it did not look like an English bracelet.

Merewyn clenched her hands beneath her cloak, and said steadily, "My Lord Abbot, I want only information. We've been captured so long, and just escaped. We know nothing of our homeland. Can you tell me is the atheling Lord Rumon still here?"

The Abbot was startled. So indeed was Orm. Who was Rumon? When he was a child at Langarfoss, was there not someone called Rumon, who came to visit with a skald?

"Lord Rumon left here, some years ago," said the Abbot, after a pause. "I hardly knew him. I was prior then. Segegar was Abbot, he who is now the Bishop of Bath and Wells."

Merewyn's fingernails bit into her palms. What did she care about the Bishop of Bath and Wells! She spoke with control. "Lord Rumon is at Court then with King Ethelred?"

"Oh, I shouldn't think so, lady," answered the Abbot with a thin smile. "The King's Men are not composed of priests, nor yet," he added, "of warriors" — and instantly checked himself. It was not wise to seem critical of the King. "Madam," he said anxious to get rid of them, and also observing with annoyance that the girl had plucked a climbing rose from outside the window and was scattering the petals over his Turkey rug. "Madam, I trust you'll be comfortable at the hostel. And it does now occur to me that an old Irish monk called Finian may know something of Lord Rumon. Brother Finian lives in one of the new cells we've built halfway up the Tor. I'm sure you'll find him."

The Abbot rose and smiled dismissal, a smile which faded as he saw Thora stamping the rose petals into his rug and singing a breathy little song. "Your daughter —" said the Abbot who had a passion for tidiness. "She is simple-minded?"

Merewyn winced and colored. "No!" she said angrily. "She's been bewitched by a pagan fiend!"

The Abbot made the sign of the cross as he stepped back quickly. "You have my sympathy, lady." He disappeared through a painted curtain into his own quarters.

"Come on, Mother," said Orm, who saw that there were tears in Merewyn's eyes; desolation in her face. "That's all you'll get from him, whatever it was you wanted."

"I'd like to find Rumon," said Merewyn in a small voice. The courage and authority she had shown since landing were dimmed.

She let Orm propel herself and Thora out of the Abbot's lodgings.

They wandered back towards the hostel and heard the monks chanting for Nones, as they passed the great church. "These Christians do a lot of singing and praying," Orm remarked. "Not a life I'd like."

"No," Merewyn agreed, and sighed. "But they've got something we haven't. I used to have it. I've lost it."

This did not interest Orm, who was eager for his dinner. "Why do you want to find a Lord Rumon, Mother?" he asked as they went through the precinct gates.

"Because —" she said in a dragging voice, "I once loved him very much. Later — too late — he loved me. He sailed to the West — sailed finally back to Iceland, trying to find me. I was married to Sigurd, oh, I loved your father, never forget that — but he's dead."

"Your friend Rumon may also be dead." Orm spoke tartly, and hustled his mother towards the hostel.

"I don't *think* so," she said. "I believe I'd know somehow."

She yanked her arm from Orm's, and spoke with sudden resolution. "Take care of Thora, see that she gets her meal when you
do. I'm going to find Brother Finian!"

Merewyn went up the Tor on foot, as she had with Rumon
years ago. Halfway up she saw a modest cluster of stone huts,
which had not been there before. She approached the nearest
one, and knocked on the wooden door.

It was opened briskly by a monk. "You want to buy candles
for St. Michael? You want permission to make pilgrimage to
the top o' the Tor?" said the monk. "That'll be fourpence."

Merewyn shook her head. "I want to find Brother Finian."

"Last cell down," said the monk pointing, and putting away
the candles he had been ready to sell, "but you know he's gone
blind?"

"No," said Merewyn, this time faintly. "I don't know
anything about Brother Finian."

"Two years ago he lost his sight, but he's sharp enough for all
that. Three o' us here we care for him, whilst we collect from
the pilgrims."

"Wouldn't he do better in the Infirmary?"

"He didn't want to be there, and our old Abbot — Segegar
that was — said he might as well live here, if it suited him.
Which it does."

Merewyn said "Thank you," and walked uncertainly to the
last stone hut. Its occupant was sitting on a stool outside the
door, sniffing the autumn air. His scalp was mottled above the
grizzled fringe of tonsure. There were deep crow's feet around
his closed eyes. Yet there was an expression of peace on the
long-lipped Celtic face.

"Brother Finian?" asked Merewyn.

"Sure and that's who *I* am," he answered. "And who may you
be, Lady?" He cocked his head, and smiled. He was accustomed
to occasional female visitors, especially those from the Irish
group who lived by the Meare.

"I am the Lady Merewyn," she said, "of royal British blood."

Finian started. He touched his cross, and murmured, "Jesu, Domine —"

"Have you heard of me?" she asked, astonished.

"Aye, my daughter," said Finian. He thought of the frantic chase with Rumon, looking for this woman through Devonshire, through Cornwall, and he thought of the tragic ending at Padstow.

"I'm trying to find Lord Rumon," said Merewyn hesitantly, puzzled by the monk and expecting disappointment again. "The Abbott said you might know about Rumon."

"Come here," said Finian. "Gi' me yer hand!"

She obeyed, and the blind monk felt all over her hand carefully. Then he reached up and touched her face. Since his blindness, he had learned to understand things about people if he could touch them. As the earthly sight had gone, it seemed as though an eye had opened in his mind.

"Ye're in trouble again," he said. "Poor child, why be ye looking for Rumon when ye didn't want him in Iceland?"

"You know *that?*" She was appalled and excited.

"I know that, and many thing else too. There's another stool in the cell, it's special for the ones who come to see me. 'Tis a luxury permitted by the Abbot. Fetch the stool and sit here, i' the sun." He raised his wrinkled face, and spread his arms out as though the sun would give him blessing.

Merewyn saw rain clouds gathering behind the Tor, but she said nothing as she scurried into the dark hut and brought out the other stool.

Finian groped for her hand again as she sat down beside him.

"Is Rumon dead?" she asked in a white, dry voice.

"Wasn't a month ago," said Finian. "I'd a message from him." He gave her hand a pat. "Years ago, m'daughter," he chuckled, "I met ye on the way to here, an' ye were lookin' fur Rumon then."

"To be *sure*," she suddenly remembered the subprior who had been guiding foreign pilgrims to Glastonbury. "And you found him for me —" she added hopefully. "Where is he now?"

"At Tavistock Abbey in Devon, m'dear, and they think a lot o' him too. Lord Ordulf fair dotes on him."

"What's he doing there? I thought he'd be at Court." Finian felt her hand suddenly tremble. "Jesu!" she added. "Lord Ordulf — Queen Alfrida's brother? I thought Rumon was finished with Alfrida forever!"

"So he is," said Finian gently. "And 'tis a long story, but afore I tell it —" He hesitated, then decided that she must get the bitter draught down at once.

"Rumon," he said, "was ordained by Dunstan, several years afore our blessed Archibshop died in '88. Rumon is a Benedictine monk, m'child, and you must not think of him in any fleshly way."

She was silent, staring up at the Tor where the clouds were growing blacker. "It's going to rain," she said. "May we sit inside your cell, Brother Finian? And you'll tell me the saga of Rumon?" She used the Norse word with a deliberate, and sad irony.

Once inside his whitewashed little hut, Finian stood up before the empty fireplace while she sat hunched on a stool, her head bowed against her clasped hands.

Finian said that having seen Rumon but a few times during the years after his return from Iceland, he naturally did not know all the details, but the substance was this.

Rumon had stopped in Glastonbury, then traveled east to Canterbury and visited Archbishop Dunstan. Rumon immediately entered the novitiate, and in due course took his final vows. He then asked permission to become a hermit somewhere.

"I know what happened," said Finian, "because the dear old Archbishop, knowing how fond I was of Rumon and that I had gone to Padstow with him —"

"PADSTOW?" she interrupted with a gasp. "You were at Padstow?"

"Aye," said Finian solemnly. "We got there just after the Viking raid, when ye were captured, yer servants killed."

Merewyn shuddered. There was a silence. He heard her breathing sharpen. "Did you talk to anyone at Padstow? Was there anyone left?"

"Did Rumon not tell ye when ye saw him in Iceland?"

"No, we hardly spoke, and I didn't ask. I *don't* want to think of what happened at Padstow. It's a long-ago nightmare. Forgotten."

The old monk reflected; had his eyes been open and sighted there would have been a quizzical glint in them.

"Ye are afeard," he said. "Ye're passing yerself off, as ye once did unknowing, as a British lady of high birth. For why do ye do this?"

"Because," she said in a rush, "I want to help Orm and Thora; knowledge of my true birth would make it impossible. England is so terrified of the Norsemen."

" 'Tis the truth. And why not? Vikings've raided and plundered and murdered and burned everywhere in the South. Ethelred he buys them off for a time, but they come back. And they say the Danelaw might be rising. I hear these things even in me cell. I understand your reasoning," added Finian slowly. "An' nobody in England knows who ye really are, except Rumon and me, who'll never mention it. Dunstan knew, but he's gone on to his reward, God rest his soul."

Merewyn got up and began pacing the clay floor. "Ketil-Firebeard *was* my father. I grew fond of him, despite the dreadful things he did to my mother. And I loved Sigurd, my husband, but they're dead. And they died as heathens. I wish to forget it."

Finian sighed. He understood the turmoil she was in, and her wish to forget her recent years; but forgetting was none too easy, nor was starting life over again easy. He guessed that she had hoped to find Rumon still unwed and powerful by reason of some position at Court. That she had, however foolishly, counted on the love which had sent Rumon a-thirsting after her to Ireland; to unknown lands in the West, and finally to Iceland, where she had not been glad to see him. Up and down, up and down, Finian thought, like a child's seesaw. But now the seesaw was broken.

"Ye're ambitious for yer children," he stated. "How many?"

"Two. A boy and girl. Though it is for Orm I want help."

"And for yerself? Waiting lady to the Queen? Ye were once."

"One can have influence when living in Court circles. I learned that long ago. This Queen of Ethelred's is from the Danelaw, isn't she?"

"Aye, from York. But she's a shadow, a little ghost. I saw her some years back when she came here on pilgrimage. Praying at the shrines that her infants would live. She's had one every year. 'Tis *something* the King can do, it seems. Make babies."

"Can't he do anything else?" she asked, staring at the serene old face with its shut eyes.

"The King is a coward, God help him," said Finian calmly. "An' he's the tool of any vicious man who wants to use him. He's always been afraid of his mother, and felt guilty for young Edward's murder. Rumon told me that after the murder, Alfrida beat Ethelred with a candle. So now he's afraid o' candles and they use fish-oil lamps at Court."

They were both quiet while rain spattered around the hut. Merewyn sat down on the stool, and said, "What did Rumon do after he was ordained? Did he become a hermit?"

"In a manner o' speaking. Our beloved Dunstan spent many a prayerful night for Brother Rumon, whose whole life he well knew. Then he sent him to the Lizard, at the tip o' Cornwall — I expect ye know it?"

She shook her head, and realizing that Finian could not see, said, "No, that's a long way from Padstow."

"There was still a heathen bunch down there, making blood sacrifices on standing stones. Rumon, when he was shipwrecked from France, had been with them a while. Dunstan never forgot anything important, and the state of Christendom in Cornwall had always disturbed him. He sent Rumon down there as a missionary. Rumon had now vowed obedience of course, and he went right off.

"Three years later he came back here to Glaston, and we talked for hours. He had lived in a wattle-and-daub hut he had built near a fine spring. He had converted and baptized sixty people and started a church. He had made them pull down their standing stones, and help him carve crosses. He traveled up and down the east coast o' Cornwall. I believe there were four parishes named for him, only I think the Cornish called him 'Ruan,' some priest having confused his name with an early saint. Rumon smiled when he told me, and said that since leaving Provence he'd never heard his real name pronounced exactly.

"I could see then," Finian added, "that Rumon's smile'd become very sweet. It warmed ye. Nor was he vainglorious over his successes, he gave all credit to the glory of God Triumphant, and to the Holy Ghost. When he was living as a hermit in Cornwall, a dove had flown in and landed on the roof of his well, which he thereafter deemed sacred. He put a cross on the well. He'd sometimes had visions of the Holy Ghost, he told me."

"So," said Merewyn slowly, "then what did he do?"

"Dunstan sent a priest to replace him, and Brother Rumon traveled back to Canterbury in early spring. 'Twas 988, the year the Archbishop died, on May 19th. A holy death he had while he was chanting a psalm, but before this he had a further order for Rumon, who he thought should give up a missionary life which had become too easy and remote. He thought Rumon's soul should meet more challenge." Finian smiled, "Our sainted Dunstan was ever concerned with what was best for a soul. Tavistock Abbey badly needed a Brother who could write Latin and make illuminations. It also needed a harpist who would set the pitch for the chants and accompany the carols on festival days. Rumon, as ye know, had both talents."

"Yes," she said. "No wonder they think so much of him at Tavistock."

" 'Tis not so much for that, 'tis for something happened three years ago. The Vikings came up the Tamar to Tavistock Abbey. Lord Ordulf was at Lydford, an' by this time Rumon was in charge of the Abbey. When those Norse pirates went a-stravaging and yelling into the church, Rumon felt fury come on him. He told me this himself. He'd never felt anything like it before. He ran for his sword, which he had put in the sacristy, an' when he saw them climbing the altar to get at the beautiful gold crucifix, when he saw 'em jumping high to grab down the silver dove, emblem o' the Holy Ghost, he attacked them, alone. The other monks were afeared — trying to hide."

"Rumon attacked the Vikings," she said in a shaken, wondering voice. *"Rumon . . ."*

"Aye," said Finian. "An' he killed two o' 'em."

Her mouth went dry. She could only whisper, "Rumon shed blood in the Abbey church . . ."

"He did. There're times, m'daughter, when a man must fight fur what he believes in."

"What happened?" she whispered. "Why didn't they kill *him?*"

"A miracle, it might be, but on the airthly plane, they seem to've been so astonished by a Christian monk giving them battle, and besides he'd killed their leader, that they scuttled out o' the church, giving Rumon time enough to take the relics, the treasure an' the silver dove to Rumonsleigh, inland — a parish he'd founded."

"And then?"

"Oh, the Vikings came back that night wi' reinforcements and burned the Abbey and monastery, but they got no real plunder; Rumon had saved what belonged to the church. It seems that they've nearly rebuilt the whole Abbey now, an' Lord Ordulf he keeps a guard around it all the time — fighting men. 'Tis a pity," added Finian, "that the King doesn't copy his uncle. Anybody but a rabbit would know 'twouldn't work to keep paying off those divvils. An' now they're landing from Normandy too."

"The Normans are Norsemen?" asked Merewyn absently, trying to understand how Rumon could so much have altered.

"The Normans were Norsemen once," said Finian, "but they've got 'emselves Frenchified. The King o' France he gave 'em Normandy, an' they were quiet for a bit, but that Danish King Sweyn, he's stirred 'em up to want conquests. England's the likeliest conquest, because we don't fight together an' we've got the Danelaw already."

Merewyn sighed deeply. "I wonder if I went to see Rumon, if — even now —"

"He'd help ye at Court? I doubt that he could, if he would. An' to see him, ye must first ask pairmission, m' dear. Have ye no other place to go?"

Her answer came from some deep part of her, through a layer of thought which was combatting disappointment. "Romsey Abbey, I suppose," she said. "They'll remember that my Aunt Merwinna was Abbess there —" She stopped short. "But she wasn't really my aunt — Oh Blessed Mary —"

Finian heard her discouragement, and was sorry. He reflected that Dunstan had kept her secret. And her ambitions were not for herself, but her son. That was no mortal sin, hardly even venial. And the poor woman had endured much.

"Elfled is now Abbess o' Romsey," he said quietly. "Did ye know her?"

Merewyn started. "She was my dear friend."

"Then go back there, child, an' I think it pairhaps better that ye don't tell her yer true story. The Vikings raided Romsey too, but the nuns escaped to Winchester. The Danish King

Sweyn was on his way to London, and scarce bothered wi'
Romsey where he found poor pickings."

"Blessed Mary —" said Merewyn again. "Is there no peace
in this country where I so longed to return?"

Finian was growing tired. He groped for the other stool and
sat down. "Well, m'dear, many think that this year 1000 from
the bairth o' Lord Jesus Christ'll bring the end o' the world. Ye
must live one day at a time, never forgetting the Mass, prayers,
an' submission to God's will fur us. 'Tis loike the loss o' me
sight. God's Will."

Merewyn was humbled by this brave old man who had
patiently given so much information, and who had in essence
agreed to her continuance in the role of Lady Merewyn.

She was uncertain, miserable, but she reached over and took
the mottled hand and kissed it. "Thank you, Brother Finian.
I shall try to submit to God's Will, whatever it brings."

Merewyn and her children arrived at Romsey Abbey in
Hampshire three days later. After many waits, and the observance of protocol, they were received by the Abbess Elfled. Not
in Merwinna's parlor, that had been burned by the Vikings,
but in one very like it, except that Elfled had her walls painted
a buttercup yellow, instead of the usual whitewash. This was
a peculiarity which Merewyn later discovered disturbed some
of the nuns.

In twenty years, Elfled had changed. She had grown meager,
the Abbess's black habit hung lankly about her — the habit once
worn by Merwinna, who was never stout, but never as skinny
as this either, even at the end.

Elfled constantly disciplined herself. She still bathed in the
freezing carp pond, and ate only a chicken wing, or a morsel of
fish on fast days.

She spent so many hours praying on stone floors that her
knees had stiffened and developed calluses.

When Merewyn finally got in to see her old-time friend, Elfled welcomed her warmly enough, and smiled when Thora, who had learned this game before, made a grab at her hand and kissed the gold ring.

"Ah, there, Merewyn —" said Elfled. "Where have you been all these years since you set forth to carry your sainted aunt's heart to Cornwall?"

Merewyn explained briefly — capture by Vikings, a forced marriage. She omitted reference to either Iceland or Greenland, places she had now discovered that the English knew nothing of.

Elfled made a rather perfunctory sound of pity. "So now you're back, and welcome, of course. These are your children?" Her sharp mouse face turned from the frowning Orm to Thora who was happy and stroking the yellow wall.

"Pretty . . ." said Thora, "like a butterfly." She had seen a brimstone butterfly outside of Bristol, and Merewyn had explained what it was. One never knew what Thora could or could not learn.

Elfled knew that the yellow in her walls had been criticized by many; she was not sure herself why she had ordered such a deviation to be made. She had searched her conscience about it; now she saw that Thora was one of the simple, and perhaps holy ones in this world. Elfled, swamped by the problems involved in running a large abbey, was touched. She looked kindly at Thora, and allowed her old affection for Merewyn to revive.

"I never wanted them to elect me Abbess," she said. "The job scarce leaves me time for worship, but they couldn't agree on anyone else."

"Can't you resign, lady?" asked Orm, suddenly interested. His mother kept dragging him to black-robed clerics, male and female, and it startled him to think that they might have feelings.

"No, I can't," said Elfled. She turned back to Merewyn. "So

the dream I had about you and the great big yellow-haired man came true?"

Merewyn nodded. "Orm looks just like him. Do you still have those dreams, Elfled?"

"Not since the one which warned of the second Viking raid, when we got all the treasure to Winchester in time. It was your Aunt Merwinna who sent me that dream, I expect."

The church bell began ringing for Tierce, and Elfled glanced rather nervously towards the open window where tree shadows were lengthening. She tinkled a cow bell, and when a nun appeared, said, "Fetch Sister Herluva." At Merewyn's exclamation of surprise, Elfled said, "Yes, she's still here, and runs the hostel. The Infirmary got too hard for her, she's over sixty now. — Do you remember, Merewyn, that twenty years ago we thought Herluva was already old?" There was a faint ghost of the elfin smile which had suited her name.

"I remember," said Merewyn, "but look, Reverend Mother —" she added hurriedly as Elfled smoothed her habit and adjusted her cross preparatory to entering the church, "we mustn't be a nuisance to you, but I do need advice. I don't know what to do, and I've no one. *No one*," she repeated with frightened emphasis, "but you to turn to."

"You could pray," said Elfled acidly, "or perhaps that's one thing you *don't* remember." She turned in the doorway and said more gently, "Go to the hostel, I'll see you again after supper."

During the next days at Romsey much happened fast to Merewyn and her children. Thora developed an attachment to Sister Herluva, who was kind, protective, and discovered that the girl could be put to gathering herb leaves and flower petals for drying in wooden frames; that if carefully directed, she would neither spill nor damage.

Then Orm, being very much bored at the nunnery, went

riding by himself in the countryside, and had a lucky encounter with one of the King's thanes, called Wulfric, who was stag-hunting in the forest with his housecarls. When Orm heard the approaching gallop of many horses, he drew his horse aside from the path and waited for the others to go by.

But Wulfric spied Orm waiting behind a giant oak. "Hola, friend!" he said jovially. "Did you see anything of a stag? The hounds've lost the scent." He indicated the hounds which were sniffing here and there, and running in circles.

Orm shook his head and blushed. He knew nothing of hunting in a forest. A seal, or a walrus would have been another matter. He wasn't even sure what a stag was.

"You're a likely-looking lad," said Wulfric. "Are ye hawk-ing? No, ye can't be," for there was no leather gauntlet on Orm's wrist.

"I'm just riding," said Orm.

Wulfric was a kindly soul, stout, middle-aged, with a red nose, and no perplexities. He owned land in a dozen counties, all inherited from his rich father, Wulfrun. All the reeves who administered his properties seemed competent. Wulfric had no need to bestir himself except on quarter days when he was pre-sented with the revenues. On his home Manor at Ashley he liked to have a handsome well-born retinue around him — drinking and hunting companions.

He was at once pleased with Orm, whom he found exception-ally good-looking with his blond hair and steady blue eyes. A very big youth he was too, as tall a man as Wulfric had seen. "We've lost the stag," he said. "Come on back to my Manor and dine with me."

Orm was pleased, and said he would like to.

The ensuing visit was a revelation to Orm. He had never seen such fine lands, such a huge stone manor house, so many retainers, housecarls, servants. He had never tasted such food. Eel pies, beef and kidney pies, custard pies, and marchpane sweets studded with raisins. All washed down with either mead or wines imported from across the Channel.

Orm asked how wide that "channel" was. Wulfric answered, "Oh, I don't know — half a day's sail; sometimes I think a bit near to those villains in Normandy. I don't see why they don't leave us alone. They've got plenty over there for themselves."

Orm accepted this in silence. He had already explained himself in the way his mother wished. He said that he was half descended from a royal British line, and his accented English was due to years in Ireland.

Wulfric scarcely listened. He grew befuddled with mead, wine, and huge helpings of the excellent food. He liked Orm, as he did almost everybody, and anyone staying at Romsey Abbey was naturally to be received. Soon he wanted his nap, and yawning, said to Orm, "Would you like to join me here, lad? As one of my retainers? I can find something at Court for your mother, the King's a good friend of mine."

Orm said "Yes . . ." in a hesitant voice. He knew that this was great good fortune, and exactly what his mother had hoped for, but he saw nothing exciting about joining Wulfric's entourage. Except good meals and whatever this kind of hunting might be. Also there were no girls to be seen except the servants.

Wulfric was a widower of some years standing, his children had married and gone to other parts of England. He had not bothered to find a new wife. He enjoyed himself on the Manor while occasionally attending upon the King. Wulfric was a placid man.

Orm waited until the Thane had his nap. All around the Hall on cushioned benches, the housecarls and thane's men set to snoring. Orm did not sleep. He went outside and walked around the gardens, slightly aware of the beauty of the English countryside while wondering what to do. He thought mostly of himself, but he was also trying to understand what his mother's life had been before his birth. He began to realize that it had been a grim life in Greenland — even before that in Iceland. He had promised his father to take care of the women, he had made a vow to Thor. Yet nobody here believed in Thor. It was confusing.

Later he consented to become one of Wulfric's men, on condition that his mother was given a place at Court.

Wulfric amiably agreed, and suddenly remembered that because of Queen Elgifu's illness — she had been ailing a long time — there was probably room for another lady at Court. It would be simple to arrange, said Wulfric. The King was due back from a foray in Cumberland, in which he had been fighting his vassal prince Malcolm.

"What did he do that for?" asked Orm, puzzled by everything he had heard of this English king. "Why fight one of his own? Why not pull the country together, and fight the — as you call them — Danes?"

"Oh, I don't know," answered Wulfric. "Those Norman pirates have gone away again, the King gave them some money. I had to pay in a hundred pounds m'self, but it's worth it for peace. Have a bit of wine?"

Orm courteously declined. He rode back to Romsey Abbey, and at dawn roused his mother to report on the day's events.

Merewyn was at first enchanted. These were certainly the steps towards importance she had hoped to get through Rumon. They had happened by chance through Orm. Elfled had done nothing during the days they'd been there, except to say that they could stay on indefinitely at the hostel, and to pray with Merewyn. Merewyn mumbled along with Elfled the old familiar Latin prayers but they gave no warmth. Nor did Elfled. The two women had lost much of their old attraction for each other. Their lives for twenty years had been too different. Elfled's had been entirely bounded by the Abbey, and the administrative duties there, for which she had no real bent. Merewyn could see many untidy details which had not happened in her aunt's time. She still thought of Merwinna as her aunt.

When she went to Mass on the morning of Orm's return, she said special prayers to Merwinna, who had been canonized in the Abbey; whose body was enshrined in an elegant marble coffin; and whose obit day, May 13, was observed with due ceremony. She spoke directly to Merwinna, reminding her that the requested expedition to Padstow with the heart had resulted in Merewyn's capture, and that therefore she wished for blessings on the new venture.

She did not know whether St. Merwinna heard her or not, but there was a feeling of peace when Merewyn left the church, and later in the afternoon there seemed to be a definite answer, for Thane Wulfric turned up at the Abbey with an invitation to stay at his manor house while negotiations with the Queen at Winchester were concluded.

Merewyn was impressed by the stout little man. He was kindly, he had kept his word, he was hospitable, and useful. Moreover, though she had thought herself finished with all that, it was pleasant to see a kindling in his small bleary eyes when he first met her. Pleasant to hear his remark to Orm, "You didn't tell me your mother was a beautiful woman."

Orm smiled a little, and shrugged. "It might be," he said, hoping that his mother would deal with another amorous thane as well as she had handled Odo.

In the end they left Thora behind. The girl did not want to leave Romsey. She clung to Sister Herluva, and prattled of all the pretty leaves she had gathered today.

Elfled had little to say. She was worried about a muddle in the accounts which would have to be shown to the Bishop. She was worried about one of the nuns who had been found in a novice's cell after Compline, her habit off, her wimple crushed into a ball, and her remarks of a kind that the Mistress of Novices said she was ashamed to report.

Elfled was not sorry to see Merewyn and Orm go. Rooms were always needed in the hostel. Nor did she mind that Thora stayed. Sister Herluva would care for her, teach her what devotions the child's mind could understand.

"I wish you very well, Merewyn," said Elfled at parting. "Your rank is such that you deserve the best of a secular life. I shall remember you in my prayers. You and your son," she added, with a tight, rather disapproving, smile.

Merewyn thought of Astrid, of the warmth, understanding and womanly experiences they had always shared. Motherhood. Wifehood. But Astrid was on Greenland, months of sailing away.

She immediately extinguished thoughts of Astrid, or Greenland.

"Thank you, Reverend Mother," she said, "for all your hospitality. I've given silver to the church, and if I get to Court, I shall try to use influence for the advancement of Romsey Abbey. I've seen that you do much good here amongst the neighboring poor. And then there is Thora. You shall be recompensed for her board."

Elfled glanced anxiously at the pile of vellum sheets on her table. "I don't seem very good at keeping accounts," she said. "Nor does my Cellaress —"

They kissed each other on the cheeks, and Merewyn rode off with Wulfric and Orm.

Like Orm she was dazzled by Wulfric's Manor. She was given a whole Bower to herself — the one formerly occupied by Wulfric's wife. She was assigned a skilled maidservant to tend her. She enjoyed the food she had dreamed of during all those years of dried fish and whale blubber.

She enjoyed being called "my lady," and the deference in Wulfric's attentions. There was never anything violent or lustful about Wulfric. He never tried to enter her room as Odo had. But she knew from his looks that he admired her. That was agreeable. He might, she thought, want to marry the Lady Merewyn — this round, good-natured little thane.

Well, that might be not so bad, sink into a luxurious peaceful life. She began to be instinctively alluring with Wulfric, but in a very dignified way. Orm felt differently. Already he was bored and restless. One day he attacked his mother. "What about your place at Court? Wulfric won't move until you make him. What about your promise to me that I could become a thane myself? This is the same thing, day in, day out. I hear," he added quietly, "that King Sweyn of Denmark has landed in England with a vast host. Sweyn is a man I'd like to meet."

"Don't you dare!" she cried. "You're English now. You must fight for England."

"But they *don't* fight here," said Orm plaintively. "And my blood, Mother, whether you like it or not, is Viking."

"Hush!" she said sharply. "I'll get us to the Court at once. Then you'll see things differently. But first we'll baptize you very quietly in the little parish church over the hill."

"No," said Orm. "King Sweyn was baptized, and it didn't last. He now believes in the old gods again, and they are giving him victories."

Mother and son glared at each other. Merewyn gave in. He looked so much like Sigurd. Her thoughts ran this way and that, and from the muddle one thing emerged clearly. She wanted to see Rumon, but oddly enough she wanted to see Alfrida again. Why? She wasn't sure except that hatred and jealousy made a deep-lying canker which had festered underneath for years. She would like to rid herself of it.

"We'll go to Court, I'll see that Wulfric arranges it. Be patient another day, Orm; for tomorrow I shall ride to Wherwell Abbey."

"What's that?" he asked. "What for?"

"To see the old Queen — Alfrida, to whom I was once a lady-in-waiting."

"You think she'll help you at Court," asked Orm eagerly, "if she's the King's mother?"

"No. I don't know—" she replied. "It's not for that, it's for a reason I can't explain. She was evil once, she caused the death of Edward, but Elfled says she's bedridden with dropsy, and has done many good works. I loved her once — for a time."

Orm's neck blushed. He was uncomfortable and barely condoned his mother's eccentricity. She had shown several eccentricities since their arrival in England. Yet critical as he might be, she commanded respect.

They had no further conversation.

The next day there was a drizzle, but Merewyn, taking one of the Thane's men with her, rode to Wherwell.

She was appalled by her first sight of Alfrida, who was propped up in bed, panting a little and enormously bloated. Her golden hair had been cut short, and had turned a muddy color. Her belly raised a hump under the sheet. Her fine-boned face had become a full moon, the eyelids puffed over the sunken violet eyes.

She greeted Merewyn, but said at once in an invalid's whine, "They tap and they cup, and I've had dozens of leeches put on me, but still I swell. They gave me the last rites again last night."

"I'm sorry," said Merewyn awkwardly, wishing she hadn't come.

"You look well," said Alfrida with a flash of malice. "Not changed much."

"Thank you," said Merewyn temperately. "I've had a rather rugged twenty years out of the country, perhaps they were good for me."

"Did you marry Rumon?" asked Alfrida. "After I got through with him I did think you might."

"No, I did not marry Rumon. I married a Norseman who captured me in Cornwall. Don't you know that Rumon is now a monk?"

Alfrida moved restlessly, and a hovering infirmaress came rushing over to put a fresh leech on a swollen vein in the Queen's leg.

"I don't know anything about Rumon," said Alfrida. "I don't know anything about Ethelred either, and considering what I did for him —" She stopped and had a choking spell. "Nobody comes to see me, and yet I helped raise Ethelred's son by that mewling little Elgifu."

"Well, *I'm* here —" said Merewyn briskly. "Would you like me to comb your hair as I did once?"

"My hair —" whispered Alfrida. "My long golden hair, and you used to stroke me all over. You were the best lady-in-waiting I ever had." She added in a faltering voice, "I shouldn't have taken Rumon from you, should I?"

"I don't know that you could help it, I'm not sure what we can or can't help. I think that humility and trust in God, are all there is to guide us."

Merewyn heard herself saying this with astonishment, which was cut by Alfrida saying in the old tone of command, "Comb my hair!"

Merewyn combed Alfrida's now lank, sparse hair. She felt pity and repulsion too. She wondered again why she had come. She came away from the visit only with sadness. And a sense of the last farewell.

chapter fourteen

In the year 1002, Merewyn and Orm made two decisions, neither of which pleased the other.

Merewyn had duly become lady-in-waiting to the feeble Queen, Elgifu, and helped with the constant nursing. During this time the Queen delivered a dead baby, and thereafter had a bloody flux from her woman's parts. She dwindled, and whimpered, and at the end often shrieked with pain. Merewyn was sorry for her, but never felt deep attachment, nor could she manage to get the land grants and title of Thane she had wanted for Orm.

Ethelred said "Yes" one day, and "Perhaps" the next; a week or month would pass, and finding that he had forgotten all about her petition, she would have to start over.

Most of Ethelred's early comeliness had vanished like his mother's. He was often drunk, and thereafter became either raging or maudlin. He enjoyed the company and advice of two men, both of whom were repulsive to Merewyn. One was Cild Aelfric, the son of Alfhere, who had arranged the murder of Edward. The other was a sleazy braggart called Edric Streona.

In the meantime Viking hordes attacked all parts of England.

They were led by King Sweyn of Denmark and his stripling son, Canute.

Ethelred cowered in his palace at Winchester while messengers brought news of fresh raids in Devon and Somerset and Essex. London was attacked, and managed to defend itself, without any help from the King. The Vikings harbored on the Isle of Wight, which they found convenient, or in Normandy. Ethelred decided to buy off King Sweyn. That wily Dane demanded twenty-four thousand pounds but consented to leave his sister, Gunhild, her husband, Earl Pallig, and their little son as hostages. Sweyn eventually went back to Denmark and Orm went too.

Before he left Orm announced his decision to Merewyn on a February day of thin sunlight and the smell of warming earth. She was sitting in the ladies' section of the Palace gardens, and was embroidering gold armbands for the Queen's funeral. No more twirling spindles or weaving. The servants, dozens of them, did that.

"I'm leaving here, Mother," said Orm. "I've had my bellyful. I've joined up with Sweyn. I'm to be steersman on one of the longships," he added proudly. "They tried me out."

"Oh . . ." she said. The nowadays unaccustomed tears gathered in her eyes. "You're not joining England's *enemy* . . ."

"England is nothing to me. It's soft as a rotten plum. I want to be fighting with my own kind."

"Fighting," she repeated, "plundering, raping, murdering . . . oh, my son . . ."

"Well," said Orm with one of his rare smiles, "isn't that all better than doing *nothing?*"

"Of course it isn't," she said angrily. "Besides, Wulfric has been good to you, and by all reports you have been doing plenty. How about those two village girls who claim you fathered their babes?"

"Possibly I did," Orm shrugged, "but those girls had lain under many a hedgerow before I laid them, and I gave them each some silver."

Merewyn sighed, and changed the subject. "What did you think would become of me? Now that the poor Queen is dead?"

"Can't you stay on here?" Orm had not really thought at all. He had a comfortable feeling that his mother was established in the Court life, however unproductive it had been for himself, and he knew that Thora was safe at Romsey.

"King Ethelred," said Merewyn, putting down her embroidery, and glancing sharply around for the eavesdroppers who infested the Court, "has already sent off to request the hand of Emma, the Duke of Normandy's sister, one of those harebrained indecent moves which come natural to him. He defied most of the Witan to do it."

Orm started, then burst into a roar of laughter. "A Norman Queen!" he cried. "A descendant of the Vikings! Oh, this is too funny! Ethelred wants to make doubly sure that he never has to fight us. First he buys Sweyn off, then he gets himself allied with Normandy!"

"Hush!" she cried sharply. "Very few know this yet. The Duke of Normandy may refuse. But I've learned that if Emma comes, she'll bring many Norman ladies with her, and a lot of retainers. There'll be no place for me at Court."

"Well, then," said Orm briskly. "Go back to Romsey Abbey."

"I don't want to." She paused, her voice was very low. "I think I shall consent to marry Wulfric."

"Thor's hammer!" Orm cried, his jaw dropping. "That prosy, fat little thane! D'you mean to say he's still after you?"

Merewyn was silent, turning her embroidery over and over on her lap. During her time as Queen's lady, Wulfric had come often to Court, he had sought her out in a shy way, he had stammered nervous compliments, he had twice stroked her hand, and asked her to wed him. He said that he knew he wasn't worthy of such a high-born lady's affections, but that he would try to keep her comfortable and contented. And once in the Palace Hall, when Ethelred's chief bard chanted a poem about the wondrous exploits of King Arthur, Wulfric looked at her with meaning, and Ethelred, who was in a good mood today, called from the throne, "There, Lady Merewyn, you have a ballad just for you about your royal forefather."

Merewyn picked up her needle and plopped it into the canvas. "Thane Wulfric may be dull, but he is kind, as you well know," she said. "And if God would send us a child, we'd both welcome it."

"Mother!" The back of Orm's neck blushed, as it still did when he was embarrassed. "You're too old for such thoughts! It's outrageous!"

"I think not, elsknan min." She smiled faintly at his annoyance. "You're about to do as you wish, and I deplore it, but now you must not mind my doing as I wish, too. I'm not too old to bear a child."

Her dignity silenced Orm, who hated the idea of her marrying Wulfric. He wanted to cry out that Wulfric might not be quite so enamored of her if he knew that she had no royal blood, and that she was betraying his father and her own. He said nothing of this though he was angry.

"Farewell, Mother." He gave her a half-mocking salute, kissed her hand, and twirling the expensive blue cloak Wulfric had given him, hurried to the gate where his horse was tethered.

Merewyn sadly watched her son ride away, then she picked up her needlework again. Jesus Christ, Our Lord, bless him, she thought, even though Orm is not one of Thine. Keep him safe! Yet she was conscious that her prayers were ineffectual. They never seemed to have any clear answer. Since coming back to England she had prayed that Orm should be secretly baptized and settle here into a high-ranking position. And now look — he was going off to join the enemy host. She could only hope that Ethelred would never know of this. He was capable of cruel revenges. And he was capable of forbidding the marriage to Wulfric which she had now determined on. The King's permission to wed was necessary to people of rank.

And then her prayers about Rumon. She had so much wanted to see him, even through a grille. Soon after her establishment at Court she had sent a messenger to Tavistock Abbey, asking if a visit from her would be satisfactory. The messenger returned in only four days, bearing a letter which she had great trouble in deciphering, partly because she had had no practice in reading for years, and partly because she did not really want to understand it.

It was addressed to the Lady Merewyn at King Ethelred's Court, "for so I understand you are again called — my compliments. My life has much altered since we met on Iceland. I deem it best that we should not meet again. I'll remember you in my prayers."

Merewyn had felt as though she were slapped across the face with a leather thong. She had been furious and unhappy for weeks, then she had gradually begun to appreciate Wulfric's attentions. They were a salve, a balm, and never more so than now when he appeared at the garden gate looking for her as he often did at this hour.

What matter that he was short and round, and had small twinkling eyes like a kindly bear; what matter that, as Orm said, he put his housecarls to sleep with rambling stories of long-past stag hunts, or carried on about his ancestry — his grandfather had been an earl in Mercia, his mother the daughter of a bishop, before Dunstan, Ethelwold, and Oswald imposed clerical celibacy on the land.

What did these matter against the joy in his round face above the chestnut beard when he saw her start forward to greet him.

"Wulfric —" she said, holding out her cheek, "do you still want to wed me?"

"I do, my lady," he kissed her cheek and gave her a tentative squeeze around the waist. "Are ye ready?"

Her brilliant sea-green eyes looked gravely down into his. "As soon as we can," she said.

* * *

Merewyn and Wulfric were married in the Thane's manor house chapel by Wulfric's chaplain. Ethelred had absent-mindedly given permission when Wulfric and Merewyn arrived one evening in the Palace Hall to find the King surrounded by a dozen oil lamps. He was hurriedly signing charters and grants, which were diffidently put before him by an anxious young clerkly monk who was new to the job. The King remarked to Wulfric that the Lady Merewyn seemed to have no dowry anywhere but if the worthy Thane would overlook that, and after all she brought a better lineage to the match than did Wulfric —

The Thane said he was prepared to overlook the lack of dowry.

"But —" interrupted Ethelred who was delighted at the arrival of a herald from Normandy with acceptance of his own marriage proposals, "since the lady served my late mother and my late wife, I'll make her a wedding grant. Let's see." He beckoned to the cowled clerk who came running. "What've we got free that's suitable for the Lady Merewyn who is wedding Thane Wulfric?"

"In Somerset, sire," said the monk nervously, "or near Abingdon, or in Hampshire — the New Forest."

"That's it!" cried Ethelred. "She shall have ten hides from the New Forest. She can get the trees cut down and sell 'em. Plenty of trees anyway."

" 'Twill lessen your royal hunting preserve," said the monk, still more nervously. "But in Corfe there is much free land which you never visit, sire."

At the word "Corfe," the young monk saw that he had made a terrible mistake. Ethelred's still young but puffy face darkened. He started to make the sign of the cross, then stopped himself. He glanced at the oil lamps, which always replaced candles when he was in residence. He had a horror of candles. Merewyn saw the gathering irrational anger which she had known for years. She saw coming the petulant ruin of all her hopes.

"My lord," she said quickly, "I shall be deeply grateful for anything, or nothing, that you grant me, but I do wish you happiness in your own marriage. I have heard that Emma of Normandy is a young and most beautiful woman. The gem of Normandy."

The King's temper subsided. His rages could always be diverted if one said the right thing, and the coming of Emma was a twofold pleasure. Not only getting a fresh young girl in his bed, but as a political victory over the Norsemen. He saw himself an astute, wily ruler of England. Even his mother would have approved. Though she was dead, and he had often feared her, yet behind most of his actions there was a reference to Alfrida.

Merewyn and Wulfric waited quietly behind the table where the King was sitting. The monk withdrew a little. "Very well." Ethelred impatiently returned to the matter in hand. "Ten hides of land in the Forest around Bramshaw for the Lady Merewyn, you'll know how to define the boundaries," he said to the clerk. "And get the usual signatures from some of the Witan."

"Yes, sire," said the clerk. "And —" Ethelred added, "see that the lady gets a mancus of gold for a wedding present." His full pink lips smiled, as he was conscious of generosity, and he inclined his crowned head graciously in acknowledgment of their thanks. He even said he would certainly come to the wedding, which Merewyn did not believe for a moment.

She had known Ethelred since childhood. There had always been easy promises, immediately forgotten, and there was nothing of possible advantage to Ethelred in attending a thane's marriage.

As they left the Hall, Merewyn glanced back to see that the writing table had been removed, and that the King was lolling on Cild Aelfric's shoulder, his arm around the neck of this present Earl of Mercia. Aelfric was the same meager, sly, insinuating man he had been as a youth, long ago at Corfe

Castle. He had not always stayed in favor with Ethelred; there had been banishment for "treachery"; there had been reinstatement. Merewyn had wondered if Ethelred knew how much Aelfric had connived in the murder of Edward which put Ethelred on the throne. And if it were true that Aelfric had arranged this coming marriage to Emma.

At her last glimpse, Ethelred and Aelfric with arms interlocked were sipping wine from each other's lips.

"Ugh!" said Merewyn. She was very glad to be leaving that slimy miasmic Court, and correspondingly grateful to Wulfric for being the means of rescuing her.

Merewyn's wedding day passed without incident. She wore a blue silk gown, heavily embroidered with gold bands, and a gold tissue veil over her looped auburn braids. The stuffs had been sent for to London, and made up very quickly by the most skilled of Wulfric's handmaidens. Wulfric gave her a garnet necklace and she wore that. She looked charming and younger than she was. She was calm, far more than Wulfric who sweated heavily in his new velvet tunic.

"After all, dear," said Merewyn with the amused indulgence she felt for him, " 'tis the second time for us both —" and only a faint jab reminded her that she had not really been married to Sigurd. Nobody knew this. She had let everyone assume that during her unfortunate years in "Ireland," she had been forcibly wed to one of the Christianized Norsemen there. Wulfric was not one to probe or question. At the age of forty-five he had fallen in love, and been awed by the exalted object of his love. His first wife had been a simple reeve's daughter.

He did not even question Orm's disappearance. He said it was a pity that Merewyn might not have her son at the wedding, but perhaps Orm would return in time, and anyway young men were like that.

Thora came to the wedding with Sister Herluva, though the Abbess Elfled sent polite regrets and best wishes, also thanks for the gifts Merewyn had recently been sending to Romsey.

The King's grant and the mancus of gold had been promptly transferred to Merewyn, thanks to the clerical monk's efficiency, and to the fact that Ethelred had not had to think of them again.

Herluva had dressed Thora in ivory whites with a soft blue mantle. The girl herself, vaguely knowing that she was going on a journey for a special occasion, had made a wreath of daisies which became her.

Merewyn saw the lewd glances from most of Wulfric's housecarls, and finally decided not to take Thora to live here. In the convent, the child was safe, and Herluva as solid and affectionate a guardian as one could wish. The sinister memory of Freydis darted through Merewyn and she shuddered, giving thanks for escape. Though all was not perfect here in England, there had been gains. Many of them.

And now I shall be content enough, Merewyn thought, looking at her bridegroom — if it weren't for Orm.

There was no such thing as pure happiness. How many years it took to learn that! Always some dark fretted thing which unbalanced the ease one had laboriously found. So now it was Orm, and this worry must be hidden. It occurred to her that other things must be hidden too.

She put them all aside, and resolutely enjoyed the moment.

She had just become the wife of a rich English thane. This was the Bride-Ale party. Two bards provided music, and an occasional ballad. The guests were getting properly drunk on the unending flow of mead, ale, and wine. Merewyn, herself, was sleepy and anxious to be done with the duty which remained to her. She knew that it would not be like the first night with Sigurd. Nor was it.

She had to help Wulfric, who was at first very timid. She felt nothing beyond a rather maternal affection, and was pleased when his grunts showed satisfaction. She was glad that her body still gave pleasure and that she could repose herself in the little Thane's arms. It was comfortable there — and safe. The lavender-scented linen of the sheets made her feel safe. And the distant night noises of the huge Manor. You could hear the servants shuffling about as they put new rushes on the Hall floor. You could hear a serf whistling in the bakehouse where the wonderful white loaves were rising. She never let herself dwell on all the years when a loaf of fresh crusty white bread had been a constant longing. She now looked towards a placid future, where luxuries would be taken for granted. Not that she would be idle; there was plenty for the Lady of a large Manor to do, and she expected to move Wulfric towards more interest in his many other properties. They would travel together and inspect them. The journeys would be agreeable and so would the regulation of any laxity they found. There was no doubt that Wulfric was indolent, but that was a very small fault compared to others she had lived with.

Again she thought of Orm. Dear Lord, stop him somehow from doing violence to others, wherever he is!

Ashley Manor was less than ten miles west of Winchester. Servants were constantly sent back and forth to buy sundries from the capital which the Manor could not supply. Particularly the Burgundy wine which Wulfric loved. Thus Merewyn kept up with the news. She knew when the new Queen-to-be arrived at Southampton from Normandy, and how Ethelred had gone there to meet her. That he took a thousand housecarls and thanes and earls with him. That he wore, not only the elaborate crown Dunstan had made for his father, but Athelstan's sword, and a velvet mantle so thickly embroidered with gold that he could scarcely walk under the weight of it when he dismounted.

She heard that Emma was small, dark, and pretty. That she looked downcast and spoke only in whispers to the bevy of Normans who accompanied her.

Merewyn heard that the wedding was to take place on Easter Day, April 5th, and was pleased when a messenger from the Palace arrived with an invitation. Though there was no reason for surprise, a King's thane and the royal Lady Merewyn would hardly be overlooked by all the clerks deputed to issue invitations.

There was a small bustle as to what they would wear, and Merewyn was heartily thankful that her husband was rich enough to send to London where they bought new mantles, and Wulfric proudly presented her with a gold coronet to hold down her veil.

"Ye've a right to wear it m'dear —" said he. "Anyone wi' royal blood has."

Merewyn's heart gave a heavy thud. "I haven't really —" she began. "That's only for the descendants of the right line of Cerdic, I think," she added lamely.

"There were two of the late Queen's ladies wore 'em," said Wulfric giving her a loving doggy look. "And you did too sometimes, only it was brass. I used to want to give you a real gold circlet and now I have."

"Yes," she said, then smiling put her hand on his plump knee. "Am I making you happy, Wulfric?"

This kind of question puzzled him. Whyever did she put it? Of course he was contented. She was a willing bedmate when he occasionally wanted that; she didn't interfere with his hobbies — drinking, stag-hunting, dice-throwing. She was an immeasurable improvement over his first wife who had whined. Besides he was proud of Merewyn, and loved her, only one didn't go on saying so week after week once the marriage was over.

"You make me happy," he said awkwardly, as she seemed to be waiting for an answer, her head a little to one side, her remarkable blue-green eyes fixed on his face. He got up and stumbled over her new dog.

This was a puppy from Spain, wherever that was, which a peddler had brought to the Manor one day. It had long floppy ears, with silky ivory-colored hair which tangled into knots unless Merewyn spent much time smoothing it out. None of the Manor hounds were anything like it. Merewyn was immediately enchanted by the puppy. She said that she hadn't had a dog of her own since she was a girl, and that had been Trig who died. Wulfric negligently bought the little beast for her, and she named it Foss. Wulfric was too incurious to ask why — and Merewyn knew only in the back of her mind that it was because "Foss" meant waterfall in Icelandic. The dog's curly, hanging-down pelt reminded her of Langarfoss. Or did it? She wasn't sure. She did not wish to remember Iceland. But she loved the dog, and it loved her.

On Easter Sunday Wulfric, Merewyn, and their retinue went to the wedding of Ethelred and Emma in Winchester's new Minster.

The ceremony did not take long, even though both Arch-bishops officiated, with Elfeah, Bishop of Winchester. The Nuptial Mass was soon over, but the bridal feast was not. Mere-wyn, seated with Wulfric towards the bottom of the Great Hall, had few glimpses of the new Queen but what she did see con-firmed an impression of misery. Merewyn knew that the girl — she was scarce eighteen — had been wed against her will. The big dark eyes were somber, she had drawn as far from Ethelred as she could, she did not speak to him. When Ethelred obviously suggested that they go to bed now, she broke into sudden viva-cious chatter in French with one of her entourage. She spoke little English, and pretended not to understand the King's meaning.

The Hall resounded with quick Norman-French voices. The English ones could scarcely be heard.

Ethelred looked baffled, he was not sure what to do, and as always in moments of indecision, turned to Cild Aelfric for guidance. The Earl of Mercia's lean sardonic face showed amusement. He had certainly promoted this marriage himself, acted as go-between, and profited greatly from both sides. It was a simple matter to interest Ethelred in the idea, harder to convince the Duke of Normandy, through an interpreter. In essence, Aelfric's success was due to the same political argument

which he used with both Ethelred and the Duke. The alliance
would make it impossible for the Vikings to base themselves in
Normandy anymore. The Duke was tired of entertaining his
Norse cousins. They cost too much, did too much casual damage. Richard was a peaceable man with a strong interest in the
welfare of his country. Moreover, he was pleased to make so
important a royal match for one of his eligible sisters. Aelfric had
received substantial gifts from Ethelred and Richard.

Now it appeared that Ethelred could not communicate sufficiently with his bride to end the interminable feast.

So the Earl stood up and made a speech so commanding that
his shrill voice silenced the crowd. It was time to put the royal
couple to bed, he said, but first they would tour the Hall and
greet their guests individually. He put out his hand and forcibly
pulled Ethelred from the throne, then he did the same to Emma.
Her dark eyes sparkled with resentment, but she dared not disobey. Ethelred pulled her arm through his, and they commenced the tour around the curtsying or bowing guests.

Emma had been married as "Aelgifu" because the bishops and
the Witan had insisted upon an Anglo-Saxon name for their
Queen. She was greeted now as "our Lady Aelgifu" by the
English. And each time she winced, tightening her pretty
mouth. She murmured "Merci" at intervals to the sea of Saxon
faces.

She gave only one smile — to Gunhild, the hostage, King
Sweyn's christianized sister, who kept an arm around her young
son while she curtsied, and the Queen paused a moment when she
came to Merewyn — holding Ethelred back, she turned to Count
Hugo, her interpreter, who followed discreetly behind. "Qui
est celle-là?" she asked, eying the gold coronet. The Count
made inquiries, and reported that this was a royal lady who had
served under the last two queens. "A-ha!" said Emma. "Je
l'aurais cru nordique, c'est un bon visage." She gave Merewyn
a thoughtful look, and passed on, tugged by the impatient
Ethelred.

Wulfric was delighted by the Queen's notice of Merewyn. "I'll wager she'll want you for Bower Lady," he said, "but I don't want ye to go m'dear, I want you to stay with me."

"So I shall, Wulfric. I never want to go back to Ethelred's Court, and I never wish to see another of his unhappy wives. Queen Emma *will* be unhappy, I know that as surely as I know that Foss is barking." She picked up the little dog, and quietened him with a kiss on the muzzle.

The summer slipped away; days so warm and comfortable that it was only now and then that Merewyn realized that she was bored. She took Foss on walks, she supervised her household, she rode sometimes to see Thora at Romsey, and found the girl unchanged. It always took her a while to remember her mother, then she would giggle and stroke the brooches or necklaces Merewyn now wore. Merewyn gave her an amber bracelet to play with, and Sister Herluva reported that after tearing the bracelet to bits, Thora spent many an hour fingering the smooth yellow beads and singing one of her wordless songs.

On these visits Elfled was polite and hurried. They saw little of each other.

In September something happened. The little Queen Emma came to visit the Manor, accompanied by several of her Normans, amongst them Count Hugo.

Merewyn was proud that she could immediately summon enough serfs and housecarls to serve the Queen properly. But the dark little lady wanted nothing to eat or drink. She had come, said the Count, because she wondered if Merewyn would like to join her Bower. The King himself had suggested this, thinking that the Lady Merewyn was experienced at Court, and might be a good person to teach English to Emma.

"*I* 'ave done my best to teach 'er," said the Count, twirling his mustaches which were shiny with unguent, "but I am leaving the Court for a time." He smiled, and nodded. "For the south of your land."

The Queen had received the customary "Morning Gift" after the marriage was consummated and now owned several towns and parts of shires. She had appointed Count Hugo to be Reeve or Governor of Exeter. She had appointed other Normans to important positions. Ethelred was too lazy to care at the moment. Besides he was enamoured of her and found her distaste for him exciting.

"I thank the Lady," said Merewyn, and hesitated. The Queen's offer had its merits. Three months ago she would not have considered it, but there had been nothing much of interest since then. She had not even been able to persuade Wulfric to the inspection of his northern properties yet, and now the weather would soon make that impossible.

Nor had the pregnancy she had hoped for happened.

"I hesitate to leave my husband . . ." she said weakly.

Hugo translated this, and Emma, with sudden vivacity, spoke at some length.

"You need not leave him all the time," transmitted the Count. "The Manor is so near Winchester that you may go back and forth as you please. And the Queen's taken a fancy to you. You look like 'er Norse grandmother."

"What!" cried Merewyn, reddening.

"Please not to take offense," said the Count, bowing. "Madame la reine does not mean it so. She knows very well who you are — a British princess."

"O Jesu —" said Merewyn beneath her breath. A qualm of nausea churned her stomach. I'm dreary, I'm not content, she thought. Everything is empty. No serenity at Mass, no answer to my prayers for Orm, he may be dead. And Wulfric — out hunting as usual, if he gets home tonight — well there may or may not be THAT to endure.

She picked up Foss who had stopped barking at the strangers, and was lying on her right foot. "If I come to Court, may I bring my dog?" she asked, almost childishly.

The little Queen hardly needed translation. And she laughed, seeing this small victory won. "C'est un joli petit chien," she said, "Je veux bien le reçevoir avec sa maman."

Merewyn rode to Winchester Palace on St. Michael's Day to wait upon her third Queen of England. Wulfric had been somewhat distressed, but then soothed to hear that she would be away only part of each week. And she knew that Wulfric and the Manor would get along very much as they had before she became mistress there.

She found many changes at the Palace — beautiful new tapestries on the walls, French armchairs in place of stools, even rugs on some of the stone floors, and the Queen had ordered an extraordinary fireplace made for the main room of her Bower. Instead of a little central fire from which the smoke got out as best it could through the roof, Emma had sent for a mason from France. He directed a handful of serfs in building a hooded fireplace on a wall, and the smoke went up an outside chimney. Very odd, the English thought it. And Merewyn thought it very comfortable.

Ethelred's children by his first wife were all housed in a separate building on the Palace grounds. They had their own retinue and nobody bothered with them much, especially Ethelred.

Merewyn gave daily lessons in English to the Queen and began to admire the girl, who was constantly unhappy but also had spirit and intelligence. Emma-Aelgifu, she was called the latter by the English but made it clear that she detested the peculiar name, showed in many ways her dislike of the husband they had foisted on her. Yet she was pregnant, as was her duty, and could therefore keep Ethelred out of her bed by representations as to unwholesomeness and danger presented through Count Hugo from a French midwife who had been sent for. There was a great deal of sailing to and from Normandy even in autumn; and Emma, being much the stronger character of the couple, continually got her own way with Ethelred. She was no Alfrida, she used no lures of the body, though it was a charming one, but she made the best of a situation she hated by favoring her countrymen.

Ethelred, denied his wife's bed at present, assuaged himself with some of the thanes' ladies, and possibly a handsome young stableboy, rumor said. Emma shrugged, and said, "Alors—" Her Norman waiting ladies shrugged too. Not one of them liked England. But they accepted Merewyn after a while, and the English lessons went fast since they were all simple conversation.

On Thursday, November 12th, it was drizzling rain and sleet. Merewyn had expected to ride home that day, but the weather made it most unwise, especially as Merewyn had a cold. She started for the Queen's Bower to ask permission to stay the night, and was startled to see through the winding stair windows that there were many horsemen in the courtyard below. Ethelred's private courtyard. A hunt? she thought, yet not at twilight in this weather. And there were no horns. The men were all full-armored with swords, shields, and spears. Ethelred was nowhere to be seen. The Earl of Mercia was circling amongst the warriors, and seemed to be telling them something. Merewyn leaned against the window, and even through the distorting wavy glass she got an impression of sinister mystery. What were all those men *doing* down there in the sleet?

She climbed to the Bower, and found the Queen mournfully strumming a lute while her ladies were embroidering by the light of several tapers. Emma smiled when she saw Merewyn and Foss. She held out her hand to fondle the dog, and said, "Alors . . . you vill stay 'ere tonight?"

The little Queen had learned far more English than she had let Ethelred know.

"I'll stay here if I may, Lady —" said Merewyn, "but there's something strange going on in the private courtyard. So many men — 'hommes.' " She indicated a multitude by spreading her arms, and showed shield and swords by gestures.

Emma sucked in her breath. She stared at Merewyn, then went out to descend the stairway to the same window Merewyn had quitted.

When she came back her face was white. "I vas varned," she said. "It vill 'appen, le roi est fou, *pire* que ça."

Her Norman ladies raised their heads and gaped at the Queen.

"But what IS it?" asked Merewyn fearingly, for she saw that Emma was extremely upset, that she was shivering.

"Massacre," said the Queen, "du Danois. Il est fou. Il est lâche. O mon Dieu!"

By the time Merewyn was able to understand what the Queen guessed was about to happen, they saw through a Bower window a file of armed men, some carrying torches, and all heading into Winchester town.

In a while Merewyn understood that Emma had a few days ago passed a small chamber near the Great Hall and had heard the King's voice shouting in a hysterical way, "We'll kill all the Danes. Get rid of them forever!" and another voice murmuring, agreeing. Emma had thought this was simply Ethelred in one of his crazy drunken rages.

Then one of her ladies — Marie de Caen, who was in love with the King's dish thane, had made a frightened report to the Queen two nights ago. Something dreadful was brewing; the dish thane had overheard the King and Cild Aelfric muttering about Danish treachery, and as Emma herself knew, Ethelred had taken to eating or drinking nothing unless the dish thane had swallowed some of it several minutes before he did, and he had closed himself in his private apartments, and ordered armed housecarls to sleep near him.

"But —" said Merewyn, puzzled, to Emma, "King Sweyn was paid off. He went away —" her voice wavered as she thought of Orm. "He left his sister, his brother-in-law and his nephew as hostages. There's nothing for the King to fear now."

Emma understood only a part of this, but she rushed to the Bower window which overlooked the town. "Regardez —"

she said, and her ladies crowded in beside her. The taller Merewyn looked over their heads.

They saw the torchlit procession head for the pleasant manor
house which had been allotted to the royal hostages — Gunhild,
her husband, Palig, and their son. Presently they saw the house
burning.

Queen Emma opened the window, and through the drizzle
they heard distant screams.

It was twilight of the following day, St. Brice's Day, before
anybody but a Bower servant came near the frightened ladies.
He brought a basket of bread and a keg of ale, and said it was
"Horrible, horrible." Every Dane in the kingdom had been
slaughtered, or was being so right now. That his own mother'd
been from the Danelaw, thank the Blessed Lord she was dead,
and he scuttled away.

"Bar the door, madame," said the Queen to Merewyn. "The
King's première reine était Danoise . . . he may now vish to
massacre also the Normans."

Merewyn barred the door. "I think not," she said dully. "He
will get over the madness, and repent. All his life he's had fears
and rages, but never like this . . ."

"Dieu me console," whispered the little Queen, and fell to
praying on her carved ivory prie-dieu. Her ladies clustered
around her, also devoutly praying. Merewyn could not pray.
She stood by the Bower window and looked down on Winchester where now many fires were burning, and in the smoke
which came down the chimney and seemed to seep through
crannies, there was the smell of roasting flesh.

At twilight, there was a knock on the door, and Merewyn
heard Wulfric's voice calling to her, and crying, "Open up,
ladies. 'Tis safe!"

Merewyn drew the bolt cautiously and peered through the
door. Wulfric was alone. She let him in. "I've come to fetch
ye," he said as he bent his knee towards the Queen. " 'Tis a

dreadful thing's been happening." His ruddy face was drawn, his little eyes were distressed, as she had never imagined they could be.

"By the grace o' God I've been four days hunting in New Forest, they couldn't find me, or I'd've had to go out wi' the other King's thanes —" He warmed his hands at the fireplace. "I've just seen the King." Wulfric spoke a trifle incoherently. "He's sobbing in the Council Chamber. He is blaming it all on the Earl of Mercia."

" 'Sobbing,' " the Queen interrupted sharply. "Qu'est-ce que c'est?"

Merewyn made a hopeless but explicit gesture with sounds. "Il pleure . . ." said the Queen. "Ha! But vat 'as 'appened, vraiment, messire," she said to Wulfric. "Expliquez-moi!"

Wulfric told them what he had learned. Ethelred had called an emergency meeting of the Witan; only of those nearby and whom the Earl of Mercia controlled. Ethelred had said that he was in imminent danger of assassination by the Danes in his kingdom, and that when he died the Witan would be murdered too. Therefore he was going to send secret messages to all trustworthy English earls and thanes. They were commanded to exterminate every Dane they could get at on St. Brice's Eve. And this was to be a lesson to the traitors.

" 'Ow many 'ave died?" asked Emma quietly.

"I don't know, Lady. Hundreds, I suppose. And I think it a great pity, aye — I think it dangerously dishonorable —" He paused; his nose grew redder at the thought of criticizing the King to whom he had sworn fealty. He went on, "Dishonorable, to have slaughtered the royal Danish hostages."

"So they are dead," whispered Merewyn. "We saw their house burning. Earl Pallig . . . the boy . . . and Gunhild of Denmark . . ."

"They are dead," said Wulfric, crossing himself. "I saw the bodies as I rode into town. Cut-off heads next to bits of the bodies. From the stink I judge they were burning the bodies."

He turned to the Queen, and began, "Lady, if you can spare Merewyn now, I'd like to take her home . . ." He stopped in consternation, as he saw that the Queen was vomiting into a chamber pot. Yet she finished very soon, and wiping her mouth on a linen cloth, said, "Take Madame Merewyn — Messire, she 'as taught me much English, I shall know 'ow to deal vit a king who ees 'sobbing' and 'as made the vorst crime I ever 'eard of — nor le bon Dieu non plus!"

Merewyn looked back at the valiant little Queen. "Ethelred is not all bad," she said with difficulty. "He has too many fears and too much power. His mother gave him both — God forgive her. You are not only strong, Lady Emma, but I know that you are good. You can rule your husband, if you can force yourself not to draw away from him, nor leave him to villains —" she chose the word carefully, knowing that Emma would understand it, "like Cild Aelfric or —"

"Hush, Merewyn!" said Wulfric, glancing back towards the stairs. "Have done!"

Queen Emma stood very still. She had understood most of Merewyn's speech. "You are wise, madame," she said. "You speak for the man you've known since child'ood, the man who 'as done 'orrible thing — non — pas lui, 'e did not, 'e vas 'idden in a chamber whilst others did it."

"God will punish him," said Merewyn.

The Queen inclined her pretty and determined dark head. "Le bon Dieu vill punish *England*," she said. "Of that I am sure."

chapter fifteen

TERRIFIED excitement over the St. Brice's Day Massacre died down by Yuletide. To be sure, a few hundred Danes in the southern shires had been killed. This was justified in English thinking by the many Viking raids from Norse countries which England had endured. Even the slaughter of the Danish royal hostages was generally condoned. After all, King Sweyn had been paid 24,000 pounds to depart with his fleet, and if he were foolish enough to leave some of his family behind, that was his lookout.

Nobody had ever found the Danes who infiltrated south from the Danelaw, or Northumbria, particularly obnoxious. Many of them had intermarried with the English of Mercia, Wessex, or Kent. Nonetheless, one did not question a king's commands, and if, as was understood, he had been physically threatened, well, there wasn't much to do but get rid of the foreigners.

By Yule, such reasoning was also Wulfric's. Merewyn said nothing. Even when her husband remarked that they were lucky to live under such a vigorous king, she said nothing. But she thought about little Emma with sympathy, and listened eagerly to the gossip the servants brought back from Winchester.

She was not summoned to Winchester Court again. The King
and Queen seemed to be constantly on the move around England.
Merewyn was not sure if Emma had been offended by the speech
about Ethelred she had felt bound to make. But it looked as
though the Queen were pumping some energy into Ethelred.

Merewyn did not succeed as well with Wulfric.

Life at the Manor was comfortable, but dull and Merewyn
found herself drifting into a flirtation with one of the housecarls.
An enterprise so aimless and humiliating that Merewyn soon
cut it off.

In March there came news that the Queen had given birth to
a lusty boy, named Edward, and produced him in Oxfordshire.
Wulfric and Merewyn were not invited to the christening, which
took place at Ely. Merewyn was disappointed. Wulfric was
glad; he was never inclined to go anywhere, unless it was for
hunting, and even this no longer interested him as much. He had
hurt his back by a fall in December, and whiled away the long
winter by dice-throwing and listening over and over to his bard
— Merewyn got very tired of the "Lay of Beowulf" — or by
playing at darts with his retainers. Merewyn tried to busy herself with the peasants of their village, but there was little hardship amongst them, nor did they seem particularly grateful to
receive the Lady of the Manor.

On Ashley Manor the serfs and a few free cotters lived their
own lives, though they went to the village church on Sundays
and enjoyed the May Day and Yuletide feasts Wulfric provided.
They paid to Wulfric their quarterly fees — Wulfric's bailiff
saw to that — paid over certain bushels of corn, or geese or a
lamb, or plowing days' work, or the produce of a certain field,
or even pennies. They paid as had their forefathers, because that
was the way things were done. They had great attachment to
the land they did not own, but Merewyn at last understood that
they felt little interest in their feudal lord, or his lady. The gulf
was too wide. She finally took to sending a house servant with
the gifts she continued to make at times. And her spirits gradu-

ally grew very low. There seemed nothing to get out of bed for
in the mornings. She would lie there for hours, staring at a
strange mark in the wood of one of the rafters. Sometimes it
looked like a grinning face, and sometimes it looked like a cross.

She lost her appetite, and began to get thin. She scarcely
noticed this, but Wulfric did. He worried about her when he
was not worrying about the health of his best gelding.

She enjoyed in a remote way the coming of spring again. The
green shoots pushing through the brown earth, the catkins hanging from the alders and hazels, the anemones and primroses
starring under the trees in the copse by the house. Then the drift
of bluebells.

She saw all these things through a glaze. They could not quite
reach her. Even Foss seemed remote. She cuddled him, and let
him lick her hand, but she did not tend his coat as carefully as
she had. Everything was unimportant. Once on an evening of
particular depression she spoke to their chaplain. Examine her
conscience as she did, there never seemed to be much to confess.
She had made the most of her flirtation with the housecarl, but
that was finished, and she had done penance.

"Father," she said, "I don't know what's the matter with me.
Nothing seems worthwhile."

The priest was a local man who had been ordained at Winchester. He enjoyed his sinecure at the Manor, thought of little
but the good food the Thane provided, and did the minimum of
his duties as a shepherd of souls. "Perhaps, you should pray to
the Blessed Virgin Mary," he said.

"I have," she answered forlornly.

"There couldn't be any sin on your conscience," said the
priest, looking eagerly out the chapel window towards the
Manor where the dinner bell would presently ring. "You've
made full confessions, I'm sure."

Merewyn was silent. Supposing she said that she had actually
committted adultery with the housecarl. Would that disturb this
smug little priest? But she had not. It would be a lie. A lie . . .

She got up. "I hope you enjoy your dinner, Father — I believe I ordered roast kid and saffron pastries."

At the end of April there were disquieting rumors. It was said that King Sweyn had returned, had landed in Devonshire with an enormous fleet, and was devastating the countryside. Wulfric refused to believe it — the peasants and churls were always spreading rumors which flew upward to his servants and then to housecarls.

"I think it very likely, Wulfric," said Merewyn in a weary voice. "Don't you think Sweyn might want to avenge his sister?"

"His sister . . . ?" repeated Wulfric, frowning. It took him a moment to understand. "Oh, you mean St. Brice's Day? But that Danish King got twenty-four thousand pounds. He wouldn't bother to come back here just to avenge a sister." Wulfric was fingering a new Norman spear he had bought. It seemed more deftly made than the English ones. Better balance, and the hasp tightened in a different way. Wulfric's back had improved and he was looking forward to hunting again.

"I think he might," Merewyn said.

Wulfric did not listen; he was thinking about his new hobby — a falcon mews. He had bought several peregrines, and ordered one of the great white gyrfalcons from the North. From Iceland maybe, Merewyn thought, and felt the familiar inner shrinking.

Wulfric gave her an absentminded pat on the shoulder, and went out to inspect his mews and consult with the new falconer.

At dusk there was a banging on the great portal. Merewyn was in the Hall doing needlework. Her head ached and her eyes strained to find the right colors for the hunting scene Wulfric had requested. It was to be of St. Hubert, patron of the hunt, with a crucifix shining between the stag's antlers. It would grace the chapel if she could ever finish it.

A housecarl came in, looking flustered. "There's a man at the portal, m'lady," he said. "Porter told me. Man wants to see you. But he looks like one o' they Danes to me. Has a helmet on."

Merewyn became very still. "Did the man say his name?"

"Orm, m'lady — I think it was."

"Let him in," said Merewyn. While she waited, the Hall spun around her. She tried to stand up, then sat down again.

Orm came striding in. He was bigger and blonder than ever. He wore chain mail and a helmet. There was a great double-edged sword hanging from his hips. She saw at once that he had a scarcely healed scar on his chin.

"Elsknan min —" she cried, rushing towards him, and falling on his chest, began to weep.

"So . . . Mother, so . . . Mother," said Orm, hugging her and speaking as though to soothe a restive horse. "I wasn't so sure you'd be glad to see me."

"Not sure?" she said between sobs. "When these years since you left, I've been wondering, waiting, praying. I thought you might be dead."

"I nearly was once or twice," said Orm with a certain relish. "Good fighting. But I'm here now with Sweyn. We've overrun the western shires. Sweyn's camp is near here in Wiltshire. I received permission to visit my mother for the evening." He examined her. "You've grown a bit thinner. Hasn't that little Thane you married been taking good care of you?"

"Oh yes," she said distractedly. "Orm — are you safe here? I don't mean Wulfric, he'd never assault a guest, but the house-carls might rise, they're English. They've not forgotten St. Brice's Day."

"Nor have we," said Orm, his young mouth hardening. "That's why we're here. You're supposed to be Christians, oozing justice, honor, and mercy for all. Instead, the murder of harmless Anglo-Danes, and especially the murder of royal hostages — the worst deed ever done by the feckless English."

"Yes, I know," she said, "and almost as bad a deed was done at Corfe, when Edward was murdered to get Ethelred on the throne."

"Perhaps so," said Orm, who was not interested in English

events before his birth. "Mother, in this great Manor you must have food and drink. I need some. And don't worry about my safety. I assure you I've learned to defend myself."

"Please," she whispered, "take off your helmet in the Guard-room, hide the chain mail, and leave your sword behind — you can put it in my Bower . . ."

"My dear mother . . ." said Orm. He was twenty-two now, and much more mature in every way than when she had seen him last. He was even able to understand Merewyn a little. He reached down and kissed her on the cheek. "So you are still playing the old game," he said. "Poor Mother," he added, "I don't want you to be anxious. I'll leave my helmet in the Guard-room, I'll cover my chain mail with my sark, but I'll keep my sword with me. I call it Ormstunga, and I got it off a great big German when we were raiding up the Elbe."

"You killed him," she stated.

"To be sure, it was a battle." Orm looked surprised. "And what better name for this wonderful sword than 'Serpent's tongue' since you named me Orm."

"I never thought about it," she said faintly, "that Orm means serpent in Norse. It was Sigurd's grandfather's name, and he wanted it."

All those years when she had not really thought at all. Golden years of mutual pleasure with Sigurd. The little homestead at Langarfoss, presided over by the Snaefell glacier, by the snow-peaked gabled mountains, by the distant and fey cone of Baula, by the singing swans which flew overhead, by the arctic fireweed she gathered in summertime, while baby Orm trotted beside her. I was happy then and did not know it.

"Orm —" she said with difficulty, "I have so prayed that you were not killing people."

"And what good are Christian prayers?" said Orm. "Anyway Christians constantly kill each other. Look at King Sweyn's sister, Gunhild, she was Christian. And you people do not even honor your sacred oaths."

"That was Ethelred's doing — the massacre, and he is King."

Orm said, "Tcha!" exactly like Ketil, and departed for the Guardroom.

When Wulfric came back from the mews, Merewyn hastily explained the reappearance of Orm. She said that Orm had a liking for the sea, and had been on several long voyages. She did not explain with whom Orm had gone. The Thane was incurious as ever. He was pleased to welcome Orm, and then talked interminably about his falcons; the mews should be enlarged, he would need another falconer; the perches were not of the proper height, and the leg tethers would have to be remade.

Merewyn was used to this, but Orm was beginning to yawn into his flagon. The bard came in, and Orm revived as the man began to chant the "Lay of Beowulf." AGAIN, Merewyn thought, but saw that this story of blood and battle and underwater monsters held Orm's attention. She also felt an intuition that there was something he wanted to tell her, something private which had not yet appeared, and was not entirely to do with a filial visit.

It didn't take very long to be quit of Wulfric. Staggering slightly, for he had drunk an extra flagon of mead in honor of the guest, he said that he was for bed. "Have a good chat, you two," he said amiably as a housecarl steadied him, and to Orm, "Your mother's been pining to see ye, many's the long day."

Merewyn told one of the housecarls to build up the fire, then dismissed all the servitors. She and Orm sat down in armchairs near the warmth.

"You've something to tell me," she said, restraining herself from leaning over to kiss him. "Would it be that Sweyn is going to attack in Hampshire? Have you brought a warning?"

"That may be," said Orm after a moment. "Sweyn's host is mighty. They've just taken Exeter."

"Exeter, which was governed by the Queen's Norman Count, Hugo?"

Orm nodded. "He delivered the town up to us. We hardly had to draw a sword."

"Did they go to Tavistock Abbey again?" she asked very low.

"Why, no," said Orm astonished. "The army is moving east for London and you won't be molested here. I've seen to that. Stay tranquil, Mother, on your own very fine Manor. And I'm sure that Wulfric'll not bestir himself."

"He will if the King calls on him!" She had a flash of anger. "So you and your Danes want to destroy England!"

"We are all Norsemen," said Orm. "So are the Normans for that matter, and soon you'll see that they'll join with the rest of us. As Count Hugo has done at Exeter. I told you before that England was a rotting plum. Squeeze it here, it squirts there. Soon it will collapse into mushiness."

Merewyn was silent; she knew that Orm was coming to the real object of his visit.

"Mother," he said suddenly, leaning forward. "You remember Leif Erikson? We now call him Leif the Lucky."

"Of course I remember," she answered tartly, "though I prefer not to think about that time on Greenland."

"Well —" said Orm, brushing this silly remark aside, "there's a Greenlander on my ship — I told you I was steersman?"

"You told me."

"His name in Einar, and he was one of Leif Erikson's crew when they set out from Brattalid to find Vinland."

"What's *that?*" she said since he paused, looked at her with excited eyes, and seemed to be wanting her to say something.

"That place to the west. It's a whole new country, Mother! A very big one. And a rich one. They went south and south for days along a coast lined with beautiful trees. They wintered in a freshwater lake, the berries grew thick around it, nothing froze much all winter, not the way things freeze in Greenland, and besides all that free timber, they found wild grapes. That's why Leif called the place Vinland."

"So . . ." said Merewyn after a moment. "That must be the place Jorund and — and Rumon got to when Ari Marson's ship was blown there."

"Oh yes, Mother. They found that place too! Einar says they sailed into a river called 'Merrimac' by the skraelings of which there were many in little pointed boats made of birch bark. That Ari Marson himself came down the bank to greet them. He was cordial enough and gave them supplies, but did not want them to stay there. He seemed to be a sort of chief of this place, both skraelings and a lot of wizened old 'Papas' who hid in some rocky caves. Einar says these 'Papas' were like the kind who used to live on Iceland ages ago."

"And what does all this lead to?" asked Merewyn.

"That I wish to go there," said Orm simply.

"Why?" she asked. "I thought you were settled with King Sweyn's avenging horde."

"I've talked to him," said Orm. "I got enough plunder myself to buy the boat I'm steering. Einar too has some to buy his way out of Sweyn's army. And also —" he paused, she saw the youthful blushing of his neck, "there is a girl . . . in Dublin, where we provisioned our fleet. She's part Norse, part Celtic like you. She even has a kind of red hair like you."

"Oh, has she indeed," said Merewyn in a neutral voice. "And she's willing to voyage towards this Vinland with you?"

"She says so."

"Is she Christian?"

"She's been baptized," said Orm defiantly. "But what does all this water-sprinkling matter! We Norse do it too."

"I'm not sure how much it matters, if the Spirit isn't there," said Merewyn slowly. She sighed. "So you wish to be a colonist in the new world. I wish you luck, and am glad that you will be fighting nobody except maybe skraelings. I wish I could meet your betrothed," she added wistfully.

"But she's in Dublin! Einar has a girl there also. We'll hire a crew in Exeter, that's where my ship is, and pick up the two girls in Ireland, then around to Greenland, join one of the expeditions. Einar says that they were planning at least a yearly boat of colonists from Brattalid."

"So far . . . so far away . . ." she said, putting her hand over her eyes. "Orm, aren't you sorry that you went a-viking?"

"Not a bit, Mother, but I'm sorry you sold the *Bylgja,* though I've learned to make this *new* ship of mine daunt Aegir's nine fierce daughters."

"I'll never see you again," she said, looking into the fire. He had not asked her to go with him; it would not be reasonable that he should, but even if he had she knew that she no longer felt the courage to brave the dampness and the danger, and the interminable rocking of the sea. She was used now to dainty fare, and even that sometimes disagreed. She had headaches. She grew chilly often. I'm no longer young, Merewyn thought. I feel young inside but my body doesn't.

"It's late, dear Mother," said Orm, brushing his golden-bearded lips across her forehead. "I must get back to King Sweyn, and take my final leave of him."

"Orm," she said, scarcely daring to look at him. "You didn't — the Danes didn't land in Cornwall this time? You've killed no Cornish?"

"No. Nor English. Though I would if I had to. I'd rather not. Sweyn understands, even young Canute does. These are not rulers like your precious Ethelred; they are warriors but they're not lazy or treacherous, and they honor their oaths."

"All the English are not like Ethelred," said Merewyn. "You know they aren't."

"Whatever they are, I want none of them, and they're no kin to *you,* really. Never mind, Mother, don't look so — so white. May the Norns decree a pleasant fate for you!"

He was gone.

She sat very still looking at the fire. Then she picked up Foss who was stretched out by her feet, and held him against her cheek. Foss had not barked at all while Orm was there. The

little creamy-coated dog must have known that the stranger was
someone she loved.

During the next week Merewyn felt ill, and concealed it from
Wulfric. The only satisfaction she had was in telling him of
Orm's departure to lands which had been discovered over the
western ocean.

Wulfric was mildly interested to hear that Orm was thinking
of going there. He could understand no place outside of England
nor saw any need to. He was pleased by the arrival of the
crated white gyrfalcon from up north and talked of little else.
He was glad that his new falconer seemed to be able to train the
bird.

By May even Wulfric had to admit that Sweyn's army was
overrunning Wiltshire. That they destroyed Wilton and Salisbury with very little opposition. Merewyn suspected that the
Queen had managed to put some of her Normans in more key
positions. The King gave no order to fight, but the men of
Wiltshire rose and looked to Cild Aelfric, Earl of Mercia, as
their natural leader. As might be expected, Aelfric accepted the
general's post, and then when actually confronted by the enemy
with their war helmets, their chain mail, their double-edged
swords and battle-axes, their berserker yells, Aelfric started to
vomit, saying that he was too ill to lead the counterattack. He
turned tail and fled. His demoralized squadron became panicky.
They fled too. Sweyn had it all his own way, and got so much
plunder from the southern shires that his ships were overloaded.
He decided to abandon the east coast for the present, and go back
to the Isle of Wight, and its harbor at Cowes where he had
already made a snug retreat for himself, with shelters for the
men, and nausts for the ships. A good place to winter before a
spring attack on Norfolk, and then London.

The news soon spread that the Danish horde had sailed away.
Wulfric said comfortably to Merewyn, "I told ye they would,

m'dear. Naught to fear. D'ye want to come and look at the mews? But don't bring the dog, it upsets my falcons."

"Very well," said Merewyn dispiritedly. She did not like the mews, which she had seen often. It smelled, and the frenzied, inimical batting of two dozen wings disturbed her. All those chained birds, and especially the white gyrfalcon, which had cruel eyes.

As they crossed the courtyard, they both looked around. There were two men at the portal — Benedictine monks.

They want hospitality, she thought, can't make it into Winchester.

There were quite often chance-comers through here from the west. Wulfric never stinted them, nor did she. Any change was agreeable.

But their visitors had never before been black-robed monks.

Wulfric went forward eagerly to greet the two monks. "May we help you, Brethren? You're welcome to anything we have." He looked at the tethered mules, outside the portal, and said, "One of 'em gone lame? We've a smithy on the Manor."

The taller monk smiled and bowed. "I am Brother Laurence from Tavistock Abbey, this is Brother Gwyn. We're not in need of help, thank you, we are seeking the Lady Merewyn."

When Merewyn heard "Tavistock Abbey," she stiffened. She bit her underlip so as not to make a sound.

Wulfric looked mildly astonished. "Here is the Lady Merewyn, my wife."

Brother Laurence bowed again. "We have a rather strange request to make of you. There's a holy monk at Tavistock. His name is Rumon. He's an atheling of the blood royal, yet is a humble man. We wished to elect him Abbot, but he wouldn't have it. He has known you, lady, in his secular life . . . ?"

"Yes."

"Who was that?" Wulfric asked, his honest face creasing in a perplexed frown. "You never told me about anybody called Rumon."

No, she thought, and there are a great many things I haven't told you.

"Brother Rumon," continued the tall monk, "has been smitten in his legs. He cannot walk. And he feels death near. He wants to see you again, lady."

"What a very odd thing," said Wulfric. "You mean she's to visit him?"

"That is Brother Rumon's hope."

"Well," said Wulfric, mulling this over. "Don't make any sense to me."

"I want to go, Wulfric," said Merewyn.

Everybody waited while Wulfric thought.

"You've been a bit in the dumps lately," he finally said. "The journey might be good for you. But ye can't just go off with these monks. I'll send two or three housecarls too."

"Thank you, my husband." She kissed him on the cheek. "You are always good." A good man, a dull man, but a *good* one.

Underneath her heart began to sing as it had not in years. Rumon has sent for me! Rumon cares again that I exist.

It was a morning in early August when Merewyn arrived at Tavistock. On the journey she had heard from Brother Laurence the tale of Rumon's great courage. As she had heard it halfway up Glastonbury Tor from Brother Finian, but with additions. Rumon had saved the Abbey treasure, he had killed two Vikings, yes, but one of them had inflicted some sort of blow on Rumon's back which did not show up very soon as an injury. It had now, and the monk-physician at the Abbey thought it the source of Rumon's trouble. This Infirmarer had given Rumon all the herbs he could think of, but Rumon's legs had gone numb and cold. His heartbeat labored.

"He never complains," said Brother Laurence. "We all admire his fortitude, and when we confess to him, everyone is comforted by his kind, inspiring words."

Merewyn pondered on Brother Laurence's praise of Rumon

as they rode through the last of Dartmoor, before descending to the Tavy.

It was a day of brilliant sunshine, as brilliant as it had sometimes been in Iceland, and only small white puffy clouds were drifting northward. This whole day on which I see Rumon again will be fair, she thought. On Iceland, one might never be sure, there the skies could darken so fast. Light and shadow. Light and shadow —when had she thought that before? Long ago with Rumon in the moonlight on Glastonbury Tor. Of late, for me, there have been deep shadows.

It was warm as they crossed the solid new stone bridge over the Tavy. She unpinned her mantle. From her present considerable wardrobe, she had chosen the gown which she felt was most becoming. It was dyed a very dark green like the foliage of a yew tree, it had been woven in France, like her mantle, and both were of a woolen more delicate and light than anything which could be made in England. She wore most of the jewels which Wulfric had given her. The garnet necklace, the gorgeous enamel brooch, the rings, the girdle clasp. All these were set in gold, except the slender chains of silver and crystals which she braided into her long plaits. As they neared the new Abbey, again whitewashed, though this time built of stone, she put on the royal circlet she had worn for Ethelred and Emma's wedding. Then she took it off again, and told one of Wulfric's housecarls to guard it. Three minutes later she demanded it back and placed it over her short white veil.

They made quite a procession as they approached the Portal — the two monks, three of Wulfric's housecarls, and Merewyn. Little Foss had been regretfully left behind.

She let Brother Laurance do the talking to the Porter, and it soon developed that Brother Rumon was lying in the monks' special garden, as he often did.

Merewyn dismounted, and made a gesture to Brother Laurence. "Please lead the way."

She heard that her voice quavered, she felt that her palms were wet, her knees wobbled as she followed the monk through a stone gate, past a brook and a dovecote, where a score of gray pigeons were flying in and out of their holes in the masonry. Merewyn and the monk entered a very small brick-walled garden. Merewyn was dimly aware of yellow flowers climbing up the walls, of moss under her feet as she stepped across a tiny rill, of a rowan with masses of scarlet berries, of tall blue flowers, of late roses, and the smell of lavender.

She saw at once the chairlike litter that was propped against the far wall, and contained a man.

"Here is the Lady Merewyn," said Brother Laurence gently to the man. "Brother Rumon, I've brought her as you asked."

Rumon, who had been drowsing, and thus forgetting the pains in his back, sat bolt upright. "I'm glad to see you," he said. "Forgive me that my useless legs will not let me get up to greet you properly."

"Oh Rumon —" Merewyn whispered. She was appalled by the emaciation of the face she scarcely recognized, of the black circles beneath the dark eyes. And it was strange to see Rumon in the habit of a Benedictine monk. Brother Laurence murmured something and left the garden.

"Why do you think I wanted you to come to me, Merewyn?" said Rumon, his voice getting stronger.

"Because —" she said slowly, "Because I suppose there has always been a sort of love between us. First me, then you. Crisscross. But underneath — always something."

Rumon nodded. "I see now that's true. I'm glad that you came to me; after my last message to you, I wasn't sure. It was rude. I regret it. But I see also that you did not need my material help." He glanced at her dark green gown, at all her jewelry. "Nor has a Benedictine monk anything material to help *with*."

"Of course not."

"Merewyn!" he said abruptly. "Did you know that I killed

two Vikings when they were raiding Tavistock Abbey church?"

"I've heard it," she answered very low. "And you saved the treasure. It was brave."

"Brave," he repeated with contempt. "I was mad with fury. I discovered strength I never knew I had, and the wish to kill. It was to save the treasure and the silver dove, yes — but do you know another thought I had in me?"

She did not answer; she sat down on a little mossy boulder near Rumon, and waited. He finally spoke in a thin dry voice. He did not look at her, he gazed over the garden towards the dovecote. "When I killed those two in the church, I was really killing Ketil and Sigurd. I did not know it for a long time. And it's because of this that God has willed that I be smitten. And I welcome His Will."

"Oh, poor Rumon —" she whispered. She put her hand on his shoulder. Then there was no sound in the garden but the cooing of doves, the purring of the little rill.

His head sank into the cowl, his breathing had become the fast shallow type she remembered all too well having heard from her Aunt Merwinna.

"Neither Ketil, nor Sigurd died by your hand," said Merewyn with force. "And as for the two you did kill, I've not a doubt they richly deserved it."

He let his arms rise and drop, a gesture she remembered piercingly from the long-ago. "When I was a boy in Provence, I vowed to the Blessed Lord Christ, to the Saintes Maries that I would do no violence. I broke the vow."

"So what if you did!" she cried. "You must have told all this to your confessor!"

"And was absolved at once, no hard penance. I told him of the murderous bloodlust I suddenly felt, and he would scarcely listen. He thought that my confessions about Ketil and Sigurd were nonsense. That they were vaporings from my injury. They made a hero of me at the Abbey. I wish Dunstan were back. He'd understand."

"*I* understand," she said stoutly. "Rumon, you were always questing, searching for a blessed place called Avalon. I see that you have not found it, and for that I'm sorry."

Rumon suddenly sat upright again. "Unless it's here," he said with a faint smile. "In this little garden, or anywhere that one can find peace."

"The garden's very pretty," said Merewyn uncertainly. "It's not an island though."

"Always we live on islands of one kind or another," said Rumon, his voice deepening.

His cowl slipped back, and Merewyn was startled by the gleaming blackness of his hair around the white-scalped tonsure.

He looked much younger, and as his dark eyes now examined her, she saw in them a look of sorrow.

"You are very well dressed," said Rumon, "and bejeweled. I observe also that you wear on your head a royal golden circlet."

"It's necessary . . . I mean everyone thinks so . . . especially Wulfric and it seemed so much easier . . . since everyone believes . . ." She touched the circlet, then snatched her hand away, frightened by the sternness of Rumon's face.

"THIS is why I sent for you, Merewyn! My concern for your soul's welfare. I have love for you, as for many years, but I'm a priest, and that love has begot more prayers for you than I can tell. I summoned you here to ask of you a brave act. Braver than *I* have ever done, for *these* motives will be pure."

Merewyn shrank inside. "What?" she said.

"Confess your deception."

"To — our Manor chaplain?" She recovered quickly, and said, "What deception?"

"You are *not* of royal British blood, my daughter," said Rumon. "And you well know it now, though you did not before your capture at Padstow, and are blameless for those early years. But now you are profiting from what you know is untrue. You have no right to wear that atheling's circlet. And it is not only for your soul's sake I say these things, but I think you are unhappy in this life. Nobody can live a continuous lie and find serenity. I can see that you are not at peace with yourself. It shows in your mouth, and in your eyes."

"What do you mean, Rumon?" she said stiffly.

"I mean that you should go and tell your real parentage to the King and Queen first — and then to Thane Wulfric, your husband."

"Oh . . ." said Merewyn with a gasp which was half a sob. "I couldn't. I can't. You're cruel, Rumon. They would be so angry, and Wulfric so disappointed, he'd repudiate me."

"Perhaps," Rumon was still sitting up and looking at her. "Then you can go to Romsey Abbey?"

"Elfled and I are not close anymore. She wouldn't want there a rejected wife with no money — and, and — no lineage."

"*I* wanted you, I followed you to the very end of the world, when all the time I knew your true birth."

"Oh, Blessed Jesu, yes," and she began to cry.

Rumon leaned back again and gave an involuntary grunt of pain as he did so.

He listened a moment to the sounds of the garden. The brook back there, the rill here, the doves, and the bees buzzing to their skeps laden with nectar from the flowers. Also to small choking sounds from Merewyn.

"This request is for *you*, Merewyn," he said, "and you may remember that you were put in my charge by your mother, a long time ago. I did fulfill my vow to her, and now I wish you to answer my request. It is also a dying request, as you must have heard from Brother Laurence. I can't last much longer."

She wiped her eyes on her dark green skirt. Relief had come to her, a feeling of lightness and surety. The little garden seemed illumined by a rosy light. The yellow flowers quivered on the brick walls, the pink roses sparkled, and the berries of the rowan dotted their green tree with orange jewels.

She looked down at Rumon and saw that his quiet face was also touched with the light.

"I will do it," she said. At the joy in his sunken dark eyes, she leaned down and kissed him on the mouth. The only time they had kissed, except that moment on the Tor, when they had misunderstood each other so completely.

Merewyn spent the night in the Tavistock Abbey hostel, newly rebuilt by Lord Ordulf, and as luxurious a guesthouse as Merewyn had ever known.

She slept on a goose-feather bed, and slept well. She did not see Rumon again, but he saw her. He had been carried to a corner of the choir for early Mass, and as he looked into the nave, he saw her kneeling in her dark green hooded mantle. Something poignant stirred in him. He had seen her thus before? Not at Tavistock? Yes, at Tavistock. When he was searching for her. There had been a foreknowledge. He had thought then that one of the monks was Merewyn, now it was really she. And time did not run on neatly; it leaped ahead, or it might double back on itself. These years at Tavistock — seven of them — seemed very short.

He watched Merewyn with tenderness. Her devout face was outlined by the dark green hood. As the Abbey grew warm, she threw the hood back, and he saw that there was no circlet over the white veil. She'll go through with it, he thought. Had Merewyn ever failed in doing what she said she'd do! He looked at her a good deal, while he mechanically followed the Mass. Then he looked at the silver dove with shiny crystal eyes, which hung in the chancel near the altar. The Holy Ghost, the Comforter, the Third Person of the Trinity. The Comforter.

Under the black habit he tried to flex his numb legs. He knew that they were turning a peculiar dark color, the lay brother who dressed him had remarked on it today. He knew that the numbness was spreading up his back and would soon engulf the pain there. He heaved a long sigh and kissed the plain wooden crucifix which had replaced his gold one. "That I may be deemed worthy of being received by Thee, when the time

comes, and that from Thy great Mercy, Thou wilt help Merewyn in her ordeal."

The Mass was over. He watched as she crossed herself, and
rose. She had not seen him lying in the chair litter at the corner
by the chancel rail. She hurried out of the Abbey. She went to
the hostel to collect her housecarls. Brother Laurence met her
at the gate. "I'll guide you back across Dartmoòr," said the
monk. "The mists are rising, and Brother Rumon —" the monk
made a peculiar sound, and Merewyn who had not really seen
him as a person before, looked up at the gaunt face.

"Brother Rumon has requested this, and also that I give you a
last message, lady. That if what he has asked of you is too hard,
you may wait until you feel you can do it. And also —" here
the monk paused because he understood nothing of all this himself, "that your race will soon, very soon make a better England
. . . he had a vision, I think." Brother Laurence finished apolo-
getically. "I don't know what he meant, was it the Cornish, or
the Welsh? I know that you have the ancient British royal
blood — Arthur's."

"I haven't," said Merewyn flatly. "No royal blood of any
kind."

The monk stared at her. But any vagaries this lady had were
no concern of his. He had been told to guide her back across
the moor, and he would obey whatever superior gave him an
order. Yet this one from Rumon was especially important. He
had a great reverence for Brother Rumon, who had several times
been his confessor, and who had listened to some murky details
of his past life with compassion.

Merewyn and the housecarls arrived near Ashley Manor on a
midafternoon, and Merewyn hesitated. Down that lane to the
right would be Wulfric, and the Manor — farther on eight
miles was Winchester.

"Ask at the alehouse," she said pointing to a hut with a bush
sticking out over the door, "if the King is in Winchester now."

One of her servants went into the alehouse.

"They think the King is back at the Palace, m'lady," he reported.

"Then we'll go on to Winchester," she said. "You will amuse yourselves there, no doubt — here is a penny for each of you, to insure it."

She gave each of the three a silver penny, and accepted their thanks with a tight, remote face.

They got to Winchester as the new Minster bell was ringing the summons to Vespers. They could see black-robed monks, walking two by two through the cloister garth towards the Minster. Merewyn led the way on to the Palace. "I don't know how long I shall be here," said Merewyn to her housecarls. "If I don't return, you'll have your own ways of finding out through the Palace carls what has happened to me."

" 'Appened to ye, my lady?" said the senior of her servants. "Wot could 'appen?"

"Anything," answered Merewyn.

At the Palace gate, she was at once recognized. The Gate Ward bowed, the knot of pages, retainers and hangers-on all bowed. Several hounds barked and were shushed, while the Gate Ward swung back the huge iron gate for her to enter.

"Where are the King and Queen?" she asked the Gate Ward, who was astonished.

"Feasting i' the Hall, at this hour, surely," he answered. He had seen the Lady Merewyn come and go to Court for many years, and he thought it odd that she should ask such an obvious question. Come to think of it, she looked odd too. Her face had lost its rosiness, her eyes didn't seem to see you. Before she'd always been a courteous lady, and would even remember to ask about his sickly grandson.

He stared after her as she walked to the Palace, and Wulfric's three housecarls joined him.

"She don't seem right," said the Gate Ward. "Wot ails her?"

"Don't know," said the senior housecarl. "But she's a good

mistress. Give us each a penny, she did. Might as well drink 'em up. At the Sign o' the Boar."

Merewyn walked into the Palace. She mounted the stairs to the Great Hall. She entered it and stood for a moment by the door.

There were many people in the Hall. Ethelred's usual retinue of King's thanes, and more foreign faces than she remembered. Norman faces, no doubt, recently brought over by Queen Emma, who sat on her chair near the King, and was picking at her food in a discontented way.

Merewyn stood where she was, at the entrance. Then she heard above the din of drinking and toasting, a noise from the left.

Merewyn advanced, and her husband, Wulfric, rushed towards her. "So glad ye got back safely, m'dear," he said. "Was afraid ye might stop at the Manor, and not find me."

"I might have, but I'm glad you're here. It'll all be over sooner."

" 'Tis the Assumption of the Blessed Virgin," said Wulfric in a slightly aggrieved voice. "The King always has a special feast, you know that."

"Yes, I knew it but I'd forgotten." She walked past Wulfric, and went directly up to the thrones, to Ethelred who was half drunk but made a vague nod of recognition, and went on fondling the neck of Cild Aelfric who sat on his right. Merewyn curtsied to Queen Emma whose bright dark eyes sparkled. During the endless feasting she was glad of any novelty, and saw at once that there might be one now. Lady Merewyn's face was set in a strange way. The little Queen looked at it, and said gently, "I've been away, but now I'm in Winchester, will you come back to me as Bower Lady?"

Merewyn hardly heard. The pupils of her eyes were huge. "I doubt that you'd want me again," she said. Her voice rose almost to a shout. "I am NOT the *Lady* Merewyn! I am NOT descended from King Arthur, though I thought so once in good faith. Good faith . . ." she repeated in a much quieter voice.

"What's all this?" said Ethelred removing his arm from Cild Aelfric's neck, and drinking. "What are you talking about, Lady Merewyn?"

Emma gave a short laugh. She looked at the King. "Did you not hear vat the poor woman said? Or vere you too much occupied by the Earl of Mercia?"

Ethelred drained the rest of his flagon, and gestured to a dish thane for more. "I heard," he said angrily.

"A-ha!" said the Queen. She turned back to Merewyn, who was beginning to droop in front of the thrones. "So you 'ave come to us, to confess a long deception?"

"Yes," said Merewyn.

"Vat are you really?" asked the Queen.

Merewyn threw her head back. "I am a bastard, the product of a Cornish woman of lowly birth, and of a Viking raider. My father was Norse."

"Mon Dieu," said the Queen, after a moment, and she began to laugh. She turned to her French courtiers. "Vous avez compris? Cette dame est vraiment nordique, comme je l'avais bien soupçonné. Son père était Viking!"

The Normans all murmured and strained to look at Merewyn.

Ethelred's befuddlement was penetrated. He slammed his hand on the table and reached for his dagger. "By the Blood of Jesus!" he cried. "Treachery! She's a Dane! All these years at my Court, she's been plotting behind my back. I'll have her killed!"

Both Emma and Cild Aelfric put a restraining hand on his arms.

Merewyn drew back from the brandishing dagger, but her eyes flashed. "I've been a loyal subject to you, Ethelred, and to your mother before you, and though I was sickened at the way you got your throne, I know that *Edward's murder*," she paused and repeated deliberately, "Edward's murder was not your fault. And that you have suffered for it!"

"Oui," said the little Queen, giving her husband another contemptuous glance. "Il a des cauchemars — nightmares you say."

Merewyn's gaze was steady on the King's face. "I've known you since you were a child, King Ethelred," she said, "and I think you have enough murders on your conscience without adding mine."

Ethelred's dagger hand wavered. Suddenly he slumped back and began to weep — maudlin tears mixed with hiccups.

The little Queen said, "Ciel — vat a king!"

Wulfric had been stupefied by all this. He now came to Merewyn's side and addressed the weeping King. "Forgive my wife, my lord. It's the weather. She's just returned from a journey to the south. The heat must've addled her wits."

"No, Wulfric," said Merewyn. She unclasped her garnet necklace, she held out a large pouch full of her other jewelry, including the royal circlet. "I'm telling the truth now, and give you back these to which I have no right."

"But you're my wife," stammered Wulfric, utterly bewildered. "And I missed ye whilst ye were gone, I did."

"Remember," Merewyn spoke with tight control, "that besides having Norse blood, of which I'm proud now, yes, *proud* — I am a bastard."

The Queen, who had been following this with increasingly sympathetic eyes, now said, "*I* vas une bâtarde, until my parents married."

"Were ye now, Lady," said Wulfric, looking helplessly down at the garnet necklace and at the large heavy pouch of jewels Merewyn had given him back. "But we're wed — in the church," he said.

"Under false pretenses," said Merewyn. "You can easily annul it."

"Peut-être," said the Queen. "Eet could be done, but is that vat you both vant? You, Lady Merewyn — I still call you that — vat vould you like? Vous avez eu du courage aujourdhui."

"I don't know . . ." Merewyn whispered. Strength drained

out of her. She could think of nothing but a quiet bed in a dark room. "I might go to Romsey Abbey."

"Alors," said the Queen decidedly. "I shall geef it endowments, so the Abbess may not look down her nose at you."

Wulfric suddenly spoke up and made the longest speech of his life. "I don't want her to. I won't say this hasn't been a bit of a shock. But I'm fond o' her, whatever her birth, and I see ye are too, Queen Aelgifu-Emma. And if Merewyn will put up wi' me, and I know 'tis a quiet life for her at Ashley, I'll forget all this. And whatever she isn't, or was, she can always be a Thane's lady, mine."

"Ah — vous l'aimez —" said Emma very softly. "Tout va bien," she said to her cluster of Normans, who had edged forward as close as they dared.

Is this what I want? Merewyn thought, and at once came the answer. Yes, it is. There would be boring days ahead, but never again the depressions and miseries of before her trip to see Rumon. She felt cleansed, peaceful, and there was much gratitude to Wulfric. She would make him content in the ways he needed. And I, she thought, shall be able to turn my spirit to God again.

She put her hand on her husband's, and he with startling gallantry refastened the garnet necklace around her neck. "There," he said, and kissed her on the forehead.

The little Queen watched and sighed. Her dark eyes glinted with tears. She glanced sideways at the King, who had stopped blubbering and was now fast asleep on Cild Aelfric's shoulder.

Emma turned back to Wulfric and Merewyn. "Somes-day," she said carefully, "un de ces jours — eet vill be different here. Ven the day comes —" she broke off, "per'aps before that, ven eet ees safe, and 'e 'as forgotten —" she shrugged towards Ethelred, "I ask you again, Lady Merewyn, to come and see me at Court."

"I will, of course," said Merewyn, aware that Wulfric was pleased, also aware of how much the Queen's support had shored up his undoubted fondness for his wife. Nor did that matter.

"May God bless you, Lady," she said, curtsying again to the Queen. "And bless your little son."

Emma smiled very sweetly.

Wulfric and Merewyn quit the Great Hall just as the bards began to play their harps softly so as not to disturb the King.

Merewyn heard the harps, and at once thought of Rumon.

There was joy in this thought. She felt his approval like a benediction. "My dear, dear love," she murmured.

"What?" said Wulfric, who was looking for his housecarls. "What you say, m'dear?"

"Nothing, except that it's a lovely evening, and we'll be home before it's really dark, and that you're a fine man, Wulfric."

"Hold that bridle, m'girl. That's one of m'horses, and some blasted fool has let it loose!"

"Yes," she said smiling. "Yes, Wulfric." And took the bridle.

afterword

THERE may be some who will want to know what happened historically after the personal story of Merewyn and Rumon. The facts can be dug from dozens of source books but they are conflicting. Those who consult the great *Dictionary of National Biography* must be warned that most of these people are inserted under diphthongs. "AE, or EA" are particularly confusing. Queen Alfrida, for instance, is listed as "Aelfthryth." But Ethelred, also spelled "Aethelred," is found under "E". I have simplified names throughout.

But the facts, in so far as they may be found through the chroniclers, who wrote much later than the events they were describing, are briefly as follows.

England went to pieces under the rule of Ethelred the Unready, who finally died in London, April 23, 1016. By natural causes or not, nobody is sure. Even during Ethelred's lifetime, the conquering Danish Sweyn became virtually King of England. And after him his son, Canute, whom the little Norman Queen, Emma, rather surprisingly married. He was considerably younger than she was, but she bore him at least one son — Harthacanute.

Edward the Confessor, her son by Ethelred, came to the throne, and either could not or would not produce children. The great line of Cerdic and Alfred petered out.

The Norman Conquest in 1066 seems to have been inevitable, and the wedding of Emma and Ethelred was the spearhead.

I have tried to trace these people who lived so long ago. For this purpose I have as usual made many trips to England, to the places one can still see, such as Corfe Castle in Dorset, to Padstow in Cornwall, to Tavistock, Shaftesbury (where one will find little King Edward's pathetic broken bones), Romsey Abbey, and Winchester, of course.

I also made a trip to Iceland, where I went to the North with a dear Icelandic friend and saw the present-day homestead at Langarfoss in the Borg District.

There seems to be no doubt of Norse discoveries in America, long before Columbus came. The recent finds in Newfoundland by Dr. and Mrs. Helge Ingstad certainly prove Norse occupation around A.D. 1000. I share the opinion with many others that the successive Greenland colonizers (including Leif Erikson "the lucky") explored, and tried to settle, a good deal of the American eastern seaboard. And that later on, the Norse even got inland. Many mysterious runestones have been found besides the "Minnesota" one. There are what seem to be Viking mooring holes all over the coast in New England. There is the disputed "Newport Tower" which, from the evidence, can NOT have been a mill, *constructed* by Governor Arnold of Rhode Island, though he used it.

As the Sagas, and the Icelandic "Landnámabók" are so accurate on genealogy, why should we distrust the essentials of their traditional facts?

Ari Marson's unexpected voyage to the West comes straight from the "Landnámabók."

There *is* some doubt about the extraordinary "Place of Stones" on the Merrimac, at North Salem, New Hampshire. I've examined it three times myself, and have chosen the most reasonable theory. But it is today aptly called "Mystery Hill."

Rumon is, at present, considered a sort of presiding saint at Tavistock Church, in Devonshire; as he is remembered in various Cornish places, particularly on the Lizard. I have done quite a lot of research on Rumon, and traced him back to Provence, with the help of a French librarian at Avignon.

My chronology for the years covered by this book is as accurate as the sources would let me make it — notably "The Anglo-Saxon Chronicle," "William of Malmesbury," "Florence of Worcester," and the splendid *English Historical Documents* edited by Dorothy Whitelock.

With deep gratitude I append a list of credits to some of the people who have helped me personally.

In England, to Sir Frank and Lady Stenton, with a bow to his classic *Anglo-Saxon England*. (London: Oxford, 1943.)

To Sir Thomas and Lady Kendrick, with thanks for hospitality, and help at the British Museum.

To Mr. and Mrs. John Ryder who live at Rempstone Hall near Corfe Castle.

To the Prideaux-Brunes at Padstow.

To Mrs. J. M. Foster of Bristol, and Geoffrey Ashe of Maidstone, Kent.

The latter's *Land to the West* (London: Collins, 1962) and his other books greatly enlarged my thinking, as did Mr. Ashe's friendly interest.

In America, I am indebted to Charles Michael Boland's *They All Discovered America*. (New York: Doubleday, 1961.) It was Mr. Boland's provocative book that first sent me to the stone caves at "Mystery Hill," New Hampshire, and I am also indebted to him for introductions in Iceland.

Iceland was fascinating. Everyone was warm and hospitable. Particular thanks to the two sisters — Selma and Blaka Jonsdottir. And to Professor Einar Sveinsson, who gave me generous time, and straightened out for me the genealogies of some of the men who went from Iceland to Greenland.

I have used many history books for this venture into Tenth Century England, and the Norse Discoveries of America.

I have all the *Lives of the Saints* by S. Baring-Gould; I have Charles Oman's *England Before the Norman Conquest* (London: 1910); I have the invaluable, though somewhat biased third edition of *The History of the Norman Conquest of England* by Edward A. Freeman (London: Oxford, 1877); Eleanor Shipley Duckett's *Saint Dunstan of Canterbury* (New York: Norton, 1955).

In the effort to reconstruct history in an era so far removed from us, there are two things to remember. The task of an author is to communicate, and since this book could not be written in Anglo-Saxon or old Norse, one must accept an approximation of our present-day speech.

And the other thing to remember is that people's psychology and motivations do not change very much through the centuries. Though the expression of these may.

At any rate I have tried to tell an accurate story, and to illuminate a shadowy corner of the past.

GREENLAND

Brattalid

LABRADOR

newfoundLand

MERRIMAC RIVER
New Hampshire Coast
Cape Cod

THE SEA VOYAGES of
RUMON and MEREWYN
.... Rumon's Voyage
------- Merewyn's Voyage

0   400   800 MILES

S·H·B